A NOVEL BY

Dorothy The

Uhnak

Investigation

Simon and Schuster · New York

With love to my family . . .

Tony and Tracy
Mother and Dad
Mildred, Harold and Susan Ellis

PART
One

CHAPTER 1

IF Tim Neary hadn't been late for our appointment that morning, or if I hadn't been early and alone in the office with Sam Catalano, things might have turned out differently. Just *might* have; in some ways the end was determined by the beginning. For instance, if there had been a team of detectives at the 107th that morning, the call never would have been relayed to our office, the District Attorney's Investigating Squad. We wouldn't have been the prime investigators responsible for the ultimate outcome of the case. The pressure wouldn't have been on us and on Neary in particular.

But Neary *was* late and I *was* early and Catalano *did* take the call from the precinct about the missing Keeler kids. Even then, there was no *real* reason why Catalano couldn't respond alone. Except, given what I had learned about Catalano during the ten months we worked as partners, prior to my working alone on Neary's "special" special investigation, and sensing Catalano's reaction to the phone call, and seeing right through his attempt at being casual and nonchalant, and maybe just going along with a feeling—the kind you develop after twenty years on the job—I folded my report, shoved it into my inside jacket pocket and told him, what the hell, I'd take the ride over to Fresh Meadows with him.

The Keeler apartment was about what you'd expect for the Fresh Meadows housing complex: a living-room suite consisting of a sofa with two matching chairs, identical lamps perched on identical end tables with a coordinated cocktail table. The Keelers were not what you'd expect; at least Kitty Keeler wasn't.

She was very young; not as young as I thought at first glance, but when compared with her husband she was practically a kid. A very beautiful kid who knew exactly how to emphasize her best features. She had large dark-blue eyes, carefully decorated with a pale-beige shadow and heavy dark liner, and very thick, very long eyelashes which may or may not have been real. No other makeup except for a touch of lipstick that made her mouth look moist. When she dragged on her cigarette, as though sucking in oxygen, a dimple appeared at the corner of her mouth and another in her right cheek. After she blew out the smoke, her lips remained just slightly parted and a glint of white teeth showed.

Her figure was more than good and the blue knit jersey pants suit took its shape from her precise contours rather than from any structuring undergarments.

Her hands were long and restless; a collection of silver rings covered her fingers. Matched the jangling silver and turquoise bracelets which slid up and down along both of her wrists as she plucked and fidgeted and finger-combed her hair, which was, as she well knew, her best feature. It was shoulder length, straight and the white-blond of an albino. It surrounded her dark-browed, oval, high-cheeked face like fine sheer curtains. The color was natural; the center part showed a delicate pink scalp.

Her voice had a low, hoarse street sound which shattered the illusion created by her face. She rolled her tongue around inside one cheek for a moment, shook her head, folded her arms across her body and said, "This is terrific, George. This is really terrific. I hope they give you a summons or something, George." She dropped sideways into one of the chairs, her legs dangling over an arm. She looked from Catalano to me, then back to Sam. "Hey, isn't it against the law to make a . . . what do you call it? A false report?"

"Tell you what," Catalano said in his warm, friend-of-the-family voice, "why don't we start at the beginning?"

George Keeler began spouting words, but he was almost incoherent.

Sam held his hand up; not in an offensive way, but easy, soothing. "Hey, Mr. Keeler, look. We're strangers here. We don't know what's going on; we're here to help. Come on, sit down. Let's all stay calm, okay?" Softly, he lulled Keeler, who nodded and let himself be gestured into silence. Catalano turned to the woman again. "Mrs. Keeler?" It sounded like an intimacy.

"Okay. Okay, George wants to play some stupid game with me." She looked directly at Catalano and said quickly, "I woke up this morning and went into the boys' bedroom and they were gone. I called George and told him to bring the kids back and—"

"What do you mean, you *called* George?"

Instead of answering me, she nibbled on her thumbnail.

George Keeler leaned forward, eager to help. "Well, see, I wasn't sleepin' here the last coupla nights." He risked a quick look at his wife, but she was watching Catalano to see how he was taking this information. "See, I own a ginmill over in Sunnyside; I own the whole building and I got a small apartment over the place. And, well, sometimes I stay over. In the apartment. Like the last few nights."

"Okay, Mrs. Keeler, at what time did you realize the boys were gone?"

She did one of those long, slow slides with her eyes, from Catalano, across her husband, around to me. She swung her leg back and forth and rubbed the back of her neck for a quick massage while deciding whether or not she was going to bother to answer me.

Catalano leaned toward her with his lighter; he made a production out of lighting her cigarette and held eye contact with her when she blew the first drag of smoke at him. It's part of Catalano's routine; he uses it on any female he comes in contact with; I've heard that he's sometimes successful.

"I called George at about seven-thirty," she told Catalano, "and told him to bring the kids back. Instead of that, *he* comes over, swearing on a stack of Bibles that he doesn't have them and doesn't know where they are."

This was George Keeler's cue to repeat what he'd said for maybe the fourth time since we arrived. "I don't have the kids, Kitty. I swear to God, I don't have the kids."

His wife blinked once or twice, but didn't answer him.

There was no point in letting them go around again; this could go on all day. Catalano picked up my signal easily; he is quick and intuitive —among other things—I'll give him that. He settled comfortably on the couch with the long, tall blond mother of the missing little boys and I took a firm but friendly grip on George Keeler's arm and suggested we get a little fresh air.

We strolled along the grounds of the Fresh Meadows development, which is a vast complex of two- and three-story garden-apartment buildings designed to fit in with the semisuburban character of the Queens community. It is a low-crime area with a population mostly of white middle-class people who migrated from the Bronx and Brooklyn after World War II. There are wide lawns surrounding the complex, thick healthy trees and ample parking spaces for residents' cars. Included in the 107th Precinct are quiet streets of one-family homes where honest, hard-working people live and raise their families.

We walked along without speaking, then settled on a bench. George was having some problem breathing: a noisy wheezing sound escaped first when he inhaled, then when he exhaled. He dug in his pocket and came up with a nebulizer. He apologized, as though what he was doing was shameful and private. He squirted and sucked the medication loudly, and though he didn't sound any better, he said that he was. We talked a little about asthma and allergies and medications, and he relaxed; a little.

George Keeler was a badly preserved forty-nine, fifty; more than twenty years his wife's senior. He was an obese, balding, sloppy middle-aged man who was well aware of his own shortcomings. It must have been tough having to measure up to a twenty-six- or twenty-seven-year-old wife who looked like Kitty.

"Tell me something, George," I said in that easy familiarity we develop on the job. Then it occurred to me, this guy doesn't even know my name. I stuck my hand out. "By the way, I'm Joe. Joe Peters. My partner back there is Sam Catalano." We shook hands and he nodded. "Tell me, George, how come your wife is so sure you have your boys?"

He shook his head and said, "I swear to God, I don't have the kids. *Not this time.*"

When he added the last three words to his routine denial, something small and tight in the pit of my stomach, like a little fist of apprehension getting ready to hammer at my duodenal ulcer, relaxed and began to unclench. You never *really* know where these family disputes might lead.

Keeler went into a long, drawn-out, hard-to-follow recitation of an incident that had happened last November, more than five months ago. He backtracked, went ahead, stopped, filled in details, but what I finally pieced together was that his wife, Kitty, worked as an assistant manager at the New World Health Spa on Northern Boulevard, just over the Nassau County line. The spa was one of a franchise, and last November Kitty went down to the Bahamas to celebrate an anniversary of the island spa. There was some trouble getting the regular baby-sitter, and against George's wishes Kitty left the kids with a young Scotch girl she hardly knew.

"I could size this girl up real easy," George winked, man to man. "A swinger-type kid, ya know? I checked the boys every day, see; I stayed at my apartment, but still I had a funny feeling about this girl."

His funny feeling was justified. After putting in late hours at his bar that Saturday night, he woke early the next morning and went over to check on his sons. It was a cold, snowy Sunday, not quite eight in the morning, and when George pulled into his parking slot he saw his two little kids, one just about three, the other not quite six years old, playing in the playground. Dressed in their pajamas and robes, with rubber boots over their bare feet. They were building a snow man.

"Terry, that's my oldest kid, he tells me that Patti, that's the Scotch girl, is asleep and she has a man in bed with her."

George bundled the two kids into his car and kept them at his gin-mill apartment for the next few days. The baby-sitter never called him to check on the kids; probably too scared, George said. When Kitty came home, three days later, the girl was sitting, staring at the TV and chewing her nails. All she could tell Kitty was that she hadn't seen the kids since Saturday night.

"When Kitty called, I told her, 'No, I don't know where the kids are.' See, I gave her a hard time then, ya know."

He sounded apologetic for having given Kitty a hard time. George was apologetic about everything where his wife was concerned.

"What was the beef about this time, George? How come you've been staying over at your ginmill the last few nights?"

George said that Kitty was planning to fly out to Phoenix to assist in the opening of another New World Health Spa. The regular baby-sitter, a Mrs. Silverberg, was in the hospital. Kitty couldn't get anyone to fill in. She was planning to take the kids with her, and George objected; they argued; George kept his distance until Kitty cooled off. Then the younger kid, Georgie, got sick.

"I talked to Kitty yesterday afternoon, on the phone, and she said she'd call me after the doctor came and let me know what's doin' with the kid. It looked like the measles. So anyway, last night at eleven-twenty, Kitty called and—"

"The doctor didn't come until that late?"

"Oh, no, it wasn't that. It was just that . . ."

George went a little red; every time he revealed something that Kitty did to him, it was with a combination of apology and acceptance. Hell, he only got what he deserved from her, right?

"Ya see, I guess she was still sore at me, so she didn't call me right after the doctor left. Like, to make me keep waitin', ya know?"

I decided not to ask George if he, personally, had given the kid the measles. He'd probably say, "Yes, if Kitty says so."

"Okay, so you spoke to her last night at eleven-twenty?"

"No, no. I couldn't come to the phone right then. See, I was in the middle of a hassle with these Irish folk singers I got working on Wednesdays and weekends. They're havin' this real donnybrook, because they're supposed to be on a break, from eleven-fifteen to eleven-thirty, and one of them started doin' an old-country song for one of the old-timers and the other guys got sore, yellin' how he was breaking the rule. That it was eleven-twenty and they were supposed to be off until eleven-thirty and all." George Keeler shrugged; apparently, nothing in his life went smoothly.

"So that's how you know Kitty called you at eleven-twenty? Okay. When *did* you talk to her?"

Poor George (I had already begun to think of him as "poor George") kept dialing his home number all night long, from eleven-twenty-five to well past two this morning. All he got was a busy signal; Kitty had obviously taken the phone off the hook.

"So you didn't talk to her until this morning? When she called you? At about seven-thirty?"

"Yeah, right. Boy, I was sound asleep, but the minute I hear the phone ring, I come wide awake, like that!" He snapped his fingers. "The minute I hear it, I say, Oh, boy. Kitty."

And that was when Kitty told him the kids were gone and he better show up with them and fast.

"And I tole her that I didn't have the kids, so I got dressed, and come right over here, and looked around the grounds and all, and called you guys."

George Keeler threw his hands up; his heavy eyebrows came low over his light-gray eyes and he chewed on his lip waiting for me to tell him what to do. I leaned back against the bench and took it slow, so George would realize that none of this was anything unusual to me.

"Look, George, let's do it this way. We'll go over to your place and bring your boys home and forget the whole thing, okay? I mean, as far as I'm concerned, this isn't a police matter. We'll bring the kids back and you and your wife work it out between you. Nothing to do with us. What do you say, George?"

George Keeler stood up, shook his head, looked around as though trying to orient himself, then he leaned down into my face. His voice was raspy and strained as though he was talking over a very sore throat, but it was the look in his eyes that really said something to me.

"Jesus Christ Almighty, haven't you been listenin' to me? I *don't have* the kids. I don't know where the hell they are. They're just two little kids and I don't know where they are!"

Everything about George Keeler convinced me that his anguish was real. Of course, the source of this anguish was still unknown, but he was a deeply disturbed man. There was one other suggestion.

"Look, George, maybe Kitty took the kids someplace? Maybe to get even with you. You told me she was sore at you in the first place, and then you didn't come to the phone when she called. Maybe she packed the kids up and took them to a friend's house, to give you a hard time?"

His face didn't relax into that bland, accepting expression. He shook his head abruptly and said in a positive, hoarse voice, "Kitty don't play them kind of games."

I believed him and suggested we return to his apartment.

.

It was obvious the minute we walked into the living room. Catalano leaned forward and put his coffee cup on the cocktail table with the casual ease of a man who has made himself at home. When he spoke to Kitty Keeler, it was in the comfortable way of an old friend. That was among Catalano's gifts: to become an instant old friend.

The first thing that Kitty said to her husband was, "Well, George, you finished playing games? You ready to bring the kids home?"

Sam distracted her, a hand on her arm, a certain persuasive pressure, a let-me-handle-this wink. He told me what Kitty had told him: the pediatrician came at around seven last night; diagnosed measles; left about seven-thirty. The sick boy went to sleep; the older boy, Terry, had supper with his mother, stayed up to watch TV until about ten and then was put to bed.

"Did either of the boys get up again during the night?"

Instead of answering me, Kitty Keeler flicked her thumbnail against her front teeth and narrowed her eyes. She finally pulled her thumb away from her mouth and said, "Look. Did George tell you about how he did this to me before? Did he tell you about the last time he took the kids on me?"

"Yes, he did. He also told me that he didn't take the boys last night."

"And you believe him?" Her moist mouth twisted downward in an expression of contempt. She moved her head so that the long silky hair swished around her shoulders. "You really believe him, after what he did the last time?"

"Yeah, but this is *this* time."

She stopped shaking her head, leaned back against the couch, reached for a loose pillow and hugged it to her body, all the time biting down on her lower lip, holding it between her teeth, then letting it roll back into place.

"All right," she said, doing me a favor. "Georgie woke up when Terry went to bed. His fever was up again, so I gave him a baby aspirin, rubbed him with alcohol and took him to the bathroom." She stood up, crossed the room to the window, stood motionless, then spun around with a dancer's ease. "There's no point to any of this. George has the kids."

It was hard to figure if the hostility was directed at me or through me to her husband. Kitty seemed to have chosen sides: her and Catalano against me and George. Matching her stare, I said, "George, do you have the kids?"

Keeler went to his wife, hands reaching for her shoulders. "I swear to God, no. Kitty, I don't have them, God is my witness."

She shoved George away, folded her arms across her body, threw her head back and studied the ceiling. She gave a loud, irritated sigh.

Kitty had been dealing with George for too long. I figured, the hell with this. I snapped my notebook closed, put it into a rear pocket. "Look, lady, if this whole thing is just too boring for you, that's all right with me. They're *your* kids."

We both ignored George's sudden gasping panic. She said, "I didn't send for you."

Catalano jumped up. "Kitty, hey, we're just trying to help." Then, impartial referee, "She's just upset, Joe."

He gave her the benefit of his complete attention; his voice hummed around her, soothed her, convinced her to "put up with" me. She crossed one leg over the other, nibbled on her pinky and asked, "What was the question?"

"When was the last time you saw your sons last night? And under what circumstances?"

She thought it over, then shrugged. "Terry got up later in the night for a drink of water. He dropped the plastic cup and that woke Georgie. So I took Georgie to the bathroom, then had to change him and his sheet because he was soaked with sweat. Then I took a coupla sleeping pills and a hot shower and went to bed."

"Those things aren't good for you, Kitty," George told her; she ignored him.

"What time was that?"

"What time was what?"

Catalano interpreted for me. "What time was it, Kitty, that you last saw the boys last night?"

She examined her pinky carefully, then nibbled on it some more. "One o'clock. That's when Terry got up. About that time. And it was about one-thirty when I took the sleeping pills and my shower and went to bed."

"Did you see your sons at all after one-thirty this morning?"

She shifted some hair from her shoulders to her back. "Nope."

"From the time you went to bed until you woke up this morning, did you hear anything, anything at all, unusual in the apartment?"

She smiled at Catalano, awarding him points. "That's just what *you* asked me, Sam." Then, blank-faced, to me, "No, nothing at all. No noise, no nothing."

"Did you leave your sons alone in the apartment at any time last night?"

"No."

"As far as you know, did anyone, anyone at all, come into the apartment last night?"

She closed her eyes, tapped an index finger against her temple, then snapped her eyes open and said, "Yeah. The doctor."

Catalano said softly, "No, Kitty. Joe means anyone besides the doctor."

"Oh. Is that what Joe means?"

The little mother was just a little too cute for me. I pulled out my notebook and didn't look up at her again. "Let's have a description of the boys, Mrs. Keeler. Start with the older boy, Terry."

The descriptions were of two unextraordinary boys: three and a half and six years old. Both tall for their ages; very blond hair; blue eyes; fair skin. Both dressed in two-piece cotton knit pajamas. Terry's pajamas had yellow smiling moon faces; Georgie's had a big yellow duck face on the front of the top half and a big yellow duck bottom on the back, with little yellow ducks on the pants. And Georgie had a measles rash all over his face and body.

"Is any of their clothing missing, Mrs. Keeler?"

"I don't know. I didn't look."

"Well, look now."

She apparently considered this another challenge, something she had to decide to do or not do. Finally she got up. "Sure, why not?"

It took her four or five minutes. Nothing was missing. When asked, she came up with an eight-by-ten studio photograph of the boys. They appeared to be little versions of their mother, with small teeth showing through plastic smiles.

When the telephone rang, George Keeler jumped as though he'd touched a live wire. It was loud and he grabbed it in the middle of the second ring; he listened, then said, "Detective Peters, it's for you."

"I'll take it in the kitchen." There was a yellow wall phone offering a little more privacy. Keeler hung up as soon as he heard my voice.

"Joe? Can you talk?"

I had left the Keelers' phone number on Tim Neary's desk; he probably was going to ask what the hell I was doing in the middle of a domestic quarrel, which is what I had been asking myself.

"What's up, Tim?"

His voice went flat and expressionless; the official kind of voice used to relay the kind of information Tim Neary had.

"Joe, I'm going to read the descriptions of two D.O.A.s that just turned up over on Peck Avenue. That's about six blocks from where you are. I haven't been there, but I'll relay what I just got from the precinct. Two male Caucasians. Subject number one—approximately three to four years old; death apparently by strangulation. Subject number two—approximately five to six years old; death apparently caused by an as yet undetermined caliber gunshot wound at the base of the right side of the skull. Both victims blond hair, blue eyes; both dressed in yellow-and-white cotton knit pajamas."

"One kid's pajamas has smiling moon faces; the other kid's has a yellow duck face." I tried to swallow the sour lump that had become wedged in my throat.

There was a long silence, then Neary said, "Them's our babies." He gave the exact location. "You got the father there, Joe? For an identification?"

"Yeah. Is there a doctor at the scene, Tim? The guy's an asthmatic. I think he's gonna need some help."

"Probably someone from the M.E.'s office. Listen, get back to me with the confirmation—or whatever—as soon as you can. And, Joe? Put Catalano on for a minute; I want him to seal the premises. We're dealing with a double homicide." He couldn't resist adding, in an irritated voice, "Christ, Joe, that's just what I need right now, huh?"

I couldn't think of anyone who really needed a double homicide, now or at any other time. I went back into the living room. "Sam, captain wants to talk to you. He's not happy about the report you did on the Flushing bank heist."

Sam's eyebrows shot up, but he didn't say anything; both Keelers were watching us closely. I went over to George and said, a little too loudly, "Hey, George, tell you what. Let's you and me take a ride over to your ginmill in Sunnyside. That way, we'll have touched all the bases and your wife will believe that you haven't been conning her. What do you say?"

When Catalano came back from the kitchen, his color had changed. He was still smooth and easy and he kept coming on with the blond mother, flexing his body, holding attention to himself, keeping it all under control. But his color had changed. And, for some reason, I think Kitty Keeler noticed it. I looked at her over my shoulder, just before we left the apartment and caught something: something in her eyes, some glint of terror or pain or anticipation. Something I would have to think about later.

.

There were a number of official vehicles in the immediate vicinity when I pulled my Chevy alongside a squad car which had been parked haphazardly on Peck Avenue. There was an ambulance with the word MORTUARY printed front, back and on both sides. The whole area had a look of urgency.

"I gotta check on something for a minute, George. Be right back."

There were uniformed personnel to deal with the curious neighbors, who really presented no problem: they were frightened middle-aged women for the most part. The homicide people were at work, measuring, photographing, cooperating with the forensic people, who were taking invisible samples of whatever substances they deemed should be brushed or scraped into the inevitable plasticine envelopes. A CBS-TV camera crew had just arrived; a crew from the *Daily News* was flashing pictures.

Captain Chris Wise of the Queens Homicide was present and in charge. Chris had been my boss for nearly four years and we knew each other for longer than that. He nodded to me, then jerked a thumb to indicate where the bodies were.

"Understand you guys took a call, Joe, about two missing kids this morning?"

"Yeah."

"Well, I don't think they're missing anymore." He turned toward the street, where my car was parked. "Who ya got, the father?"

"Yeah."

Captain Wise led the way and motioned his men aside. He reached down and pulled back the tarpaulin which had been tossed over the bodies. "This what you're looking for, Joe?"

The lower torso, pajama clad, stuck out from beneath a small body wearing white pajamas with round, smiling yellow moon faces. Face down in earth softened by morning mist, then slightly hardened by the sun. The head of the child on top seemed peculiar; it had swelled to twice normal size as the result of the brain having been penetrated by a foreign object. A bullet in the head causes various fluids to flow; the child's head was bloated as though air had been blown unevenly into a balloon. There wasn't very much blood, just a thick, dark, wormlike mass at the base of the skull on the right side, site of penetration, and a few trickles down the thin neck. The pale-blond hair lifted in a breeze, then settled back into place. The huge head was slightly to one side and the face had turned the color of a bruise; the features were swollen and distorted.

The face of the younger child was covered by his brother's body. There was a strong, peculiar yet familiar odor. Captain Wise said, "Dog shit, Joe. The smaller kid is lying with his face in dog shit."

Automatically, my hand began to massage the biting pain in my stomach. "Captain, can they be turned over yet? I mean, that's their *fa-*

ther in my car. It's bad enough without him having to see them like that."

"Give it five minutes more, Joe." He put a hand on my arm and we turned away from the bodies. He spoke while looking down at his well-polished shoes. "What's the story with the parents?"

There wasn't very much to tell, and when we circled back the bodies had been placed on their backs, side by side.

"Can't they wipe the kid's face, for Christ's sake, before the father sees them? I mean, dog shit in the kid's mouth."

Chris Wise jabbed at the smaller child with the tip of his shoe. A few pieces of dried-up brownish substance slipped down along the kid's head. Then Chris wiped his shoe along the length of the kid's pajama leg, making sure his shine wasn't ruined. Which is one of the things I never learned to do in four years of homicide work: to treat a dead human being as an object, an end product of someone's rage or craziness or greed or jealousy or revenge or whatever the hell else. Which is one of the reasons why I have ulcers.

Chris finished wiping his shoes on the dead kid's body, then watched me with that tight close smile of his. "Want me to comb their hair too, Joe? Maybe I should travel with a cosmetic kit."

George Keeler looked up blankly when I approached my car. "What happened here, anyway? Boy, lots of cops, huh?"

"George, would you come with me for a minute? George, there's been an accident. It's very bad. Both of your boys."

George Keeler stared at me for a split second, then yanked his arm free. He spun around wildly, then lunged to where they waited for him, just behind the bushes. George stood over them, stared down at them. He stretched his arms out in an empty, meaningless gesture, then dropped to his knees. He looked up at the circle of men who watched him. Who stood and watched him and weren't doing a goddamn thing for his boys. He flung himself over the small bodies, protecting them from view, covering them, hiding them from the expressionless stares. He grabbed the smaller, Georgie, by the shoulders and tried to pull him into a sitting position; he began to shake the body; he began gasping and yelling.

"Help them. There's something wrong with them. My God, help them, don't just stand there staring, there's something the matter with my boys. Georgie! Terry! Help them, help them!"

It took two other cops besides me to pull his child's dead body from his grasp and to drag George Keeler to the ambulance.

"Heart attack, heart attack," the white-faced young intern muttered.

He jumped into the ambulance and instructed a uniformed cop to help him with the oxygen mask.

Captain Wise placed himself between the intern, who looked terrified, and George Keeler.

"You goddamn fuckin' fool, this man's hyperventilating. You give him a whiff of oxygen and he's dead. *Asthma,* dummy, he's having an asthma attack."

The intern was stricken by the terrible possible consequences of his near-mistake. His face and mind seemed to go blank. Chris Wise turned him around and shoved him back toward the ambulance, and apparently the intern remembered what to do. He emerged to give George a shot of adrenalin.

Within a few minutes, the loud wet sucking sounds eased and George was breathing easier. He suddenly pushed the intern back and reached out to me. I helped him up and the pressure of his hand was numbing.

"We gotta tell Kitty," George Keeler said. "Oh my God Almighty, we gotta tell my poor Kitty."

We practically burst into the apartment, a flying wedge of policemen, but Kitty Keeler didn't seem to notice. She leaped from her chair, mouth opened, eyes wide and seeing only her husband. She reached out for George, her bracelets clanging and sliding up her slender arms. She grabbed at his sleeves, then at his shirt front.

George Keeler turned away; looked over his shoulder; over her head; looked at the ceiling, the floor, the walls, anywhere, at anything but at his wife.

"George," she called to him. Finally she pounded his chest with a clenched fist. "What's wrong, George? What's the matter? My God, George, Georgie, talk to me!"

He inhaled slowly and steadily to the fullest capacity of his lungs. Then, arms dangling at his sides, he looked directly at his wife and in a terrible voice he told her, "They're dead, baby. They're dead. Both boys. Both of them. They're dead."

Kitty shook her head slowly from side to side and said, "Don't say that. Don't say a stupid thing like that. What the hell's the matter with you, to say a dumb stupid thing like that? Don't say that. *George!*"

He stood against her onslaught of fists and words and protests, and his mouth kept moving, saying the same words, over and over again.

"They're dead, baby. They're dead."

Mary Hogan was a small pear-shaped woman whose delicate features bore a striking resemblance to her daughter's. There was some confusion as to who had directed that Mrs. Hogan be picked up from the Bronx bakery where she worked and brought to the Keeler apartment. The reason was obvious: it was felt that Kitty Keeler might be needing her mother.

Mrs. Hogan brought a Father Kerrigan from St. Simon Stock along with her. He was one of those Irish priests of indeterminate age: perpetually boyish, smooth-cheeked, tenor-voiced, a few silver speckles in his blond-red hair. He kept informing everyone that Mrs. Hogan was hard of hearing, and would we speak carefully, she was good at lip reading.

George Keeler came from the bedroom and went directly to his mother-in-law. She virtually disappeared from sight in his embrace, and the one muffled cry came from him. She carefully disengaged herself and studied his face with great intensity. Her eyes, obviously from years of serving partially as her ears as well, were sharp, somewhat glassy, but whatever tears they contained were frozen inside her sockets.

"George," she said in a soft flat brogue, "where are they? Where are my little ones? George, what's happened here?"

Kitty Keeler staggered into the room. Her face had gone dead white. She pushed George aside, pointed at the small stiff-backed woman and said to her husband, "What is *she* doing here? What the *fuck* is *she* doing here?"

While Mrs. Hogan could not see what her daughter had said, she felt the impact of her anger. As though believing that no one could hear her unless facing her, she waited until her daughter turned to her and then, softly, almost in a whisper, she said, "Kitty, Kitty, Kitty. *What have you done?*"

CHAPTER 2

Tɪᴍ Nᴇᴀʀʏ has been one of my closest friends from the time we were kids playing street games in the north Bronx. After high school, while I was learning how to lay lines for the telephone company, Tim was spending three years at a seminary learning that he didn't really want to be a priest. We came into the department together; Tim passed every promotion exam right at the top of the list. He's a very deliberate, careful guy and we trust each other completely. With a few reservations.

Sometimes what Tim Neary doesn't say is more important than what he does say.

"What's this thing look like, Joe?" That's what he said.

"How is this thing going to bounce on me?" That's what he didn't say.

"It's a little early to tell, Tim."

The Keelers were sitting on the bench in the squad room. Catalano was keeping himself between them and anyone else in the squad, as though the Keelers were his private property.

"Jesus, Joe, this couldn't have happened at a worse time."

"Want me to run over to Peck Avenue and tell those kids that their timing was pretty bad?"

"Don't be a goddamn wiseass, Joe. I don't need that right now." Then, as though he just thought of it, as though it wasn't of great importance to him, he said, "How about that other matter, Joe? You come up with anything?"

I reached inside my jacket without answering him; handed over my report with a shake of my head.

"Shit. Nothing? Nothing at all?"

"Give me a little time, Tim."

What Tim had assigned me to do was to get information of an incriminating nature on the District Attorney of Queens County in order to force him off the primary ballot for the upcoming mayoralty election. Tim's wife is a law partner of the campaign manager of the D.A.'s rival. Tim and I are both eligible to retire at half pay on November 28 of this year. Twenty years down the drain. Or whatever. Tim has a big future promised if the right man wins. He is also certain that my future, left in his hands, if the right man wins, will be nothing short of terrific.

Of course, Tim ignores facts that don't fit with his plans. He considers it no big deal that my wife and I have sold our home in Queens; bought a condominium in Florida, where my wife is waiting for me to join her come the end of November. She fully expects that I'll pack up and leave the two-room apartment we took on a short-term lease in one of the old buildings near the Forest Hills Tennis Stadium. And go down to Florida. And take a job in her brother's construction company. Her brother, as far as I'm concerned, is a crooked, smug, stupid bastard who thinks the same of me. I'm not sure how all of this came about. It just seems to have happened, according to a plan worked out so long ago I can't remember when it wasn't part of our understanding. Once the girl was married, and she was last year, once the boy graduated high school and was set in college, which *he* was, once my twenty years were in, that would be it. All set. The rest of my life. Except that now that it was practically reality I have been taking a good hard look at what the rest of my life would be with brother-in-law Fred, and I don't like it. At all. And another strange thing. After twenty-three years of marriage, of living with Jen and the kids, this was the first time I'd ever lived alone. In my whole life. I had gone from my parents to the Army to Jen. Now I wasn't accountable, in any way, to anyone. I had thought I'd be lonely. Jen thought I'd be lonely.

The funny thing was, I wasn't lonely at all.

"All right. Let's take a statement from the parents, Joe. We'll talk about the other thing later."

In a monotone, Kitty Keeler answered Neary's questions. She stared at the reels of the tape recorder on the desk and seemed to pace herself to the slow revolutions. She repeated what she had already told us. That she had last seen her sons between one and one-thirty this morning. Had taken sleeping pills; showered; gone to bed. Woke up at seven-thirty. The boys were gone.

"I thought George had the boys. I thought—" She didn't cry or anything. She just stopped speaking.

She had changed; she was a different version of the same woman. She seemed translucent. Her paleness had gone almost to the bones of her face. Her cheekbones seemed to shine and protrude through the tightly stretched skin. She reminded me of a small, shining, transparent glass animal: fragile, breakable, easily shattered. And yet she had a curious strength, directed toward her husband.

George Keeler, in his grief, seemed to bloat and swell; the lines of his body became indefinite and unclear. He turned to his wife, his face totally trusting and dependent. Kitty took control of both her husband and herself with a hard tenderness, direct and businesslike and effective. It was a surprise, this tough concern for George. She had been totally uncaring of him earlier. Before the bodies of their children had been found.

"Mr. Keeler, do you have any idea, at all, who might have done this to your sons?"

A wildness came into George Keeler's voice. He waved his arms in front of him as he spoke, then stared at his hands, which trembled violently.

"Look at that," he said, needing to account for his hands. "The adrenalin shot makes them shake like that."

His wife reached over, touched his arm, her fingers closed on his wrist. Her touch settled him. He told his story for a second time in almost the exact same phrases. He had come over to the apartment after Kitty called him; searched briefly; called the police. He raised his arms in a terrible, empty gesture, then let them fall heavily onto his thighs.

"And then he took me to that park." Keeler looked at me for confirmation. "And then I saw them. The boys. I saw them. My boys."

His meaty shoulders heaved forward, his hands dangled and shook between his knees. He began to gasp for air.

Kitty Keeler reached into her husband's pocket, then adjusted the nebulizer. She instructed George firmly and patiently; directed his breathing, his inhalation of medication. There was an oddly maternal quality in her way of handling him; she had an assurance, a willingness to be leaned on; her strength seemed to expand as his need increased.

"Could someone take us to my brother's house now?" she asked Neary.

Catalano moved toward the Keelers, comforting arm extended.

"Sam, tell Tom Flynn to drive the Keelers. Where is your brother's house, Mrs. Keeler? You said Yonkers?"

Catalano extended a slip of paper. "I have the address, Captain. I could drive—"

Neary spoke right over Catalano. "You stick around the office and handle the telephones, Detective Catalano. Sergeant Gelber called in sick."

There was no way Sam could argue or protest. Neary was the boss.

And Sam Catalano was the District Attorney's spy. He had been in the squad just less than a year. Within two months of Sam's arrival, our eminent District Attorney, Jeremiah Kelleher, began needling Tim Neary about the way certain facets of certain investigations were being handled. It had long been Jeremiah's hope to get rid of Neary, who had been, of course, a political appointment. It had taken some pressure on Kelleher to accept Tim Neary in the first place and he had done so with malice. The position of squad commander of the District Attorney's Investigating Squad called for the rank of deputy inspector. Jeremiah refused to promote Tim from captain. Everyone was waiting everyone else out until Primary Day, which would decide who was washed out and who was on his way up. The only information Catalano had been able to pass along "upstairs" for the last ten months was bits and pieces of an inaccurate nature which I slipped him from time to time.

Aside from splits based on politics, racial, religious and ethnic backgrounds and specific personality differences, we're just one cohesive team.

Catalano risked a quick semidirty look before he left the office, and Tim said between his teeth, "That sneaky son-of-a-bitch."

We drove over to Fresh Meadows. There was a large group of curious people gathered in front of the three-story garden-apartment building where the Keelers lived. A young patrolman, posted at the entrance, quickly saluted Neary's captain shield, which was pinned to his dark-gray suit jacket. The patrolman looked very tense and young and eager.

Neary motioned him closer with a jerk of his head.

"Yes sir!" The kid saluted again.

"Officer, why don't you tell all these good people to go on to their own homes." Neary waved at a second uniformed patrolman who was standing at the curb. "You and this other officer clear this entire path from the building to the sidewalk. Just let residents in; and no loitering, residents or not. And pull that damn patrol car up straight. It's taking up two parking spaces."

Both patrolmen saluted and looked excited at having something to do. As we entered the building, Tim said to me, "Twelve years old, for God's sake. They're taking them on the job at twelve years old."

Which is how you tell you're getting old on the job. A few years ago, the new cops looked fifteen.

We stood in the living room, taking it in, getting the general effect. Tim, who married late in life and doesn't have children and lives in a luxury apartment on Queens Boulevard in Forest Hills, glanced around and said, "Tacky."

Captain Wise appeared in the entrance of the children's bedroom and waved us across the living room. We walked carefully around the technicians who were still dusting and squinting and photographing and testing. We stood in the doorway and absorbed the essentials: the room, approximately twelve feet by fifteen, contained twin beds, separated by a small night table on which stood a night lamp (yellow duck base, white pleated lampshade); half-empty plastic cup of water; box of tissues; a small lump of chewed-up and hardened pink gum.

There was a long, low chest of drawers built under the windows which faced the beds. On either side of the window, shelves had been built over the chests, up to the ceiling. The shelves contained an assortment of toys, games, stuffed animals and books. Directly in front of the windows, about two feet from the chests, there was a small round white table with two small white chairs. On the table was an open coloring book with a picture of an astronaut. It was carefully colored, not quite finished. The astronaut wore a red space suit, and the surface of the moon was purple against his green space boots. His space ship was partially filled in with a silver color; the silver crayon rested carefully in the center of the coloring book along with a large box of Crayolas.

The windows were curtained with sheer white cotton, decorated along the sides and edges with pale-yellow daisies, the same color as the dust ruffles on the beds. The walls were sunny yellow; the floor, a bright yellow-and-white plastic pattern. There was a thick oval Rya rug between the beds; it was white and yellow and red. The room and everything in it was very clean. There was just the slightest indication that the beds had been slept in: the Keeler boys had obviously been very quiet sleepers. It took something of an effort not to visualize their distorted, bloated faces resting on the clean yellow pillowcases.

Neary moved the curtain with his fingertip and studied the window. About four feet wide; casement type. The center pane was stationary. The panes on either side could be cranked open with a handle.

"It's okay, Tim," Wise told him, "we've dusted that already."

Tim cranked one pane open as far as it would go, then measured it roughly with his hands.

"Ten and a half inches," Wise said.

Neary nodded and leaned forward, looked out the window directly into the eyes of a homicide man outside.

"How far a drop?" Neary asked him.

"Six feet from the sill to the ground, Captain." The detective saw me. "How ya doin', Joe?" Then he shook his head. "Not a mark around here; no signs of footprints, no ladder, nothin'."

"C'mon," Captain Wise said to us. "You seen the parents' bedroom, Joe?"

"Uh-uh."

We trailed him through the apartment to the second bedroom. Wise stood to one side, watching our reactions as though he had offered us some kind of a treat. It was a room without any connection to the rest of the apartment. The carpeting was thick and soft, slightly lighter than the rose-beige color of the heavy satin bedspread and matching drapes. There was a chaise longue of the same satin, with an assortment of pillows tossed casually against the back of it; it faced toward a small portable color television set which was perched on the corner of a huge triple dresser.

"French provincial," Tim told us. He looked at himself in the ornate mirror over the dresser. "This is good stuff; expensive." He checked with Wise before touching, lightly, the assortment of perfume bottles which were displayed on a mirrored tray on the dresser. Tim leaned forward, sniffed, then said, "Sixty bucks an ounce. It's the real thing." He sniffed at a couple of other bottles, reeled off some French names. Tim was impressed. He pointed at the empty double-picture frame.

"We removed the pictures of the boys, Tim, for reproduction. I'll see your squad gets copies." Wise pulled at Neary's arm, anxious to get on with his show.

"Real silver; heavy, good quality," Tim said about the picture frame, then turned to watch Wise.

Using one finger, like an impresario, Wise opened a folding louvered door to expose one half of a custom-built closet which took up the whole long wall.

Aside from the sheer amounts of garments and items, what was fascinating was the organization of the closet. Everything was in an assigned place: every dress, blouse, pants suit, short or long skirt was precisely placed for quick reference. Two shelves over the hanging bar were filled with clear plastic boxes, through which an array of colors showed. It took a few seconds to realize that everything had been arranged according to color: from pale cream sweaters to pale yellow to bright yellow to gold to beige; from palest blue to sky blue to deep blue.

Wise gave us about a minute, then went to the other side of the closet and repeated his performance, opening the louvered door with a flourish. Here was the other side of the spectrum: deeper, darker, more blatant colors of clothing of all kinds, including a selection of long and apparently expensive gowns, carefully enclosed in clear plastic garment-protector bags. Shoes were arranged on slide-out trays along the floor of the closet.

Neary whistled between his teeth.

"Where are George's clothes?"

Wise winked at me, then reached up and shoved some of Kitty Keeler's clothes to one side. There was a section, approximately two and a half feet wide, of double hanging bars filled with men's clothing. Tim pulled out the arm of a butter-soft suede jacket, let his fingers move expertly. "Expensive stuff," he told us. "Not very much here, but what's here is good quality." He fingered through the rest of George Keeler's clothes. Tim, since his marriage to the lady lawyer, had taken to wearing custom-made suits, jackets, slacks, shirts—maybe custom-made socks and shorts too. He's developed a passionate interest in clothes, and one of the things he had against Jeremiah Kelleher was that "the phony bum buys his suits at Barney's, then has his wife sew in good labels."

I checked the windows underneath the heavy drapes and filmy curtains. Same-type casement window; directly ahead and to the left was a fairly new twenty-story building just at the edge of the development of garden apartments. To the right, at a distance of about a hundred yards, was a circular playground where some kids were shooting baskets. To the back of the playground was a thirteen-story apartment building, also set just outside the border of the development. I closed the window, let the curtains and drapes fall back into place. The voices of kids playing could still be heard; muffled, but still audible. Wise closed the bedroom door, and the three of us stood motionless, listening. The voices of the detectives in other parts of the apartment could be heard again, softer, but clearly audible, so that while the heavy carpeting and drapery buffered noise, they didn't eliminate it.

"Want to show you something," Chris Wise said, offering us another treat. He reached up and adjusted something on the inside of the bedroom door, then stepped back so that we could examine it.

It was a bolt lock, installed at eye level. Neary tested it, whistled tunelessly between his teeth, which is what he does when he's not ready to comment on something.

"Unusual, huh?" Wise asked. "Now, Tim, Joe, take another good look at this room. This is exactly as Mrs. Keeler left it."

The implication was clear, but Wise spelled it out anyway. "Not a thing out of place, right? The mother wakes up, looks around, sees her kids are missing, calls her husband, right? Then," Wise turned and gestured toward the bed, "she very calmly turns around and makes up the bed."

"How do you know she was calm at that point?"

"C'mon, Joe, don't be a wise guy, you know what I mean. Some distraught mother, huh? And how did she look, Joe, when you first got here?"

"Not bad if you like the type."

"You know what I mean, Joey. Makeup on, hair combed, nicely dressed, right? *Some distraught mother*," he repeated.

Neary watched the technicians at the door to the apartment. It had been dusted, prints lifted, photographed from all angles.

"This lock wasn't forced, Captain, no sir, no way."

"No signs of forced entry, Tim," Captain Wise told us. "Not via door or window." He turned to me, took a few seconds to control his annoyance. "Collins gave you that?"

He was referring to a pink-leather-covered telephone book; stamped in gold script letters on the cover was the name "Kitty Keeler." Just a quick scan through the pages revealed a lot of men's names; just first names and telephone numbers.

"Well, you *are* senior man in the team catching this, right? So I guess it's rightfully yours, but make sure I get a Xerox of every page, right, Joey?"

Neary said, not kidding, "You can have the case, lock, stock and whorey bedroom, Chris. Just say the word and it's all yours."

"Well, it would be the first time I got handed something as easy as this." Wise recited the facts for us. "Mama is alone with the kids. Mama goes to bed and sleeps through the night, doesn't hear a thing. Wakes up in the morning and the kids are gone. No forced entry; no signs of violence. Nothing. Kids are found dead six blocks away. And Mama didn't hear nothing at all." He leaned close to me, winked and said confidently, "Come on, Joe, show Captain Timmy here what you learned working for me for four years. Give him the answer to the whole damn thing. Give him the windup, Joe, before we go further." He poked me in the ribs with his elbow. "Who done it, Joe? In one word."

The first place you look for a perpetrator is within the immediate family: husbands kill wives; wives kill husbands; brothers, sisters, uncles, aunts, nephews, nieces, sons, daughters, mothers, fathers, in-laws, all kill each other. Only after they've all been cleared do you start looking at the wider circle of friends, old friends, new friends, ex-friends; then the circle widens and you begin to look at strangers.

In most cases, you don't have to go that far.

In most cases, the murderer is found right inside the four walls of the victim's home. Instead of stalking the streets looking for new victims, the murderer is usually at home helping to make the funeral plans.

I rocked back on my heels a little, looked toward the Hollywood-style bedroom, thought about the clothes and then about the woman and the little boys who had been taken from their beds without anyone hearing anything unusual at all.

Wise had stopped smiling. I gave him his one-word answer.

"*Mama.*"

Tim Neary whistled thoughtfully between his teeth, and Chris Wise said in a raspy, certain voice, "You betcha balls it's Mama."

CHAPTER 3

D R. ALEXANDER FRIEDMAN was a neat, compact man with a clipped precise manner and intelligent eyes. He was Viennese. According to the various framed documents decorating the wall of his office, he was a pediatrician with diplomate status, which meant he was qualified to teach pediatrics.

His time was tightly scheduled. Every morning, between 7 and 8 A.M., he was available for telephone consultation, and, barring emergency, he would not discuss symptoms with parents during another person's scheduled appointment. He made hospital rounds between 8:30 and noon; had lunch between noon and 1 P.M. His first office appointment was scheduled for 1 P.M. He took no break between appointments; he saw patients at his office until 5:30 or 6 P.M. His house calls began at 7 P.M., allowing him an hour for dinner. House calls were limited to communicable diseases, high-fever patients and emergencies.

I knew all this because when we spoke on the telephone Dr. Friedman told me his schedule and also that 2 P.M. was available to me, since there had been a cancellation.

So far, Dr. Friedman was the last known person, besides Kitty Keeler, to have seen the Keeler boys alive on the night they were murdered.

"Sit down, Detective Peters." He checked his wristwatch against his desk clock. I was right on time.

Dr. Friedman extended two cards. Each card was a precise, accurate record, containing every known medical fact from date of birth—to date of death—re Terence Thomas Keeler and George William Keeler.

"I have photostated copies of my records on the Keeler boys for you, to save time. If you have any difficulty in understanding any of my notations, please let me know."

The neatly printed series of dates, facts and figures seemed clear enough. "I'll look these over later and call you if there's any question."

Dr. Friedman leaned over and handed me his card. "Please try to call between seven and eight A.M. Unless, of course, it is some sort of emergency."

"Right. Doctor, what time did Mrs. Keeler call you yesterday?"

He glanced down at his daybook, then tapped his index finger at the information. "She called yesterday morning, at just about eight A.M."

"And what did she say?"

"That George, the younger child, seemed to have all the symptoms of the measles. It was no surprise. The child had been exposed to the measles approximately two and a half weeks ago." He nodded at his copies of the Keeler boys' medical records. "At that time, Mrs. Keeler brought the children in for gamma-globulin shots. She had missed their last regular appointment, in September. They were scheduled to have measles shots on . . ." Dr. Friedman held up a wait-a-minute finger, then opened his 1974 appointment book to a place marked by a paper clip. "Yes, on September twenty-fifth, but Mrs. Keeler canceled the appointment. She had to be out of town, with the boys. I cautioned her to see to it that she reschedule the appointment, but she didn't. They should have been inoculated against the measles." He added in a severe tone that defied argument, "There is no excuse whatever for a child to get the measles in this day and age."

"Did Mrs. Keeler miss appointments often?"

"No, very rarely. In fact, that is the only one I can recall offhand. At any rate, Mrs. Keeler telephoned me on April first," he checked this with his current appointment book, "and told me the boys had been exposed and she asked if it was too late for inoculation. I told her that it was, but to bring the boys in." He glanced at his book again. "Yes, later that day, after five, they came for a shot of gamma globulin each."

"And what would that do?"

"In the event the boys did come down with the measles, the gamma globulin would tend to lessen the duration of the illness. They would have a case of shorter duration. When Mrs. Keeler telephoned yesterday morning, she reported that George had a sore throat, high fever and was flushed. I scheduled him for a home visit."

"And at what time did you see him?"

Dr. Friedman held up his hand to let me know that I'd interrupted him. "At about four-thirty yesterday, Mrs. Keeler telephoned again. George's temperature had shot up to over a hundred and four and he had come out in a rash. I instructed her to give the child a child's aspirin, which is what I had earlier instructed her. One every three hours for a high fever. And she was to give the child an alcohol rub and cool water to drink; cold cloth on his head. Keep him as comfortable and quiet as possible. As is usual with a high-fevered child, I made the

Keeler apartment my first stop last night. I arrived at precisely seven-o-five P.M."

"And it was definitely the measles."

"Yes, of course. Mrs. Keeler seemed upset because she felt George was having a very *bad* case, despite the gamma globulin. I explained to her what I meant by a mild case. The *symptoms* aren't mild; the *duration* of the serious symptoms are shortened by the cautionary shot. I told her to anticipate a difficult night, the child would be uncomfortable, but by morning the child would probably have a lowered temperature, continuing sore throat, possible upset stomach, but the worst would be over. I did caution her to keep close check on the child's temperature."

"Through the night?"

"Until such time that it remained below the hundred-and-two-degree point. After that I wouldn't advise disturbing a sleeping child."

"And what about the other boy—Terry?"

"I checked him, then told Mrs. Keeler there were several possibilities. One, that he would come down with the measles within hours, or a full day at most. Or that he might have a natural immunity and not come down with measles at all. Or that his initial exposure hadn't been enough to cause the illness. But that, without a natural immunity, which is rare, he would probably come down with measles in about two weeks as a result of his exposure to George."

"Which would have been just about when George would have been up and around?"

"Yes."

We stared at each other, but it was impossible to guess what Dr. Friedman was thinking. I dug a cigarette from my pocket and looked around for an ashtray.

"I don't permit smoking in my office. Or in my home." He opened his top desk drawer, reached in, then scattered lollipops toward me. "They contain no sugar. Won't rot the teeth or the lungs." He studied me, then said quietly, "Your cough is very indicative, you know."

"My cough? What cough?"

"Apparently it's become so automatic that you're not even aware of it." He shook his head slightly and I suppressed a sudden need to cough. He checked his watch and desk clock, clasped his hands on his desk and asked, "Detective Peters, what else can I tell you?"

"Dr. Friedman, to the best of your knowledge, what kind of a mother was Mrs. Keeler?"

"Nonabusive, if that's what you mean. The children were brought in to me regularly from the time they were born. Their physical and mental and emotional development has always been well within normal range. The older boy, Terry, was an extremely bright child: very precocious as an infant. Early walker, early talker, very fluent. The younger child, George, was somewhat slower by comparison, but that's always a risky sort of judgment and I don't encourage it. The boys were well-fed, well-clothed; they never exhibited any indication of being abused children, if that's what you're asking me."

"How would you characterize Mrs. Keeler's behavior last night? How did she seem to you?"

Carefully, Dr. Friedman said, "That is a very subjective thing, you understand. Not knowing the young woman very well, it is a surface observation. I have found her to be a competent, level-headed young woman. Certainly not among those young mothers I classify as my 'hysterics.' She wasn't overly alarmed by the illness. She exhibited what I would call *proper concern*. There was one thing, though."

"Yes?"

"Well, she *did* ask me if it was possible that George could travel in two or three days."

"*Travel?* Did she say to where?"

"She said she'd been planning to go to Phoenix, Arizona, this coming Saturday and thought about taking the boys with her. Said something about . . . didn't I think the weather there might be beneficial to George. I told her what I'm sure she already knew. That it was unthinkable. Bearing in mind not only George's illness, but Terry's potential illness as well."

"What was her reaction to that? Did it seem to upset her?"

"I think she regretted having asked me."

Dr. Friedman's look of disapproval must have stopped many young mothers from asking obvious questions about as effectively as it stopped my lighting a cigarette.

"How long did you stay at the Keelers'?"

"I left at seven-thirty. Of course, I did make two phone calls prior to leaving. First, to check with my service and to alert them as to my next call in case of emergency. Second, to assure the parents of the next patient that I was on my way." He shrugged slightly and almost smiled. "With children as patients, emergencies pop up from one minute to the next. I like the parents to know I can be reached in short order."

There was a soft chiming sound; he glanced at his desk clock, then selected one of the cards from his desk blotter. "Mrs. Ellis. Ten minutes early."

I took the cue and stood up when he did, extended my hand and was surprised again by the firmness of his grip.

He didn't release my hand immediately. "This . . . this whole thing, Detective Peters. Those two children . . ." There was a totally unexpected look of deep, personal pain; the Keeler boys *had* been more than two index cards filled with precise, bloodless notations.

"Dr. Friedman, I told you when I called earlier the circumstances under which these children's bodies were found. Just between us, strictly off the record, one experienced man to another, what do *you* think might have happened to those boys?"

His eyes never left my face as he shrugged and walked to the door leading to his outer office and waiting room. He held his hand on the doorknob for a moment, then said, "All kinds of terrible things happen in this world. I try to keep them alive and healthy. You try to find out who kills them. I don't envy you your job. If I can be of any help, please don't hesitate to call." He added quickly, "Any morning, between seven and eight."

CHAPTER 4

As soon as Sam Catalano heard my voice on the phone, he started complaining. "I don't know why the hell I'm stuck in the office, Joe. It's *my* case as much as yours. Actually, *I* took the initial call and . . ."

"Sam? Sam. Is Captain Neary there or what?"

In the silence, I pictured Sam lighting a cigarette with his flashy silver lighter; heard him exhale in a wounded sigh.

"No, but he left a message for you, Joe. You're to go over to 447 Woodhaven Boulevard and see a Patti MacDougal. She called the Keeler apartment about an hour ago. She'd heard about the murders on the radio and wanted to know what she should do about Kitty Keeler's car."

"Kitty Keeler's car?"

"Yeah, Joe. Kitty loaned this girl her car yesterday. A white Porsche. How about that, Joe, a *Porsche*."

"That's terrific, Sam. Now repeat the girl's name and address so I can write it down."

Sam gave me the information, then launched into a recital of all the reasons why he shouldn't be in the office, but should be out in the field. I wasn't really listening; what I was thinking about was that the Porsche would have to be driven to the precinct. And then the girl would have to be driven to the squad office for a statement. A police officer should drive the Porsche, just in case it contained any evidence of any nature whatever. If I drove the Porsche, with the girl, to the precinct, then I would be stuck without my car.

"Tell you what, Sam. Is there anyone else in the office to handle the phones?"

I knew there was; I could hear talking and typing in the background.

"Yeah, sure. Finn's here, and Young and—"

"Okay, Sam. Tell you what. Meet me at the girl's apartment in about twenty minutes. Then you can drive the Porsche over to the 107th."

"Right, right, Joe." Then, trying not to sound concerned, but sounding concerned, he said, "Hey, Joe. What about Captain Neary? Ya know, he *did* tell me to stay in the office and take the phones."

"Don't worry about it, Sam. You'll be back before he is. And I'll handle it." To make sure he'd show, I added, "A white Porsche, huh, Sam? Boy, that's *some* car."

"And how. I'll meet you there, then, Joe."

I should have just hung up at that point, but through force of habit I couldn't resist. My voice went low, almost a whisper. "Hey, one more thing, Sam. Anyone around the office say anything about the narcotics thing?"

"The narcotics thing?"

"Jeez, Sam, not out loud, for Christ's sake. Listen, just forget I said anything, all right? It may or may not pan out. But if it does, Sam, man. Imagine us walking into a two-million-dollar narcotics deal. Listen, listen, just forget what I told you, Sam. See you later, okay?"

It would be interesting to see how long it took for that tidbit to bounce around.

The house on Woodhaven Boulevard was one of those big old frame buildings that had, in its heyday, been the home of a large and prosperous family. Although the sixty-odd-year-old porch sagged a little, all in all the house was kept in good repair. Even the long dark hallways and narrow tall staircase held remnants of a respectable past: the shoulder-high oak panels were still beautiful and the plaster walls above had been recently given a fresh coat of light-green paint.

The division into rooming units was somewhat awkward and the doors were unnumbered, but Patti MacDougal was expecting someone and as soon as the outside bell rang she came out and waited on the landing.

The girl was a slob. Without the slightest indication of embarrassment or any attempt at apology, she waved me into the most incredibly filthy room I've seen in a very long time.

Not just cluttered, but filthy. An assortment of dirty clothing was strewn about the room; dirty underwear was looped on doorknobs; dresses with layers of armhole stains were hung lopsidedly on hangers which had been balanced precariously on the hinges of doors. There was a small utility kitchen unit in one recessed wall. The small sink was filled with a collection of dishes, pots, cups, scrapings of various foods. There was a cold, dry, half-eaten old-looking piece of pizza, half wrapped in aluminum foil, on the top of the three-burner stove. Also, a package of brownish chopped meat, still in the supermarket wrappings, on a plate set on one of the burners. Two large black cockroaches were making forays under the foil to get at the pizza. They darted back and forth, back and forth.

The girl politely offered me a choice of seats: the unmade, gray-sheet-covered daybed, the lumpy armchair or a hard wooden chair. I sat on the very edge of the wooden chair and watched some sort of tiny black bugs race across the back of the armchair. Patti noticed them, too, and slapped at them with the flat of her hand, then smiled at me as though we were partners in the constant battle against nature.

She began to tell me the story of her life: how she had entered the country two years ago as a domestic from Glasgow, Scotland, with a guaranteed job in the household of an unsuspecting New Jersey doctor and his family. How she had spent most of her time eating, polishing her nails and entertaining the Avon Lady while ignoring any number of household catastrophes. She patted her hips, which seemed about to burst the overly stretched blue stretch slacks, then her cheeks, which were puffed out as though someone had put an air hose into her mouth and just kept pumping. Then she dug around through a collection of pictures and papers on her dresser top until she found what she was looking for. It was a photograph of a tall, slender smiling pretty girl who might have been a distant relative of the current Patti MacDougal, but it was, of course, a photograph of the previous Patti MacDougal, less some fifty pounds she had put on while enjoying the good life. Judging from the way her clothes fit her, she hadn't gotten around to shopping for larger sizes.

"How do you know Mrs. Keeler, Patti?"

"Oh, I met her through my friend Marge Kennicutt. She came out a year before me, you know. I've been through so many different jobs, you see." Patti grinned at her lack of ability to settle down. "And last November I was really out of it, if you take my meaning, and Marge let me move in with her for a bit, but she was newly married, and I was in the way and all, but so anyway. See, Marge got a call from Mrs. Keeler, that she was needed for a few days, or could she recommend a girl to stay with the boys—"

"You're the Scotch girl."

Patti gasped and pushed her lips out as though to whistle. "You mean you've heard of me! A policeman, and you've heard of me!"

"Not officially, Patti, don't worry about it."

She considered that for a moment or two, then ducked her head down and looked up at me from under her eyebrows and a lock of dark hair that had fallen over her face. "It's *Scots*," she told me. "Not

Scotch. Scotch is something you drink; I'm not something you drink, you see?"

It was a few seconds before I realized that Patti was being coy; that she was fluttering those stubby, blue-beaded mascaraed eyelashes for my benefit.

All the time we were talking, Patti MacDougal was feeding herself one of the creamed varieties of canned soup. She walked around, one hand holding the handle of the greasy white enamel pot filled with the lumpy stuff, the other hand guiding a long-handled wooden spoon from the pot to her mouth. Before she resettled on the bulging, buggy armchair, she extended the pot toward me: wouldn't I like some? Then she sat down and proceeded to lap up the thick soup with an obvious, total enjoyment.

"You and Mrs. Keeler are on good terms, then, Patti? In spite of what happened last November?"

The sight of Patti delicately biting at a solid glob of soup didn't do my ulcer any good.

"Oh, she's that nice, really she is. No, she wasn't angry with me." Patti shrugged her shoulders and laughed girlishly. "It *was* bad of me, though, and I was *that* sorry."

From time to time, Patti baby-sat with the boys, but only for an evening or a morning. She admitted, with a grin, she wasn't that trustworthy to baby-sit for longer periods of time.

"How come you borrowed Mrs. Keeler's car, Patti?"

A few days ago, Patti had had an accident with her Volkswagen and she called Mrs. Keeler for help. Mrs. Keeler apparently knows any number of men who can handle any manner of catastrophes. On Mrs. Keeler's advice, Patti called a Mr. Mogliano, and within half an hour a tow truck arrived and the battered VW was taken away for repairs, which, she had been assured, would cost her only a nominal fee.

"Well, so, that was over the weekend, and, see, I had this very important appointment for last night, and my car wasn't ready, and there I was, up the creek. Without a car, do you see?"

She called Kitty Keeler for advice; was advised to hop a cab to Fresh Meadows for the loan of the Porsche. Upon her solemn promise to be very careful.

"Oh, and it's a beautiful machine, the Porsche, you know."

"What time did you see Mrs. Keeler yesterday, Patti?"

She had arrived at 4 P.M., stayed with the boys for about forty-five minutes, while Kitty went marketing, then stayed on to have a cup of tea.

"How was Mrs. Keeler, Patti? Was she upset, because George was sick? And she couldn't go to Phoenix because of that?"

Patti stopped licking the last of the soup from the spoon. "Oh, my, you do know all sorts of things, don't you? Well, she was upset, some, I'm sure. Because, see, Mrs. Silverberg, the old lady from next door, is in hospital and all—"

"Did Mrs. Keeler ask you if *you* could stay with the boys?"

Patti laughed indulgently at her own shortcomings. "Oh, noooo, she wouldn't want me for that period of time. I'm not all that reliable, I admit it on myself, you see."

"What time did you leave the Keeler apartment?"

"At just after five, it was. Oh, and I drove the Porsche, and I don't mind telling you, my young man of the night was that impressed."

Very carefully, I led her into a discussion of the kind of mother Kitty Keeler was. According to Patti, Kitty was about on a par with the Virgin Mary.

"I'll bet you didn't know I'm Catholic," Patti bet me. "Most people are surprised to learn that there are Catholic Scots."

She sure had me there; I'd never have guessed. She continued her testimonial, then launched into a detailed account of her date, which really sounded terrific.

"So then, this morning, when you put on the radio you heard about what happened to the boys, to Terry and George?"

Patti stopped speaking in the middle of a word; she shrugged her shoulders and shuddered as though a chill ran down her back. Her small eyes filled with tears and they spilled down her round cheeks, leaving long royal-blue streaks of mascara.

"And you haven't seen or spoken to Mrs. Keeler since . . . what was it, five o'clock last night?"

She nodded absently, then jerked her head at me. "Oh, no, wait, that wasn't what I said, was it?"

"I'm sorry. I must have misunderstood, Patti. Did you see or speak to Mrs. Keeler after five last night?"

She became evasive; her face screwed up with indecision. I leaned forward and reached for her hands; they grasped mine with a surprising tension.

"What's wrong, Patti? What is it you're not sure you should tell me?"

"How did you know that?" she asked in wonder. It's been a long time since I was so impressive.

"Because you're a nice girl and I can see you're worrying about something. It'll be better if you tell me; then you won't have to worry about it anymore. Patti?"

"Well, you see, last night I drove my gentleman friend to his place and left right away. He's coming down with the flu and didn't want me to stay around. He lives in Manhattan, you see, so as I was driving over the bridge to Queens, I fell to thinking that why ever should Mrs. Keeler be without her car in the morning? It was good enough of her to lend it to me; the least I could do was to return it, and take a taxicab home, you see?"

"Very thoughtful, Patti." Very carefully, I asked her, "So you went back to Mrs. Keeler's apartment late last night? What time would that be?"

"It was two-thirty. This morning. I pulled into the parking lot, see I know her parking space, it's all reserved and all, and I knew it was two-thirty, the news was just coming on and all."

"And what happened then? You went to Mrs. Keeler's apartment at two-thirty?"

"Well, yes." She hesitated; this was the tricky part; the part of it that had her worried. I squeezed her hands lightly; they were very cold.

"Did you see her at that time? Patti?"

"Well. No. See, that was the funny thing. I went to the apartment door and tapped. I didn't want to wake the boys, so I didn't ring the bell at first."

"What about waking Mrs. Keeler? Didn't you think she'd be asleep at that time?"

"Oh, no. Mrs. Keeler is so used to working late-night hours, at the spa, you see. She hardly ever gets to sleep before three or four, she'd told me that. Besides, I'd seen her bedroom light on, around the back, you know, when I came from the parking lot."

"Okay, what happened then?"

"Well, she didn't come to the door. So finally I rang the bell. I hated to do that, it's such a loud bell, but, you know, I thought maybe she'd the telly on and couldn't hear me tapping."

"Did she come to the door?"

Patti shook her head, staring at our collection of fingers.

"Then what did you do? Did you hear anything from inside? The boys crying or calling out or anything?"

"It was quiet inside. From what I could hear with my ear at the door."

"Then what did you do?"

"Well, then I drove home. Back to here, and I got ready for bed. And then . . ." She wavered; drew her hands onto her own lap.

"Come on, Patti, then what?"

Apparently she couldn't talk unless I squeezed the words out of her hands. They were still cold, but, at the same time, now they were sweaty.

"Well. I was sort of worried, you know. Her not coming to the door and all. So . . . I went out into the hallway there, where the phone is. And I called her. Mrs. Keeler."

"And . . . ?"

"She answered; on the first ring, in fact. I was relieved to hear her voice. That she was . . . all right, you know?"

"What time was this, Patti? And what did she say?"

"It was a minute or so after three; the news was on again." She gestured vaguely toward her table radio. "And so, well, I told her that I had stopped by, with the car for her, and all. But, well, I think she was angry with me. Or annoyed."

"Why? What did she say when you told her about knocking on the door and ringing the bell?"

"Well, she said that she'd been under the shower and had the radio on in the bathroom and didn't hear me at the door."

She looked up at me with her small runny eyes, waiting for me to ask the right question; unwilling to volunteer anything more.

"But you didn't believe that, right, Patti?" I took a calculated guess. "The bathroom window faces the parking lot, doesn't it?" She nodded. "Was the light on in the bathroom at that time?"

Patti shook her head. She looked at me hopefully. "Maybe she was bathing in the dark? Do you think that might be possible?"

I shrugged; that made her feel a little better.

"Patti, did you see anyone, anyone at all, either in the parking lot or near the building? Did anyone see you there at two-thirty this morning?"

She hadn't noticed anyone; it would take days of bell-ringing and hundreds of interviews to determine if anyone in the vicinity could confirm the fact of Patti's presence in Fresh Meadows at the time she claimed.

When I told her that I'd drive her to the squad office, she smiled, shoved the tears from her cheeks with the back of her hands, and dug through a morass of garments in the small closet until she finally bent down and yanked out a short bright-blue fake-fur jacket. When she put it on, she looked like a stuffed blue teddy bear.

We hit the street just as Sam Catalano got out of his car. He waved and called to me. I waved back, got the Porsche's keys from Patti, tossed them to Sam just before I got behind the wheel. The Porsche was parked right behind my car.

"See you later, Sam. They're waiting at the 107th for the Porsche. Try to get back to the squad before Captain Neary."

I couldn't hear what Sam was calling out to me, so I just waved as we drove past him.

CHAPTER 5

W HILE I was in Neary's office giving him the essentials of what Patti MacDougal had told me, Patti was making friends in the squad room. To keep her happy until her statement was typed and ready for her signature, she'd been provided with a bag of Burger Kings and a couple of chocolate milkshakes.

"Jesus, Joe, let's get her story confirmed."

"I've notified Wise. And I pulled Collins and Schwartz from the Peck Avenue location and told them to question the owner of every car in the Fresh Meadows parking lot. Maybe we'll get lucky."

It wasn't that Tim was generous with his authority as squad commander; he wasn't. At the point where the case was ready to be all pulled together, he would remind us both that even though I was the senior first-grade detective in the squad, he was the boss so far as credit was concerned. District Attorney Jeremiah Kelleher waited upstairs to remind Tim that in the event of failure it was also all Tim's.

"I wish the goddamn Medical Examiner would call. Even with tentative information." Tim was cracking his knuckles; a sure sign of building tension. "Have you seen the early edition of the *Post?* They got someone working in my squad or what?"

Some enterprising, ambitious anonymous reporter, trying to earn his byline, had gotten hold of the fact that there were more than a hundred men's names in Kitty's pink leather telephone book. And that of the names checked so far, more than half were known to the police in connection with various interrelated criminal matters. That was how this anonymous reporter described it: "various interrelated criminal matters."

"The paper got that almost as fast as it was relayed to me, Joe." Tim whistled softly between his teeth, and his eyes glazed over for a moment. Then he blinked and smashed his hand down on his desk. "Hey, where the hell is that dago son-of-a-bitch Catalano?"

Tim Neary has nothing against Italians. His wife, Catherine, is Italian. It was the first thing he told me about her, years ago when he asked me to be his best man: "She's Italian, Joe, but a terrific girl."

I convinced him that Sam was safely out of the way. After turning it over in his mind, Neary said, "Good. Good. In fact, Joe, give him a call over at the 107th and tell him he's to stay with the Porsche. He's not to let it out of his sight."

"He's probably on his way back here by now, Tim."

Tim smiled tightly. "Good. The minute he gets here, tell him to turn his ass around and get back to the Porsche. The son-of-a-bitch." Then, just in case, he asked, "You don't think the car has any connection to the case do you, Joe?"

"At this point, I doubt it. But someone used a car to carry those bodies over to Peck Avenue. While Jefferson is typing up the girl's statement, his partner is checking out how and where she spent the night. I'd say she rings true."

"We gotta keep right on top of this case, Joe. You realize that, don't you?" For about the third time in three minutes, Tim checked his watch. "If we don't wind this thing up fast and clean, that bastard upstairs could replace me, Joe. He could justify it, and how the hell would that look in my credentials? Getting bounced over a headline case could screw me up, but good." Tim stood up, swung around and kicked his wastebasket. It was metal and the ringing sound lasted for about fifteen seconds. Then he shoved his hands into his pockets and turned around to me.

"We're going upstairs in about ten minutes, Joe, to brief him. From what's been coming in all day, this Keeler dame is a flat-out tramp. If her husband didn't help her, and if she didn't have her car last night, the chances are that the guy who helped her is someone listed in her pink book, right?" He rubbed some coins together inside his pocket and whistled tunelessly. Then, "According to the neighbors, Keeler hardly spent any time at all with her kids. This elderly woman—Mrs. Silverberg?—practically raised them from the time they were born. I want you to talk to Mrs. Silverberg first thing tomorrow, Joe. She's at the Long Island Jewish Hospital. She can probably give you the lowdown on the little mother and some of her playmates." His eyes got that glazed look again, then, as though talking to himself, he said, "No one else could have done it. It *had* to be the mother."

Tim turned and faced the traffic outside his window on Queens Boulevard and seemed to go into a trance. I glanced absently at the collection of black-framed photographs that took up most of the wall over the green leather couch that Tim's wife had bought him for a birthday present. Most of the pictures were of Tim shaking hands with someone or other who was in the process of presenting Tim an award in the shape of an engraved brass plaque mounted on wood. Most of the awards were hanging along the back wall of Tim's office over the long narrow conference table.

There were a few familiar faces in the pictures besides Tim's: Bobby Kennedy standing off to one side as Tim accepted the Irishman-of-the-Year Award from some hearty-looking Irishman back in the early sixties; Tim and his wife, Catherine, flanking stocky Richard Daley (they had been engaged then and Catherine had been a delegate to Chicago in 1968; the occasion of the picture had been some Communion breakfast in New York). Daley's expression was murderous, his eyes glinting and tough, and both Tim and Catherine looked reverent and impressed.

The only outsized memento was the framed, yellowing front page of the old *New York Mirror*, the thick black headline saying HERO ROOKIES SAVE 10 KIDS IN B'KLYN BLAZE. There we were on the front page, Tim and me, the hero rookies, our faces younger and more innocent than either of us had ever been, handing over the last-saved kid into the arms of an ambulance attendant. Three of the kids died subsequently, but we both got first-class commendations anyway. It was that particular incident that more or less determined the direction of Tim's future career in the department.

"Hell," Tim had said to me the next day in the hospital, where he was resting up from smoke inhalation and I was awaiting surgery on the torn cartilage of my right knee, "I'm not going to end up burning my ass for a bunch of little nigger kids left alone by their whore of a mother. I'm signing up at Delehanty's for the next sergeant's exam and if you have any brains at all you'll come with me."

I spent three weeks on sick leave and then four weeks on light duty while my knee was healing. I was assigned to a desk job at the old Bureau of Criminal Identification, where I made a few useful contacts and performed a few "favors" for a couple of people in positions to reciprocate if and when I needed a favor. Which is something that Delehanty's doesn't teach you: how and under what circumstances to pile up favors owed. And when to call in debts.

In the next couple of years, while I worked foot patrol out of the old Twenty-third Precinct in Harlem, Tim was collecting sergeant's stripes and managed to get himself assigned to a spot in Manhattan headquarters, which gave him plenty of time to study for the lieutenant's exam. I liked my job; I liked the people up there. It wasn't the way it is now, when even a black cop's life is on the line the minute he sets foot outside the precinct house. If you were a good guy, you made a certain number of friends—among the local shopkeepers, ginmill owners and customers, neighborhood working stiffs as well as neighborhood sharpies. It was like any other situation: people were suspicious at first, then once they sized you up, once they accepted you, once you had an established working relationship and people knew what they could expect from you, you knew what to expect from them.

I delivered a lot of babies; broke up a hundred family Saturday-night fights; arrested more than twenty rapists even though I knew that when it's black on black the case is odds on to be dumped. I saved—or at least prolonged—a couple of lives, using first-aid techniques. I collected twelve more commendations before I killed a man and nearly got killed myself.

I went into a tenement to try and reason with some lunatic who had slashed his wife's throat, then castrated and stabbed her lover. Before I said one reassuring word, he managed to sink his knife into the side of my neck so that within seconds we were in close, intimate contact, his knife in me, my revolver dug into the soft tissue of his throat just beneath his jaw. My shot blew half his head off, and as he died he dragged his knife down along my neck and across my chest. I got a first-class commendation for killing that guy, although the general opinion was that I was a dumbbell for having allowed myself to get cut: that I should have come in shooting and saved conversation for later. An opinion with which, of course, I finally agreed.

While I was recuperating, with thirty-six stitches making a jagged pattern down my throat and chest, Tim Neary came to wise me up. He had just passed pretty high on the lieutenant's list and was already beginning to study for the captain's exam. Tim was a lot smarter than me in a lot of ways. For instance, he knew how to use what I had collected over the years. About a week after I spoke with Tim, a lieutenant from the Bureau of Special Services visited me on behalf of his newly appointed squad commander, a deputy inspector I had done a favor for when he was still a captain. I followed Tim's instructions: said all the right things, looked blank at all the right times. I was assigned to the B.O.S.S. as a third-grade detective when my recuperation was over.

The squad handled all kinds of undercover surveillance assignments, ranging from illegal activities of various political dissidents to wildcat-strike threats by leaders of municipal unions, to discreet background investigations of individuals proposed for high city-government appointive office. We acted more as an information-collecting unit than as an enforcement branch of the department. The squad also handled security assignments, and since I spoke a passable French (my wife, Jen, is

French-Canadian), I drew a lot of the glamour escort jobs: seeing to the safety of visiting foreign dignitaries or heads of government attending sessions of the U.N.; keeping between the body I had to protect and the various emotional demonstrators who had carried old political grievances to the streets of New York on behalf of citizens still in the mother country.

I felt sorry for the uniformed cops assigned to handle the political protesters; for the most part, the guys assigned to these various functions didn't know what the hell the whole thing was all about, but they ended up being the only visible form of "oppression." While the poor slobs on the street were yelling and shoving and provoking their own arrests, I was with the targets of their anger, be they Russian or Chinese or Cuban or Israeli or whatever, who were usually socializing politely with one another, drinking and eating at any number of gourmet luncheons, dinners or receptions. The closest thing to antagonism at these affairs would be one diplomat bragging to another about the marvelous custom tailor he had located in New York and then smugly and undiplomatically refusing to give the name of said tailor.

Occasionally, some nut in Hollywood would come up with some kind of gimmick to publicize an about-to-open film, and, the Mayor being ever anxious to attract film-makers back to New York and being himself one of the beautiful people who loved to mix it up with movie stars, we would be handed over as taxpayer-paid personal bodyguards to an assortment of producers, directors, male and female stars and celebrities. Some of the guys got sore about these assignments. I found them interesting: like a visit to a foreign world.

Even the hardest old-timers in the squad, the impossible to impress, would always remember the special assignments to the Secret Service contingent traveling to New York with John F. Kennedy. Usually, when you're assigned to a top government official, you never get beyond a polite "Good morning," but at the end of a day J.F.K. would wave a mob of us into the hotel suite, kick off his shoes, yank down his tie, break out the booze and egg us on to tell him our "war stories" about life on the streets of New York. I always had the feeling he was a buff; that under other circumstances he'd have been one helluva Irish cop, with that quick sharp wit and incisive way of getting right to the center of things with a few fast remarks.

The department went higher-education crazy in the late sixties and started to replace members of the various squads and bureaus, regardless of experience and performance, with college-educated men. Half the guys I worked with began hustling back and forth between assignments and classes at John Jay College of Criminal Justice, frantically compiling credits. I figured that either my years of various police experience qualified me or they didn't qualify me for the job I had been doing for the last five years; which had earned me promotion to second-grade detective.

I got bounced—without prejudice—from the B.O.S.S. at the beginning of 1967, and Tim, who had just made captain and was assigned to a precinct in Brooklyn, arranged for me to be assigned to the Queens Homicide Squad.

I hated Homicide. I hated everything about it, including some of the guys I worked with who liked to pretend that they were instrumental in "solving" a case. Any cop worth his shield knows that unless a homicide is committed by someone close to the victim, the odds are that the perpetrator will remain at large. Unless you get lucky and an informant comes through for you. Informants—what the Hollywood cops call "snitches"—are the backbone of any successful police department. The informant is generally the scum of the earth, and when his usefulness is over, any cop would throw him to the wolves without a blink. Which is not exactly the cute relationship of the television-series Homicide Squad hero who sleuths out solutions week after week, using ten bucks' worth of information and a head full of clever ideas. And who feels an off-the-cuff affection for his "snitch" and vows to revenge his death, should he get caught by his fellow hoods.

I worked Homicide for four years and was promoted from second to first grade, which meant my salary was at captain's level, same as Tim's. Of course, I could always be dumped all the way back to patrolman. Tim, with his civil-service rating, could never be lower than captain and had a wide-open future into the upper-echelon appointive ranks. Once his political friends were in position to help.

On the wall space between the two windows behind Tim's desk were mementos of his graduation from the sixteen-week-long F.B.I. training session which Tim had attended in Washington, D.C., in 1969. There was a two-foot-square replica of the F.B.I official insignia, all blue and gold with white lettering: DEPARTMENT OF JUSTICE at the top of a circle; FEDERAL BUREAU OF INVESTIGATION at the bottom of the circle. Inside the circle, a badgelike emblem, the top half gold with a blue scale, showing, I guess, the quality of justice, the bottom half striped red and white like a peppermint stick. Beneath the badge was a sort of unfurling ribbon divided into three sections, proclaiming FIDELITY—BRAVERY—INTEGRITY.

Centered beneath this was an expensively framed photograph of Tim Neary having his hand shaken by J. Edgar Hoover. Tim's face was wooden, his eyes riveted on the somewhat pop-eyes that seemed to look right through him.

Tim had confided to me, years ago, after a couple of drinks too many, that there seemed to be something a little "strange" about the Director. (That's what you called him if and when you talked about him at all: the Director.)

Tim told me how he and the other graduates of the F.B.I. training session had been rehearsed for the graduation ceremony to the point where every man in the room, regardless of his age, rank, experience and professional position, was reduced to a dry-mouthed nervous little kid afraid to so much as blink or swallow when in the Presence. Not to mention the emotional condition of the F.B.I. instructors responsible for their training and their successful completion of the prescribed course. They had been rehearsed as to the precise number and length— in inches—of the steps to take when approaching the Director for presentation of the diploma; the exact distance to maintain between them; how far to extend the left hand for the diploma and the right hand for the handshake. Which had been, Tim confided, warm, moist, loose and heavy. They had been told to say nothing more or less than "Thank you, Mr. Director"; to release the handshake immediately, drop the eyes respectfully, turn and noiselessly return to their assigned seats. There was to be no coughing, throat-clearing, whispering, slouching; there were to be no crossed legs; feet were to remain motionless, neatly aligned, whether standing or sitting. No excess movement of any kind in the room, including blinking or facial twitching.

The Director did not care for any of the above behavior.

Today, everyone and his publisher is telling "strange" J. Edgar Hoover stories, making accusations and telling jokes right on television, but this was in 1969. Tim came over to my house at six the next morning after our little drinking session, woke me up, held my arm in a killing grasp and made me swear to God, on the foundation of old friendship, that I would forget that he had ever mentioned anything at all about the Director. Of course I swore, and we never mentioned the matter again.

There wasn't much that Tim's wife could do with the color of the walls in Tim's office. As squad commander, he rated a sort of municipal bluish gray as compared to the municipal greenish gray of the squad room. I don't know where the hell the city buys its paint, but somehow they managed to get a dirty color to swab on the walls so that the room looks exactly the same before and after painting. Tim's venetian blinds were gray metal city issue and were some improvement on the squad room's yellowing heavy cloth window shades. His wife had supplied the custom-made heavy green-and-blue drapes and the heavy flat green-and-blue tweed wall-to-wall carpeting, whereas the squad room has no drapes and we make do on the municipal brownish-gray rubber-based floor tiles. Tim's medium-size wooden desk came with his job, but his wife had dressed it up with a collection of executive-type furnishings from Bloomingdale's: a good leather-edged blotter holder; matching green leather pencil cup; silver-framed photo of herself; a couple of gag-type paperweights. The gold-plated pen-and-pencil set had been a presentation gift to Tim from the Sergeants' Benevolent Association. The rest of the stuff on the desk, metal file trays, battered intercom, four-button black telephone, was standard city issue.

Tim turned from the window, checked his watch for maybe the tenth time, touched the knot of his tie, then carefully put on his suit jacket. He shook his head at me and resettled the lapels on my jacket. "Joey, Joey, you still dress like a Bronx boy. Where the hell do you buy your clothes, Alexander's?" He tried to sound casual, but he was as tight as wire.

Even the District Attorney's secretary's office had paneled walls and real leather couches and wall-to-wall carpeting. The secretary's desk was bigger than Tim's and she clicked away on her living, breathing new red electric typewriter. She told the D.A. we were waiting, and his loud voice boomed from the intercom over the soft hum of the typewriter. She raised her eyebrows brightly and jerked her head, adding her permission for us to enter the realm.

The D.A.'s office was not only paneled, draped and carpeted, it was also chandeliered with a huge brass affair hanging from the center of the ceiling, giving off a warm amber glow. There were built-in bookcases along one wall, filled with what looked like real-leather-bound sets of lawbooks. Which looked like no one had touched them since the day they had been installed. The furniture was all dark and heavy. There were a couple of oil paintings on the walls, each with its own little brass light and heavy frame. In one corner of the room, there was an antique mirror framed in dark heavy brass, with a small matching console table on which rested the D.A.'s silver hairbrush and silver clothing brush. They were engraved with his initials, as were his silver letter opener and his outsized silver fountain pen. I knew this because Jerry Kelleher liked to make a public point of the fact that he was used to all this: to real leather furniture, wall-to-wall everything and his initials on old silver. His father had been a judge, so he was a second-generation "successful" and accustomed to the finer things in life.

The D.A. was winding up his telephone conversation with the kind of reassuring, nonmeaning sounds you make when all the business has been discussed and you're into the socially required niceties. He leaned back in his tall expensive executive chair, laughed into the receiver of his ultramodern telephone, winked at us as though we were party to the fraudulently good-natured remarks he was making.

Tim's face was stiff and cold, accepting as an insult the fact that we had been summoned prematurely and had to wait while the D.A. finished his conversation. Finally, after a hearty laugh, Kelleher hung up. The telephone disappeared on the surface of his huge, cluttered ornate desk: the judge's desk, as everyone knew. The kind of old desk you can't buy for love or money anywhere because they don't make them like that anymore; the kind of desk you have to be second-generation successful to appreciate. People like Tim and me thought it was a pretty ugly old hunk of junk.

The District Attorney of Queens has always been openly pleased with his nickname: Gorgeous Jerry. An attractive man with high pink color, bright-blue eyes and an unruly mop of lemon-colored fluffy hair which he finger-combed from his forehead in a calculated way, he greeted us, literally, with a wide opening of his arms as though we were long-missing friends he was happy to see. It took him about thirty seconds to greet us, offer us any of the comfortable leather chairs in front of his desk and our choice of Scotch, Jack Daniels or coffee. It took us another thirty seconds to sit down, get settled and politely refuse his hospitality.

Even if he did switch labels on his clothes, I thought he looked pretty good for a fifty-four-year-old former college athlete who for years had overindulged and underexercised. Jerry Kelleher was very popular in Queens and could have spent the rest of his life being reelected to the D.A.'s office. But Jerry figured eight years was long enough; it was time for the big move. To City Hall.

Unfortunately for Jerry, he came across as too much of the chameleon pol to inspire the disillusioned, weary and battered voters of New York City. Despite his pink cheeks and golden hair, he carried the atmosphere of the smoke-filled back room. He might have been as clean and pure as he claimed, but the voters wanted, if not the substance, at least the appearance of purity.

At least that was how one powerful section of the Democratic Party read things, and since Jerry couldn't be persuaded that he had a nice setup where he was, a Democratic mayoralty primary was set for early June.

Gorgeous Jerry was pitted against the noncontroversial if somewhat unknown figure of Marvin L. Schneiderman: forty-six years old; former member of the City Council; former Assistant Commissioner of Public

Works; former Commissioner of Investigation, with an accumulation of credits for having cleared up a certain amount of corruption in various city agencies. He was presently in private practice. He was a relatively attractive man; a widower with two very photogenic, well-behaved little girls. He was inoffensive; bright without being too intelligent; ambitious as hell without letting it show too much.

The key to the outcome of the primary rested with Ken Sweeney, the young Democratic Party leader of Kings County. Kenny had weight not only in Brooklyn but in the city, in the state and, in fact, nationwide. He considered himself to be, and was in fact, a king-maker, and he had come out a few weeks ago for Marvin L. Schneiderman, pledging the considerable support of his organization and, of course, of himself. Ken had had the decency to take his old pal Jerry for a decent meal at Gage and Tollner's, the well-known Brooklyn political watering place, and to tell him, face to face, man to man, that there was nothing personal involved; it was just "politics."

I knew about the meeting because Ken Sweeney had told his law partner, Tim's wife, Catherine; Catherine told Tim and Tim told me.

And Jerry Kelleher knew that Tim knew about the luncheon; and Tim knew that Jerry knew he knew. But Jerry didn't know that *I* knew, because I wasn't involved, directly, in any of their games.

To an uninformed spectator, the two men would appear to be cordial, even fond of each other. They exchanged some small talk, then the D.A. told his secretary, via the intercom, that he wasn't to be interrupted until further notice. He sat in his high-backed black leather chair, settled himself in, clasped his hands over his stomach and carefully rearranged his normally happy face into an appropriately sad expression. He jutted his chin toward the afternoon *New York Post*, which had been placed on his desk, the headline facing us: QUEENS BOYS FOUND MURDERED.

"Bad business, bad business, Tim." He shook his head and studied the upside-down headline for a moment, then unclenched his fingers and carefully touched the corner of his mouth. His diamond pinky ring caught a spark of light from his desk lamp and cut right into Tim's eyes, but Tim never even blinked.

"Well, wadda ya say, Tim? We got some kind of nut running around Queens, sneaking into the bedrooms of sleeping children in the dead of night and stealing them away and murdering them? What the hell are we dealing with here, Tim?"

That, of course, would be the worst possible situation to deal with: terror would spread into the heart and mind and home of every vulnerable citizen of the Good Borough, the Safe Borough, the Borough of Homes.

Neary gave a quick, concise rundown of what he knew at this time, turning now and then for my comments. Jerry Kelleher nodded from time to time, as though not listening too closely but just waiting for us to finish. He picked up his silver-handled long-bladed letter opener and toyed with it, then dropped it on his desk. His eyes stayed on the opener for a moment, then he looked directly at Tim with his clear, wide watercolor-blue eyes.

"There's something I'm afraid I don't quite understand in all of this, Tim. Maybe you can help to clarify it for me." His tone wasn't one of confusion; it was of accusation. "Tim, why the hell, why the living, breathing, fire-burning hell, are *we* stuck with this goddamn case in the first place? Why the hell can't it be bucked to Homicide where it belongs?"

"You've heard of budget cuts, I take it," Tim said tightly. "And of layoffs; and of the department being seriously understaffed. And of the whole Detective Division being screwed up and dissipated by nondetective assignments? That's where the fault lies, Jerry. There were no detectives at the 107th when the call originally came in, so it was bucked to my squad. And since members of my squad caught the case, it's ours until completion."

All the time Tim was speaking, Jerry Kelleher stared at him with a slight, unpleasant smile turning up the corners of his big pink mouth. There was about thirty seconds of silence when Tim finished, which can be a very long period of silence in certain circumstances.

"I'm speaking, Captain Neary, of practicalities, not technicalities," Kelleher said softly. "I am aware of the fact that technically a case of this importance rests with the responding detectives and hence their squad. What I'm wondering is, why can't some arrangement be made so that maybe Joe here," he jutted his chin in my direction, but his eyes stayed on Tim, "could be assigned to the Homicide Squad for the duration of the investigation. Surely the two of you are tight enough with Chris Wise to work something out."

The funny thing is that such an arrangement could have been worked out and it would have taken the pressure off Neary as well as off Kelleher. But Tim, when his back is to the wall, goes for the jugular even though his own best suit is going to get all bloodied and ruined.

"No way, Jerry," he said tersely. "It's against departmental rules."

"And we all of us, of course, operate solely and totally within the framework of 'departmental rules,'" Kelleher said carefully.

"I can only speak for myself, Jerry. I know that I do," Tim shot at him.

Kelleher was better at this kind of thing than Tim would ever be. He just smiled, nodded and said, "Well, then, so be it. Now, Tim, you haven't *really* questioned the *mother* about all this, have you?"

"We have a preliminary statement. It hasn't even been signed yet. It was taken in my office this morning. Both parents gave us statements, but they haven't told us anything significant yet."

One thick yellowish eyebrow shot up Kelleher's forehead until it disappeared underneath the silky yellow lock of hair. He spread his large, soft pink-palmed hands over his desk.

"Wouldn't this be the ideal time to push them a bit, Tim? Before their stories have a chance to harden. Given what I would assume to be their emotional state at the moment, regardless of their involvement or noninvolvement, might not this be the time to question them—especially the mother—a bit more closely? Or do you think they were in on it together?"

Jerry's eyes were clear blue marbles, staring directly at Tim. He didn't blink once while Tim spoke. For that matter, neither did Tim.

"Anything they might possibly say at this time wouldn't be admissible, as I'm sure you know, Jerry. I wouldn't think of questioning them intensely without recommending that they have an attorney present. Any attorney would advise them against cooperating at this particular time. As I'm sure you would agree."

"I don't need you to teach me my law, Tim." They held the stare for a long count, then Jerry glanced down at his hands. When he looked back at Tim, his whole expression had changed; his voice sounded reasonable, helpful. "I would think if your investigation is thorough and properly done, as I naturally expect it to be, you'll have enough, soon enough, to persuade them, lawyer and all, to come forward to corroborate all you know, wouldn't you say?"

"As of now, all we *know* is that there are two murdered children."

"Well, you know a bit more than that, Tim." Kelleher considered his fingernails for a moment, then picked at a cuticle as he spoke. "You know that the mother, this Kitty Keeler, seems to have a very active extracurricular love life." He gnawed at the loose sliver of skin, then wiped his lips. He picked up the newspaper and held it in front of us as though it was an exhibit. "Why, it says so right here in this news story, Tim. Seems to be common knowledge, if the newspaper reporters already have it."

"I'm not sure that was a particulary wise thing to do, Jerry. For that information to have been leaked to the papers."

"Then why the hell was it leaked?" Kelleher demanded.

"I wouldn't know, Jerry. Would you?"

Not even a casual, uninformed spectator would think these two were anything but opponents. They went into another staring match.

The D.A. slowly shook his head from side to side. The lock of hair floated over his eyebrows. He shrugged his shoulders to express his innocence and bewilderment in the matter. Then he said softly, "A terrible thing, Tim. Terrible." He sucked in his lower lip, then said, as if to cue Tim on his response, "It does look like this whole thing, this terrible tragedy, is *very close to home*, though, doesn't it?"

"I wouldn't say that at this point, Jerry. I *especially* wouldn't say it to the *media*."

Kelleher tossed it right back at Tim without missing a beat. "I'm saying it to *you*, Tim, and you're not the media." He widened his eyes, gave a slow innocent blink, then: "At least, *as far as I know, you're not*."

Tim was both cracking his knuckles *and* whistling softly through his stretched lips. It sounded like a soft hiss of steam.

Jerry tapped his fingers in a little dance step along the edge of his desk and studied them with grave interest as he spoke. "I would say, Tim, from my experience with the human situation, and the nature of things, barring some really unlikely happenstance, that this entire matter would probably be cleared up within the walls of the Keelers' apartment." He looked up, first at me, then at Tim, then he hunched over his desk and said in a friendly one-of-the-guys voice, "This is unofficial, of course, Tim. Just so I can assure my wife that our three little grandchildren are safe on the streets of Forest Hills and she can call our daughter and tell her there's no real worry that some mad murderer is stalking for children in the dead of night."

Even though it was as important to Tim as it was to Kelleher that what the D.A. assumed was accurate, Tim got back a little of his own by not agreeing.

"We're not overlooking *any* possibilities. We've made assignments to check on known degenerates; we're checking on neighborhood incidents of any kind. We've got door-to-door inquiries both at the Fresh Meadows complex and in the area where the boys' bodies were found. We're getting close cooperation from the Homicide Squad and we're utilizing personnel from the 107th and 110th precincts. Plus my men will all be on considerable overtime."

"All the overtime you need, Tim, all the overtime and additional personnel you need." Kelleher rested his clasped hands on his desk and jerked the hair off his forehead with a schoolboy's toss. "The only thing

I'm concerned about, Tim, is that when the headline comes out, 'Keeler Case Closed,' the story beneath the headline emphasizes that the solution rested with the District Attorney's Squad. And I am willing to speculate that it will all prove out to have happened within the home of those tragic little boys. And my hope is that the solution, whatever it may be, will be arrived at *soon*."

"We're right on top of this investigation, Jerry. We'll find out what the story is."

I could read Tim's expression. His main regret was that both he and Kelleher had a vested interest in the within-four-walls solution to the case.

Kelleher rested the palms of his hands on his desk and stood up, leaning forward. "Fine, fine, of course you'll find it all out, Tim." Then casually, his eyes steady and enjoying the impact of his words on Tim, "Oh, by the way. I'm assigning young Quibro—you know Ed Quibro, don't you?—to handle the case. He'll be working closely with you, Tim. Keep him posted and up to date."

Assistant District Attorney Edward Quibro was a protégé of the D.A.'s: sharp, tough, devious as hell and a well-hated son-of-a-bitch. He and Tim had had a couple of go-rounds in the past. Kelleher must have felt very confident that this was going to be a fast, open-and-shut case if he gave it to Quibro. Quibro was in the process of collecting credits so that if Kelleher won the mayoralty primary he would resign in favor of Quibro. Kelleher would then devote himself to the fall election; Quibro would appear on the ticket as the incumbent—almost a sure thing to be officially elected the new District Attorney of Queens County.

The D.A. shook my hand firmly, then held on to Tim's and studied him with great sincerity. "Get the bastards, Tim. You men go out there and get those bastards."

"We will, Jerry. You'll be the first to know."

"Good, good, Tim." Kelleher waited until I had opened the door to his secretary's office before he added, as a casual afterthought, "By the way, Tim, what's this I hear about drugs? The mother involved in pushing, is she?"

Tim went blank, but recovered quickly. He shrugged his shoulders, indicating there wasn't enough yet to talk about. "We're going in several directions, Jerry. Time will tell."

"Yes. Yes, right, right."

Since I'd forgotten to tell Tim I'd dropped a drug rumor with Sam Catalano just to see how fast and how far it would bounce, when he asked me about it in the elevator I shrugged and said I'd look into it forthwith.

Tim said, in great pain, "There is no way that bastard isn't going to benefit from this case. If we crack it fast, he takes the credit. If we don't, he blames me. And all I've got going for my whole, entire future career is that bland jerk son-of-a-bitch Marvin L. Schneiderman."

"Who?" I was needling Tim; I really did remember the name of his man in the coming mayoralty primary. Tim kept staring at me, so I offered, helpfully, "Maybe we could arrange for Kitty Keeler to get together with Marvin L. and give him her confession."

"Just shut up, Joe, okay? Just shut up."

CHAPTER 6

By 8:30 P.M. the squad room was crowded and the air as many parts cigarette, cigar and pipe smoke as oxygen. A cleaning woman pulled her wagon to a halt outside the door, glanced in and turned around to leave. One of the guys called her back and asked her to at least empty our wastebaskets and ashtrays, which she did grudgingly, her thin whitish lips moving in some kind of incantation.

Vito Geraldi, a squat heavyset man with a cigar in the corner of his mouth, said, "Hey, c'mon, Momma, you're not doin' us a favor, that's your job, huh?"

Whereupon the cleaning woman dropped the full ashtray she was holding into an overflowing wastebasket, turned and walked out empty-handed, muttering something about "the union."

Vito winked, ran after her and, after a short whispered conversation with the woman, brought her back into the room; one heavy arm was thrown over her shoulders and she was laughing and blinking up at Vito like he was just the living end and they had come to a real meeting of the minds. She emptied all the ashtrays and baskets, opened a window, made a pass with a dustcloth over the gray metal, black-rubber-topped desks and finally left, smiling to herself.

"Vito, Vito, you could charm a witch on Halloween," his partner called out.

Squad members were checking their work schedules against the instructions Tim had posted on the bulletin board: all other investigations were postponed unless otherwise specified; all vacations were canceled; there was to be one day off in ten; the squad was to be prepared to put in heavy overtime.

By the time Tim stepped from his office, everyone had more or less settled down. He leaned against a desk, shoved his reading glasses up to the top of his head and spoke very quietly. It was effective. No one in the room so much as coughed or struck a match.

"Every member of this squad is to go down to the morgue and view the bodies of these two children. Find the time, regardless of your assignment. I want you to see them in the condition in which they were found this morning. Take a good long look at them. Then, every man here is to find the time to go over to the Peck Avenue location where the bodies were tossed like so much garbage. When you go home at the end of your tour, take a good long look at your own kids. Then think about the Keeler kids."

Tim wasn't going to let any of us get jaded; calloused; offhand. Not about these two little boys. He looked around the room, made sure we all got the message, then, briefly, brought everyone up to date on the investigation so far.

"About an hour ago, we received a tentative report from the Medical Examiner's office. Now, the times given are an approximation, give or take an hour either end, so keep that in mind." He turned to me. "Joe, pick it up from here."

"Victim number one, George Keeler, was manually strangled sometime between eleven P.M. and midnight." I glanced up at the men, who were all taking notes. "Add an hour at either end, which gives us roughly sometime between ten P.M. Wednesday and one A.M. Thursday, April sixteenth–seventeenth.

"Victim number two, Terence—Terry—Keeler: thirty-eight-caliber Smith and Wesson bullet in base of his skull, penetrated to a depth of . . . you don't need all this right now. Death occurred sometime between one and two A.M.—again, give or take an hour either end. Gives us sometime between midnight and three A.M. Thursday, April seventeenth."

Vito Geraldi, second senior first-grade man after me, was about to say something, but I held up my hand. "Hold it for a minute, Vito, let me finish this. Now, indications are that the first victim, George, was not killed at the location where the bodies were found. And that the second victim, Terry, was *shot* at the location."

"*Shot* at the location, Joe?" Vito was sharp. "You didn't say *killed* at the location, Joe?"

"Right. Cause of death hasn't been absolutely determined on the second boy. It appears that this kid, Terry, was either comatose or dead when he was shot. Apparently, he had ingested a large amount of sleeping pills," reading now, "time of ingestion and amount of ingestion not yet determined." I held my finger in place and looked up. "Tests will, hopefully, determine if the boy died of respiratory failure or whether he was still alive when shot."

A couple of the men asked questions, made comments, but Tim told them, "Hold off for a minute more, let Joe finish."

"It should be noted that neither victim shows any obvious or clinical signs of sexual molestation. An abrasion was found on the forehead of Terry, victim number two. It is approximately two inches long by a half inch wide." I looked up from the report. "The head is so swollen that it's difficult to determine at this time what might have caused the abrasion. No other wounds or abrasions on either body except for a minor scratch or two, not recent, considered normal for a child."

There was a thoughtful silence; little by little, everyone turned toward Vito Geraldi. Vito chewed on his cigar and studied the bitter, curling smoke, then he looked at Tim. "Captain, there's a discrepancy in the mother's statement, no? According to her, she saw the kids alive and well as late as one to one-thirty. How does that stack up against the M.E. report?"

"There is the strong possibility," Neary told them, "that at one A.M. George was dead; had been dead anywhere from an hour to three hours. And that Terry, the second boy, was comatose, if not dead, from the ingested drug. We'll have the times of death more accurately by sometime tomorrow, but the M.E. said we can work pretty close to the eleven-to-midnight and one-to-two-A.M. time slot."

Vito squashed the stubby remnant of his cigar into a full ashtray, neatly brushed ashes from the top of the desk into the palm of his hand, then turned his palm to the floor. He watched the ashes as they floated to his shoes.

"Number one, Captain," Vito said carefully, "we gotta look for a motive, right? Who the hell's got a *motive*? Who's got a grudge against little kids, three and six years old? Number two, we gotta look for opportunity. How the hell could someone come into an apartment and steal *two* kids? Without a sound? Maybe one kid. Maybe. But two? Uh-uh."

"No signs of breaking and entering, Captain, right?" Jim Jefferson, second grade, law-school graduate, one of the four black guys in the squad, began kicking it around. "No signs of sexual molestation. No one in the area heard any unusual sounds during the night. Probably because there weren't any. What time was it that the MacDougal girl claims to have gone over to the apartment?"

"Two-thirty; then called Kitty Keeler at three A.M."

"How do you see the sequence, Captain?" Vito asked.

Neary turned to me. We had discussed it already; pretty much agreed with each other. "I would say the first kid, George, was strangled in his bed. The second kid, Terry, witnessed it. Was given sleeping pills. Maybe just to quiet him."

"Ya mean it was all a big accident?" Vito asked without any particular emphasis.

"I mean I can see how it could happen. A kid's sick all day; restless; crying; demanding. Ten or twelve hours of that can drive you nuts."

The room became silent; a few men were doodling along the edges of their notebooks. Vito took out a new cigar and unwrapped it, but didn't light it. He held up his beefy hand, studied it.

"Ya know, Captain, when my kids were little I never laid a hand on them. I figured, hell, I wanna give the kid a smack in the ass, with this hammer of mine, I'da put him through the wall." He looked up and said, "It don't take much strength to choke a three-year-old kid."

"What we are talking about, then," Neary said, "is that the likelihood is that the mother, Kitty Keeler, killed the children. Or at least killed the first kid, George. Joe, you want to say something?"

"My guess would be that if the M.E. finds that sleeping pills killed the second kid, she actually killed both of them. In a fit of anger, or frustration, or whatever, she choked the first kid. Probably not meaning to; then the other kid might have gotten hysterical, and to quiet him she gave him some sleeping pills. And the kid died. And she panicked. Two dead kids and just her alone with them."

"And did what then?" one of the younger men asked.

I shrugged. Vito turned heavily, his small beady black eyes dancing around until he found who had asked the question.

"And did what then?" Vito repeated. "Then she picked up her little pink telephone book and called one of her boy friends to help her get rid of the bodies."

"She called George at eleven-twenty," I reminded them. "He couldn't come to the phone right then. When he tried to call back, the line was busy. She could have been calling around, trying to get someone since she didn't connect with George." I lit a cigarette and then added, "Which could narrow down the time of the first killing to somewhere before eleven-twenty, if that's why she called George."

"And," Vito suggested, "we could also figure that she didn't get any help until much later. She apparently wasn't home at two-thirty but was home at three A.M."

"What about the bullet in the second boy's head?" Walker, Geraldi's young partner, was a little puzzled.

Vito swung around heavily toward me. "Joe? Show him how to account for the bullet."

"Either of two ways: One, that the kid was dead from the sleeping pills, and the bullet was an afterthought, to make it look like someone took him from his bed to kill him. Or, two, that the kid wasn't dead, and the bullet, again, was to make it look like someone took him from his bed to kill him. The bullet in the kid's head was a cover."

Neary mentioned some of the names found in Kitty's phone book. "I'm having all names checked by Paul Sutro. Joe, you know Sutro, right? Used to work in Special Services, then retired and is working for the State Organized Crime Unit."

"Yeah, I know Paul."

"Joey," Vito said, "what's your impression of the little mother? You seen her before and after the kids were found."

None of them had seen Kitty Keeler yet; just her picture in the newspaper; just her quick appearance on the TV news. I remembered the inappropriate hostility, the unprovoked challenge, the blatant sexuality in her every move. I wondered if a woman who had just killed her two children could have carried that performance off. And then I remembered a certain look, a frozen instant when her eyes sought mine, just before I left the apartment with George. To identify the murdered boys. It had been a look different from the rest of her behavior, but I still wasn't sure.

"She looks like the kind of girl who would have the kind of names in her telephone book that Kitty has." That was true.

"What about the husband—George? You think he's involved?" Geraldi's partner asked.

"He seems to have an alibi," Neary answered.

I thought of George for a moment; remembered his anguish when the kids were missing. It had seemed real, but it could have been caused by knowledge of the children's murders. Except if his alibi held up. Thinking of George, I remembered Kitty Keeler; her unexpected tenderness and concern for George. That had seemed real, too.

"Now, I want to point out," Neary told the squad, "that there is *very heavy pressure* from the top floor on this case. And that pressure bounces right on me. So, from me to you: get out there and bust your asses on this case. If you all like working in this squad, that is."

Neary spent the next half hour giving out assignments. The men were instructed to ring doorbells systematically; were told to hit the bars, drugstores, food shops, beauty parlors, barbershops, dry-goods shops, restaurants; hit every department in Bloomingdale's Fresh Meadows branch; check the movies. Reinterview every person who had already been interviewed by the uniformed force. They were to determine if anyone at all had seen anything at all that might relate to the Keeler case. If anyone had seen any of the Keelers, mother, father, either child, anytime, under any circumstances at all, after 7:30 P.M., Wednesday, April 16. The men were additionally told to ask about the presence of the white Porsche and Patti MacDougal. Teams were assigned to check out the names of all persons listed, male and female alike, in Kitty Keeler's telephone book.

"We have to find out who helped Kitty Keeler. Someone did. She didn't do it all by herself." Neary voiced the common feeling in the squad. In effect, the investigation we were undertaking was not to determine *who* killed the Keeler kids, but to prove that *Kitty Keeler* killed them and to locate her accomplice/accomplices.

Tim, Vito and I went into Tim's office. Vito crushed the lit end of his cigar between his fingers, then slipped the dead stump into his pocket. Vito and all of his clothing always smelled of cigar butts. Vito leaned over, picked up Tim's reading glasses and studied his notes.

"Jeez, Timmy, I better get me reading glasses. My eyesight's gettin' bad as yours."

"That's old age, Vito," I told him.

Vito is a very physical guy. He punched me on the arm with what *he* thought was playful force; the pain ran down to my elbow and up to my shoulder.

Tim pulled open a bottom drawer and took out a bottle of Dewar's. He didn't bother to ask; we each had a shot in silence, then Tim leaned back in his chair.

"I want Kitty Keeler taken down to the morgue. I want her to see those kids *before* the funeral home pretties them up."

I nodded. "Right, Tim. What time you want me to pick her up?"

Tim shook his head slowly, then pointed his chin at Vito. "You, Vito. You're to take her. I'll let you know when. Probably late afternoon tomorrow. I'm hoping to have enough to bring her in for interrogation by tomorrow night. There are a hell of a lot of questions that we haven't asked, and that she hasn't answered. Including the fact that she called her husband last night at eleven-twenty; and that she got a phone call at three A.M. Vito, get over to the phone company tomorrow. Find out if she made any out-of-town calls."

Tim checked out my morning assignments, but he kept looking at me as though he wasn't paying attention to what we were talking about. Like he was thinking about something else; about me. Finally he said, "Joe, you're gonna be the *good* guy. To Vito's *bad* guy."

"That's not a good idea, Tim. I don't think Kitty would consider me in that role."

"Why not?"

"I don't know; she and Catalano hit it off pretty good. Do you think maybe . . ."

Tim automatically said, "That son-of-a-bitch. Forget him, he stays buried as far as I'm concerned."

"Then one of the younger guys, Walker or—"

"*Joe. I said you.*" Tim held a stare. I wasn't about to start playing eyeball games with him.

"Look, Tim. I don't know why, maybe because I stuck with George this morning, but this broad doesn't seem to like me any better than I like her, so—"

"Joe," Tim said sharply, "I'm not *asking* you to go *steady* with the girl. I'm *telling* you to play *good guy*, to Vito's bad guy." Tim let his authority sink in.

What the hell; he's the boss. His head was on the line, not mine. "Tell me when and where, Cap. You call the signals."

Tim took out his bottle and refilled the shot glasses. This time it hit me right in the midriff with a blast. The ulcer wanted milk, not booze; the rest of me wanted booze and sleep, because it was pretty clear that we were all going to be keeping long hours for a while.

CHAPTER 7

THE Bronx may have taken longer than some other boroughs to change, but when change started, it went fast. Almost en masse, those white middle-class citizens who hadn't already moved out to Long Island, Westchester or Jersey poured into the fortresslike skyscrapers of Co-Op City. The only people left when the blacks and Puerto Ricans came spilling in were the old people who still paid nearly the same rents as they had for more than twenty-five years. Who had been fixed in income, fixed in a particular neighborhood, in a particular building, in a particular apartment. They stayed as though serving a life sentence; their next and only move would be in a box. For the first time in their lives, people like Kitty Keeler's mother, Mary Hogan, became conspicuous: part of a minority of white, elderly, vulnerable, frightened people.

Mrs. Hogan carefully reset the three locks inside her door, then led me down a long dark hallway toward the living room. She hesitated at the doorway to the kitchen, asked if I'd like some tea, then continued into the living room.

It was from another era. The overstuffed furniture had probably been recovered several times, but it was in perfect condition, with handmade doilies on arms and along the backs. It was all dark and serviceable. The end tables gleamed with high polish and were topped with ornate lamps whose shades were covered by cellophane wrappers. Heavy clean curtains covered the windows; there were some dark-green plants and some artificial flowering plants; an old black-and-white television set; a small bookshelf that held some religious statues and some children's books. There were photographs of children everywhere: baby pictures, Communion and Confirmation mementos, class groups, rows of kids in dark parochial-school uniforms; gawky adolescents, girls thin and shy, boys looking sheepish in Navy and Army uniforms; wedding pictures, graduation pictures; a couple of yellowing newspaper clippings with a blurred picture of the high-school basketball star. More baby pictures, one generation overlapping the other. A studio portrait of Kitty taken in cap and gown: face a little fuller, much softer, lips slightly parted, sensuous but at the same time innocent; nothing innocent coming from her eyes, which stared directly at the camera, something challenging and knowing and cool coming from her eyes. All the time I spoke to her mother, Kitty watched me, lips parted, eyes shrewd and clever.

Mrs. Hogan's eyes riveted on my mouth; I had forgotten she was hard of hearing. Even so, her concentration was unnerving; it had the quality of a frightened animal trying desperately to figure out what was expected of it; anxious not to miss a clue. She had something of the dazed, shocked look of an accident victim who hasn't yet fully understood or experienced the extent of her injury. There was something abstract and vague about her. She ran her hand nervously down from her neck, caught at the rim of her apron.

"Oh, my, I didn't realize," she said, staring down at herself. She untied the apron and folded it into a neat square, which she held on her lap and fingered and patted.

"I just want to talk with you a little, Mrs. Hogan. About Kitty. And her family."

She nodded dumbly; there was no objection, no resistance, no resentment, no wariness. Just a resignation and an expectation. It was hard to see her eyes; the reflection from the lamp by my side glinted them out under her glasses.

"Mrs. Hogan, George Keeler is considerably older than your daughter, isn't he?"

She nodded. "Yes. Yes, old enough to be her father. More than old enough, I guess. Kitty's father died when she was an infant," she added. "There were the four boys. And Kitty, the last."

"It must have been hard for you, Mrs. Hogan, all alone like that."

Mrs. Hogan's mouth tightened; her hands folded narrow pleats into the apron. "I worked to support my children; I never took anything from anyone. And I wasn't ashamed of the work I did; there's no shame in honest work. Kitty was ashamed of it, that I worked as a waitress downtown in Schrafft's. None of the boys felt that way. Just Kitty."

She bit down on her lip to keep the words from spilling out unchecked.

"How did Kitty get to know George?"

"Well, he owned his own establishment then, up on Webster Avenue. And my oldest son, Richie, worked for him. And Kitty was good at figures, arithmetic and bookkeeping and the like; so when she was in her last year of high school, she worked several hours each day, doing the books for George and all."

"And they started to see each other then? Go out together?"

For a minute, I thought she hadn't caught the question, but before I could repeat myself she shook her head.

"No. It wasn't like that at all. She quit working for George when she finished high school. And was very put out that no one had thought to set money aside for herself, to go on to college if you please. Four other children, four sons, and all together they never caused me the heartache from that one girl."

Mrs. Hogan pressed the palm of her hand over her mouth tightly; turned her head to one side; brought herself sharply under control.

"She was raised in a decent home. Really she was. I don't know where she got all her fancy ideas from. Always *wanting, wanting* all kinds of things. Maybe from the movies, or the television, I don't know. But my Kitty was never satisfied, never. She left one good job after another. She was *bored*, she said." Mrs. Hogan looked at me questioningly; as if I might have the answer. "*Bored*. She'd leave a well-paying job, time and time again, because she said it was *boring*." It was incomprehensible to her.

"Well," I offered, "young girls are like that."

"No one ever asked me if I was *bored* with carrying trays of food and cleaning up after people and then coming back here to do for the children." She shook her head sharply, admonishing herself.

"How did she come to marry George?"

She thought for a minute or so, watched her hands crushing the apron, then finally, resigned, weary, she said, "Well, it was no secret; not to anyone. My Kitty never felt ashamed of herself in her life, only ashamed of her mother and brothers. She . . . she worked for . . . some man in an office, I don't know exactly. But . . . he was married, you see. And . . . there she was. Pregnant." Mrs. Hogan raised her chin, held her head up. "And he, the man, left New York; lock, stock and barrel. Had been planning to all along. And George. Poor George, he loved Kitty; he worshiped her from the time she was a child. Married her; gave her anything she wanted. That beautiful apartment in Fresh Meadows, just like in the country. All the clothes she wanted, anything at all. But not even being married and having the babies settled Kitty. Not my girl. She just wanted—*something*, I don't know. God knows. So she got that job, at that . . . that 'health spa.'" Mrs. Hogan sighed without realizing how loud and terrible the sound was. "I don't understand any of it, any of the kind of people Kitty knows. She's just lucky she has George to put up with her at all."

"Do you see much of Kitty, Mrs. Hogan?"

She kneaded and twisted and released and clutched the apron. Her mouth tightened and she shook her head. A long thin strand of grayish-red hair had come undone from the knot at the back of her neck and fell on her cheek. She reached up ineffectually and tried to smooth it back. "No. We don't see each other. Not much."

She knew nothing of Kitty's plans; very little, actually, of Kitty's life. When asked what kind of mother Kitty was, Mrs. Hogan was sharp and bitter.

"Oh, the *best*, according to herself," she said sarcastically. "You've only to see how nicely dressed her boys are; all the fine things they have, all the places they've been. But she's hardly ever with them herself. Hires baby-sitters everywhere she goes. It's easy for her, she can come and go as she pleases with hardly any time for the boys and—"

Mrs. Hogan stopped speaking abruptly as the realization hit her. Her mouth fell open; she blinked rapidly, but no tears spilled from under her glasses. Her hands shook and she buried them under her wrinkled apron.

"Mrs. Hogan." I wasn't sure how to ask her. Her face had gone totally pale. She seemed suddenly fragile, her strength drained away by reality. There really was only one way to ask the question: ask it.

"Mrs. Hogan, yesterday when you first arrived at your daughter's apartment, when you first saw her, you said to her, 'Kitty, *what have you done?*' Why did you ask her that, Mrs. Hogan? Why did you think Kitty had done something to her boys?"

Her mouth fell open; her face froze. She stared at me with magnified eyes behind her smudged glasses. Slowly she began to move her head from side to side. Her hand clutched at empty folds of skin along her neck. "No, I never. I *never, never* said such a thing. Sweet Mother of God, *I never.*"

She hadn't realized that she had actually spoken the words; really believed she had only thought them. Beyond her, the graduation portrait of Kitty caught my attention: the uneven combination of innocence and challenge; a certain gleam coming from the eyes that wasn't merely a reflection of the photographer's lights; the slightly parted, moist lips, about to speak. To say something. But I couldn't think what.

This woman didn't know anything about her daughter's life; they had been separated from each other by more than years. I stood up, apologized that I had been mistaken. She took my extended hand awkwardly for a limp shake and led me down the hallway to the door.

After I stepped into the outside hall, I turned to see her once more;

there was something vaguely familiar as she turned her face upward. Something I had seen before: a fleeting reminder of a long-gone beauty eroded by a hard and bitter life. Mary Hogan still had a hint of her daughter's beauty.

.

Mrs. Sophie Silverberg was a patient at Long Island Jewish Hospital and was considered seriously ill. The young bearded doctor who confronted me had exhausted, bloodshot eyes. He told me that Mrs. Silverberg could not be questioned; she had had surgery four days ago and had gone into shock when she heard about the Keeler boys on the radio.

"I'll be brief; I'll do my best not to upset her."

The doctor shook his shaggy curly head. He brought his hand up to his wide sweaty forehead, trying to think of a simple way to get his message across. "Look, there is *no way* you can see her. She practically raised those kids. Aside from the emotional shock, she's had a real physical setback."

"Okay, Doctor, I understand. Don't worry about it. I'll come back tomorrow."

He let out a long, annoyed groan. "No, you *don't* understand. It won't be any different tomorrow. I will not let you see her tomorrow either."

"Sure you will. I'll have a court order, Dr. Wood." His name was on a white nameplate with black letters hung sideways on his white jacket. "If you refuse to honor it, you'll have to get all tied up in a court proceeding which will be a pain in the ass for you and me both."

He believed me. He listed a few warnings. "She's an elderly lady, would you keep that in mind? I mean, you won't come on strong with her or anything?"

"I *was* planning to kick her around a little. You know, just to keep in practice. I haven't worked an old lady over since last Thursday."

He narrowed his bloody eyes at me and said, "You know, I *believe* you."

Mrs. Silverberg was propped up on pillows and her knotted hands trembled as she moved her fingers along the edges of her blue quilted bed jacket. She kept a wad of crumpled tissues in each of her hands and dabbed at her eyes from time to time, pushing her rimless glasses up and then back into place.

The odor of illness, medications and sadness surrounded her. At the center of everything else, undisguised by her freshly bathed and powdered body, clean nightgown, hint of cologne, fragrance of fresh flowers, there was the unmistakable, undeniable odor of impending death. Mrs. Silverberg did not have long.

She sucked loudly on a peppermint Life Saver which she had first offered to me. We spoke quietly; she was a lot tougher than the young doctor gave her credit for.

She had loved those boys. She had taken care of them almost from the first, even when Terry was brand new and there was that little Scotch girl, Margie. Almost from the day they were born. The boys went as naturally to her apartment as they did to their own. They had two homes; they called her Nana.

"They were more family to me than my own grandchildren. My own, they live in California and once a year, maybe once every two years, they come here or they ask me to fly out there. Why would I want to fly out there? Five, six hours on the plane, and then they don't know me, I don't know them. Strangers; they're all growing up, my grandchildren, teenagers already. They drive their own cars. We don't know each other; they're uncomfortable around me. What do I need that for?

"My Georgie, my Terry. My beauties," she said, "from the time they were infants, I would go next door with a little gift, a little sweater, a pair of booties, a hat. I used to do very nice work before the arthritis. I knitted, I crocheted. But now the fingers are too stiff. Too stiff."

"They were lucky to have you, Mrs. Silverberg."

She moved her head from side to side. "No. Me. Me. I was the lucky one. Oh my God, those poor babies, those poor babies."

"Mrs. Silverberg, tell me something about Mrs. Keeler."

Her breath caught, her eyes blinked, she dabbed at the tears which ran down her face. "Kitty? My darling, darling Kitty. Oh, that is a good, lovely, lovely girl. The face, so beautiful, like a movie star. And good as good. The last time, last year, when I was in the hospital for the gallstones, every day my Kitty came or she sent George. And flowers, and bed jackets she brought me. And when I came home, there was a nurse to take care of me. A nurse she got for me and paid for, herself. My children, my college-graduate daughters, you think they thought of such a thing? A *nursing home*, they said." She lifted her chin and with a flash of spirit and pride told me, "My Kitty said *no!* No nursing home. My children, they told me, it's all arranged, a very nice place in Long Beach by the ocean. What do they know, three thousand miles away? They see a booklet and the pictures all look pretty, so send Mama there and that's that. But Kitty, she sent her friend out to see for himself and he sees what's what, behind the pictures. And I stayed in my *own home*, with a nurse to take care of me."

"Do you remember the name of Kitty's friend, the man who checked out the nursing home for you?"

"Who remembers? Kitty is a wonderful girl. People, you know, they see her, all the time going, running, going out, dressed so nice. So they say things." She studied me shrewdly. "You know what kind of things I mean. Because she knows a lot of men. They're jealous because she's young and beautiful and so . . . so alive. They don't know her, my Kitty. But *I* know her. She is beautiful not just on the outside." She tapped her chest. "In here, where it counts, my Kitty is beautiful."

She seemed to have gotten stronger with the need to tell me about Kitty Keeler.

"She works hard, that girl, so hard. Like little movie stars she dresses her children. The best clothes, not just for herself, but for them too. And for George. Beautiful suede jackets she got for him, and suits. At discount, from friends she has. When she was a girl, ah . . ." Mrs. Silverberg moved her hands, turned them palms up. "She was so poor. All her childhood, only wearing school uniforms and hand-me-downs. Now she works so hard for good things. Nothing cheap, no junk. She has such good taste, my Kitty."

I remembered the closet filled with all kinds of clothing: the obsessively arranged colors.

"Mrs. Silverberg, what about George? George Keeler?"

She sighed, then carefully studied me. "You're thinking in your head, why did she marry George? He is so much older, like a father he is to her. And that's part of it, yes. Kitty never really had a father. So young she lost her father. And for most of her life, she has known George. No man in the whole world could be as good to Kitty like George is. And she, she is good for him, too. Don't listen to the little gossips around the neighborhood. What they don't know, they make up. Kitty is a loving, loving girl." She pressed her trembling hand over her pale thin lips for a moment, then said in a thick voice, "She is my daughter. To me, *Kitty is my daughter!*"

The shaggy, bloody-eyed young doctor looked in and blinked at me a few times. I had been planning to leave anyway, but I let him think it was his idea. I reached out and held the bony, gnarled hand lightly on the flat surface of the bed; applied a gentle, light pressure.

"Mrs. Silverberg, do you think you could try to remember the name of the man that Kitty had check out the nursing home for you?"

She shrugged. "One of the men from her place where she works, I think. I don't know. A lot of men Kitty knows. A rough-looking man with dark hair." She frowned, straining to recall. "With a face, it was so mean it would scare you on the television. But he was so nice, so kind, so good. He said, 'No mother of mine would go to a place like that.' That's what he said. A good man, you can't judge a book by its cover. He can't help he has a mean-looking face. My daughters' husbands, smart, handsome professional men, they dress like the magazine pictures, with the fancy haircuts—they go to 'stylists,' if you please, for a haircut and they go to Europe and Mexico and Hawaii for vacations, but when it comes to *caring*," she moved her shoulders, "forget it. Forget it." She blew her nose and pressed the tissue into a wet ball in her hand. "For *caring*, thank God, thank God, *I have my Kitty*."

CHAPTER 8

WHEN I checked with my office, Neary told me that the Porsche was cleared and had been released to the Keelers. Patti Mac-Dougal's boy friend and a few other people had confirmed that she had spent the evening with them, but still no corrob on her having gone to the Keeler's apartment at 2:30 A.M.

"It would really be nice if someone remembers seeing the Scotch girl in the parking lot."

"*Scots* girl," I told Tim. "*Scotch* is something you drink."

"Screw you, Joe. Listen, I sent that son-of-a-bitch Catalano over to Keeler's place in Sunnyside to check George out. Meet him over there, Joe. See if you can get a line on George. Then send the s.o.b. for statements from *everybody* who was at Keeler's Wednesday night. That oughtta keep him busy."

A couple of years ago, Sunnyside had been mostly Italians, Irish and Jews, in that order. It was a small, tight Queens community that had formed its identity around a couple of churches, an orthodox and a reform synagogue and a collection of Irish bars, Italian bakeries and restaurants, kosher butchers and delis. It was also the home of Sunnyside Garden, scene of less than notable boxing and wrestling matches. The neighborhood was still hanging on, but changes were taking place, slowly and surely. The corner pharmacy now had a small sign in the window announcing that Spanish was spoken here; there were a couple more bodegas than a year or so ago, to cater not so much to a sprinkling of Puerto Ricans as to a growing number of Cubans who were buying the comfortable attached one-family homes on the side streets. There were several Greek food and specialty shops, apparently run by a huge family: all the muscular dark-haired young guys looked related. Some of the nonethnic grocery and chain stores carried what was called "Caribbean specialties" to lure the illegal immigrants from the islands, an uncertain number of phantoms who creeped out at dawn to factory jobs and came back late at night to sleep in a crowded subdivided apartment for which they paid a greedy landlord an exorbitant rate.

George Keeler owned the two-story building where his bar, Keeler's Korner, was located. The building also housed, at street level, a somewhat dirty-looking French-Italian bakery, a small lamp store, a Hebrew printing company. Upstairs, on the second floor, George had his apartment and two small offices which were rented out, one to a lawyer and one to a C.P.A. Both of those tenants used the offices primarily as a mail drop.

The building had been erected in 1906 in what was probably considered at the time to be a highly handsome style. The gray stone façade was heavily ornamented along the top edge with what appeared to be a bunch of fat cherubs dancing with a bunch of mythical fat animals. Here and there were masklike faces of what looked like grinning devils: probably thinking dirty things about the cherubs and the animals.

Keeler's Korner was exactly that: a tavern with the doorway set into the corner of the building. Keeler had bought the entire building in late 1968 and had refurbished what had been a seedy neighborhood tavern into his idea of an Irish pub. He had installed heavy leaded-glass windows, surrounded by simulated old beams of wood in a crisscross pattern. Here and there were some diamond-shaped inserts of glass scenes depicting what looked like Crusaders on horses. Over the entrance was a gable, apparently supported by the same type of simulated beams to give an old, authentic, real-Irish-village-pub effect. Surrounded by bright-green metal shamrocks was a sign, directly over the doorway, KEELER'S KORNER. The entire facing had been stuccoed over and painted a dull beige to fit in with the wooden-beam décor.

Sam Catalano was leaning comfortably at the bar, talking with two new good friends. He introduced me to them with the warmth reserved for members of a secret society.

The barman, a big chunky guy with a round soft pinkish face that went right back to his balding skull, was Danny Fitzmartin. His grip was bone-crushing and at odds with his nice soft sweet Irish voice and easy smile.

The waitress, Lucille something, had a wet limp handshake. Even in the dim light, it was obvious that Lucille had known better days. She was so thin she was almost transparent, and the great bubble of bright-red hair overwhelmed her sharp narrow face. Her makeup was vivid and the mascara ended in little lumps at the ends of her false eyelashes. She and Sam had already established a certain understanding. When he sat down again on the bar stool next to hers, their knees touched.

"Nice place," I told Fitzmartin. "Bigger than it looks from outside."

"It's a real family place. The old-timers still come round steady from the neighborhood. And we've been gettin' a lot of younger people, some from as far away as the Bronx. To hear them folk singers we got, three times a week, ya know."

"Yeah, I hear they're pretty good. Except for a show of temperament now and then."

The barman shrugged and grinned. "Crazy Irishmen, what can ya expect?"

"You were both here Wednesday night?" They both nodded and their faces became serious. "And George Keeler was here, all night, Wednesday into Thursday morning?"

"Oh, George was here," Lucille answered. "Poor George, them poor little kids, poor George."

She didn't say "Poor Kitty."

"George was here until about two and a little after, maybe ten or fifteen after two," Fitzmartin said.

"And did you see George, all during that time? Was he absent for any length of time at all?"

Lucille poked at her hair and leaned a little closer to Sam. "Oh, Georgie was here the whole time, here and in and out of the kitchen. Like I already told Sam." The last with a wink at Sam.

"How about a little something to make the day go by?" Danny gestured to his entire stock. We settled for beer, and as an afterthought he drew one for Lucille and himself as well.

Lucille sipped the beer with small, dainty little swallowing sounds, then licked her lips. "George works the bar right along with Danny and he even works the tables with me, if the part-timers don't show. We got two part-timers; young kids. Ya never know if they'll show or not, ya know how kids are."

The part-timers were all present Wednesday night; could vouch for George Keeler.

"Jesus," Danny said suddenly, his meaty shoulders hunching over his arms on the spotless bar. "Who'd do a thing like that to George's kids? That guy'd give you the shirt offa his back you asked him. He's one in a million, that guy. Everybody loves George."

"Yeah, everybody but Kitty," Lucille said tightly.

Danny turned to her. "All right, Lucille."

"Yeah, well, it's not all right. It's true." She added, softly, "That little bitch."

"Lucille, I understand you spoke to Kitty Keeler on the phone Wednesday night?"

"We were just up to that when you came in, Joe." Sam wanted me to know he was right on the ball.

"That's terrific, Sam. Lucille?"

"Yeah, well, like I started to tell Sam, ya know, she called him at eleven-twenty, on the button."

She verified what George Keeler had told me: the Irish folk singers had gotten into an argument because one of them wanted to sing something for an old-timer and the others objected because it was eleven-twenty and they had a break until eleven-thirty.

"What did Kitty say when you told her George couldn't come to the phone?"

"I just asked her that, Joe, when you came in," Sam told me.

No doubt about it; Sam *was* right on the ball.

"Well, like I started to tell Sam," she spoke directly to Catalano as though they were alone and sharing a confidence, "her ladyship tells me, 'I don't care about that he's involved with those singers, you tell him to get his ass over to the phone, right now!' " One thin hand rested on a sharp hipbone and her face and voice were expressive as she imitated first Kitty, then herself. "So I tell her that George would get back to her as soon as he was free and she says again, 'Get him on the phone right *now!*' " According to Lucille, Kitty's voice had been high-pitched and screechy; Lucille's had been warm and polite. "So, okay, I call George again, and poor George, he's up to his eyebrows in trouble with them singers, so I just hold the phone up high so's *she* can hear the noise and all and then I tell her, I says like this to her, 'As you can hear for yourself, Kitty, George ain't free to come to the phone at the moment.' And I tell her, 'He'll get back to you as soon as he's free.' And then I hung up on her." She nodded a righteous jut of her chin. "Before she could do me, ya know?"

"She got a bad temper—Kitty?"

"She's just so useta George gotta jump when Kitty says jump is all." Lucille made a clicking noise against her teeth. "Huh, too bad about her, *Mrs. Keeler.*"

"How did she sound, Lucille, when she spoke to you? Any different from how she usually sounds on the phone? Upset? What?"

"I was just gonna ask her that when you came in, Joe."

This time I ignored Sam.

"To me, she always sounds bitchy," Lucille admitted. "She sounded the same as always, only more so, if you take my meaning. Just mad as hell that George didn't come to the phone right away."

"Did she sound worried? Upset? hysterical?"

Lucille bit on her lip in thought. "Naw. Just sore as hell. Boy, poor

Georgie, he tried to call her back like in five minutes, but from then on, the phone was busy-busy. She musta took it off the hook for the resta the night. She's some bitch, that Kitty."

"Okay, Lucille," Danny said, not so softly, "you done your little number. Take care a that old couple in Booth Three. They look like they're dryin' out."

He leaned on the counter and confided, "She just don't like Kitty is all. Hell, I guess most women don't like Kitty much. She's a real beautiful girl."

"How do you figure Kitty and George?"

Danny pulled back, stiffened. "None of my business, ya know. I've known George fifteen, sixteen years, and he's the nicest guy I ever known in my life. Kitty? Well, Kitty's George's business, the way I figure. How they live ain't none of my business."

Spoken like a true bartender. While Danny and I shot the breeze, Lucille took Catalano upstairs to check out George's apartment. Homicide guys had already checked out George's .32, for which he had a permit.

"Jeez," Danny said, "I unnerstan the older kid, Terry, was hit by a thirty-eight." It overwhelmed him for a moment and he rubbed his water-reddened hand over his face. "Jeez. What an awful thing."

"Yeah. You think of anything, Dan, anything at all, give me a call, right?"

He assured me that he would and I believed him. Lucille brought Catalano back through the door from the hallway which led to George's apartment. She was playfully poking at her bubble of hair; Catalano leaned close and said something that sent her into high ripples of laughter. Then Sam pressed her hand and left her regretfully.

"Anything?" I asked him when we hit the late-afternoon street.

"Naw. Nice neat little place, though. Lucille told me that in all the years she's known George, he's never once played around. She says Kitty is enough for George, but that it don't work both ways. She says she can't figure how George, or any other man, would put up with the way Kitty plays around. Like she don't make no secret, no excuses or anything."

"Well, that's how some people are, Sam."

"Well, I wouldn't put up with it if it was *my* wife." Then Sam flexed his shoulders, settled his jacket and told me, "Ya know, I bet I coulda made out with her in another five minutes; if I wanted to."

"Lucille knows a good thing when she sees it." That made him feel good; at least until I told him his next assignment.

"But that don't make any sense, Joe. Hell, we don't need all those people to verify that George was at his place all night. Joe, I wanna talk to you about something been bothering me."

Sam Catalano was bothered by the fact that he was only a third-grade detective; that he rarely had an opportunity to prove that he was worthy of promotion to second grade, which would merely be a stepping-stone to first grade, which was what he *really* deserved. For some reason he was beginning to sense that Captain Neary didn't like him very much, and could I maybe put in a word with Tim on his behalf? But be subtle about it, like it was all my own idea. "After all, Joe, *I* was the one who caught the case, even if you are senior man. It isn't even as if we was partners anymore, it's just the way things worked out, ya know?"

I promised I'd mention his name to Neary, but he didn't seem too cheered up by that. "Hey, Sam, you know a guy named Steve Werner? Second-grade guy in Narcotics?"

"Steve Werner?" Catalano was memorizing the name. "Hey, Joe, anything to do with the . . . the 'drug thing'?"

I winked and patted Sam on the back. There was a new spring to his step as he headed for his car. The son-of-a-bitch was in a hopeful mood again.

•

Vito Geraldi's beady little eyes were gleaming with excitement when I reported to Tim Neary's office. Even Tim looked a little cheered up, but Tim keeps a tight rein on himself.

Vito wrapped a heavy arm around my shoulders and escorted me across the room. "Pay dirt, Joey," he told me. "We're starting to hit pay dirt, kid."

"That's terrific, Vito." I eased myself from his grip and glanced at Tim.

"Vincent Martucci, Joe. Familiar name?"

Either they were going to tell me or they were going to make me guess. "Owner of the New World Health Spa; Kitty Keeler's boss. Right?"

"Minor mob figure, with a record going back some thirty years," Tim said. "Owner of the New World Health Spa; Kitty Keeler's boss; *and* Kitty Keeler's *lover*." Tim picked up his reading glasses. "He's out in Phoenix, Joe; where Kitty was supposed to be going. On Wednesday night, April sixteenth, 1975, Kitty Keeler made a person-to-person call to Vincent Martucci, out at the spa in Phoenix." He checked with a slip of paper, then said, "They talked from eleven-thirty P.M. until twelve-five midnight."

Tim paused significantly to let me consider the timing of the call; before I could say anything, he held his hand up, looked down at a second slip on his desk, then up at me.

"She called him a *second* time, person to person, from three-ten A.M. to three-twenty-five A.M., Thursday morning, April seventeenth."

We stared at each other, then Vito slammed me on the back. "Wadda ya think, Joey?"

I sat down on one of the chairs in front of Tim's desk; slouched way down with my legs going under the desk and my shoulders even with the top of the chair. There was no portion of me that Geraldi could punch, pinch, jab or pat.

"Run through it, Joe."

I closed my eyes and started. "First kid is killed between eleven and midnight Wednesday. Kitty calls George at his bar at eleven-twenty." When I opened my eyes, I saw that Tim was checking me against a page of jotted notes. He nodded when I continued. "We can assume the first kid was killed sometime between eleven and eleven-twenty, right? She can't get to speak to George. She calls Martucci and talks to him between eleven-thirty and twelve-five midnight. At around this time, the older boy, Terry, has apparently ingested a certain amount of a barbiturate, so he's either dead or comatose at this time."

"Comatose," Tim said. "He was still alive when he was shot; the M.E. confirmed the tentative times of death and that the thirty-eight was the cause of death of the second boy."

"Right. Then this Scotch girl—"

"*Scots* girl," Tim said coldly.

"Right. Patti MacDougal claims she was at the Keeler apartment at two-thirty A.M. Apparently, no one home; at least no one came to the door and she didn't hear anyone inside. Still not confirmed, Tim?"

"No, but presuming the girl had no reason to lie, she then returned to her apartment and called Kitty at three A.M." He nodded at me to continue.

"Right. Kitty talks to Patti at three A.M.; says something about having been under the shower earlier. Then, at . . . what? Three-ten?"

Vito came behind me and rested a hand on my shoulder. He began to squeeze his encouragement. "From three-ten to three-twenty-five, Joe, she and Martucci talk on the phone again."

"By which time both of her children are dead, Joe." Tim stood up and shoved his hands into his pocket and began clinking coins together; he stared out the window for a moment, then turned and leaned against the sill. "My guess would go something like this, Joe. In some kind of . . . anger, maybe, she strangles the first kid. Probably didn't mean to do it; give her the benefit of the doubt, at this point. The other kid witnessed it; maybe he starts to cry, is all upset, so she gives him a couple of sleeping pills." He interrupted himself. "No question that the sleeping pills came from Keeler's medicine cabinet: Doriden. She just picked up the prescription about a week ago. That's what 'someone' gave to little Terry. Okay. Now let's say she's in a panic; calls George to come over to help her out. Can't connect. Calls Martucci in Phoenix and they talk for more than half an hour."

"Did he call her at any time?"

Vito massaged my numb shoulder. "No, Joe, we checked with the Phoenix P.D. Martucci didn't make no New York calls, no one from the spa made *any* long-distance calls those two days."

"He probably calms her down." Tim sounded like he was talking to himself; his eyes were glassy and unfocused. "Tells her who to call for help; who'll help her get rid of the bodies." He stopped speaking and just stared, then rubbed the back of his neck and looked up at me. "Her own kids, Joe. Jesus, this girl has got to be cold-blooded."

"She's nothin' but a little whore, Tim, wadda ya expect?" Vito declared. He dug at me with his thick fingers. "Time of death for the second kid, Joe, from the bullet: estimated sometime between two and three A.M. Thursday morning."

"It can even be narrowed down," Tim said. "To sometime between two-twenty and three A.M. Figuring they were out of the apartment before two-thirty and Kitty was back by three. Takes maybe five minutes to load the kids into a car, drive them down to Peck Avenue, dump them, shoot Terry, drive back. Kitty gets out of the car and back into the apartment and answers the phone at three." He rubbed his face roughly, first down, then up. His eyebrows were all rumpled. "What we have to find now is who helped her. That'll pull it all together."

"Then she calls Martucci back at three-ten until three-twenty-five, to tell him the score," Vito told me.

"What's the matter, Joe?" Tim's voice was sharp and tight. I wasn't nodding enough or something. "What the hell's going on inside *your* head?" He made it sound like treason. Which is how Tim acts when *he's* satisfied with a solution and you don't agree with him with enthusiasm. Which could also mean he's just a little shaky and needs reassurance from everyone.

"Just trying to get it straight in my head is all, Tim."

His jaws tightened as he clenched his teeth and the thin whistling started. The whistling and his stare were directed right at me.

"Just wondering . . ."

"Wondering what?" He waited, daring me to have any questions about anything. At all.

"Just wondering why they dumped the kids so close to home. And why . . . Kitty didn't realize how easy it would be for us to trace the long-distance calls. And . . . why she didn't come up with a better story than just 'I went to bed. Got up. They were gone.' Period."

"That what's bothering you, Joe?"

Vito began explaining. "The girl acted in a panic, Joe. She musta got somebody just as scared as she was; just got rid of the bodies at the first possible spot. Dumped them, shot the older kid, to make it look like a kidnapping or something. Then came back and wanted to tell Martucci about it. He probably told her to stick with as simple a story as possible."

Tim watched me, but I didn't move a muscle. This guy has had my loyalty and my reassurance from the time we were in the second grade. It was time he started acting like a big boy.

Finally Tim asked, "Doesn't that sound reasonable, Joe?" This sounded more like a question than a demand.

"Yeah, Tim, I'd say so."

Vito wasn't sure what the hell was going on and he looked a little puzzled, then figured whatever it was was between Tim and me. And it was finished; for the time being, anyway.

"Martucci is coming into Kennedy via TWA in less than an hour, Joe. Vito has the flight information. You guys are going to pick him up and bring him back here." Tim leaned forward and squashed a cigarette into his large black onyx ashtray. "I want us to be very well prepared when we question Kitty Keeler later tonight."

"Right, Captain. *Absolutely.*"

Tim turned that over for the needle and decided not to acknowledge it. He was absorbed in jotting down notes when Vito and I left.

•

On the way to the airport I read through the folder Vito had given me. Vincent Martucci's yellow sheet began with his first arrest for felonious assault when he was eighteen years old. The mug shot showed a close-cropped, unformed young face, mouth self-consciously pulled into a tough-guy sneer. He'd been sent to Elmira for two years; was out in fourteen months. Despite a total of nineteen additional arrests on charges ranging from auto theft to murder, Martucci had never again been convicted of any criminal charge.

According to a background report prepared by Paul Sutro, Vincent Martucci was a man of many business interests. He was a sixty percent owner of the New World Health Spa Systems, Inc.; he had a fiscal or controlling interest in several real-estate and land-development companies; owned a women's-dress manufacturing company, a few machine shops, a small printing company; a substantial interest in a scrap-metal yard, a private garbage-collecting company, two industrial laundries, four bowling alleys, three restaurants, a large well-known caterer's in Brooklyn, an equally well-known, classier caterer's in Nassau County; a piece of a luxury hotel in Miami; interest in a couple of racehorses; a fifty percent interest in an up-and-coming welterweight, a commercial paint-manufacturing company as well as three retail outlets for the paint, a heavy trailer-parts supply company and a demolition company.

Outright, he owned a food-supply organization that catered exclusively to concessionaires in all the major racetracks and indoor sports arenas within a fifty-mile radius of New York City.

Several of the organizations in which he held a substantial interest had ongoing and future contracts with various city and state governmental agencies. A company in which Martucci owned thirty percent of the stock supplied all bed linens and towels to all municipal hospitals in New York City. Another company in which he held an undetermined interest had been awarded, through competitive bidding, the purchase of major Transit Authority scrap iron for a period of two years; given all his other interests, it wouldn't be hard for Martucci's company to underbid more legitimate organizations.

Vincent Martucci didn't deserve to look the way he did. At fifty-three years of age, he had a full head of carefully styled black hair with gray at the sideburns. He had black eyebrows over startlingly blue eyes, and even white teeth which flashed in his Arizona-suntanned face. He wore a conservative, expensive dark suit, immaculate white shirt with small gold cuff links and a carefully knotted dark silk tie. At the end of a five-hour flight he left the plane looking crisp and fresh and pleased to leave behind him a group of pretty smiling stewardesses. When they called out cheerfully to him, "You come back soon, now, you hear?" they sounded like they meant it, and he seriously promised that he would.

He spotted us the second he set his foot on the ramp, but he didn't even bat an eye as we approached him. He finished his conversation with an impressed-looking businessman, and they exchanged cards and good wishes before Martucci acknowledged us.

He glanced at our shields, nodded politely, then spoke to someone behind us. "Willie, you follow behind us, I'll ride with these gentlemen." He said it as though it was a decision he had made. "We're going to Kew Gardens, yes? You will wait for me outside the court there, Willie." And then, as if reassuring a child, he told his chauffeur, "Go, go, it's all right, Willie."

He settled himself comfortably in the back seat as though we were his employees acting on his orders.

We let him sit in the squad room for about twenty minutes, but it was a waste of time. When Geraldi finally brought him into Tim's office, he was cool and polite.

He leaned over Tim's desk, hand extended. "I am Vincent Martucci. Anything that I can do to help in this matter, anything, I will be willing to do." When Neary ignored the outstretched hand, Martucci just smiled and shrugged slightly. He glanced behind him. "May I sit down?"

Tim's eyes got that glassy look they get when he's giving someone the business. "Sit down, Martucci," he said. "This is an informal meeting, Martucci. You are here on an entirely voluntary basis, is that right?"

"Yes, of course." Then, with a slight smile that could have meant anything, Martucci said, "Let us *both* remember that fact, Captain Neary is it?"

"Exactly what is your relationship with Kitty Keeler?"

Martucci remained absolutely motionless, but there seemed to be a tightening process going on; everything about him was rigidly still. Quietly, in an intimate voice, he said, "With Kitty, as I'm sure you've learned already, it is a 'special thing.'"

"Explain what that means," Tim said coldly, not accepting any mutual knowledge between them.

Martucci smiled; his right shoulder moved just a fraction of an inch, an elegant shrug. "Very well. You could say that she is my mistress."

"Really? Well, from what we've learned, Kitty Keeler has a 'special thing' with a lot of men besides you. Which leads me to believe that the 'lady' isn't very 'special' at all."

"You pimp for her?" Vito asked roughly.

Martucci's head snapped toward Vito and his eyes narrowed and considered the large, squat man, then dismissed him with a soft click of his tongue against his teeth and turned back to Tim as though expecting to find an ally.

"Detective Geraldi asked you a question," Tim said. "I haven't heard your answer, Martucci."

Martucci's eyes, fastened on Tim, seemed less blue now; grayer; icier. His hands tightened on the chair arms and he became rigid with control. He gave off waves of emotion, tightly held back, clenched between his teeth and under the palms of his hands.

Vito moved menacingly toward Martucci. "I asked you a question, buster." Then Vito said something in Italian; an expression I'd never heard before, but the impact was immediate and obvious. Martucci went two shades lighter beneath his tan; his lips pulled back into what looked like a snarl. He started to rise from the chair, but Vito put one hand flat against his chest, didn't seem to exert any pressure at all, and Martucci hit the chair so hard he almost went over backward.

"Sit down, Vito, c'mon, take it easy." I pulled Vito away just as he seemed about to go for Martucci again. Vito turned away from me with a sound of disgust, then concentrated on lighting a mashed cigar end.

Martucci started to straighten his jacket, then let his hand drop to the arm of the chair, refusing to acknowledge that Vito had had any impact on him. He pulled back his lips into what wasn't quite a smile, though that's what he seemed to be trying for.

"Do not play games with me, Captain."

I don't know how Tim can go that long without blinking, but he'd never stopped his stare right at Martucci, who finally seemed aware of it and seemed just a little uncomfortable, which is the effect Tim tries for when he pulls that bit.

"I am not a pimp," Martucci said.

"Not anymore, huh?" Vito noisily fingered through Martucci's yellow sheet, making obscene comments after every page.

"Tell me something that puzzles me, Martucci," Tim said in a reasonable voice, but without blinking. "You say that Kitty Keeler's your 'mistress.' Well, apparently you're a well-informed man, no one can put something over on you. You must know that Kitty *fucks around* a helluva lot." He waited for the reaction to his words; there was none. Martucci's face had hardened into a steely blankness; the color of his eyes, over which he had no conscious control, had changed again; just slightly; gone a little more gray. "Doesn't that bother you, Martucci? I mean, if she's your mistress, doesn't she owe you more loyalty than that?"

"I don't own Kitty. She is free to do as she pleases, when she pleases, with whoever she pleases."

"Jesus, you're just another George Keeler, ain't ya?" Vito said.

Martucci deserved a couple of points for style; no question about it. His eyes had gone almost as colorless as his lips. The rest of his body had tightened, but the minute he became aware of the white-knuckled grip of his hands on the ends of the chair arms he made his fingers relax, go slack. There was a visible easing of the tensed muscles of his body. His breathing, which had become sharp and fast and audible, slowed to a more natural, silent rhythm. He raised his chin slightly, swallowed once and reset his face into an expectant, interested, well-mannered half-smile. I wondered if he displayed his polite good manners to his victims, maybe an elegant shrug of his shoulders and a soft apology just before he blew their brains away. I wondered if it had made any difference to his victims.

Tim blinked once; his eyes went directly to me. I responded by pulling a chair up alongside Martucci and leaning toward him.

"What did you and Kitty Keeler talk about when she called you on Wednesday night? Between eleven-thirty and twelve-five midnight, what did you two talk about?"

"Business," he said quietly, showing no surprise at the question. "Kitty wanted to know all about the opening; how things were going and all. She would have been there but for the illness of her child. She wanted to know everything that was happening."

"She talk business to you again when she called you a second time? What did you have to talk about from three-ten until three-twenty-five on Thursday morning?"

Martucci turned to me and smiled; man to man. He showed his white teeth, but his light eyes weren't smiling at all. "You know how it is."

"I don't know how it is," Tim Neary said. "You tell me."

Martucci faced Neary and spoke softly, politely, as though explaining an obvious situation patiently to a stupid child. "Kitty had been planning for a long time to attend the Phoenix opening. It was an exciting event; we had many movie people there, and many politicians. I can give you the guest list, if you wish." When no one asked him for it, he continued. "Kitty was to have been not only the hostess but the assistant manager of the spa. It was to be a training period for her, Phoenix was. If she could handle it, I'd promised her that position when our Westchester spa is open and functioning." Neary was staring again; this time he was also tapping his thumbnail against his front teeth and softly whistling. When he didn't ask any further questions, Martucci went on, almost against his will. "Kitty was naturally disappointed that she was unable to be there. She is, in some ways, like a child. She wanted to hear everything, to know what was going on." A bit impatiently, he explained, "There is, as you know, a time difference, New York to Phoenix. It was only eight-thirty Phoenix time when she first called; it was only after midnight Phoenix time when she called the second time. She just wanted to know all the details of the opening. Nothing unusual in that."

Tim's eyes moved about an eighth of an inch toward me.

"When Kitty called you the first time, Vincent," I waited until he turned his head to me, "when she called you at eleven-thirty, New York time, did she tell you then that she had just strangled her son Georgie?"

Martucci gasped as though he'd been hit in the stomach. He shook his head, said first to Neary, then to me, "That is crazy! That is insane. Kitty *loves* her children. She stayed home with them because the little one was sick. She has always been a devoted mother, she—"

"And did she tell you at that time," Tim's voice was hard and cold and he'd stopped staring, "did she tell you that she'd given Terry sleeping pills? And that she was afraid he was dead, too?"

"No. No, that's not true. Nothing like that was discussed, you are wrong."

"When she called you back the second time, Martucci, did she tell you it was all taken care of? She'd gotten rid of the bodies?"

Martucci started to rise toward Tim. "All taken care of? I don't know what you mean. You are wrong in all of this. Kitty loves her children."

Vito Geraldi planted himself alongside Martucci's chair, and Martucci sat down again, at the edge. "Who'd you tell her to call, Vince?" Vito put a friendly hand on Martucci's shoulder and said in a raspy, personal voice, "In the old days, you used to have Louis Galgonzola."

"Galgonzola? What are you saying? Galgonzola's been dead for ten, fifteen years. What—"

Vito spoke right over Martucci; he told Tim, "His top hit man in the old days, Captain. They used to call Galgonzola 'the Beast,' which will give you an idea of the guy if punks *like this one* called *him* a beast." He turned his full attention again to Martucci. "Who's your beast now, Vincent? Because it would have to be one helluva beast to have done these two little kids."

There was a fine line of moisture over Martucci's upper lip, and he blotted it with the back of a manicured hand, twisting away from Vito's grip on his shoulder. "Captain Neary, I came here in good faith, hoping I could help, but . . ."

I moved Vito away and sat down again next to Martucci, who wasn't sure if he should try to leave or not. "Look, Vince, I personally think that Vito's wrong. I think the whole thing was a mistake, an accident." I turned to Neary. "Tim, remember what we talked about before, how the whole thing might have been just a terrible accident."

"It's possible," Tim said.

"Look, Mr. Martucci," I said. "The way I figure it, Kitty choked the first kid by accident; hell, it's easy enough to do to a little kid. Then she gave the second kid sleeping pills, to quiet him down, and then she realized what she'd done and panicked. Then she called you; you're a good friend, why wouldn't she call you? So you told her who to call; someone you could trust, who would fake a kidnap-murder, to get her off the hook. Look, I'm not saying what you did was right, hell, I don't know. Maybe I'd do the same thing in the same situation."

"If that's the way it was, Martucci," Tim Neary said, "tell us now. Right now. Because, technically, you're an accessory to the fact. Three thousand miles away or not, the minute Kitty called you and told you what happened, you became legally responsible. Keeler will probably be able to get away with manslaughter. She was under emotional pressure; maybe she can even pull off a temporary-insanity plea. But you won't have anything to go with, Martucci. This one isn't going to just go away. We're gonna deal, Vincent; we don't deal with you, we deal with Keeler."

He wasn't buying. Not that anyone expected he would. He realized that no one was going to stop him from leaving this time.

"Since I have nothing further to say, Captain, I am going. The next time we speak, if there *is* a next time, my attorney will be present. He'll be very angry that I accompanied your two men here tonight, but I let my concern for Kitty and my sorrow for her children overcome my good sense. It will not happen again."

He stood up, turned and walked out. Neary nodded at Geraldi, who went to the window and signaled a waiting team of detectives that Vincent Martucci was on his way. They would be with him wherever he went.

"Okay, Vito," Tim said, "pick up Kitty Keeler and show her what her kids look like."

CHAPTER 9

I gave Vito about an hour and a half to get up to Yonkers, pick up Kitty Keeler, then drive down to the morgue in Manhattan. By the time I got there, reporters, photographers and TV cameramen were standing around casually as though they had been waiting for a long time.

The old guy behind the desk at the door squinted at my shield, then checked my face and made me sign a sheet of paper attached to a clipboard. In case any stiffs are missing, they know who to question. There were two names between Vito's and mine, so my timing was pretty good. The old guy looked like a collection of worn-out bones jangling around in a baggy navy-blue uniform. I didn't ask him if he was a former cop; I was afraid he'd say yes.

I spotted Vito before he saw me. Even from halfway down the long corridor, it was obvious that he was upset. He paced back and forth, head thrust forward and down, one large hand massaging the hell out of the back of his neck. He spun toward me and stamped down the hall. There was a dull red flush in Vito's face, down his neck into his sweaty shirt collar. He was breathing in loud short snorts and he grabbed my arm and shoved me into an alcove where there was a series of telephones.

Vito's eyes were blazing and he flexed his heavy jaw a few times, like he was testing it for biting. "Jesus Christ, Joey. Swear to God, this bitch is iron, Joe. I tell ya, she's iron and stone." He positioned himself for a good view of the corridor.

"What happened, Vito? Where is she? You been downstairs yet?"

"Yeah. We been downstairs. Where is she? I'll tell ya where she is, Joe. She's in the ladies' room, Joe, fixing her makeup. Swear to God, Joe, fixing her makeup. She says, 'I have to fix my makeup for those cameramen.' How about that, Joe, huh?"

Vito bit the end off a cigar and spit it to the floor. He drew on the cigar and finally, behind a haze of bitter smoke, he decided to tell me what made him so upset.

"It was like this, Joey, see, we go downstairs." He interrupted himself. "Jeez, I hate this damn place, ya know? Like the minute I walk into this building, it gets to me. Okay, okay, so we're headin' downstairs, this bitch and me, and I'm beginning to feel, like tight inside, ya know, Joe? and I look at her and nothin', Joe. No expression; nothin'. Like, she *knows* where we are by now, she *knows* what we're gonna see; so I'm thinkin', Okay, lady, just wait. Then that guy down there, Jenson, Johnson, whatever, that little guy in charge of the stiffs, Jeez, he looks like somethin' out of a Frankenstein movie, right, so he comes and takes us to where the boys are."

Vito swiped his hand over his wet red forehead, then blotted it on the side of his jacket. He dropped his cigar and covered it with his huge shoe absently. "Joey, I gotta tell ya, I seen those kids yesterday and I thought it was pretty bad then. But it's worse today, Joe. Them little kids . . . them corpses, they've been working on them, Joe. They been slicin' and cuttin' them all up for the autopsy. I could hardly look at them myself. I felt a little sorry for her, Joe, God's honest truth I did. So I moved aside for her and she stands there and she looks at what's left of her two kids. They was beautiful kids, Joe. I seen the pictures of them, they was dolls. And she looks at them and then she looks at me, swear to God, Joe, she says to me, 'They're so dirty. Couldn't someone clean them up?'" His voice was a bitter imitation of a woman's. Vito squeezed my arm, just below the elbow, to relieve some of the horror he was feeling. "On my mother's grave, Joe, that's what she said—'They're so dirty. Couldn't someone clean them up?' That's what bothered her, Joe. They was dirty."

I tapped Vito's hand and he released my arm just before the bone could snap. "Maybe she was just in shock, Vito."

"Shock my ass," he muttered. "That dame didn't bat an eye, Joe, God's truth. She says then, 'Where's the ladies' room, I gotta fix my makeup for those cameramen.'" He moved his foot, then stared at the crushed, shredded cigar in surprise. "Jesus, Joe, that was my last one. Gimme a cigarette."

Kitty Keeler walked toward us, a slash of electric blue against the sick-green walls; her platform shoes clicked and echoed in the empty corridor.

Vito turned away. "I'll see you back in the office, Joe, I don't wanna look at her right now. Swear to God, this bitch makes me sick to my stomach."

She had her hair pulled back softly at the sides, and her eyes picked up the color of her dress with a hint of green from the walls. She stood nearly three inches taller in her platform shoes, and she held her head to one side, waiting for me to say something.

"Mrs. Keeler, you weren't supposed to be brought down here. Your husband already made the necessary identification. Your being here was a mistake."

"Really? Is that what it was?"

I offered her a cigarette and she let her hand rest on mine as she touched the cigarette to the match. Her touch was cold and dry and she looked up at me as she blew the first smoke from her lungs.

Vito had been wrong. She wasn't iron and stone, though she hardly seemed flesh and blood. Beneath the fresh layer of makeup she had just applied, she was the color of putty. It showed through just a little, along the edges and sides of her face. There was a fine blue-white circle around her mouth, which glistened with a bright, moist lipstick. And there was something in her eyes, not easily seen, but it was there. Some touch of horror or expectation which I had seen just before George and I left the apartment to identify her dead sons.

She made a subtle but determined effort to shield herself in anger, not unlike the sort of anger she had directed at me when I had first questioned her. Before the boys were found. She fixed the anger coldly on her face and along her thin, rigid shoulders as we walked briskly through the mob of newsmen. I was puzzled by what was under this crisp, controlled façade, but I knew, even if Vito didn't, that she *had* been affected by what she'd seen.

•

Assistant District Attorney Ed Quibro had probably been the kind of kid other kids punched around when they had nothing else to do. The first thing he did when Kitty Keeler and I arrived at Tim's office was to consult his wristwatch, elaborately, pointedly, and even then he had to say it. "We expected you at least fifteen minutes ago."

"Well, we're here now."

He was a precise, compact man and he carefully checked the various cards and papers he had meticulously set out on Tim's desk. He looked like a large midget with that peculiar tissue-paper skin wrinkling around his pale button eyes. He could be anywhere from an old twenty-five to a young fifty and he was probably somewhere in the middle. His thinning black hair, worn in an old-fashioned style with short sideburns, was combed straight back from his high forehead; it looked damp. He wore a dark suit with a buttoned-up vest on which was displayed his Phi Beta Kappa key, which he frequently fingered. The collar of his white shirt was as stiff as cardboard and dug into his neck, causing an angry red mark. While everyone in the room waited and watched, Quibro went through a ceremony involving his steel-rimmed eyeglasses, breathing on each lens a predetermined number of times, scrubbing them with a large, clean linen handkerchief. Finally, glasses clean and in place, he pulled some heavy rubber bands from several stacks of three-by-five index cards, which he then tapped on the desk.

"Now. For the purposes of this interrogation," he informed the stenotypist, a hulking mountain of a guy who hunched over his machine like it was a delicate toy, "let it be noted that present besides myself—that's Assistant District Attorney Edward M-for-Martin Quibro, that's Q-U-I-B-R-O—on this date, Friday, April eighteenth, 1975, at, yes, at eight-forty P.M., was Captain Timothy Neary, commanding officer of the District Attorney's Special Investigating Squad, and Detectives . . ."

Quibro snapped his fingers at us; Geraldi, Jefferson, Walker and I gave our names and shield numbers.

Slowly, methodically, chronologically, Quibro led Kitty Keeler through a recitation of her activities and the activities of her children on the night of Wednesday, April 16, beginning at 7 P.M. with the arrival of Dr. Friedman. He stopped her response at several points, demanding more specific information.

"What, besides hamburgers, did you and your son, Terry, have for supper that night, Mrs. Keeler?"

She had been answering softly in a flat tone, the way a kid repeats something that has been memorized. This question puzzled her and she leaned forward slightly. "What else did we have for supper?" When Quibro nodded, she broke the rhythm she had established for herself. "What *difference* does that make? What does that have to do with anything?"

She drew on her anger, carefully, just testing for the sound of it.

Quibro took off his glasses and directed his blank beige eyes at Kitty. In a nasal monotone, as though reading a set of directions, he said, "It is essential that we know what food or other matter was consumed by your children to your knowledge. Then this information will be checked against the contents of their stomachs when they were found."

Her mouth fell open and she brought her hand up, but dropped it to her lap before it made contact with her lips. "The contents of . . . their stomachs?" She clenched her teeth and pressed her lips together.

Quibro tapped his index cards lightly against the desk and continued to wait. No one said anything and I was about to move when I caught something from Tim: Let this come from me, not you.

"Mrs. Keeler," Tim explained, "there is the possibility that whoever took the boys might have given them something to eat, some candy or cookies or something. If we know, for a fact, that you didn't feed them something they apparently ate that night, well, that gives us just one more thing to work with."

She glared at Neary. "One *more* thing to work with? You mean *one more thing* besides my *telephone book?*" She slid around in the chair and blazed at the men standing on the side of the room. "You bastards been having fun? Listen, *you,*" she turned back to Neary, "you want to know about my love life, my sex life, you just ask me. *Ask me* and I'll tell you whatever the hell you want to know to get your kicks, to make your day." She leaned back in the chair, folded her arms, tilted her head to one side. "And that'll save you time, so you won't have to send all these goddamn overpaid sons-of-bitches digging into my private life. And then maybe, *maybe,* you can start finding out who killed my kids!" Her anger fed itself, generated an even greater fury, strengthened her, made her more than equal to deal with all of us. She gave each of us one quick, scornful glare; she passed Quibro with a small, bitter laugh. "That's what this is supposed to be all about," she told us tightly. "Or did you *forget* that two little boys were killed? You so caught up in *my* sex life that you just forgot all about my kids? You all so fuckin' hard up you gotta get it secondhand?"

Vito Geraldi pulled away from the windowsill, lowered his head bull-like. "You're really all broke up about them kids, aren't you, Kitty?"

She made a deep gagging sound, like she'd just been hit in the throat, but she pulled out of it and concentrated all of her energy and strength at Vito. She stood up, rigid, and jabbed an index finger at him. She whispered something harshly in Italian; all I could make out were the words "your mother." Geraldi seemed to swell toward her rather than lunge. I caught him full against my chest and heard Kitty, behind me, saying coldly, "You keep that fat mother-fucking bastard away from me!"

Vito's face had gone purple, and when I put my hand on his shoulder and tried to kid him out of it he pulled away, crossed the squad room and headed toward the men's room. When Vito played bad guy, he went all out. Walker, Vito's young partner, came from Neary's office.

"Captain wants ya, Joe. Jeez, Vito got sore, didn't he? She shouldna said that about his mother."

"John, any guy over fourteen who takes that kind of remark to heart has a problem."

Walker started to protest, but I went past him back into Tim's office. Quibro was collecting his index cards, and Tim told me he'd called a

ten-minute coffee break. Apparently Ed Quibro didn't trust us with his
cards and he checked his watch just before leaving the room. Neary
went to the electric coffee pot and poured two mugs which he brought
over to Kitty, setting one on the edge of his desk. He took one sip from
his cup, looked up, and excused himself when Walker called to him
through the opened door. Tim closed the door quietly behind him.

"You want the coffee?"

She waved a hand at me. "Go ahead, drink it."

"Can I get you something else?"

Kitty Keeler dragged on her cigarette, pursed her lips and blew the
smoke in a steady beam right at me. She pulled her mouth to one side
thoughtfully. "It's a helluva way you people have of making a living.
Do you have a lot of fun digging into people's private lives?"

I thought about it for a minute, then told her, "Not much."

"It really shakes the hell out of you. All of you. Doesn't it? That a
woman can have a full, active sex life. It's different when it's one of the
boys, right? Then you all think, boy, this guy's great. But let a woman
live the way she wants and—"

"Mrs. Keeler, you're talking to the wrong guy. All I want to know is
what happened to your boys. Anything else, I couldn't care less. It's
you, not me. Right?"

She ran her tongue around the inside of her cheek and studied me
carefully, shrewdly. A small dimple worked in and out of her cheek and
she pointed a finger at me and said in a phony sweet voice, "Hey, now I
got it. You're the *good guy*. The rest of them," she waved her arm
around the room, "all the rest of them are the *bad* guys. And that pig,
that Geraldi, he's the bull, the *main bad guy*, right? And you're the
soft-soap artist, the one I turn to, right? Joe Peters, that's your name?"
There was nothing soft left in her, and her voice was ice. "Well, I'm
wise to you, Peters. I'm wise to all of you."

For some reason, it really got to me; made me really sore as though
she wasn't right about anything. I shoved the chair back and said,
"Look, lady. I don't know what the hell games you think we're playing
or what games you're playing. I don't give a damn about you, your sex
life, your life style or any other goddamn thing. I'm a cop and I've been
assigned to find out who the hell killed your kids. With or without your
cooperation. I've been working my ass off for the last two days trying to
get some leads. It would probably be easier *with* your help, but with it
or without it, we'll find out what happened."

She said softly, "What's the matter, Peters, did I hurt your feelings?"

I don't know if I was pissed off because she saw through us so easily,
or if I really did feel offended; after all, *I* hadn't given her a hard time.

The interrogation resumed, without Vito. When Quibro asked her what time she had called her husband the night of the murders, she replied, "It was ten-fifteen."

Quibro looked up. "Are you sure?"

Kitty took that as a challenge. "Yeah, I'm sure. It was ten-fifteen."

"Could it have been later? Maybe closer to eleven o'clock? Maybe even later than that, say eleven-fifteen or eleven-twenty?"

She leaned forward and spoke directly to the stenotypist, who didn't know what to do, so he just kept taking down words. "Hey, you. You at the machine. Read him back my answer. He doesn't seem to have heard me. I told him I called my husband at ten-fifteen. Isn't that what you took down?" Then, to Neary, "Is that guy hard of hearing or does he need permission to speak?" Then, to the stenotypist, "Speak! C'mon, good boy, speak!"

The stenotypist hunched himself closer to his machine and just kept hitting the soft-clicking keys; he never looked up at Kitty.

She was prepared to be questioned about the telephone calls to Vincent Martucci. They had discussed business: the opening of the new spa; nothing else.

When Patti MacDougal's statement was read to her, the portion describing her visit at 2:30 A.M. to the Keeler apartment, Kitty held up her hand. "You have to know Patti," she said. "She didn't come near my apartment that night. She probably *thought* about it by the time she got home. Patti *means* well, but she hardly ever follows through on a good impulse. She did call me at three A.M. and gave me the story about having tried to return the car earlier, but I knew she hadn't."

She told this calmly, shrugging Patti MacDougal off without much trouble. What I had seen of Patti didn't really contradict Kitty's view of her: a girl who means well, but.

Finally, Quibro rested his elbows on the desk and leaned forward. "Just a few more questions, Mrs. Keeler, but I must urge you to consider them most carefully. You have previously stated that you last tended your two sons between one and one-thirty A.M. Thursday, April seventeenth, 1975. Is that right?"

Her voice seemed tired, stretched thin. "Yes. Yes."

"At that time, Mrs. Keeler, how did your son George appear to you?"

"Appear to me?" She pulled herself straight in the chair and became sharper, more alert. "What do you mean? Georgie had fever. He threw up a little and cried. It always upsets him. And I cleaned him up, changed him and all, and he went back to sleep. That's all."

"And your son Terry. Did your son Terry appear to be in a normal condition?"

"Normal condition?" She regarded Quibro carefully, weighing the questions, trying to find the direction they were taking. "I don't know what you mean, normal condition?"

In his monotone, flat and irritating, Quibro said, "According to your earlier statement, you saw Terry in the bathroom and then back in his bedroom. In any way, did he appear to be different than he normally was?" When she didn't answer, just stared at him, Quibro said, with a touch of impatience, "Did he appear to be hurt, or injured? Did he seem to be . . . drugged?"

"Drugged?" Kitty frowned; she glanced from Quibro to Neary to Walker to me, then back to Quibro. "I don't know what you're talking about. He was . . . sleepy. He went back to bed and went back to sleep. What do you mean?"

"Mrs. Keeler, did you at any time during the night of Wednesday, April sixteenth, and Thursday, April seventeenth, 1975, leave your children alone in the apartment?"

I might have imagined it, but she seemed to falter, to hesitate for about a split second, as though coming to a decision; no one else noticed; Tim's face was still set and unmoving.

Kitty Keeler shook her head and her voice sounded weary, exhausted, tired of it all at last. "No, I didn't leave them alone at any time."

"Mrs. Keeler, do you have any idea, at all, as to who may have been involved in this matter?"

"In 'this matter'?" She mimicked Quibro coldly; he didn't react, just stared at her blankly. "Is that what you people consider the murder of my two children? Is that how you refer to it: *this matter?*"

"Mrs. Keeler, I believe your husband is waiting for you in the outer office. Detective Walker will drive you to your brother's house. That is where you're staying, isn't it?"

She stood up without answering Tim and started for the door, then stopped as though she'd just remembered something. "Captain Neary, when will we be able to get into our apartment and get some clothes? I have hardly anything with me. Can we go in and take out some clothes?"

"In another day or two, Mrs. Keeler; we'll let you know."

I opened the door and stood back for her to pass. She stopped again, bit her lip, inhaled and seemed to hold it. She turned again to Tim.

"Captain Neary, when will they release the boys' bodies? We have to make funeral plans and no one's told us yet."

"We'll let you know as soon as we know, Mrs. Keeler."

Vito had been standing just outside the door, in the squad room. He stepped back elaborately to let her pass and she never blinked at him.

He went into Tim's office and said, "Holy Christ, Tim. *First* she asks when she can get some of her clothes. And *then* she remembers to ask about her kids' bodies."

It hadn't seemed exactly that way to me; it seemed to me that it was too hard a question for her to ask. That she worked up to asking about the boys by asking about her clothes first. Vito hadn't seen the dull center of her eyes at that moment; he hadn't seen the slight twitching of a nerve ending in the corner of her mouth.

Ed Quibro packed and buckled his briefcase, then fondled his head to make sure every hair was in its assigned place.

"Well, boys," he said, "what do you think about that? According to Kitty Keeler, there was nothing wrong with either of her sons between one and one-thirty A.M. According to the Medical Examiner, one kid was dead and the other was drugged unconscious by that time. And she never noticed anything unusual about them." He pulled his thin lips back into what he thought was a smile. His teeth were little and dingy. "I think that little lady is going to hang herself."

Tim said, cautiously, since the burden of finding proof was squarely on his shoulders, "We have a helluva lot of work to do before that happens, Ed. We're just at the beginning of the investigation."

"Well, I hope you'll move right along, Captain Neary. Time is of the essence in this particular case."

Quibro never noticed the way Tim's eyes glazed over, the way he was breathing through his teeth in a soft, dangerous whistle.

"Hey, Quibro," I asked him, "you got a cousin in the Bronx? Name of Teddy Riley?"

Teddy Riley was the Ed Quibro of our neighborhood when Tim and I were kids. He was the kid we used to punch when there wasn't anything else to do.

Tim laughed and turned away from Quibro. Quibro's beige eyes blinked, but he couldn't find the joke. "No, my family is from Westchester originally."

He started out of the office, but couldn't resist stopping and saying, more for his own benefit than ours, "Yes, sir, I'll tell you how this whole thing is going to end. *I'm* going to get that little lady indicted on two counts of murder one. Just you wait. You'll see."

It was at that exact point, if Ed Quibro had been Teddy Riley, he'd have gotten one right in the mouth.

CHAPTER 10

THE minute the phone rang, I remembered that I hadn't called Jen. Before she could say a word, I said, "Hi, babe. Sorry I didn't have a chance to call you last night. Tim's got us working long hours."

There was a short silence, then, "You've really got me pegged, haven't you, Joe?" She sounded sharp and tense, like this was the opening line of an argument, but she dropped it and said, her voice trying for lightness, "Hey, I saw you on the late news last night. You really looked good, Joe. How come you're on that case?"

We talked for a little while about how come I was on the case. Then about our kids: she'd heard from our daughter; she was planning to call our son tonight. We made polite conversation, like two strangers being very careful not to say the wrong thing and not really certain what the wrong thing might be.

Jen quit City College to marry me; she'd been an art major and always planned to go back someday for her degree. We were married nearly three years before I got on the job and we felt we could manage on my salary alone. Instead of going back to college, Jen got pregnant with our daughter. Then we put a down payment on the house in Queens; then we had our son. Jen kept up with her work on her own. She sold some watercolors and a few oil paintings from time to time at different summer art shows. But it always seemed that the more she worked, the less satisfied she was with what she was accomplishing. When the kids reached school age, Jen worked, on and off, in an art gallery; as a free-lancer for an advertising agency; as an instructor in an adult-education community center. But she said she always felt "on the fringe of things"; not really into the center of what she felt she could do.

Last year, our daughter got married in June; our son went off on a two-month jaunt across the country before establishing himself at the University of Michigan in September. In August, we did just what we'd promised each other, years and years ago when it was far enough in the future to look like some terrific goal: we sold our house in Queens and bought a brand-new four-room condominium in Florida. Jen went down there and enrolled in the University of Miami as an art-education major. And I'm supposed to retire from my life next November and start "living" down in Florida.

I spent a week with Jen at Christmas. She seemed settled in and happy and busy with classes. I went down for a four-day weekend last month and something happened that I don't think either of us anticipated. At least, I didn't.

It was the last night before I was to return to New York. We started to make love. *I* started to make love and Jen seemed to stiffen up, to draw back.

"Why, Joe? Because it's the last night we'll see each other for a long time? The way it was always on the last night before you changed tour, for the same reason?"

That was how it started. By the time we parted, it was like I'd never really known Jen at all. Maybe living on her own for the first time in her life, maybe because there'd been so many changes all at once in our lives, maybe because she was spending her days around kids half her age with a whole different life style, Jen seemed all caught up in the fact that she was forty-four years old and that there were more years behind her than ahead of her.

Two years ago, Jen went with our daughter to a women's consciousness-raising group at Hunter College. Jen dropped out after about three sessions. What she told me was, "Those women scared the hell out of me, Joe. They're all so crazy and angry and frustrated." My daughter accused her of being afraid of what she might discover about herself, but Jen shrugged that off.

I think maybe our daughter was right; and maybe Jen knew that all along and finally has had a chance to take a good look at herself and her life. I think she feels a little confused and scared. I know she feels cheated. She's made that pretty damn clear, one minute blaming her own background ("I guess the nuns in Montreal really did a number on me in all those years they had to shape my life"); the next minute blaming me ("How could you *not* know it was never the same for me as it was for you? How could you honestly say you didn't know?").

Of course I defended myself by going on the offensive: "You mean in all these years you've never been able to be totally honest with me about this? to let me know? Christ, I'm not a goddamn mind reader."

And then went further: "You were always so damn inhibited about sex, about your body, about my body, how could I have ever tried anything different with you? And I did try, Jen, you know damn well, and you know goddamn well what your reactions have always been anytime I ever—"

"Right, right. Poor Joe. Stuck with a cold frigid wife, which of course would drive any hot-blooded normal male into the arms of other women . . ."

"I never said . . ."

"You never had to . . ."

We both went too far and neither of us knew how to undo whatever harm we'd done the other. I tried.

"Look, Jen, this is the first time in our whole lives that you and I have even *approached* discussing our sex problems. Maybe this is the first step—"

"Or maybe it's the last step, Joe."

In all this time, we've spoken on the phone regularly, on schedule, and never once has either of us acknowledged in any way what happened that night. But it isn't as though it never happened; it's there, for both of us. If we were living together, seeing each other every day, it would have been resolved, one way or the other, by now. But we're a thousand miles apart, so we talk like careful strangers.

Jen questioned my diet: Was I eating enough bland foods? Had I cut down on my smoking? Was I getting enough sleep? Then, softly, almost like she was thinking aloud, "She's a pretty girl, isn't she, Joe?"

"Who?"

"That girl, the mother. Kitty Keeler. She looked beautiful on the news last night."

I felt the tightness working down my throat, a steady pressure against my windpipe. "Yeah, she's a pretty girl."

"What an awful thing, Joe. Those poor babies. How could she have done it?"

"What?"

"That girl, Kitty Keeler. How could she have killed her own children?"

"You've got that all figured out, have you?"

"Well, *she did it*, didn't she?"

"That's terrific, Jen." I felt anger pulling my voice tight and thin. "I mean, you're what? about a thousand miles away from Fresh Meadows and you caught the late news and I guess you read the morning paper and you've got the case cracked. I'm up here, working twelve hours on and twelve hours off, and this is the start of the third day of investigation and you know more about it than I do. That's really terrific."

I don't know why I said any of that. If I could have taken it back, I would have taken it back. In the silence, I could feel Jen's hurt; her faraway hurt and anger. I was sorry. But I was tired of being sorry and I was tired of these strained, forced conversations on the telephone.

After a long silence, Jen said, "I guess I shouldn't believe everything I read in the papers, Joe."

"Well, they've got it all figured out, too. In fact, *everybody* has it all figured out."

"Well, don't you think she . . ."

"I don't know, Jen. Damn it, I don't know. No one really knows anything at this point."

But they *were* all certain. Who the hell else would have killed those two kids? All you had to do was take a look at Kitty Keeler. Everyone said that; everyone felt that. Tim knew she did it; Vito knew; even the girl's own mother knew. So why the hell was I so mad because Jen knew, too?

Because Jen had said she was a pretty girl and I know what Jen means by that. Because I've gone through years and years of coming home after fifteen-, sixteen-hour investigations, tired, aching, needing a hot shower and sleep, and there was Jen, trying not to but always asking me: "Does she mean anything to you, Joe? You spend more time with these people than you do with us; with the kids; with me. Sometimes you *must* feel *something* for one of these women you get involved with on a case."

Jen wasn't asking me if Kitty killed her kids; she was asking me how I felt about Kitty. And at this point, although I hadn't even acknowledged it to myself, I *was* beginning to feel *something* about Kitty.

"Listen, Jen. You caught me on my way out. I have an interview right in Forest Hills Gardens."

"You mean *policemen* have to work on *Saturdays?*"

"Well, the *bad guys* work on *Saturdays,* don't they?" It was an old joke between us, going back to when we were young and laughed a lot together.

We said a few more safe things to each other, then Jen said, "Talk to you Tuesday night, then. Love you, Joe."

"Right. I love you, Jen."

Whatever the hell that means.

I had another cup of coffee, another cigarette, a couple more antacid tablets. I doodled circles and arrows on the notepad next to the telephone and then I began to trace large and small question marks with little circles underneath.

If Kitty Keeler didn't kill her kids, then who did? She was the only logical one, but there wasn't anything logical about any of her actions, assuming she did kill them.

Keeler wasn't a stupid girl; why the hell would she have dumped the bodies so close to home?

Why the hell didn't she come up with a better story than just "I went to bed; I went to sleep; I woke up; the kids were gone"?

Why had she called Martucci, person to person, twice that night? She must have known that would be easy to check out.

Why was she coming on so hard, antagonizing everyone who might possibly help her? The media could go either way: make you want to hang the bitch or make you want to jump on a white charger and save her.

Why the hell did I come up with that particular image? There was *nothing* helpless about Kitty Keeler. Maybe something a little vulnerable beneath the surface toughness; maybe something a little injured in the dead center of her beautiful cold eyes. There *was* another Kitty, another facet we hadn't seen: a girl who was loving and concerned about that lady, Mrs. Silverberg. I'd seen a flash of it when she'd reacted to George's near-collapse after he'd found the boys. There had been something pure and selfless and uncontrived about her concern for George.

All of our assignments had been to prove that Kitty Keeler killed her kids, instead of a wide-open investigation, which would ultimately prove she did it if in fact she was guilty. What bothered me was that we seemed prepared to prove her guilty even if she wasn't.

If I was feeling somewhat protective of Kitty Keeler, it was more because someone had to play devil's advocate rather than because the girl seemed to want or need a protector.

I think.

•

One block into Forest Hills Gardens and you're in another world at another time. It's a protected enclave of private tree-lined streets untouched by the incredible development of the rest of Forest Hills. There are no thirty-two-story apartment buildings, no bachelor pads or groupie-stewardess setups. Although the enclave is a part of the borough of Queens in the City of New York, the Gardens Association maintains a private sanitation service, a staff of gardeners and maintenance men and a force of security guards who patrol on foot and motorbike. Unauthorized vehicles—without a numbered Gardens sticker—get window-sized, iron-glued notices pasted over each window informing the owner that "Forest Hills Gardens is not a parking lot." The second violation, and the car gets towed away at the owner's expense. Not friendly, but effective.

Most of the homes were either Tudor or Normandy mansions set back among trees, shrubs, velvet lawns and formal gardens. The home of the Vincent Martuccis was imposing by any standards. It was a huge old castle set so far back and so concealed by hedges and twisting brick pathways that I wasn't sure where the front door was located until I was nearly on top of it. I ignored the small neat sign advising "All Service to Rear Door"; the sign beneath it, just as neat but more ominous, advised me to "Beware of Trained Dogs." As soon as I touched the buzzer, the chimes and the trained dogs went off. Even through the heavy door, I was convinced that the barking was of the no-fooling-around variety.

There was a slight variation in the small round mirror set at mouth level in the door: I was being viewed. There was a small clicking sound, and a voice came at me from a cluster of tiny pinpoint holes set into the doorjamb. I held my shield up to the mirror and gave my name to the pinholes.

"You wait dere please jus' a minute." The accent was West Indies. The dogs barked again, but a sharp command shut them up.

Another sliding of the viewer; a different voice. "I'm Mrs. Martucci. What is it, please?"

I identified myself again; there was the sound of heavy locks being undone. The door opened on a chain and she asked, politely, for some identification, which she checked quickly; then she shut the door, undid the chain and allowed me into a huge marble entrance hall. The trained dogs, two sleek Dobermans, sat quivering with emotion; a deep rumble vibrating in their throats and four glassy, vicious eyes convinced me not to offer them a pat on the head. They waited for me to follow Mrs. Martucci, then they backed me up, one on each side. I put my hands into my pockets; I didn't want them dangling behind. She led us into a huge room with a stone fireplace that stretched from floor to high ceiling across one entire wall. A young girl sat against the velvet-topped railing in front of the fireplace and she stopped in the middle of a sentence, so that a second girl, poised at the edge of a velvet chair, became curious and turned toward me.

The dogs ran, one to each girl. The younger girl, against the railing, closed her eyes and offered her face to the dog nearest her. I thought the kid was crazy; her whole head could easily fit inside that dog's opened mouth.

"Lucia," Mrs. Martucci said sharply, but with a maternal pride, "don't let him do that to you." The dog was slobbering a thick pink tongue all over the girl's face. "Girls, you must excuse yourselves now." She told them in Italian to take the dogs with them. I added a silent *grazie*.

"I hope I haven't interrupted you." There was a breakfast tray set between the two velvet chairs.

She waved her hand: it was of no matter. A very small, very black woman in a light-gray uniform stood in the doorway waiting.

"Bring another cup, and some fresh coffee, Pearl, and some of the small glazed cakes. Thank you."

She snapped on the lamp beside her chair, and for the first time I saw her clearly. Maria Martucci was a Madonna. She was totally unexpected. She had a pale, unbelievably elegant face with high prominent cheekbones, a regal nose, wide lips and the blackest, brightest eyes framed by thick long lashes. Her hair was black and very heavy, worn off her face, twisted into a knot at the back of her neck. She wore a dark wine-colored long velvet gown which clung to her tall body sensuously. The only jewelry she wore was a narrow gold wedding band, and at her throat, just in the hollow, rested a tiny gold crucifix.

It was hard to figure why the hell Vincent Martucci was at this moment having coffee in a crummy Yonkers luncheonette with Kitty Keeler when he could be here, with this magnificent woman. Kitty had a fresh, cute, girlish beauty. Maria Martucci was the real thing: a woman whose beauty increases with time.

She moved her head to one side politely; apparently she was accustomed to the effect she had on people.

"Mrs. Martucci, I'm sorry if I've intruded on your breakfast, but I must ask you questions about a very serious matter."

"Yes?" Her eyebrows, black against her white skin, raised expectantly.

"You've heard about what happened to the children of Mrs. Kitty Keeler?"

A shudder went through her body, working across her shoulders, then down along her spine. Her hand went to her throat; she touched the tips of her fingers to the crucifix. "Terrible. Terrible. Little babies." Then one shoulder moved forward and she said softly, flatly, "The will of God is difficult to comprehend sometimes."

"I don't think God's will had anything to do with this, do you?"

"*Everything* is God's will."

There was a certain tension coming from her, but it disappeared as she turned, polite, expectant, to watch the maid set a silver tray on the coffee table. Mrs. Martucci leaned forward, indicated that she would handle it from here. The maid disappeared without a sound, as though she vaporized. Mrs. Martucci concentrated on pouring coffee into the large thin cups, added sugar, cream, stirred it quickly, then, half smiling, handed the cup and saucer to me. "You must try these little cakes; I make them for my children. They are so fond of them."

I tasted the coffee, then put saucer and cup down on the table, shook my head at the dish she held toward me, sensing she was trying to distract me. It wouldn't have been hard. There was something very erotic about her.

"Mrs. Martucci, I have to ask you some questions. About a somewhat . . . delicate matter." I don't think in my whole life I had ever used that expression: a somewhat delicate matter.

She stopped stirring the small silver spoon in her cup and looked at me coolly. "There is nothing delicate about it. A whore is a whore."

That brought me up sharp. "You know, then, about your husband's relationship with Kitty Keeler?"

She put the cup down on the tray and folded her white hands in her lap. They were startling, like ivory, against the dark velvet. "I know what goes on between such a woman and a man."

"Do you know Kitty Keeler?"

I could have sworn she made a spitting sound; at least, a sort of hissing. "I would not know such a woman." Then, in almost a whisper, telling me a secret, "There are *many men* who know this woman. Many. Married men, unmarried men. It means nothing to a . . . a woman such as this."

"Do you know of anyone at all who might have a reason to do such a terrible thing to Mrs. Keeler's children?"

Without hesitation, she flashed back, "To *her*, yes. To her *children*, no." Her back pulled away from the chair; she moved her long hands, one inside the other. "A woman like this, with no respect for marriage, for her own or another person's, brings down terrible things on her own head. A woman like this, with no heart," she brought a hand up to her breast, "who knows what such a woman is responsible for?" She was silent for a moment and I was about to ask a question, but she added, slowly, deciding whether or not to continue, "There are many women whose lives have been damaged by this woman." She hesitated, then added softly, "A poor crippled woman . . ."

I leaned forward. "I'm sorry, did you say a crippled woman? Who would that be?"

She moved her head from side to side; there was a strange light coming from her eyes. The corners of her mouth turned up slightly, but not in a smile. "Maybe you will find out something about that." She shrugged. "Maybe not, I do not know."

She sat as still as a picture; her face was serene and beautiful and yet she gave off certain sparks, tensions, signals, that were contradictory. She held up the plate of cakes toward me, and when I shook my head she carefully selected a little pink-iced square for herself, placed it on a plate, took tiny crumbs of it on her silver fork, inserted the fork between her barely parted lips, then licked the end of the fork with the tip of her tongue. All the time, she watched me, her eyes huge and amused.

"Mrs. Martucci, we have serious reason to believe that your husband is implicated in the death of Kitty Keeler's two sons."

She put the plate down, as though she'd had all the nourishment she needed. She dabbed at her mouth with a heavy linen napkin, then said softly, "My husband was in Phoenix. He only arrived home last night."

"He spoke to Kitty Keeler twice on the night the children were murdered. Immediately after they were dead."

"How would I know about this? What is it you want from me? Why do you not question my husband?"

"If we are right, Mrs. Martucci, and I believe we are, your husband gave Mrs. Keeler advice that night, regarding the boys. When we prove it, your husband can be charged with murder."

"My husband has been charged with many things in his lifetime. I do not involve myself in his affairs."

She moved one hand, brought it across her body to rest on the opposite arm, then slowly, languidly, she moved her hand up and down, from shoulder to elbow. Her face showed pleasure, the kind of pleasure a cat feels when being stroked the right way.

She had that half-smile again; an indication that she was aware of her impact on me. That she was radiating sensuality with a simple, innocent, nonsexual motion. There was a hard light in the center of her black eyes and now I could see that she and Vincent Martucci were not mismatched.

"Mrs. Martucci, where were *you* on Wednesday night, between, say, ten o'clock and midnight?"

She dropped her hand to her lap, moved back against the chair and smiled. "I was at Our Lady of the Martyrs. We are sewing and preparing baskets for the victims of the flooding in Guatemala. My chauffeur dropped me home at twelve-thirty and then he drove Father Collins to his residence on the campus at St. John's." She began the stroking of her arm again; tilted her head to one side. "Can I help you with anything else? Anything at all?"

I considered for a moment, shook my head. "Maybe some other time."

"Perhaps." The word offered something; in and of itself, a harmless, meaningless word, but from her lips the word conveyed several meanings. I wasn't sure at this point whether she was merely amusing herself or challenging me to interpret what she didn't choose to say openly. I don't mind games when I'm in on the rules, but this lady kept everything secret; kept the advantage and enjoyed my discomfiture. When she stood up, her hands lightly skimmed the outlines of her body, and she moved silently into the two-story-high hallway. I took a minute to take it all in: the sweeping curved marble staircase, the various paintings, the handsome grandfather clock, ticking steadily, softly, the dazzling crystal chandelier hanging on a gleaming chain from the high ceiling, then I turned to Maria Martucci.

Her eyes fastened on my mouth; my lips began to tingle. I tried to be casual about rubbing my thumb along my lower lip. Without a word, a sound, a gesture, the lady made me aware of her great, deep hunger. Games. The lady was playing games again.

"Oh, by the way, Mrs. Martucci. I guess you know—or would want to know. Your husband is up in Yonkers right now. In some diner with Kitty Keeler. Consoling her, probably, the way a good friend would."

Her mouth turned down; her lips parted and pulled back; her teeth glinted. Her dark eyes hardened and glowed with an ancient, undeniable hatred and demand for revenge for injuries suffered. Her hands rolled into tight fists at her side and she leaned toward me.

"She has no right to the man of another woman. No right to the father of my children." Her hands came up, together, and rested at the base of her throat. She whispered in a harsh voice as though I was someone she needed to confide in, "The nights *I* have spent alone; *my* empty bed; *my* empty body. Do you not think that *I* have suffered, while she, the whore, has drained the juices from my husband? For her, let there be no end to the suffering. Her children are in God's hands now." She let her hands fall to her sides and she smiled tightly with anticipation and said with absolute certainty, "God will see to her." She nodded and repeated, "Yes. God will see to her."

I heard the heavy door close behind me, followed by the resetting of the various locks.

So much for the Madonna of Forest Hills Gardens.

CHAPTER 11

THE last time Alfredo Veronne's name hit the papers was about four years ago when his son-in-law, Ray Mogliano, stepped into his Cadillac, turned the ignition key and, along with a young fill-in cocktail waitress, blew up all over the parking lot of a popular Nassau County roadhouse managed by Ray and his brother, John Mogliano, and owned by Veronne. The regular cocktail waitress and more or less steady girl friend of Ray had been home sick that night. If she hadn't been home sick that night, little pieces of Kitty Keeler would probably have been scattered all over the parking lot. So it was very lucky that Kitty was sick that particular night.

Not surprisingly, no arrest was ever made for the bombing; according to Paul Sutro, the word was that since Alfredo Veronne objected to divorce on religious grounds, he had little choice when his well-loved only daughter complained to Papa about her wayward husband. And as if that wasn't bad enough, it was an open secret that Ray had been ripping his father-in-law off; Mogliano had been known to brag that no one could touch him. As it turned out, he was wrong.

Until that incident, anyone interested in such things would have assumed that Alfredo Veronne, in company with his contemporaries Lucky Luciano and Frank Costello, had long since made his piece with his Maker. Although he was now deathly ill, Veronne was not yet dead.

When Alfredo Veronne's name and unlisted telephone number turned up in Kitty Keeler's little pink book, Paul Sutro's amazing memory came up with a significant detail. According to what's called "information received," the officers investigating the bombing learned that on the afternoon of the night that Ray Mogliano exploded, someone called Kitty Keeler and told her she was going to be sick that night and she better get right into bed and stay home and take care of herself.

Which could mean, apparently, that Papa Veronne didn't blame Kitty for his son-in-law's behavior; in fact, that he thought enough of

Kitty to do her a favor. Like save her life. And maybe like send someone over to Fresh Meadows to help her dump a couple of small bodies.

In the not too distant past, Alfredo Veronne, with a blink of an eye
or a flick of a finger, could have condemned a man to a most horrible
death. The mention of his name had been sufficient when money or a
service was demanded. His name, face and organization were familiar to
nearly three generations of governmental agencies which had been
formed to study and combat organized crime. There were at least three
popular writers collating material about his most colorful days which
they hoped to capitalize on once the old man was dead; which shows
there is an honest buck to be made from organized crime.

Veronne now languished in the beautiful stone house in fashionable
Great Neck where he had raised his family of five sons and one daughter. His sons had all gone to good colleges and were all established in legitimate enterprises. More or less. He had many fine grandchildren.
Impressed by the wisdom of old-fashioned American millionaires, as
each grandchild was born Papa Veronne established a million-dollar
trust fund for the infant. Something which Alfredo's stonecutter father
in Sicily never would have thought of.

Alfredo Veronne was a cordial host. From his sickbed, he waved his
hand, offering me any kind of refreshment: food, liquor, fruit, candies,
cookies, anything. The table next to his bed was well stocked and
tempting.

"I'd just like to talk with you, Mr. Veronne."

"Well, since you do not accept my hospitality," he sounded offended,
"what is it you have come to see me about?"

Veronne's voice was raspy, low in his throat, hoarse. Some nodules
had been removed from his vocal cords, but others were growing back.
He touched his wrinkled throat with a bloated hand as though he owed
me an apology for his inability to speak louder.

"Mr. Veronne, you've heard about the murder of Kitty Keeler's two
sons?"

"Terrible. Two such small children. Terrible. A bad thing."

"Do you know anyone at all who might do such a thing?"

Alfredo Veronne closed his tiny eyes and whispered, "People might
do *anything* at all, for any *reason* at all." The dark, bright rat eyes
sprang open and studied me shrewdly. "Who can know another person's mind? But you ask me this particular thing and I must say no. I
know of no one in this instance who might have done such a thing."
He moved his head slightly and added, "I have heard nothing." As if,
had there been anything to hear, it would have reached his ears inside

this beautiful dark-paneled bedroom with its massive fourposter bed, huge gold-framed paintings, Oriental rugs, stained-glass windows.

"Tell me about your son-in-law, Ray Mogliano."

Veronne's body jerked up on the pillows and his face was surprised, as though he'd been jerked upright by an outside force. He carefully relaxed and seemed in pain as he slid down slightly. His brows, thin and scraggly gray, like his remaining hair, moved close together over his thin nose, and his mouth worked, lips pulling downward as though trying out suitable words. Finally his lips twisted and deep in his throat he simulated a spitting sound.

"Dead. No great loss."

"Because he was sleeping with Kitty Keeler?"

The old man blinked quickly to clear his vision. His head tilted toward one shoulder as he stared at me. He smiled slightly, an unpleasant baring of his square yellowish false teeth, and he nodded his compliment. "Very direct. Yes. You are very direct. Sometimes, that is good. Sometimes it can be very dangerous, you know?" He considered his own words for a moment, then made a cackling, laughing sound. He held up his swollen hands, let them fall stiffly to his sides, indicating his helplessness, his inability to move from the bed, the senselessness of either threats or denials.

"What the hell, what you gonna do to me? Crazy world, anyways. They let a punk kid take a walk if he murders some poor old retired shopkeeper." He shook his head, clearly outraged. "These little punk bastards who beat old people because they're helpless." He muttered to himself, realized he had lost track of what he had started out with; came back to it. "Mogliano, that bum. It was a long time ago, what, four, five years? Time runs together for me now, it's tough to get old, huh, kid? But me, I've made my peace; I've squared my accounts, so what the hell? You know something, he wasn't even worth the effort." He scratched at an eyebrow, then shook his head. "I regret the girl, though. In the old days, it would have been a clean hit, but, like everything else, there are no more quality workers left, you know?"

"Was it a try for Kitty Keeler?"

He waved his annoyance at me; changed his opinion of me. I was stupid after all. "Ah, you have a one-track mind. Kitty Keeler, Kitty Keeler. Listen, pal," his eyes narrowed and his voice, though still painful and rasping, was strong, certain, "if it had been a try for Kitty Keeler, Kitty Keeler would have been hit. If not in the car with that bum, Mogliano, then another time. The woman was not important." He clenched his hand into a fist and shook it at me. "With that bum, it was any woman. It was for the *insult to my daughter!* He held my daughter up to public contempt, as though it did not matter that he made his affairs with women common knowledge." In a softer voice, he said, "Men are men; they will seek out women, what the hell. But we use discretion; we respect our wives. My wife, may she rest in peace," he crossed himself reverently, "forty-two years we were married when she left me for heaven, and not once, in all those years, did she ever know about any of my women. Respect; see. You gotta have respect, but this Mogliano, this bum, he respected nothin'." He leaned back, his head sank into the collection of large, soft pillows. He held out his hands, wrists together; they shook. "So, what you gonna do, cop, ya gonna arrest me?"

"What about Kitty?"

He shrugged. "Keeler is a good kid; she's a nice girl. Not like the papers are tellin' stories about her, like she was a tramp. Kitty's no tramp. She's a good girl; she's a smart girl." He poked his forehead with an index finger. "She got it up here, know what I mean. You can trust Kitty. She's a smart girl."

"What about your daughter?"

There was a sudden silence, broken by the hard gasp for breath as Veronne tried to pull himself up from the pillows. "What about my daughter?"

"Did she want to see her husband dead? For the insult to her? Did she think Kitty Keeler was a 'good kid'? Or did she maybe think there was a score to settle?"

There was a sudden, terrible strength in the old voice; even though it was still a whisper, it was a loud whisper. "You go into matters that do not concern you. Family matters—"

"Well, I guess I'll talk to her myself, then."

The emaciated body seemed to rise from the mattress in a swell of strength and bony determination; arms outstretched, clutching at air, eyes blazing, the inarticulate voice a thin, terrible howl, like an animal suddenly caught in a springtrap. At the instant of Veronne's outcry, the door burst open and two men rushed to his bedside and with small effort eased him back onto his pillows. His breath came in loud, choking, irregular swells.

A third man, an older man than the others, vaguely familiar the way you remember someone from an old, faded wanted flyer, or at least with that kind of face, with a typical expression of contempt or threat, grabbed at my arm and pulled.

"Okay, you, you've overstayed your welcome here. Now. Move!"

He might have been old, but the guy had tremendous strength and I had the uncomfortable feeling that he wasn't even beginning to exert pressure; this was only his warning grip.

I went with his pressure rather than resist it; with a quick twist, I got lucky. He went sprawling across the foot of Veronne's bed. Before he could pull himself up and before the other two, who were just a pair of thugs without any class at all, could react, Veronne's voice, hoarse and strained as it was, held them in place.

"No. No, Lorenzo." He motioned to the red-faced, fast-breathing man at his feet. "It's foolish, it's worth nothing." He waved the younger guys aside for a better view of me. "Because times have changed, because Lorenzo and me," he turned his head and spoke directly to the older man, poised at his feet, "because we respect the men now in charge, eh?," then, back to me, "because this is *their* day now, you walk out of here *alive*. A few short years ago, cop, you lay a hand, so much as one finger, on Lorenzo, and *you would be a dead man.*"

I looked at Lorenzo, who had not mellowed with age. I believed what Veronne had said. I waited until I was through the doorway, then, since you shouldn't leave your host without saying good-bye, I turned and said, "So long, Mr. Veronne. Rest in peace. Real soon."

•

Howard Beach had been built on reclaimed swampland. In the early and middle sixties, some enterprising developers realized that not all Bronx and Brooklyn people sought the good life far out on the Island or in Jersey. There was a large group of people who wanted to move, practically en masse with friends and relatives and traditions and customs, into one-family homes still within the boundaries of New York City.

Tract houses were built upon the dank land of filled-in swamp: row on row on row. Each plot was approximately forty by eighty feet, which allowed for a small front lawn, small back lawn, a narrow driveway leading to a single garage and one of three types of houses: split-level, ranch or Cape Cod. Occasionally, in times of heavy rain, the swamp seemed to reclaim its territory; basements had to be pumped, mosquitoes darted out of the floors, and mildew crept along the walls. But by and large, the residents of Howard Beach were contented with their lives.

The main thoroughfare, Cross Bay Boulevard, was lined with a variety of supermarkets, quick-food drive-ins and take-outs, kosher butchers, delis, Italian groceries, restaurants and fish markets.

There was a large lot adjoining Mogliano's Volkswagen showroom on the boulevard. I wandered among the used cars that were for sale, then back toward a shed where a few mechanics were working. There were a great number of auto bodies in various stages of disassemble scattered around.

One of the mechanics looked up, squinting through grease. "Yeah? You want somethin', Johnny?"

I touched the shiny fender of a huge black Lincoln. "This for sale?"

"Naw, nothin' here. You wanna look at cars, go around the front. Customers ain't permitted back here."

I had a good idea why not. I went around the corner and into the showroom, which was filled with bright shiny new VWs. They reminded me of the bright bumper toys in one of the old Coney Island amusement park rides: something silly and cheerful and attractive about them.

There were five men seated around a table toward the back of the room. They were hunched toward each other and I'd be willing to bet they weren't discussing the automotive industry. There was a small dark old man standing off to one side, leaning against the plate-glass window, watching the others, nodding like a wise old counselor as they spoke. A huge German shepherd, held by the old guy on a short thick black leather leash, sat warily at his feet. Every now and then, a deep growl ran up the animal's throat, as though he was humming to himself.

A kid came up to me from another part of the showroom. He was short and chunky, with a lot of thick black hair which he wore low on his forehead. Probably because it grew low on his forehead. He looked like the kind of kid who is someone's nephew: give the kid a break, for his mother's sake, ya know?

"You wan' I should show ya somethin'?" he asked me.

"Yeah. I want you should show me John Mogliano. Tell him to break from his friends and come over here."

The kid wasn't sure what his reaction should be. His uncertainty registered on his heavy features and in the way he set and reset his wide shoulders and thick neck. He made a neutral, clicking sound which could be interpreted as amusement, contempt or cool. He stood sizing me up for a minute, then turned and walked across the showroom and made his way slowly to the table, where he bent and spoke to one of the men. He jerked a thumb over his shoulder toward me. The man he spoke to stood up, looked in my direction, then patted the messenger reassuringly.

The other men at the table watched as Mogliano approached me, chin thrust out, eyes measuring me for height, weight and occupation. "You wanna talk with me? I'm John Mogliano."

I decided we didn't need an audience. "Outside, okay?"

I leaned against a black 1974 Mercedes and watched Mogliano put on a pair of huge dark sunglasses that he pulled from the pocket of his mustard-colored sports jacket. He fitted the glasses carefully behind his ears and smoothed them along the sides of his face. The thick wavy black hair was a toupee; a good one, probably very expensive, fitted precisely to blend with whatever hair was still growing, but close up you could make it for a toup. If you are particularly conscious of such things; which I am for certain reasons concerning thinning hair.

"When's the last time you spoke to Kitty Keeler?"

Mogliano's hands flew open. "Oh, Jeez, that was bad, what happened to her kids, huh?" He shook his head. "Terrible. Jeez."

"You haven't answered the question."

"Huh? Oh, yeah, Jeez, maybe a week ago or so. Kitty called me about some kid's car. Some girl over on Woodhaven Boulevard smashed her VW up pretty bad, so I tole her don' worry about it, I'd take care a it." He shrugged expansively. "What the hell, ya do a favor for an old friend, ya know?"

"You consider Kitty Keeler an old friend?"

Mogliano didn't know how to answer that. He glanced over his right shoulder as though he expected someone to tell him what to say; what was the safe thing to say. "Well, ya know, like she worked at the club, out in Nassau County, years ago. That's all." Then, in a sudden burst of enlightenment, he said, "Oh, hey, you mean was Kitty and me *'friends.'* Not like *that* we wasn't. Uh-uh. No, no. Not me and Kitty, not like that we wasn't." He shook his head for emphasis.

I lit a cigarette and held the match for Mogliano. As he ducked down, I could see a small rivulet of sweat slowly working its way down from his temple to his cheek. I also inhaled a lungful of musk-based aftershave or cologne. I waited until Mogliano straightened up.

"Tell me, John. You ever feel it was Kitty Keeler's fault that Ray got hit?"

Mogliano looked alarmed. He glanced around, first over one shoulder, then over the other, expecting to see someone moving in on him. "Oh, Jeez, you gotta be kiddin'." He cupped his hand alongside his mouth; I had a little trouble hearing him. "Listen, Ray was my brother, know what I mean, but I gotta tell you, if ever a guy was askin' for it, Ray was." He jabbed his forehead with his thumb. "Dumb, ya know. I tole him and I tole him, ya don't kid around with . . . ya know. With the big guy."

"With Alfredo Veronne?"

Mogliano's head spun around, checking again. "Hey, listen, you said that, not me. Look, it was what, four years ago, what the hell. Like I said, Ray was my brother and all, but even I couldn't tell him nothin'."

"What did you try to tell him?"

"Ah, you know."

"No. I don't know. Which is why I'm asking you. Look, John, you wanna talk with me here, or you wanna come down to my office?"

Mogliano checked his showroom, the parking lot and the passing traffic. "Naw, look, I'll talk with ya, only let's walk along a little, okay? Hey, you wanna have a sandwich or somethin'? C'mon, my cousin got a nice place right across the boulevard."

I ordered a veal cutlet sandwich, which wouldn't do my ulcer any harm at all; veal is bland. It was the spicy sauce that I should have refused, but the aromas coming from the kitchen were overwhelming. Mogliano dug into a steaming plate of hot sausages and he talked with his mouth full of food.

"Look, my brother Ray was a kid, ya know? Twelve years younger than me; he was the baby of the family, six sisters and me. We all spoilt Ray. And a good-lookin' son-of-a-gun, I tell ya, the kid looked like a movie star. Which was bad for him, ya know. Ya couldn't tell Ray nothin'; he knew it all, may he rest in peace, poor dumb kid."

I didn't have to ask many questions now. Mogliano kept eating and talking and I kept eating and listening.

"See, the old man liked the kid's looks, ya know, so he give him a job drivin' for him." Mogliano checked the wall behind him, the empty tables all around us; he leaned forward and didn't notice the large glob of sauce on the sleeve of his mustard jacket. "That's how he met the old man's daughter, ya know, drivin' for the old man. The minute the girl laid eyes on Ray, that was that. The old man give that kid anything she wanted; like we spoilt Ray, he spoilt her. She wanted Ray, the old man give her Ray. He set the kid up with the club in Nassau County and he put me in to manage it, ya know. Ray didn't know nothin' about business, he was there for show, like a host or maître d'. An' on weekends we had a little band and every now and then Ray would get up and sing a little. He wasn't no good, but, see, that was my oldest sister's fault; Angie raised Ray from when my mother, may she rest in peace, died and she keeps tellin' Ray everything he does is great, terrific, like another Sinatra. So anyway, son-of-a-gun, Ray brought the crowds in. I mean, the kid wasn't any good, but he could put over a song, ya know. He would really pitch it to the women in the audience and soon Ray starts sayin' he wants to cut a record. See, he believes all these broads tellin' him how great he was, but it wasn't his voice they was talkin' about and I try to tell him it ain't his voice that puts him over, but Ray says he's not gonna waste what he's got in a dump in Nassau County. Swear to God, it was like listenin' to my oldest sister, Angie, that's the kinda stuff she'd been givin' him all his life. And Ray, he's goin' out with these broads, all they gotta tell him is they got a uncle or a cousin in show business and the kid laps it up and I'm tryin' to tell him to watch out, ya don't play games when your wife's old man is . . . ya know."

"Then it wasn't just Kitty Keeler?"

"Are you kiddin' me? Jeez, any woman comes into the place, she gets a look at Ray and what he's advertisin', she's ready to buy. It wasn't like that with Kitty. I mean, Ray *respected* Kitty, know what I mean? *They wasn't lovers*; it's hard to explain. But Kitty's the kinda girl you could trust, ya know. Like, I never knew any other woman you could call a 'friend,' ya know, like a guy is a friend. Kitty handled the books besides being a cocktail waitress, and she knew right away that Ray was rippin' the old man off. She covered for the kid, but after a while there wasn't no way. Ray got so sure of himself, like there wasn't nothin' he couldn't get away with, ya know." Mogliano let his fork fall into his plate; he rocked his head from side to side, held one hand against his jaw. "Dumb kid, dumb kid, may he rest in peace. It still hurts me to think about it, the waste, ya know. Like, he had it all and he blew it. He'd never listen, not to anybody, he knew it all, so now he's buried in little bits and pieces, dumb kid."

I reached across the table and picked up Mogliano's napkin and jabbed at his sleeve. He stared at me, mouth opened; it took him a couple of seconds to realize what I was doing, then he finished cleaning his sleeve himself, dipping a corner of the napkin into a glass of water.

"How come I keep hearing around that Kitty Keeler was your brother's mistress?"

"Ah." Mogliano brushed that aside with a wave of the napkin, upsetting the glass of water, which he began to swab and blot. "That kinda talk is because right away, people see a girl around with a guy, especially a guy like Ray, and that's all they can think about. Like I told you, Kitty's a special girl. Look, I'll tell ya somethin'." His eyes darted around quickly and he leaned over the table. "Somethin' I never told nobody else. The night Ray . . . the night Ray got it, Kitty called him at the club. Right in the office, I was there. He talks to her a minute, then he laughs and hangs up and turns to me and says, 'Kitty says I should watch myself tonight. She got the word, which is why she stayed home.'"

"Are you kidding me, John?"

He pulled back against the leatherette of the built-in seat, looked offended. He raised his right hand and said, "Swear to God on my mother's grave, she should rest in peace."

"What about Veronne's daughter, John? You think she got the word that Ray was heavy with Kitty Keeler? You think she might have had a grudge against Kitty, held her responsible for the way her marriage was going?"

Mogliano's eyebrows shot up almost to his fake hairline. "Cindy? You gotta be kiddin' me. Hell, that girl never knew nothin' about nothin' about any of Ray's girls. She never heard none of the talk about Ray. And I gotta tell ya, he was my own brother, but he was dumb. He bragged about all the women; he said some really dumb things, like . . . well, like . . ." He debated for a moment, then shrugged. "Well, he shouldna gone around sayin' things like he did. Ya know, like how he had the old man over a barrel, he could get away with anything as long as Cindy loved him."

"And then Cindy stopped loving him?"

He shook his head and regarded me with surprise. "You gotta be kiddin' me. That girl worshiped Ray. She was all broke up when Ray got it. But her father was right, I gotta admit it, she deserved a better husband than Ray. A poor girl like that, the only thing surprised me was that her father let Ray marry her in the first place."

"What do you mean, a poor girl like that?"

"Ya know, with her affliction." He was convinced now that I was really stupid. "Ya didn't know? That Cindy Veronne is a cripple-girl. Like from the waist down. I tell ya the truth, I was tempted to ask Ray how they . . . ya know?" He rocked his hand from side to side. "But I never asked him outa respect for the girl."

The Madonna of Forest Hills Gardens' poor crippled woman.

"Where is she now? Cindy Veronne?"

"Cindy? Hell, she's right where she's always been. With the old man."

"Wadda ya mean, with the old man? With her father?"

"Yeah, sure. She's never lived nowhere else but with her father, even when she and Ray was married. That house out in Great Neck, they had a whole section to themselves, like it was a separate house altogether, all built special for the girl; lotsa privacy, ya know, but still close to the old man. I guess he's what ya call very . . . what? protective of the girl. Not that I blame him, her being the way she is and all."

I remembered something: there were ramps leading off from the main entrance hall in the Great Neck house. And the doorways had seemed extra wide. To accommodate a wheelchair?

"What's the girl's problem, John?"

He took a big lump of cheesecake on his fork; as he chewed and talked, cheesecake squirted out of both sides of his mouth. He collected it carefully with his index finger and shoved it into his mouth. "Cindy? That she's crippled, ya mean?" He shrugged. "I don't know too much about it. She wasn't born like that, if that's what ya mean?"

"Yeah, that's what I mean."

He wiped his mouth and his fingers, one by one, on his napkin. "There was an accident, see, when Cindy was just a little girl. Her mother got killed in the accident. Car accident, and the old man was driving, so you can see how he held himself responsible, why he always wanted to keep Cindy close to him; ya know, to watch out for her and all. Jeez, I remember about a year before the kid got hit—funny, I didn't think much about it until just now. But Ray and Cindy had a car accident too. Wait a minute. Yeah, they was going out to Kennedy to catch a plane to Florida right around Christmas time. The old man got a beautiful layout down in Palm Beach, ya know, and they was going to meet with him down there, and Ray skidded on the ice and somehow the door on Cindy's side flew open and the girl wasn't wearing a seat belt and she went flying out to the side of the road and all." He shook his head at the memory. "Jeez, she was real lucky, ya know. Just shook up, with a coupla bruises. Ray had a concussion, and him and the girl were taken to . . . I think it was maybe Jamaica Hospital. The old man flew back to New York and he has them both transferred to a private hospital with round-the-clock care and all that. Something funny about it, but I don't remember right now. Something Ray told me, but I can't seem to remember what. Oh well, couldn't be important, I guess."

"Tell me something, John. You know anybody got a grudge against Kitty Keeler? Anybody who would want to hurt her really bad?"

Mogliano wiped his mouth with the back of his hand. Bits of cheesecake soiled the sleeve of his jacket. "Look, I don't know of nobody, *nobody*, in the whole world would wanna hurt Kitty. Kitty is . . . she's the best, ya know? And George too; Jesus, George is the salt of the earth, ya know? I've heard a lotta people say George gotta be a little crazy or a little dumb to put up with Kitty, but people who say that are wrong, ya know? George is happy with whatever he gets from Kitty, so who the hell is to say? I'll tell ya somethin', there isn't nothin' in the whole world I wouldn't do for Kitty, she asked me."

"She call you Wednesday night, John?"

He shook his head. "Naw, it was last week, wait, I think Monday about that girl's car."

"She didn't call you Wednesday night? And tell you she had a little problem and needed your help?"

"Naw, I spoke to her—" He stopped and stared across the table, mouth opened as he realized what I was asking him. "Jesus, you gotta be kiddin' me. You askin' me if . . . if . . ."

I wasn't really asking him. "Forget it, John." When I stood up and dug for a couple of bills from my wallet, he got up heavily and caught my arm.

"Naw, this is on my cousin, it's like an insult to pay him for a meal, if I bring ya. It's like eatin' in his home, ya don't insult him."

"Okay, John. Thank your cousin for me."

He walked with me to my Chevy, looked at it with distaste, kicked at a front tire. "You ever get ready to get a real car, you come around. I'll fix you up with something really nice. At a good price."

"I'll remember that, John."

He slammed the door for me and stood outside the driver's side.

He pulled off his sunglasses and began to rub them with his handkerchief. "I'm gonna tell ya somethin' that I *know*, like ya know somethin' from in here." He spread his fingers on his chest. "Like ya know from in your heart. Kitty never hurt them kids of hers. Kitty never in her life hurt anybody at all. She loved them kids; maybe she wasn't the kinda mother all the magazines tell girls they should be, ya know, like my wife, alla time home with the kids, every minute watchin' out for them. But Kitty's not like they're tryin' to make out in all them newspaper stories. Believe me. I know."

"Okay. And, John." He bent down again and came closer. "If I were you, I'd make sure I had a purchase receipt and complete records on all those VW chassis and parts around back of your place. Or else I would keep them out of sight. Just in case some auto-theft cop takes it into his head to check you out, know what I mean?"

He pulled back, offended innocence. "Who, me?" Then he clamped a hand on my arm, which was resting on the window, squeezed it once, leaned toward me and said, "Hey, you're a good guy, ya know? Remember, when you're ready, I'll make you a good deal."

"Yeah, I'll remember, John. Thanks."

Mogliano slapped himself on the forehead with the heel of his hand and said, "Hey, ya know what? I just remembered something. About that time when Ray and Cindy was in Jamaica Hospital."

I don't think he just remembered; I think he'd just made up his mind to tell me. "What's that, John?"

He glanced over his right shoulder and leaned close to me. "Well, I don't even know if it's worth somethin' or nothin' at all. In fact, I don't even know if it's true, know what I mean?"

"I know what you mean."

"Well, see. Ray tole me that there was this doctor in the hospital, a wadda ya call them kinda surgeons, they operate on your nerves and back and things? Like all the ball teams got?"

"A neurosurgeon?"

"Yeah, yeah, like that. So anyway, Ray tole me that this doctor examined Cindy. She wasn't hurt bad or nothin', just bad shook up, but he took a whole buncha X-rays and he tole Ray that the girl coulda had a operation a long time back, like when she was a little girl, ya know?"

"What does that mean?"

Mogliano pulled back nervously and shrugged. "Hell, I don't know, ya know? But from what Ray said, it was like the doctor seemed to think that Cindy didn't have to be a cripple alla her life. Like she coulda had a coupla operations and been up and on her feet and all, like anyone else."

I thought about that for a minute. "Did the doctor say the girl could *still* have surgery, or did he say it was too late at that time?"

"Oh, hey, Jeez, I don't know nothin' more about any of that, ya know? Anyway, Ray tole me he didn't say nothin' to Cindy about it, but, well, he tole me he asked the old man about it when he come up from Florida."

"Veronne?"

"Yeah. Yeah, and Ray says the old man got very . . . agitated, ya know? and he orders an ambulance to take the girl to this private hospital and he tells Ray," Mogliano hunched down and almost came through the window onto my lap; his voice went to a thick whisper and he cupped his hand around his lips, "he tells Ray, like, forget it, it's a buncha crap, what you *think* this doctor tole you, and he tole Ray, 'You *never repeat this kinda garbage to anyone. At all.*'"

"Especially not to Cindy?"

Mogliano shrugged and pulled back out of the car, banging his head on the window frame. He rubbed at his head; it seemed to me he must have loosened his toupee; his hair seemed to slide around a little. "I don't know nothin' from nothin' about any of this, ya know? But for what it's worth, I pass it along to you."

I didn't know, either, if it was worth anything, but I thanked John Mogliano and I waited until I had gone a couple of blocks away before I brushed the little lump of cheesecake from my sleeve.

CHAPTER 12

JOHN MOGLIANO'S cousin had too heavy a hand with the spices, and I regretted the free meal by the time I arrived at the squad office. Before I had time to search for some Gelusil or Tums, Tim opened the door to his office and signaled to me. Which surprised me. After all, it *was* Saturday and Tim *was* a captain and the squad commander.

There was a clean-cut, pink-faced baby patrolman in Tim's office who leaped to his feet in what seemed like deference to age when Tim introduced him to me.

"Patrolman Carter here has come up with a witness who has confirmed Patti MacDougal's story about coming back to Fresh Meadows on Thursday morning, Joe." Tim turned to the kid and said, "Go ahead, Officer, tell Detective Peters what's in the report."

Patrolman Carter looked like he'd rather I just read the report that Tim held. He clasped his hat behind his back and seemed to rock a bit from side to side. His voice was a little shaky and his face went a brighter red.

"Yes, sir. I was assigned to interview tenants at the Monroe Arms and—"

"The Monroe Arms?" I turned to Tim.

"The thirteen-story building facing the Keelers'." He waited, then had to start the kid off again. "Go ahead, Officer."

"Yes, sir. I was assigned the ninth and tenth floors. On Thursday, April seventeenth, and Friday, April eighteenth, I attempted to make contact with resident of Apartment Nine-K, a Dr. Frank Michaels, with nil results."

"With nil results?"

"Yes, sir, with nil results. At eleven A.M. this date, I made contact with the aforementioned Dr. Frank Michaels, who stated to the undersigned as follows: that on—"

Tim took pity on the kid. "It was a nice job, Patrolman Carter. Tell you what. You drive Dr. Michaels back to his apartment or wherever he wants to go and then—"

"Sir," Patrolman Carter said, "I don't have any means of transportation. Dr. Michaels drove me over in his vehicle."

Tim led him to the door. "In that case, have Dr. Michaels drive you back to the 107th, if it's convenient for him. Otherwise, hitch a ride with someone, okay?"

In the midst of a coupla "yes-sirs" Tim threw in a few "nice-jobs," then handed me the kid's report, which he should have done in the first place.

> On the night of Wednesday, April 16, 1975, Dr. Michaels had been summoned to Queens General Hospital, at 10:30 P.M., for an emergency delivery. His patient, not expected to give birth for another two months, had been critically injured in an auto accident on the Grand Central Parkway. Within twenty minutes of his arrival, Dr. Michaels delivered by Caesarean a four-pound preemie. The mother survived for nearly three hours and then succumbed to her injuries. Dr. Michaels signed out of the hospital at 2:15 A.M., Thursday, April 17, 1975.
>
> Dr. Michaels arrived home at about 2:30 A.M. As he left his parked car, he observed a white Porsche pull into the parking lot in location determined to be the assigned location of the Keelers. Dr. Michaels stated that he was too keyed up and upset to go directly to bed; he changed his shoes and returned to the street, intending to jog until he felt more relaxed. As he exited from the lobby of his building, Dr. Michaels noticed the lights flash on the Porsche and within the next minute or so, the car pulled out of the parking lot. It was about 2:40 A.M. Dr. Michaels did not see anyone enter or exit from the Porsche. He was confirming that subject car did arrive and leave in times corresponding to statement of Patti MacDougal.

"That young fella, Carter, was right on the ball, Joe. Nine out of ten guys would have let it drop after the second attempt. I'm going to put him in for a commendation."

"Have you got any Gelusils, Tim?"

"You don't need anything, Joe. You look fine." Tim hadn't come in to the office just to congratulate this efficient cop. He saved the best for last. "I've just come down from upstairs, Joe, from a meeting with that bastard Kelleher and his weasel, Quibro. They've decided to hold

Keeler as a material witness. Hold her in protective custody. What do you think, Joe?"

I wasn't too sure what I was supposed to think. "You're the one with the college education, Tim. You tell me."

Tim shoved his hands in his pockets and clicked some coins together; he walked to the window, then turned and stared at me.

"It's a *device*, Joe. To put some pressure on Kitty. She's some tough little cooky. If seeing her two kids down in the morgue didn't break her, maybe a little restriction of her freedom might. Legally, it's feasible. Obviously there was more than one person involved in transporting the boys' bodies. Kitty would be the clearest threat to that person, therefore a possible target. Hell, to be technical about it, there have been a few nut letters and phone calls."

There are *always* a couple of nut letters and phone calls, but I didn't point this out to Tim, since he knew it as well as I did and he wouldn't have appreciated hearing about it.

"When is all this going to happen, Tim?"

"We're working on it right now. I just sent Geraldi out to pick up Judge Donlevy; Kelleher caught up with him at his golf club in Westchester. Soon as he finishes his game, he's going to come in and sign the necessary papers. Which is where you come in, Joe."

The bodies of the Keeler boys had been released that morning. I was to meet Kitty Keeler at her brother's house in Yonkers, escort her to her apartment to pick up clothes for the boys, then bring her to the Kelly Brothers Funeral Home in the Bronx, which is where the bodies were now. Then call in; if it was all set, I was to bring Keeler back to the office. Without telling her exactly why.

Kitty walked through the mob of reporters, photographers and cameramen as if she was a movie star who'd been doing it all her life. Head up, normal pace, into the car without a sign of being aware of the voices that called out to her in that strangely intimate way.

"Hey, Kitty, c'mon, Kitty baby, give us a break."

"Hey, babe, take off the glasses. Let's get a look at those big blue eyes."

"Hey, Kitty Killer, you kill any kids today?"

She pulled off her glasses and snapped her head around to see who had called out the last thing; a series of flashbulbs went off as I pulled the car away from the curb. She sat, one hand over her eyes, massaging lightly before she put her dark glasses on again.

"How come George isn't with you?"

"He's still with your partner." Then, lower, angrier, "As if you didn't know."

My partner. Catalano? "George is with Catalano?"

"With Soft-Soap Sam. He's been very helpful, taking George back and forth to the ginmill. He's all heart, isn't he?" Her voice was bitter and restrained. "I would have thought Sam would've been assigned to buddy-up with me. He's the type, isn't he?"

"He's a type, all right." Catalano; hanging around George Keeler?

When we pulled into the cul-de-sac at Fresh Meadows, there was an identical group of news people waiting for Kitty to walk from the car to the building.

"What are they, a bunch of magicians?" Kitty said; which is exactly what I was thinking.

The young cop, with a couple of days of experience behind him, cleared a path for us. There were more people here than in Yonkers; more curious sightseers who had somehow gotten the word that Kitty Keeler could be seen, in person. A few strange types, glassy-eyed with excitement: the string-bag-clutching old nuts who swarm around murder scenes hoping to touch someone, anyone, even remotely connected to tragedy.

Someone close to hysteria began to shriek, "I touched her! My God, she looks just like her pictures. We're with ya, Kitty baby, we're on your side." You couldn't even tell if it was a man's or a woman's voice; somehow, nut voices don't have genders.

I wrapped my arm around her shoulders and followed the uniformed man; he held the door open for us, then closed it and stood facing the crowd, using a strong, professional, calm voice.

Kitty dropped the bunch of keys, and when she retrieved them she couldn't seem to find the apartment door key; when she found it, she couldn't fit the key into the lock. She held the keys toward me and stepped back until I opened the apartment door, then she went inside. She hadn't been home since the morning the children's bodies were found: Thursday.

The apartment had a faintly closed-up feeling; Kitty ran her finger over a table and frowned at the dust. She picked up an overflowing ashtray and brought it to the kitchen. The technicians hadn't cleaned up after themselves. There were a few stained, empty coffee containers and a few wadded-up sandwich wrappers. Kitty snatched a brown paper bag and began cleaning up. She stopped, hand about to reach for another ashtray.

"Is it all right? I mean, can I . . . touch things now?"

"Yeah, they're all finished."

She looked around the living room with annoyance; she kept touching things, straightening things, moving items a fraction of an inch. Finally she decided that was all she could do for now.

"Did they . . . find anything?" she asked. "You know. Whatever it was they were looking for?"

"Don't worry about it. Everything's under control."

She thought about that for a moment or two, went into the kitchen with the bag of debris, then stood in the doorway. She gestured vaguely. "Look, do you want coffee or anything? Or just coffee, I guess. I don't think there's anything else in the house. I have to . . . I'll have to go shopping, I guess." She seemed somewhat confused; not quite sure if she should be a hostess to me.

"No, I don't want anything. Or do you have Gelusil? Or Tums? Or something like that?"

She shook her head; caught me pressing my hand into the burning spot where the ulcer was biting at Mogliano's cousin's spicy sauce.

"Wait a minute." She ducked into the kitchen, came back with a glass of milk.

I took a small taste; it was sour, but I didn't tell her. I waited until she went into her bedroom to get a suitcase for the boys' clothes. Then I spilled the sour milk down the kitchen drain and rinsed the glass. I could hear her banging around, opening the sliding closet doors, displaying the rainbow colors of her clothing. When she came back into the living room, she was wearing a different outfit: a dark-blue denim pants suit with a light-blue turtleneck. She had tied a small red railroad man's scarf over her hair, knotted in back of her neck. Her face was pale against the bright color. She held up an expensive leather suitcase; an overnighter.

"You think this will be big enough?"

She sounded uncertain; as if she needed reassurance, which surprised me. She was nervous and on edge; I hadn't realized how drawn and pale she really was. She looked from me to the suitcase, then back at me.

"That'll be fine. You want some help?"

She considered that for a moment, then shook her head. It seemed to take a certain determination and resolve for her to go into the boys' bedroom. But she went.

I walked to the window, looked outside at the grassy lawn, then turned back into the living room. It had the impersonal feel of a motel room; there was no evidence of the kind of people who lived here. Something caught my eye; a bright-yellow object was sticking out from beneath a chair. I picked it up: a small plastic rectangular object with little protuberances along one edge, indentations along the other edge.

A piece from a child's game, building blocks that locked one into the other. I slipped it into my pocket, deliberately not thinking about what child's hand had dropped it; and wouldn't ever pick it up. There was something odd, something I couldn't quite identify. The outside playground noises and the low humming of descending jets faded into the background as I became aware of the silence, ominous and total, within the apartment. I crossed the living room and stood just inside the open doorway of the boys' bedroom.

Kitty Keeler was standing between the two beds, her back to me. She held something in each hand; her arms were stretched outward as though she was offering what she held. She was rigid and motionless; then she swayed slightly, caught her balance; then, suddenly aware of the intrusion into her privacy, she whirled around and faced me, her arms still extended stiffly.

She glared at me suspiciously, then she said softly, in a barely controlled whisper, "Look. *Look!*" She was holding a pair of rolled-up socks in each hand. Arrayed on either side of her, on each of the two beds, was a carefully selected outfit: small navy-blue blazer, gray flannel slacks, white turtleneck, set of underwear for each child.

"Isn't this crazy?" She began to laugh. "Look at this. I'm matching the socks to the charcoal-gray pants and I'm standing here and I'm wondering if I should match the socks to their shoes instead of to their slacks." Her body shook with the deep gasping sounds of her laughter. She suddenly brought both hands up to her face and held the socks against her mouth, muting the sounds of her voice. When I moved toward her, she pulled her face up and shook her head. "No. No, don't. Please, don't touch me. But isn't it funny? I mean, I'm standing here trying to decide what color *socks* they should wear. To be *buried* in!"

It was there again, more clearly than before: the terrible expression of pain in her eyes; unblinking, unaccepting, unbelieving pain. Her mouth opened, but there was no sound now. She bent over suddenly as though kicked in the stomach, with that same kind of gasping, suffocating sound. I caught her, tried to ease her down onto one of the beds, but she pulled away and said wildly, "No, for God's sake, I don't want to sit on their *clothes!*" As though the clothes were their bodies.

She pulled herself up straight, extended the socks again and said, "What color socks should they wear?" She blinked rapidly, but there were no tears in her eyes. "Well, don't you think it's funny? Don't you?"

"What color are their shoes?"

She jerked her head back as though she'd been hit. She rubbed her cheek with a pair of the socks and stared, uncomprehending.

"What color are their *shoes*, Kitty?"

She let her hands drop to her sides and said quietly, "Saddle shoes. Blue-and-white saddle shoes."

"Navy-blue socks," I told her. "Do you have navy-blue socks?"

She nodded dumbly, then moved to the chest of drawers, switched socks, and dropped one pair on each bed. Then she knelt in the closet and dug around for the shoes. She pulled them out and held them up toward me. "They're dirty."

She fingered the soiled spots on the shoes and seemed unable to deal with the situation. She slumped against the side of a bed and was completely, totally vulnerable; defenseless. Her fingers trembled as she dabbed at a smudge on one of the shoes. A chill passed through her body; she shuddered and tightened her shoulders.

"Kitty?"

I called her a second time and she turned her face up toward me. It was devoid of all pretense, all masks, all armors; it was ragged and suffering and filled with despair.

Kitty, did you kill your sons?

Kitty, *why* did you kill your boys?

Kitty, tell me all about it; you'll feel better when you do. It will be over with once and for all. It's the only way you'll ever be free of it.

Kitty, talk to me.

All I said was, "Where's the shoe polish?"

I helped her to her feet, surprised at the fragility of her body; she seemed weightless. I put paper towels on the counter in the kitchen, painted the white parts of the shoes with the liquid polish, then asked her for small plastic bags for the shoes. As I cleaned up the counter, she put the shoes into the bags; all but one shoe.

"There's a broken lace," she said in a helpless, despairing voice. She turned her face to me: defeated; no solution.

"I'll pick up a new pair tomorrow morning." I took the shoe from her hand and put it in the plastic bag. "Don't worry about it. It'll be all right."

We went back into the boys' bedroom and she began folding the clothes, but she kept dropping things. Her hands were shaking and she tried to hide them, but without a word she stepped back and watched as I folded the clothing and packed the suitcase. Just as I was about to close the suitcase she came forward, reached a hand to touch one of the small navy jackets: just touched it lightly, wordlessly, then drew back.

"Will it be all right? The clothes? Will they look all right? I want the boys to look good. Does everything match?"

"Everything will be fine. Come on." I handed her a bag of shoes. She seemed reluctant to leave the room.

"Have I got everything? Have I forgotten anything?" Her hand went to her face. "I have the most awful feeling. Like, I'm forgetting something really important." She turned, her eyes swept the room. "Oh, God, what? What have I forgotten?"

"You haven't forgotten anything, Kitty. Come on."

She turned to the small round child-size table, touched the open coloring book, fingers slid over the incompletely colored picture of an astronaut. She picked up two crayons and put them back in the crayon box; closed the book; put it on a toy shelf. She studied the rows of toys and reached for a stuffed yellow duck. It was worn and bleached-looking.

"This is Georgie's. Do you think . . . ?"

"Sure, if you want to bring it, why not?"

Kitty took a long, slow, deep breath; she pulled herself up straight, rearranged the expression on her face; took control of herself. She tossed the stuffed duck, with a quick sharp motion, against the wall. It landed, upside down, on one of the beds.

"What would be the point?" she asked. Briskly, toughly, she said, "Let's get the hell outa here. This room is making me feel morbid."

I picked up her keys and sunglasses from the kitchen counter. "Put these on, Kitty, and keep your head low and we'll rush right through that mob out there."

She took the sunglasses, held them without putting them on. She pulled her arm from me, stood motionless. There was a visible gathering of strength filling her; she was drawing on a kind of anger. She was no longer vulnerable; that moment was over.

"I'm not worried about those crazy bastards out there, or any other bastards, Peters, so you can just stop playing Mr. Good Guy right now."

She pushed past me on her way out. The funny thing was, I really hadn't been playing a role with her.

We drove around to the back of the Kelly Brothers Funeral Home in the Bronx. One of the Kellys was there, waiting to take the clothing. He made soft, comforting, meaningless conversation with Kitty while I went into a phone booth and called the office. Tim sounded tense but excited; I tried to sound casual.

"We gotta take a ride back to Queens," I told her. We drove in silence all the way out to Kew Gardens.

Tim was behind his desk. Ed Quibro sat, straight as a stick, on one of the chairs in front of the desk. He jumped to his feet and, with a sort of sweeping motion, invited Kitty to sit in his chair. She froze him with an insolent smile, slumped into another chair, slid her legs out straight, folded her arms over her body.

"Well," she asked Tim, "now what?"

Ed Quibro walked around the desk, collected a stack of typed papers. "Mrs. Keeler," he said in his precise, flat, monotonous voice, "I'm going to give you the typewritten transcription of your statement as given to me on Friday night, April eighteenth, 1975. I ask you now to read it over, carefully, and indicate if you would like at this time to make any corrections in your statement. If this statement is accurate to the best of your knowledge, I am going to ask you to sign your name at the bottom of each page."

Kitty rubbed her eyes, then said to Quibro, "Go ahead and ask me."

"I beg your pardon?"

"You said you were going to ask me to sign my name. At the bottom of each page. So go ahead and ask me." She reached up and snatched the papers from Quibro and said, "Forget it, just forget it." She reached for a pen from the leather cup of pens and pencils on Tim's desk. "Where do I sign? The bottom of each page?"

She began flipping through the pages, signing her name without reading any of the endless questions and answers.

"Mrs. Keeler," Quibro protested, "I must caution you to read over this statement carefully and—"

"All right. You cautioned me."

Tim came alongside of her. "Mrs. Keeler, it would be wise for you to read what you're signing."

She looked up directly at Tim and said tersely, "You want these pages signed? You got them signed." Deliberately careless, she lifted the corner of the next page and, without even looking, scrawled her name. She stood up, tossed the signed documents across the desk at Quibro. "There. I'd like to be taken home now."

"There are a few things we have to go over with you, Mrs. Keeler."

Suddenly wary now, she drew back; seemed to slow herself down. She gave her attention to Quibro, first glancing at me. "Yeah? Like what?"

"There is a question of timing, Mrs. Keeler. Particularly a question as to the time you claim you last saw your sons alive. You see—"

Kitty leaned on the desk, her hands planted firmly, her face jutting toward Quibro's. "Listen, you, I didn't *claim* anything. I told you exactly what was what that night. And I signed your goddamn papers. And I'm sick of you and this office. And I'm going home, right now."

She turned to Neary. "We can go back to our apartment now, can't we?"

There was a strange, significant silence in the room. Kitty looked from one face to another, aware suddenly that no one was meeting her questioning stare. A slow, certain panic began to build; she tried consciously to control it, locking her hands one inside the other, taking deep, silent breaths. Finally she sat down again as though drained totally of energy; covered her eyes with her hand, shook her head.

When she looked up, directly at me, her expression was different from any I'd yet seen: unmasked, yet not revealing anything but a blank, empty exhaustion, appealing to me to take over for her. She had turned to me naturally, as though I was her one ally in the room. I ducked my head down toward my cupped hand, lit a cigarette, then handed it to Kitty. She took it without a word; when Tim began to speak, she forced herself to turn toward him; it seemed an effort for her to concentrate and she seemed uncomprehending, puzzled, too weary to follow what he was saying.

When Tim finished speaking, Quibro extended some papers at her, assured her of the legality of what was happening. Finally it penetrated; the knowledge seemed to give her new energy. She stood up, hands rigid at her sides.

"Wait a minute. Just wait a minute. What the hell are you talking about? Protective custody? *Custody?* What does that mean? Custody? Oh my God, my God, *you're not going to put me in jail, are you?*"

She stumbled back, unaware that she cried out. Her knees buckled and I caught her before she slid to the floor. She hadn't passed out; it was more like she'd been knocked over by a strong and unexpected wave. She struggled from me as soon as she caught her balance, whirled around, confronted me.

"What are they trying to do to me, Joe?" Her voice was low and furious, but her face looked drained and defeated. Her eyes were dark and shining and staring as though she didn't trust herself to blink. There was a slight nerve-twitch at the corner of her right eye. The minute she was aware of it, she pressed her fingers against her temple, trying to maintain control. The fingers of her other hand dug into my arm, either for emphasis or because she literally needed to hang on to someone. "What are they trying to do to me?" she demanded a second time.

"It'll be all right, Kitty," I said softly; her total focus on me created a peculiar intimacy. It was as though we were totally alone, confiding in each other. Not quite realizing what I said, I told her, "I promise, Kitty. It'll be all right."

CHAPTER 13

I<small>T</small> had been decided not to hold Kitty Keeler in a cell, although technically it was permissible. There was nothing altruistic in the decision: the reasoning was that Keeler might fall apart and have to be hospitalized for hysteria. That would make for sympathetic press coverage; the news people didn't play favorites—they went in whichever direction made the best headlines.

Since Kitty had been placed in protective custody late Saturday night, it wasn't until Monday morning that it made the newspapers. All day Sunday, radio newsbreaks gave carefully sketchy details: that Kitty Keeler was being held as a material witness in an undisclosed location.

She was temporarily housed in a motel near Kennedy Airport in a large suite with a policewoman and a few detectives. Tim didn't want me anywhere around Kitty at this time; he didn't want her to feel hostile toward me as being part of this whole custody idea. I notified George; not just because I had promised Kitty that I would but because she was entitled to have someone contacted. The first thing George did was fall apart; then he called Sam Catalano, his good friend. Sam Catalano, playing it nice and safe, called me. He didn't want anyone to think he'd been doing anything sneaky, which of course is just what he had been doing, hanging around George Keeler in his off time. He'd told George to contact a lawyer; that was the right thing to do, wasn't it?

"Yeah, as long as you didn't tell him any *particular* lawyer, Sam." There was a silence. "You didn't do that, did you Sam?"

"Not exactly."

"I think you'd better tell me what 'not exactly' means."

Silence. Then, "Well, George didn't know any lawyer to call, aside from his regular attorney, who doesn't handle things like this. So . . . I told him to call Vince Martucci. He'd know a lawyer."

When Sam Catalano becomes a friend of the family, he becomes a friend of the family. "That wasn't too wise of you, Sam. I wouldn't mention this to anyone; at all."

Sam's voice went a little hollow; I knew he was about to wheedle a promise from me that I wouldn't tell anyone; at all; about his advice to George. Before he could, I assured him that we should *both* just forget it.

"Oh, listen, Joe, before I forget. Do you think you were mistaken, in the name of that narcotics cop? You said Steve Werner? I've been calling all over and nobody ever heard of him."

"Who?"

"Steve Werner, Joe. You said he was a narcotics cop and—"

"Must have been two other guys, Sam. I don't know what you're talking about." I figured Sam must have been bothering people enough. "Look, Sam, you show up at the Kelly Brothers Funeral Home Monday; stay close to George. He might need a friend."

I assured Catalano that my suggestion was an official assignment and that I'd cover him with Tim Neary.

There were a couple of guys in the squad office on Sunday morning, none of them working too hard, all of them complaining about how hard they were working. When Tim Neary surprised us by coming to the office at about nine-thirty, newspapers disappeared, containers of coffee were forgotten, typewriters and telephones went into action. Tim browsed around for a couple of minutes, then signaled me into his office.

As he dug through the pile of updated reports on his desk, Tim asked me the same question four times, using about four different lead-ins: Didn't I think that Kitty Keeler would break? Didn't I think that the pressure of being held, on top of the circumstantial case, on top of the confirmation of the Scots girl's statement, would have an effect on her?

"Kelleher is talking about bringing the case to the grand jury, Joe. He feels we should be in pretty good shape, what with the established times of death, Keeler's statement about when she last saw the boys alive, the telephone calls to Martucci, MacDougal's statement. On top of Keeler's known reputation. Jesus, Joe, she runs with some pretty bad guys. Well, Joe, wadda ya think? Think she'll finally break at the funeral?"

"I think I better take better care of my ulcer." My right hand went like a magnet to the pain. I took a closer look at Tim's face, then said, "Look, Tim. I think we've got time. I think we haven't got a very strong *court* case yet. And I think that you agree with me, right?"

Tim got up from his desk and went to the window. He stared at the early Sunday-morning traffic for a while and I went and stared with him.

"This is a bitch of a situation, Joe. That mother fucker up there is really putting the screws in. Jesus, these kids were only murdered four days ago and he's breathing down my neck like we've been on the case for a month. Like we're supposed to have it all tied up and gift-wrapped before the kids are even in their graves."

"We're doing okay, Timmy. Don't let him get to you. How about us having some breakfast?"

Tim checked with his watch. "I gotta get going down to the Waldorf. My man Schneiderman is one of the speakers at the Columbian Society Communion breakfast."

"Schneiderman?"

"Old Marvin L. himself."

"Old Marvin L. himself?"

"Don't be such a goddamn wiseass, Joe."

"Oh, *that* old Marvin L. Schneiderman."

Tim rubbed the back of his neck vigorously, stretched his arms like they ached at the elbows, then jabbed at my shoulder. "I'm talking, old buddy, about the next Mayor of the City of New York. Trouble with the son-of-a-bitch is that he never seems to leave any kind of impression wherever he goes. We've been making him available for weddings and wakes, Communions and bar mitzvahs, graduation parties and brisses. A man for all ethnics in a city of ethnics."

"Brisses? What the hell are brisses?"

"A briss, my boy," Tim explained, "is the kind of ceremony I would like to witness being performed on the gorgeous leader of us all on the top floor. Only, with Jerry, the knife should slip a crucial inch or so."

"Oh, that kind of ceremony."

Tim stopped clowning abruptly and said in a deadly serious voice, "Well, what do you think, Joe? The Keeler girl going to crack or what?"

"I don't know, Tim." Which was exactly true; I didn't know. Which wasn't exactly what Tim wanted to hear; which meant I wasn't being supportive, the way I'm supposed to be.

"For Christ's sake, Joe. *She did it.* We all know that, right? Even *you* know she did it."

"It's what we're all assuming."

"*Assuming, hell!*" Tim planted his feet apart, tilted his head to a pugnacious angle which is supposed to assure me he means business now; no more bullshitting; get into line. He narrowed his eyes shrewdly and said softly, "What's going on, Joe? This little whore getting to you?"

Once years ago, when we were kids, Tim had said something like that to me about a girl he liked who preferred me. With the self-righteousness of youth, I punched him in the mouth and broke the tip off one of his front teeth. Of course, he'd had the tooth fixed years ago, and he did knock me out cold once he'd recovered from my unexpected attack; but I remembered what a release it had been, belting him in the mouth. That was when we were kids; we were supposed to be big boys now. Maybe it's always kid stuff when you're around someone you've known all your life; Tim is the only guy I regularly feel like punching.

Instead of that, I shook my head slowly and spoke slowly; it was one way of keeping myself and the situation under control. "No one's getting to me, Tim. I just don't think we should count on a confession. I think it's more important to build our case on evidence. Without evidence, a confession won't count for a damn thing."

"You don't mind that I would prefer to have a confession, do you? I mean, it isn't going to bother you too much, is it? That I would very much like to see a signed, sealed and delivered confession from that little bitch?"

"Want me to rubber-hose her, Tim?"

Tim banged into his desk as he whirled past it; he stopped, turned and swiped his hand at the stack of file folders containing squad reports. They fluttered all over his desk and the floor, but Tim didn't even look back.

We both knew that I certainly wasn't going to pick up after him.

I typed up a short, simple one-page ongoing report of my investigation. I always keep my interim reports very lean and sparse. Then, if I do develop something in the future, everybody thinks I'm some kind of magician. I like to deliver more than I promise instead of the other way around. Which is just one of my many trade secrets.

I read through the growing stack of squad reports, amazed at how many otherwise savvy cops could write such dumb reports: a couple of them seemed to indicate that based on suspicious behavior of the person interviewed there was reason to believe there would be a break in the case in the immediate future. My reports never promise a goddamn thing. I like my surprises to be on the plus side.

Back at my apartment, I spent the better part of the afternoon working up detailed reports for *myself*. These included my impressions, suppositions and possibilities as well as characterizations of the people I'd interviewed, along with an open question or two at the end of each report; e.g., "Check medical reports at Jamaica Hosp. re accident-John/Cindy Mogliano."

By seven o'clock, I hadn't even taken the Sunday *Times* apart. That had always been Jen's weekly ritual and I always got a kick out of watching how systematically she attacked that job on Saturday nights. I'd picked the paper up late this afternoon and it just didn't feel like a Sunday night with the *Times* still neatly packed. I didn't feel like going out for something to eat, even though there wasn't much in the refrigerator. That would be my evening: a nice hot/cold shower, a light supper and the Sunday *Times*.

By midnight, it still hadn't rained although the weather report every hour on the hour between the music and the news on WNEW forecast a storm, to be followed by clearing and cool air. I fell asleep in my chair, the magazine section opened like a tent over my face causing me to dream of suffocation and drowning. It was two o'clock in the morning when I fought my way out of the newspaper. The weatherman was repeating his cheerful prediction of a storm, then clear and cool. I looked out the window; it was so muggy and thick I couldn't see across the street. The street lights had hazy globes around them and they seemed to be floating in the air.

I swallowed a couple of antacid pills with some cold milk, then went to bed and dreamed about Jen.

She was shopping in a large supermarket, only there wasn't any food on any of the shelves, just large jars and tubes of paint and all kinds of canvas, rolled canvas, canvas board, blank canvas stretched on heavy wooden frames. Jen collected items from everywhere: from shelves, from small file cabinets that were filled with paintbrushes and sticks of charcoal and pencils and Crayola crayons. Her wagon was piled high with all the things she'd collected and she couldn't see where she was pushing it and she kept bumping into people and into the displays of art goods. She was getting hysterical and I kept talking to her, telling her it was okay, and then she walked away from the wagon and reached up for a huge coloring book, nearly as tall as she was, and she leaned it against the wagon and turned the pages. Finally she found what she was looking for. She stretched both of her arms out, holding the book away from her, and she began to cry. I came to her side and looked at the picture of the astronauts. They were cartoon figures, all dressed in silver—their suits, their faces, their shoes; the background was all silver, too, and they were moving around on the page and that's why Jen was crying.

Only, it wasn't Jen. It was Kitty Keeler and she was standing there, holding the coloring book open, and she was breathing in short, terrible gasps, asthmatic gasps, and between the gasps she kept saying over and over again, "My God, Joe. Help me. Please help me. My God, Joe. Help me." She was upset because someone had colored everything silver and she couldn't find the right crayon to fix things up.

I was soaked with sweat when I woke up. I took a quick shower and was dressed before I looked out the window and realized that Monday morning, without benefit of the promised storm, had arrived clear and cool with a blue sky. Perfect weather for a double funeral.

I arrived at the Kelly Brothers Funeral Home an hour before Kitty and her family were to arrive. The crowd outside could have been gathered for anything from a Hollywood opening night complete with stars to a down-home lynching. There was a general air of unhealthy excitement that seemed on the verge of getting out of control. The uniformed captain in charge of mob control must have thought so, too. By the time the Keelers arrived, he'd arranged for a large number of reinforcements and the mob was forced well back from the entrance by wooden barriers.

Vito Geraldi and I stood in the entranceway and watched as Kitty exited from the limousine. "Boy, just look at that bitch," Vito said. "The way she got herself fixed up, you'd think she was on her way to a party."

His remark was an exaggeration. Kitty Keeler wasn't dressed for a party, but then neither was she dressed for the mass and burial of her two young sons. As she walked, head tossed back, light hair blazing in the sun, I thought she'd worn the soft pink dress as an act of defiance: the hell with them. The reaction of the crowd outside Kelly's was explosive, especially the cries of women.

"What kind of a mother are you? A pink dress to your own kids' funeral?"

"Well, wadda ya expect: Kitty the Killer. Shame, Kitty, shame."

"How come she's not in mourning?"

"She is; maybe whores wear pink when they're in mourning."

"Wadda ya mean mourning? Murderers don't mourn!"

When I got a closer look at her face, as she walked through the hall, into the assigned room, it was obvious that she hadn't even been aware of the crowd outside, calling at her, reaching for her. A fight had developed between her accusers and her defenders; fists and elbows had been exchanged. Kitty was totally unaware of any of it. Everything about her was rigidly under control. It seemed that George clung to her arm more for his own support than for hers.

They settled on the small velvet bench at the front of the room. When old Mr. Kelly, the senior of the Kelly Brothers, approached the parents, leaned over them solicitously, Kitty shook her head and remained seated while George went forward to the two small white coffins. He leaned heavily, first into one, then into the other, obviously placing something, probably a religious medal, with each dead child. The air was heavy with the fragrance of hundreds of flowers which had been arranged behind the coffins and down along two sides of the room.

When George began wheezing badly, it was Sam Catalano who rushed solicitously to his side and escorted him from the room for some air. As they walked past me, Sam Catalano winked. The way George Keeler leaned on him, it was obvious that Sam was having a lot of success in "developing" George; wherever it might lead.

Two of Kitty's brothers listened to her as she pointed to the flower arrangements in the front of the room; they instructed one of the Kelly Brothers to remove some of the flowers; the air was becoming overwhelming not only for George but for others as well. Then Kitty's brothers turned their attention to their mother, Mrs. Hogan.

They escorted her directly to the coffins, prayed briefly with her at each one. Mrs. Hogan touched each face once, then turned and allowed her sons to escort her to her daughter. Kitty rose stiffly, leaned toward her mother; the two women made brief, uninvolved, cheek-touching contact, then the grandmother was led to a seat on the other side of the room. Neither woman had shed a tear. It was a kind of control learned at her mother's knee; not exclusive with tough-hearted Kitty Keeler.

One of her brothers returned and sat beside Kitty as she accepted condolences from an endless number of people who came to see her; to pray at her children's coffins. In the middle of an embrace from a woman, Kitty stood up, turned around and scanned the room with a look of suddenly rising panic. One of her brothers came to her side, took her arm, tried to reassure her, but she pushed him away from her with a brisk annoyance. Finally she saw me, off to the side of the room; as she moved toward me I reached in my pocket and took out the knotted shoelace and the wrapper that the new shoelaces had come in. She brushed past the hands that reached to comfort her; it was as if there was no one else in the room, just Kitty and me.

Before she could ask, I opened my hand. "All taken care of, Kitty."

She touched the knotted shoelace, nodded, then looked up at me. "I didn't forget anything, did I?" Her fingers closed around my hand, squeezed and pressed. "I still have that awful feeling; like I've forgotten something."

For one flashing instant, she appeared totally vulnerable; unguarded.

Her eyes, intent on my face, excluded everyone else, obliterated where we were, why we were here. With an extraordinary magnetism, Kitty revealed herself to me again with an intimate and complete trust.

"Everything is okay, Kitty."

It passed as suddenly as it had occurred; she dropped her hands to her side, drew back from me, turned without a word and walked back to the bench in front of the room. Tim Neary, across the room, directly opposite to me, wasn't sure what he had seen; he raised his chin, questioning, tense and alert. I shrugged, shook my head slightly, but Tim still had that alert, wary, curious expression, more than a little worried that someone was trying to put something over on him. I could practically hear him: What the hell was *that* all about?

When George came back, looking slightly tranquilized, the priest began the prayers. The room filled with the low humming sound of chanting voices and clicking beads as some of the older women fingered their rosaries. Finally there was the muffled commotion of a roomful of people trying to leave quietly.

I went down front and stood near the bench where Kitty and George sat; I wanted her to know I was nearby.

One of the Kelly Brothers came over to the parents. "Mrs. Keeler, wouldn't you like to see the boys now?" He bent forward slightly, like a headwaiter offering the specialty of the house. His voice was soft and tempting. "They look like sleeping angels, Mrs. Keeler. It will be a good last memory for you to have of them."

George slumped forward and began to sob. Departing guests politely refrained from turning back to look at him. Kitty sat motionless, waiting; one of her brothers and Sam Catalano helped George to his feet.

"Go ahead," Kitty told them. "I'm fine; I'll be along in a minute." When the Kelly Brother offered his arm she shook her head, but he didn't seem to notice.

"That's all right, Mr. Kelly," I told him. "I'm with Mrs. Keeler."

Kelly looked a bit put off, like I was depriving him of something; maybe he was waiting for her compliment on his work. He backed away and disappeared; the last glimpse I had of him, he looked disappointed and hurt.

Finally Kitty stood up, her hands loose at her sides. She walked forward and seemed to be staring over the coffins, as though just noticing the lavish array of flowers. Her face in the soft, stagy light seemed dazed; she moved her eyes from the flowers to the floor. Then, slowly, by degrees, she lifted her gaze until she focused on the face of her older son, Terry. Her mouth dropped open in surprise; she glanced up at me with a puzzled expression and shook her head slightly. Then she turned toward the body of her younger son, George; she moved closer for a better look. Again, she turned to me with that same expression of confusion and growing horror.

She spread her arms out, then let them drop to her sides. "Something's wrong," Kitty said. "This is crazy! These aren't my sons. *These are not my sons.*" There was a terrible, desperate urgency in her voice and in her words. She pulled at my arm and urged me to examine the unknown manikins in the white coffins. Her fingers dug into me with a surprising strength. Her eyes darted back and forth from one coffin to the other, and her voice went low into a chilling whisper. "They don't look like that, Joe. My children don't look like that!"

I tried to turn her away, but she began to struggle; her teeth were clenched tightly, barely holding back a deep shuddering moan. When Kelly approached, took her arm, Kitty wrenched away, flung herself against me and whispered, "My God, Joe. What's happening? What's happening? Help me, Joe. Get me out of this nightmare."

CHAPTER 14

Vito was leaving the squad office as I arrived. He grabbed my arm and warned me, "Watch out for Captain Tim, Joe. He's right up the wall."

The first thing Tim Neary said to me was, "Well, where the hell have you been?"

He damn well knew where I'd been: to the cemetery with the Keelers. I thought of about four wisecracks and decided this wasn't the time. "What's happening, Captain?"

"I'll tell you what's happening." He interrupted himself to glare at Walker, who had just tapped and stuck his head in the door. "What the fuck do *you* want?"

Walker looked like he wanted to be at least seven miles away from Neary's office. "You told me to let you know when I got Miller and Duffy on the phone, Captain."

"Yeah, and—"

"Well, I got them on the phone, Captain. On extension 122."

Tim snatched up the receiver; Walker rolled his eyes toward the ceiling and closed the door quietly behind him. Tim began to speak quickly and with short choppy sentences, which is one of his ways of telling you not to ask any questions about his instructions; just do it, whatever it is. From what I could make out, he was sending Miller and Duffy, who were what we call our "technical men," to meet Vito Geraldi at a very expensive hotel on Madison Avenue in the upper Sixties; they were to bring all of their equipment and they were to get set up fast.

"Vito will meet you in Room 406; you don't say anything to anyone, not the desk clerk, not the bellhops; no one. Be as discreet as you can. Absolutely *no one* is to make any of you guys. And for Christ's sake, get things set up fast. Vito will brief you." Apparently, Miller or Duffy, whichever one was on the other end of the conversation, tried to tell

Tim something. "Listen, I don't wanna hear any of your goddamn bullshit. Just do what I told ya." He slammed the receiver down and pulled his lips back tightly, then looked up at me, ready to take me on; all he needed was a reason.

I waited quietly; Tim rubbed the back of his neck, jammed his hands into his pockets, muttered a few unpleasant things to himself, then decided to let me in on things.

"Jay T. Williams has been retained to represent Kitty Keeler. The son-of-a-bitch is flying up from Atlanta this afternoon."

"Is that what's with the Madison Avenue hotel?"

"What the hell do you think is with the Madison Avenue hotel?" Tim turned and kicked his metal wastebasket; it was so loaded with newspapers that it just fell heavily on its side. "The minute I got into the office, Gorgeous Jerry had me on the carpet. Someone from Williams' New York office called him. They decided the motel out near Kennedy is not a suitable place for Mrs. Keeler to be held as a material witness. Gutless Jerry should have asked how they'd like to see that little bitch in an iron-barred cell. Instead, they had a conference about it, and it was mutually agreed that a suite of rooms up on Madison would be more in keeping with the style to which Mrs. Keeler has been accustomed. You know what they charge in that place? Huh?"

I had no idea.

"Seventy-five bucks a day. A suite, for Christ's sake."

Walker tapped on the door and in a soft, hesitant voice said, "Captain? Detective Casey is on extension 120."

"What does he want?" Walker went blank. Tim snatched up the receiver and said, "Captain Neary. Wadda ya want?" He listened, nodded, said okay and hung up. "The Keelers are up in her brother's house in Yonkers, packing. Then they're going to their apartment in Fresh Meadows to pick up clothes and things. Then her ladyship will be installed in her suite, waiting for her attorney, that son-of-a-bitch. I want you up there, Joe, in Room 406; tell Miller and Duffy to get their asses out the minute the equipment is set up; you and Vito stand by. Well, what's your problem, Joe? What the hell's bothering you now?"

I thought about mentioning something called privileged information, the confidentiality between lawyer and client, but I know Tim doesn't behave very well under pressure. He has a basic lack of grace that has become more noticeable as the years go by.

"Not a thing, Captain. All you gotta do is name it and you got it."

"Listen, don't you break my chops, Joe, okay? Go on, go on, get the hell outa here." Then, feeling he had to justify himself or something,

Tim said, "Listen, Joe. This Williams guy uses every trick in the book; don't have any qualms on his behalf."

"I haven't got a qualm in the world, Tim, not even one."

Jay T. Williams had a national reputation as the attorney to get when you had little more to face a jury with than a clever lawyer. If you could afford him. If not, and if the circumstances of the crime were interesting enough, he might be persuaded to take on the case provided you signed over all ensuing literary rights (including Sunday-supplement and magazine articles and interviews, and book, television and film properties) in lieu of standard fee. This had apparently worked out very much to Williams' advantage; he had two best sellers based on the real-story-behind-the-story of his more sensational cases. He was also a popular, entertaining if cynical guest on the late-night TV talk shows: a smooth, attractive performer with a quick flashy style.

The Keeler "situation" was right up Williams' alley. It had all the elements that would appeal to him: a beautiful woman with an unsavory reputation, mob connections, murdered children, a slanted press, and a politically motivated need for a quick solution. It could develop into the kind of game Williams enjoyed.

I'd seen him in action and read a great deal about him as well as both of his books, and he did consider the law a game. The trick of the game, according to Williams, was proper selection of the jury. No matter which of his offices he operated from—Atlanta (his home town), Los Angeles, Dallas, Boston or New York—he made the same point to his staff: the key to a successful trial rested, to an incredible degree, on the ability to accurately read a prospective juror. He maintained, and I believed him, that he could interpret the meaning of and reason for every gesture, twitch, cough, facial and bodily adjustment; could interpret character as revealed by selection of color and style of clothing, hair style, makeup (women), mustache, sideburn or beard (men), type of eyeglass frame. He had a sharp ear and could pick out otherwise hidden evidence of ethnic heritage and then conclude certain ingrained prejudices and leanings. Aside from the usual standard considerations of sex, age, marital and parental status, occupation, height, weight and appearance, Jay T. Williams could read the soul of an individual as revealed by the condition of hands, fingernails, shiny or unshined shoes, eager or reticent mannerisms, broad or abrupt gestures, grudging, constrained or inappropriate laughter.

Time and again, courtroom observers had been puzzled by his approval of an apparently hostile or unlikely juror, but Williams knew exactly what he was going for. He maintained that the case was lost or won by the time the final juror had been sworn in; his summation was set in his mind before the first witness was called. It was all in the or-chestration, he claimed: in knowing how and where to pitch each and every particular argument; who to intimidate; who to trust; who to flatter and court; who to challenge; when to underplay and exactly when to let out all the stops. I'd seen him on a televised law sym-posium; when some earnest young recently graduated attorney accused him of being cynical in his approach to law, Williams replied in his sweetest Georgia-boy accent, "Why, shucks, what you call being a cynic I call being a realist. The idea is to win, right?"

In nearly seventeen years of headline trials, Jay T. Williams had never lost a major case.

It was also well known, though not too commonly discussed, that to a large extent Williams' successful career depended on his unerring se-lection of associates and staff. Once they were selected and carefully tested, he relied on them totally to research, investigate and prepare the heart of each case for him. He made a point of never questioning the sources of certain bodies of information supplied to him which were not generally available, legally, to defense attorneys.

Before I left the office, Tim, to justify either to me or to himself what we were about to do, informed me that there had been a leak somewhere in the District Attorney's office and that Williams was in possession of Xerox copies of the Medical Examiner's final autopsy re-port on the Keeler boys, as well as Xerox copies of nearly every interro-gation conducted in the case to date and of the background reports prepared by the squad and forwarded to the D.A.

Not even Tim suspected Catalano; this was too big a leak, and it was Kelleher's problem as far as Tim was concerned.

•

Williams and his chief New York assistant, a six-foot-five former N.Y.U. basketball star named Jeff Weinstein, got to the Madison Ave-nue hotel before Kitty Keeler and her escorts. Which almost seemed like good timing; by the time Keeler arrived, Williams had established himself in the large sitting room and acted as host.

The team of plainclothesmen and policewoman checked with the squad office and were told to get themselves something to eat down in the coffee shop; no one but Tim and the technical crew knew that Vito and I were settled in the room next door to the suite.

"You jus' call me Jaytee, like everyone does, and I'll call you Kitty, if'n you don't mind."

Although he spoke softly, ole Jaytee came through nice and clear. There was some quiet, well-mannered commotion as the waiter distributed cups and saucers and plates; Jaytee urged Kitty to accept some of the cake he'd ordered especially for her. He was familiar with the hotel, and the staff was more than happy to cater to his every wish.

"Well, maybe you'll feel more like trusting mah judgment—in the matter of cakes—once we've talked a bit, you and me, Kitty. Now, would you do me a favor and remove those dark glasses, Kitty? I do like to see into a lady's eyes when we converse."

He was smooth and knew just how to do it; the next thing he said was, "Well, I do thank you for that. You are a beautiful woman, Kitty Keeler, you are indeed. I haven't seen any pictures that do you justice."

Vito shook his head in disgust, but I thought Williams knew what he was doing.

"Now, Jeff here tells me that you and your husband, George, and he had a nice long talk last night and that Jeff explained to you the sort of arrangements that would be made if it was decided that we would represent you. Is everything Jeff explained clear to you, Kitty?"

"Oh, it's all clear all right. There's just one thing that isn't clear to me. Why do I *need* a lawyer? Any lawyer; not just you specifically."

"Well, I'll tell you what, Kitty Keeler. Why don't you jest get right up now and go through that door and walk over to the nearest airline ticket office and buy yourself a ticket. To anywhere. To Miami. To Mexico." There was a long pause. "Or maybe to Phoenix, Arizona. And see how fast the District Attorney's people grab ahold of you. And check you outa this here real nice refined hotel, and pop you into a real safe security cell without any of the amenities." There was a deep, sorrowful sigh, then he said, "Lady, lady. Like it or not, *you* are the A-number-one prime suspect in the murder of your little boys. This protective custody thing, wal, they're just bein' a little cute with you; trying for a little psychological pressure, which we should be able to swing in your favor instead of theirs. But I think it's best that we all be very realistic about your situation, Kitty. Don't you?"

Kitty's voice was tight and careful. "Exactly what *is* my situation?"

"Well, you've made and signed a statement for the Assistant District Attorney that you'd have been better off not making."

Kitty, tough, challenging. "I just answered all their questions truthfully."

Jaytee, calm, comfortable and comforting. "You answered all of their questions at a time when you were under the greatest emotional stress possible. Why, not twelve hours or so after the bodies of your two slain little boys were found, these professional interrogators had you answering questions as to what time, precisely, did you do this, what time did you do that, what time did you do the other thing."

He sounded as though he was instructing. "Now, I'll tell you for a fact that had an attorney been with you at that time, you would have given *no* statement, at all. Not then. Why, hell, how in God's name could anyone be expected, under those terrible circumstances, to give an accurate, hour-by-hour accounting of herself? Do you generally walk around with a clock around your neck, Kitty, and check the time before you do anything and everything?"

"I only told them what I did and when I did it, that's all."

"And you're gonna stick by what you said, first time round, come hell or high water?"

She responded to the slight baiting tone of the question with a flash of annoyance. "Because I told the truth."

"And even if it was medically proven that your younger boy was dead and your older boy was unconscious during the time you said you tended them?"

"*I know what I did that night!*"

"And you're gonna stick to the time slots you said first time out, because, goddamn, you're not gonna change your story. It's yours and you're gonna stick with it, no matter what?"

"It wasn't a story I'm stuck with. It was the truth."

The mocking tone, challenging her, changed to a cold, sober, less Southern-boy voice. "You checked the clock at one A.M., did you, Kitty, and then again at one-thirty A.M., and said to yourself, I last saw them between one A.M. and one-thirty A.M. because I checked it on the clock. That the way it was?"

"No, but—"

"Couldn't have been that you took the boys to the bathroom earlier?" He didn't give her a chance to reply; his voice now went hard and tough and sarcastic. "Why, hell, no, impossible, because if Kitty said one A.M. to one-thirty A.M. first time round, she's gonna stick to that time, come hell, high water or conviction for first-degree murder!"

There was a stark silence; so total that both Vito and I leaned toward the tape recorder, afraid we had lost them. But finally there was a soft, quiet sigh, and then Kitty's voice, small, defeated, honest.

"They got me mad," she said.

"Why, hell, honey, that's what they was tryin' to do." He was on her side again: warm; protective; tolerant; understanding. "See, that's what an attorney does for a client: he gets between you and those who are proddin' you to get you to say what *they* want you to say. I'll give 'em this, Kitty, they found your weak point." He laughed softly. "You sure do stick that chin up and out when you're sore, don't you, Kitty? Took me two minutes to find it; probably took them ten minutes, seein' as how they're not nearly as perceptive and sensitive as I am. Wal, now, tell you whut, Kitty. You don't go talkin' to anybody, not anybody at all, without either Jeff here or me's with you."

"What about . . . the times I gave them in my statement?"

"Well, Kitty, you willing and ready to admit you was just guessin' and under pressure, you jes' stuck with what you said first time round, outa some kinda pride or anger?" She must have nodded, because then he said, "Well, then you jes' let me handle that end of it. When and if the time comes. It was downright unfair of them and they damn well know it, too."

"And what about . . . you know, my staying here? Being held."

"Wal, now, Kitty, this here is a very nice respectable place and I picked it for that very reason. Stayed here myself along with a President or two through the years." His tone went from bantering, kidding, easing her along, to dead flat serious. "What we are going to do, Kitty, is to insist and emphasize that you are here for your own *protection*. Never mind the 'custody' part, because the real truth is, they're not far off the mark, insistin' you might be in danger. And that leads to a final important thing, Kitty. The newspaper people—"

"Those bastards!"

Jaytee Williams, sharp and experienced. "That they are, honey, but what we're gonna do is, we're gonna make them *our* bastards. The more you growl and glare at them, the more they gonna say mean sharp things about you, and them mean sharp things are what stays in people's minds. Why, that headline in this morning's *News*—Jeff, hold that paper up high for me—'Kitty Keels Over at Kids' Funeral: Pink-Garbed Mom Passes Out.' Now, if they'd been *our* bastards, honey, that headline woulda been somethin' like 'Grief Stricken Mother Collapses,' and that story woulda brought tears to the eyes and hearts. And we want people to stop thinkin' 'bout you the way these newspaper people been doin' you. So you're gonna hafta start lettin' down a little, Kitty. Let these here photo boys and news people get a better look at you, that a deal?"

"I guess. But it'll be hard. I just want them to leave me alone."

"I know, I know. Now, I'm headin' on down home to Atlanta tonight and I have to be out on the Coast for about three-four days, and I'll be back here early next week, but don't you worry none. Jeff here'll be in touch with you every day, and him and me, we talk every night, so you rest easy. You got any questions at all, any time, you pick up the phone and call Jeff. Hey, and this is important, Jeff. You straighten these D.A. people out that Kitty Keeler isn't no prisoner. Honey, nice as this place is, you don't hafta stay here all day and all night. You oughtta take advantage of your location, nicest part of New York City, near to the theaters and good movie houses and all those nice Fifth Avenue shops not too far off, a short taxi ride away."

"Er, Jaytee . . ."

"What Jeffrey here is trying to warn me is that you really shouldn't be seen gallivantin' around too much, but I'll rely on your discretion, Miz Kitty. Remember, now, any questions at all, you get in touch with Jeff. He's tall, but he's smart."

The voice level changed as Jaytee moved toward the door. "Now here's the most important thing of all, Kitty. You don't talk on this telephone about *anything at all* that's botherin' you; you call Jeff and he'll take you somewhere, coffee shop or a park bench, but nothing on this telephone." There was a short, thoughtful silence. "And you don't say nothin' private or important in this room, ya hear? Ain't our bastards got this place bugged; it's *their* bastards." Both Vito and I pulled back from the machine and looked at each other. Vito shook his head and said a few words in Italian.

Apparently Kitty hadn't quite gotten his message. She asked him, "Jaytee, what do you think is going to happen to me?"

"Well, I think there's a good chance, at least it's what the D.A.'s aimin' at, that sooner or later, one way or another, you'll be indicted for first-degree murder. But don't you worry none, Kitty. You got ole Jaytee on your side now."

We heard them exchanging good-byes at the door, then heard Jaytee step to the elevator. Vito watched him through the peephole, and when the elevator closed on him Vito said, "That son-of-a-bitch is smart as hell, Joe. You notice something, Joe? With all that nice, charmin' sweet-talkin' he done, he never once asked her; he never once came right out and asked her."

"Asked her what?"

"If she done it, Joe, if she done it."

I didn't answer Vito. I was very busy rewinding and collecting tapes because Tim was very anxious to hear them. It really didn't make much sense, and I didn't want Vito to notice, but I felt that a heavy, pressing, steel-edged weight had been lifted from the pit of my stomach.

CHAPTER 15

J AY T. WILLIAMS didn't waste any time; he got right to work collecting his own bastards. He gave a brief, light, friendly, concerned interview at Kennedy Airport while waiting for his flight to down-home. Listening to Jaytee, you'd think he was talking about another girl entirely: he was setting the new image of Kitty Keeler before the public and he was smart as hell and very persuasive. It would be up to Kitty to follow through; I think he'd convinced her it was necessary.

A feature article in the next morning's *Daily News* quoted Jaytee as saying of Kitty Keeler, "Why, this girl has more guts than any man I've ever known. She been puttin' on a front, actin' out a role, and it's cost her plenty to carry it off. She'd made a promise to herself that she wouldn't break down in public. This kid's got a sense of pride you wouldn't believe. When I saw her in private, why, it'd like to tear your heart out, to see this girl's grief. She tole me, why, she nearly puts herself into a trance out in public, which is why you hardhearted s.o.b.'s been thinkin' of her in all the wrong ways. Look, you know and I know, every person grieves in his or her own way. Hell, I'd sure hate to be expected to carry my grief out to the public, wouldn't you?"

Relative to Kitty's being in protective custody, Jaytee Williams commented as follows: "If that there Jerry Kelleher hadn't come up with the idea hisself, I damn sure would have. Glad to see him takin' a sensible line after all the hootin' and nonsensical hollerin' I seen him doin' on the TV and in the papers. Fact of the matter is, they had this poor girl stuck in a dumb, unprotected motel out near this very airport, where every nut and screwball in the world coulda had at her. And I'm about to tell you this too, though Kitty herself will have a fit, should she read this interview. That girl is scared near to death—and rightly so, rightly so, what with the position she's in. Now, I'm not sayin' one way or t'other way, but you can all just figure it out for yourselves: any desperate sick-minded low-life that coulda done her little babies like they did, why, it wouldn't be no more than whipped cream on a cake to them to do Kitty. She's knowed that all along, but she's been carryin' her head high and you guys been callin' down all kinds a things on her for it. The burden on this girl is mighty heavy enough without you fellas adding to it, and fair-minded that I've always known you all to be, I'm askin' you all now to put yourselves in Kitty Keeler's situation. And have a little compassion for what she's been through. And a lot of admiration for how she's handled things all by her lonesome. And be advised, gents and Jerry Kelleher, she ain't by her lonesome no more."

Gorgeous Jerry Kelleher, of course, had apoplexy at being addressed by name by this mushmouthed phony bullshit artist, and he had Tim Neary up and at attention by 9 A.M. the day Jaytee's campaign hit the newspapers. Which put Tim Neary into one of his front-line, down-to-earth, we're-all-in-this-together moods.

What he said to those squad members still in the office when he returned from the top floor was, "What the fuck are all you men doing in the office? What is this, anyway, coffee and gossip time?"

The last crack was meant for me in particular. It's not that I'm overly sensitive; it's just that I *was* finishing a container of lukewarm coffee and laughing into the telephone at the exact moment of Tim's arrival.

"Whenever it's convenient for you, Joe," Tim said, "if you can fit it into your schedule, I'd like to see you in my office."

I nodded and went on talking on the telephone. It's amazing how fast nearly everyone else wound up their office business; reports were quickly stapled together, notes stuffed into pockets; Sergeant Gelber, who had been out sick for a week and looked terrible, was advised by each team leaving where they were going.

The first thing Tim said to me when I entered his office was, "What the fuck is Sam Catalano doing hanging around with George Keeler? This a secret operation you got going, Joe? Something you're gonna surprise me with or what? What the fuck is going on, anyway, Joe?"

"We're all in on it together, *Captain Neary. All of us.* It's us against you. I figured you'd figure that out sooner or later."

We stood with the desk between us, both of us breathing hard and both of us waiting to see exactly how far this stupid thing would go. Or rather, how far we'd *let* it go.

Tim shook his head and rubbed the back of his neck. "I don't think I slept more than two hours all told last night."

"Then you better get to bed early tonight, Tim. Insomnia is making you nasty."

I still felt tight and ready, but we both knew it was over for the moment.

"What the hell was that pompous schmuck upstairs telling me about Catalano 'bringing George Keeler along'? How long's that been going on?"

"A coupla days. I guess Sam feels that by buddying up to George he might be able to turn him. Against Kitty."

Tim raised his eyebrows.

I shook my head. "Not a chance. George is true-blue. Which is why I figured it wouldn't do any harm. And it would keep Sam from underfoot. He was doing it on his own time, so what the hell, let him do it on city time."

"All right, all right, makes sense. Just in the future, Joe, *you* tell me what's going on in my own squad. I don't want to be told again by that bastard upstairs." Tim took a good look at my face and said quickly, "All right, all right, Joe, for Christ's sake, don't *you* go getting touchy, too." Which, coming from Tim Neary, can be considered an apology; which is as close as I've ever known him to get.

Apparently there was nobody left in the outer office to warn Vito, because he came barging into Tim's office loudmouthed and excited. There are days when everyone, even Vito, should tap on the door and wait for Tim's invitation. This was definitely one of those days. Tim's face went right back to that tight, tooth-grinding, trouble-borrowing expression.

"Joey, Joey." Vito wrapped his arms around me from behind and squeezed once, then let me go. I felt like I'd missed two complete breath cycles. "Timmy, kid, wadda ya say, Timmy, huh? Wadda ya say?"

"*Vito.*" That was all Tim was able to say; he was cracking his knuckles two at a time.

"Hey, Tim, you got your tight shoes on again today, huh, Captain Timmy?" Vito dropped into a chair, put his large feet up on Tim's desk. "I'm gonna relieve your achin' feet, Tim. Jeez, Joe, don't he look terrible? Whatsa matter, Tim, they been givin' ya the business upstairs again? Huh?"

Tim stood directly behind his desk chair; his fingers clenched the top of the chair so hard that his knuckles cracked all by themselves. "Vito. I'll give you thirty seconds. And it better be good. Really good."

Vito let his head fall back and he looked like he was doing eye exercises, examining first one corner of the ceiling and then the other. Finally he pulled his feet off the desk, pulled himself upright and said, "It's good, Tim. Oh, it's good."

Tim walked around his chair, sat down, folded his hands on the desk and said, very quietly, "Fine, Vito. Any time you're ready. I'm listening."

Vito wanted to savor it a little longer; he shook his head, grinned, winked at Tim, then at me. He turned sharply toward the cracking sound. "Tim, you're gonna give yourself arthritis of the knuckles you keep doin' that. Tim." Vito's voice changed. "You remember you told me to keep a team on Vincent Martucci." Tim's face went blank for a moment. "Yeah, I forgot about it, too, Tim. So Haley and Finn been stayin' with him on the late shift. They been workin' six P to two A, since this guy moves around a lot at night." Vito grinned. "And everywhere that Vincent went, the tail was sure to go! Right, Tim?"

"Cut out the goddamn nursery rhymes, Vito, and get to the point."

"Well, Captain Tim, they tailed Mr. Martucci from his house to his health spa. From his health spa, he went to a nice restaurant in Manhasset where he ate his dinner. In the company of a coupla friends, right? Then, he has his driver take him into Manhattan. They pull up in front of one of those really swanky new buildings on Third Avenue. Jeez, remember the old days, Joe? When Third Avenue was like the Bowery uptown? With all them bums sleepin' on the stations of the El?"

I just stared at Vito. He glanced at Tim and shrugged. "Okay, okay. So Vincent, Mr. Martucci, gets out of his limo and sends his driver away. He heads for the building. He enters the building. Then, Tim, then, like two minutes later, Vincent pops out of the building. He walks to the corner. He looks all around. He hails a cab. The cab takes him, Vincent Martucci, down to the Village. Greenwich Village, right? Lower Greenwich Village. Vincent gets out of the cab." The words had been coming from Vito in short jabbing bursts; his head swung from Tim to me as he spoke. "And then, Tim, huh?, then, Joe, Vincent Martucci spends the next three hours, from ten P to one A, visiting . . . ya ready?—*the gay bars. Cruisin'*, Timmy."

"Cruising?"

"The gay bars?"

Vito looked from Tim to me. He stood up, placed himself behind my chair, grabbed my shoulders and pressed his clamplike fingers into me for emphasis.

"Cruisin'; cruisin' down the fuckin' river, Timmy! Vincent Martucci was lookin' for a goddamn *boy!*"

•

It took us three nights to get Vincent Martucci.

While the younger team of Haley and Finn trailed him from saloon to saloon, Geraldi and I waited, slumped in my Chevy. On the third night, when Martucci, in the company of a tall blond male hustler, headed for a local one-nighter, Vito and I became part of the tail. As soon as we entered the musty lobby of the hotel I felt a sharpening of the senses, and a sort of electric alertness wiped out the long hours of bored fatigue. Geraldi told Haley to stay with the panic-stricken room clerk after we learned that Martucci had been given the key to Room 12. Two small, thin young homosexuals entered the lobby, took one look at the little group surrounding the desk and, without breaking their arm-in-arm synchronized stride, about-faced and exited.

Vito, Tom Finn and I stood in the narrow dark insecticide-smelling hallway. Vito, his ear pressed against the door, listened, then whispered, "Now's as good a time as any."

The door splintered at the impact of Vito's shoulder and he went wheeling across the small bedroom, landing almost on top of a naked Vincent Martucci and an almost naked hustler. In the confusion, Vito grabbed the hustler and a collection of clothing and said, "You take Martucci, Joe. I don't trust myself. I might kill the bum."

I picked up the butter-soft suede shirt and slacks and held them toward Martucci, but he bent over, grabbing at his stomach, and made it into the dark little cubicle in time to vomit into the toilet. He ran the small trickle of water in the sink over his hands, dabbed water on his face, then blotted himself on the rough paper towels. Within the next five minutes, he was dressed and deposited in the rear seat of my car between Haley and Finn. Vito, who had scared the living hell out of the hustler before giving him a kick in the ass out the hotel's side door, sat next to me as I drove. Vito was breathing heavily; it was the only sound in the car.

We took Martucci to a small, quiet, unused office down a long corridor on the third floor of the Kew Gardens Criminal Courts Building. The room was dim as we entered, but Tim, who had been waiting, switched on the overhead light, which really didn't add much visibility. I pulled out a chair for Martucci; he seemed to fold into it. The man inside the beautiful suede custom-made outfit had become as limp as a scarecrow racked by blight. His hands trembled as he pressed his face into his palms.

"Vincent, look up."

Vito came behind the chair and jerked Martucci's face up toward the light, but Tim shook his head and Vito walked away.

"Vincent, do you want to call your attorney?" Tim turned and picked up a telephone from the small desk. "You want *me* to call him for you?" Tim's voice sounded concerned and serious; there was nothing mocking or mean about it. "In fact, Vince, you can leave right now.

You don't have to stay here if you don't want to. No one has placed you under arrest, have they?"

Haley and Finn both said, "No, sir." Vito and I didn't say anything. "Vince, you want me to call your driver? Have him bring your limo around? Just say the word."

Each time Tim spoke, it was as though a blow had landed on Martucci's bowed head. In a thin, breaking voice, Martucci said from between his hands, "What do you want from me?"

During the ride out to Queens, he had already offered money, any amount, anything, but he had been met with silence.

"It's very simple, Vincent," Tim said. He turned and indicated the tape recorder on the desk, next to the telephone. "We just want you to tell us, exactly, what you and Kitty Keeler talked about on the telephone the night her children were murdered."

Vincent Martucci rocked his head from side to side, not because he was refusing the request made of him, but because he knew that he could not refuse.

As much as we all knew about Vincent Martucci, as strongly as we all felt about him and his long and vicious career, no one, not even Vito Geraldi, took any pleasure in his complete and total degradation. I can't speak for the others, but I know that my own feeling, in this and in similar situations, was one of personal shame. Maybe the sight of Vincent Martucci crying and cringing like a frightened child established a kind of common humanity between us; none of us were feeling particularly superior or satisfied with ourselves.

"My poor Kitty," he whispered hoarsely. "Oh God, my poor Kitty. How can I do this to her?"

"Because you have no choice," Tim Neary said.

PART
TWO

CHAPTER 1

It took Ed Quibro six days to present the case against Kitty Keeler to the Queens grand jury. The biggest headline during that time was KITTY, GEORGE CLAM ON KIDS' KILLING, over a front-page picture of Kitty and George dashing for a car as they were leaving the courthouse, after claiming Fifth Amendment rights. The next-biggest headline was KITTY K'S LOVER BACK FOR SECOND DAY; in smaller bold print, over Vincent Martucci's picture, was the question "Martucci Key to Keeler Kids' Killing?"

On May 26, 1975, the Queens grand jury returned two indictments against Kitty, charging her with first-degree murder of both of her sons. The *News* headlined KITTY K. INDICTED! WHO HELPED KILL KIDS? The *Post* put it this way: MRS. KEELER INDICTED IN DOUBLE MURDER.

Vito Geraldi, Sam Catalano and I arrived at the Madison Avenue hotel at a prearranged time to serve the arrest warrants. George Keeler, his face the color of damp cement, stood to one side of Kitty; Jay T. Williams stood to the other side. Jeff Weinstein stood behind them, towering over all three. We all rode down the four floors in the same elevator. When we hit the lobby, there was a casual, subtle rearrangement. Williams and Weinstein eased George back slightly; Kitty came alongside me. When George reached for Kitty's arm, she turned and said firmly, "George, you ride in Jaytee's car. Go ahead; you'll be right behind me all the way." Then, with a sharp unyielding demand, "George, we're going to do this the way Jaytee said." She studied his face for a moment, as though debating which was the best approach. Her hand rested lightly on his arm; she whispered something to him, so quietly I couldn't make out the words. Then she turned from him abruptly and walked beside me without breaking pace, without looking up until she was settled next to me in the back seat of the unmarked squad car.

We booked Kitty at the 107th Precinct in Fresh Meadows. Everything was low-key and routine; at least it was for us. Kitty's face was ashen and from time to time she touched the corner of her eye where a nerve began to twitch. When the desk sergeant asked her to empty out her pocketbook, George tried to move in. Kitty whirled around and pushed him back.

"Goddamn it, George." She said to Jaytee, "Get him out of here. Make him sit down somewhere."

Jeff Weinstein took George away; Jay T. Williams stood next to Kitty radiating good will and reassurance.

"We're going to go upstairs now, Kitty," I told her. "We're going to take your fingerprints." For some reason, even to me, it sounded like an apology. When I took her arm, she yanked away from me. "It's all right," I told her.

"Why don't you go fuck yourself," Kitty said, head up, chin jutting, eyes blazing.

For the rest of the booking and arraignment procedures, Kitty was under very tight, angry control. During the ride from Queens into Manhattan, where she was photographed with a Bureau of Criminal Identification number on a plaque around her neck, then back to Queens for appearance before a magistrate, Kitty never glanced out of the rear window. She knew that Jaytee's white Mercedes was directly behind us. She didn't speak one single word beside me in the car; no one spoke, not even Vito, who chewed on an unlit cigar.

As we entered the Brooklyn–Queens Expressway, heading back toward Kew Gardens, I offered Kitty a cigarette. When she reached for it, I noticed her hands for the first time. Her fingers.

I took her left hand in mine without a word; examined it, then her right hand. Across the top of each nail was a ragged, bloody slash of soreness where she had either bitten or pulled the nail away. She stared at her fingers as though they were a total surprise to her. She looked up at me, then back to her fingertips, with that confused, puzzled expression I had seen at Kelly Brothers, when she had looked from one dead child to the other, not recognizing them. I pressed her wrist slightly and she jerked her head up, narrowed her eyes, pasted her lips together tightly and yanked her hand from mine. She folded her arms and buried her hands and stared out the window, the back of her head to me, for the rest of the trip.

Jaytee Williams was skillful at directing most of the attention from Kitty to himself as we hurried from the car to the court building. He blocked her without seeming to; protected her innocently while giving his statement to the press and television people.

The worst moment for Kitty came in the courtroom. She stood, rigid and vague, her eyes burning sightlessly into space, while the legal procedure took place all around her: impersonal, quiet, steady, routine, devoid of passion of any kind. The low humming of voices seemed to hypnotize her; not even George's dangerous wheezing sounds seemed to penetrate. I stood to her left; Jaytee Williams a comforting presence to her right. When he spoke to her, his face close along the side of her neck, his hand playing up and down her arm, she turned, puzzled, totally unprepared for what was happening, since she hadn't been following any of it; not any of it.

She twisted around; finally saw the woman in uniform standing behind her, obviously waiting. Waiting for Kitty. She turned back to Jaytee, her hands on his body, clutching and pulling in a frantic rhythm at his vest and jacket. He caught her hands in his, hunched down quietly, his head bent to hers; he walked her to the side of the courtroom, his arm around her, preventing her from seeing George, who was struggling with Jeff Weinstein—struggling for breath and struggling to get to Kitty. Sam Catalano helped Weinstein; they got George out a side door.

"Now, you are not *listenin'* to me, Kitty," Jaytee said firmly, "and you are not behavin' the way I expect you to behave. Now, you *knew* what to expect, honey. This is only gonna take maybe one, one and a half hours at the very most." As he spoke to her, he shook her from time to time; he alternated between scolding and reassuring her. "Soon's you start actin' like mah girl, honey, that's how soon Jeff and me gonna get that bail bond all arranged and get you ta hell outa here and back with ole George where you belong, y'heah?" He wrapped an arm around her shoulders; his head ducked down and he seemed to be whispering right into her ear. All I heard of it, when he drew back, was, "Now, you remember, you gotta be brave for ole George, honey. That man *needs* you."

Kitty nodded; took Jaytee's large white handkerchief, turned away to wipe her face. Her back went stiff again; she raised her head, turned away from her attorney without another word and went toward the woman court guard. I accompanied them through the barred door off the front of the court; down the flight of steel stairs, through another steel-barred door at the entrance to the detention quarters.

There was an exchange of signatures; I verified delivery of Kitty Keeler; they verified acceptance. We never looked at each other as Kitty went in one direction and I went in another.

.

Tim and I sat in his office and watched Jeremiah Kelleher on the eleven-o'clock news. "There is little feeling of satisfaction in any of this," Jerry said seriously and quietly. "The whole case, from beginning to end, is a tragedy." He was careful not to divulge any details, but he did say, somewhat smugly, I thought, "As I told the parents of Queens County right at the very start of this tragedy, we had no reason to assume that *their* children were in any danger. We never, at any time, had any serious doubt that the solution would lie within the walls of the Keeler apartment."

Tim stabbed at the television button and Jerry's face disappeared, swallowed down the drain at the center of the picture tube. Tim's eyes were red-rimmed and he didn't do them any good by rubbing at them every few minutes.

"He's terrific, isn't he? Isn't it wonderful how things are working out for him, that son-of-a-bitch. He got the indictment in time for the primary; all the goddamn free publicity in the world." Tim slumped into the center of the green leather couch. He took a long swallow of Scotch, leaned his head back and stared at the ceiling. "Jesus, Joe, wouldn't it be something if we picked up some guy tomorrow, some total stranger, someone from left field, who sits down and tells us he killed the Keeler kids? Hands over the gun, comes up with all kinds of proof. Some guy who has access to *all* the homes of *all* the children in Queens."

Grinning tightly at his fantasy, Tim continued, "And we'd work it out so this guy gives himself up to Marvin L. Schneiderman, right on the six-o'clock news." He laughed shortly. "I'd like to see old Gorgeous Jerry go on the tube and talk about *that*. Jesus, wouldn't that be something?"

"You want me to go out and find him, Tim?"

Tim pulled himself upright. His eyes centered on me and he didn't say anything for a long time. Then, "You *really* think she didn't do it, Joe? For Christ's sake, no one else *could* have done it."

"About two million people *could* have done it, Tim."

"Right. And only *one* person did do it. *Kitty*. With help from someone else. And that's where it's at right now. That's where our focus is: we have to find the guy who helped her." He stood up and walked behind his desk, pulled open the bottom drawer, took out the bottle, poured another inch, put the bottle away, sat down. He rubbed at his eyes again. He looked exhausted; his voice was drawn and tired. "Joe, you were here; you heard what Martucci told us. Line for line, exactly what we had figured out ourselves, right?"

"That's the point, Tim."

He drank some Scotch and glanced up at me as though he hadn't heard what I just said. "What? What's the point?"

"Tim." I took a long deep breath, leaned forward and crushed the butt end of my cigarette and immediately lit another one. "Tim, *that's the point. Martucci.*"

He snapped his head back slightly; brought himself sharply into focus. There was nothing vague or tired about him now; he knew I was about to tell him something and he wanted to be very prepared. Even his voice was different: sharp, renewed, tight, demanding. "Okay, Joe. Something's been bothering you for quite a while. Since the night we bagged Martucci. Either you're gonna forget all about it or you're gonna tell me what it is, right now. And *then* we'll *both forget it.*"

"Martucci didn't volunteer one single solitary bit of information, Tim." Tim's eyes were glazed and staring; he was whistling softly, but he was listening and hearing me. "Martucci gave back, verbatim, word for word for word, whatever we fed him." I stood up; had to move around. All my muscles were tensed and cramping. " 'When Kitty called you the first time, Vince, did she say, "Vince, I just strangled Georgie"?' 'Yeah.' 'Yeah what, Vince?' 'Yeah, Kitty called and said Vince-I-just-strangled-Georgie.' 'Did Kitty say, "I gave Terry some sleeping pills and now he won't wake up"?' 'Yeah.' 'Yeah what, Vince?' 'Yeah, Kitty said I-gave-Terry-some-sleeping-pills.' And blah-blah-blah!" I walked over to the window and stared out without seeing anything but flashing lights: car lights, traffic lights, street lights, apartment lights. I turned around, leaned against the windowsill. Tim had swiveled around to face me; his hands were clasped across his stomach and his face was set into a blank, noncommittal expression.

Tim knew what I was talking about. Maybe he hadn't realized it while we were doing it: all of us, we all did it to Martucci; we gave him, line for line, what we wanted him to say; what fit in with what we'd already figured out.

"Jesus, Tim, the only thing Martucci *couldn't* tell us was who Kitty called to help her get rid of the bodies. And that's because *we* don't know who she called, so *we* couldn't tell *him.*"

I sat down again; slid my legs under his desk. Tim took out the bottle and poured about an inch into my glass, none into his this time. I swallowed it and tried not to feel what it was doing to my ulcer.

"That's what we're going to do now, Joe. That's assignment number one. That's the loose end in the case. We're willing to deal with Kitty in return for whoever helped her." In a quiet, rational voice, Tim said, "In fact, finding her accomplice is almost more important than bagging Kitty. She killed the kids in an emotional state; whoever helped her did what he did in cold blood. In fact, he probably killed Terry; no one thinks Kitty fired the shot into him."

"That's it, Tim? No discussion? You have nothing to say about Vincent Martucci's statement?"

Tim shook his head slowly and steadily. "Nothing at all, Joe. Not a goddamn thing; not a goddamn fucking thing at all. Vincent Martucci's statement is going to convict her. There is nothing at all to say about it."

"I better get home before the supermarket closes. I don't have any cottage cheese or milk left." I held my hand against the digging pain.

"Joe. I think you better pick up on that 'special' assignment for me. I think you better continue checking our Jeremiah's real-estate dealings."

"That what you think, Tim?"

Tim stood up. We stared at each other across his desk; neither one of us said anything. Then Tim said, "Joe, stay off this case; it's over now as far as you're concerned. Get something on Jerry and get it fast or that bastard is just liable to take the primary. And then, buddy, it'll be a uniformed desk job for me. And Florida for you."

"Florida. Florida. You know, Tim, tonight, just tonight, that doesn't sound too bad."

CHAPTER 2

WHEN the phone rings at two o'clock in the morning, it's natural to assume that it's someone calling with bad news. No one calls to tell you something wonderful at two o'clock in the morning.

"Jen?" My eyes narrowed against the sudden sharp light from the bedside lamp. My fingers were fumbling a cigarette from the crushed pack.

"Joe?"

"Who the hell is this?" It sure wasn't Jen.

"Joe, it's me. Sam. Sam Catalano. Joe, could I come up to your place and see you? I'm right down the street; at the bar. Daly's. Right on your corner."

"Yeah, I know where Daly's is. All right, Sam. Come on up."

Sam looked fresh and wide-awake even though he said he was beat; he didn't even need a shave, although he rubbed his chin and said he needed a shave.

"Look, Sam, you didn't come up here at two o'clock in the morning to discuss your grooming. What's on your mind?"

He started rambling; Sam finds it very difficult to get right to the point.

"Cut the bullshit. What's on your mind?"

"Okay. Okay, Joe. I'm going to take you into my confidence. I'm going to trust you completely." He said it like he was offering me a rare gift.

I was in no mood for Catalano. "Sam, why don't you get the hell outa here and let me go back to sleep."

"Jaytee Williams has a transcript of the entire presentation to the Keeler grand jury."

"*What?*" It was impossible; or rather, it should have been impossible as well as being illegal, which it is.

Sam looked over his shoulder, checking the walls in the tradition of all good secret-tellers. "I told you, I been cultivatin' George. George told me. He tells me everything. Joe, according to George, Jaytee Williams has been having fits with Kitty because she won't say anything against Vince Martucci. He's been up the wall with her about it. Like one minute Vincent is her lover and now he's talking his head off about what she said to him on the telephone the night the kids were killed. He keeps asking Kitty, not if what Vince said was true, but he keeps asking her, 'What do the cops have on Vince to make him tell this story?' And George says that Williams says that Kitty has *got* to know something about Martucci and she'd better tell him so that *he'd* have something on Martucci, too."

It was funny; it hadn't even occurred to me. Kitty would have to know about Martucci. In fact, Christ, Kitty must have been fronting for him for the last couple of years: Vince was safe going out with his boys; it was common knowledge that Kitty Keeler was his mistress. What the hell was in it for Kitty? Money, clothes, probably. But now why wouldn't she blow his cover? *He* was crucifying *her*.

"George says that Williams says that without Martucci's testimony there was no real case against her. And that's why I come to see you, Joe."

"What's why you come to see me, Sam?"

Sam flexed his shoulders to adjust the perfect fit of his jacket. He glanced toward the windows, checking that no one was hanging by the fingernails, six stories up, to eavesdrop.

"Joe, like I been tellin' you, I've been buddyin' up with George. We're real close, Joe. Poor guy, he don't have hardly anyone left to talk to, ya know? His business has fallen off, all his regulars, they don't come around his pub anymore. They're like uncomfortable, ya know? They don't know how to talk to him anymore, with all the publicity about Kitty and all. So, see, he's gotten to rely more and more on me." Sam winked.

"That's terrific, Sam."

"Yeah, well, here's the thing, Joe. The way I got it figured, Joe, is this. Kitty depends on George; hell, George is all she got left. You know that old lady neighbor, the Jewish lady?"

"Mrs. Silverberg?"

"Yeah, right. Well, she died last week, George told me. He said Kitty was all broke up about that. She says like everyone she loves is dying or turning against her. All she got left is George."

"And what have you been telling George?"

"That if he wants to see Kitty walk away from this before she's an old woman, he better convince her to give with the name of her accomplice. The guy who drove the bodies to Peck Avenue. Either Kitty tells him or *he's* gonna *walk*." Sam leaned forward and spoke quickly, nervously. "Then she'd have no one. At all."

"And when you say that to George, what does *he* say?"

Sam shrugged. "Aw, George is a funny guy, Joe. Quiet; never says too much, but he's thinking; like you can tell he's holding it all inside himself. But I'm sure he can get to Kitty, Joe. And, see, here's the thing, Joe . . ."

"You want to make the collar."

Sam looked like I'd just thrown water in his face; he jumped slightly, looked around, leaned forward. "Well, after all, Joe, it's only right. Look, I don't know why Neary's always on my back, but you know as well as I do he hasn't let me near this case. Look, Joe, I'm not gonna be a third grade all my life. If I come up with this accomplice, hell, anyone else would get jumped right up to first grade. But I'm willing to take second if that's all Neary will give me."

"So George believes Kitty did it?"

"Sure he does. Oh, he doesn't come right out and say it, but when I talk to him, ya know, about getting down to cases with her, threatening to leave her, he don't object, he don't say a thing. And, see, I been emphasizin' the bright side of it: ya know, if Kitty cooperates, her lawyer can deal with the D.A."

"Sam, why'd you come to me with all this?"

Sam brushed some ashes from his knee, then checked the side of his leg. "Well, see, Joe. Well, you and me were partners almost since I been in the squad. And we *did* answer the Keeler call together. I mean, technically, it's *my* case, too, but for some reason Captain Neary hasn't liked me from the day I come into the squad. And, well, I wanna be sure no one screws me outa the collar. So, seein' as you're good friends with him, and we *were* partners and all, I wanna ask you to back me up. To make sure I don't get shafted."

"Are you that sure, Sam?"

"That George'll get it out of her? Absolutely. *Absolutely.* Look, you know the old saying, still waters runs deep and all. She got no one at all left. Ya know, Joe, I already talked George outa killing Martucci."

He said it as though it was all in line with a day's good deed. He was just full of surprises.

"And, hell," Sam went on, "that woulda blown the case, right?"

"Not to mention what it would have done to Martucci. And to George. And to Kitty."

"Right, right. That's what I tole him. So wadda ya say, Joe? Will you back me in this? Make sure I don't get screwed?"

"Sam. Go home. Go to bed. Let me go back to bed, all right?"

"Right, right, sure, sorry I got you up. But, see, I just come from George's place and I was really high on all this, ya know? Like I can *feel* the timing; that it'll be *soon*, ya know?"

"Terrific." I led him to the door, practically had to shove him into the hall.

"Joe, listen, just one thing, okay? Joe, how'd you get Martucci to turn on Kitty?"

I closed the door and went back to bed.

•

Sam was right about one thing. It happened soon. That was all he was right about.

The next day, Tuesday, I spent most of the morning checking out Brooklyn and Queens real-estate records, going back nearly twenty years, which is just about when Jeremiah Kelleher entered the public employ. During those years, he had acquired, for remarkably little money, a collection of those useless little side alleys and irregularly shaped, unusable garbage lots and corridors between buildings, which the city sold at auction. He purchased these parcels regularly, steadily, over the years, and just as regularly and steadily he sold them back to the city, and in some cases to the state, for incredibly high amounts of money, when as it just so happened expressways or post offices or police stations or public libraries were to be built in exact proximity to Kelleher's seemingly useless holdings.

This was the kind of information Tim wanted me to locate, but it was really too complicated to be of any immediate use to him; there would be delayed investigations, charges, countercharges, accusations, denials, which could go on for years, during which time Jeremiah Kelleher might well be defending himself from City Hall. However, this is what the Man told me to do with my working life and this is what I was going to do.

I had a bite to eat and went in to the office to write up my report. There wasn't anyone else in the office except Sergeant Max Gelber, who looked like he was about to start another siege of the flu that had him laid up for a week. I stopped typing to listen to him yelling into the phone. Ever since he was sick Gelber had been accusing everyone of whispering around him; he wouldn't admit his ears had been affected by the virus.

"What? What?" he kept yelling. Finally he looked up at me and said, "Joe, you pick up on this goddamn joker, I got better things to do than play games."

He waited until I picked up the phone, then he slammed down his receiver and went down the hall toward the men's room.

"Detective Peters. Who's this?"

The voice was low and hoarse; I could hardly hear what was being said. There was a gasping, wheezy sound, a strangling, desperate, suddenly familiar sound.

"George? George Keeler, is that you?"

"Where's Sam Catalano? Gotta talk to Sam. He wasn't at his home; tried to call him, but he wasn't at his home."

"George, this is Joe. What's the matter, George? You okay? You sound bad. You having an attack, George? I'll get you some help; hang up and I'll call an ambulance."

"No. No. No ambulance. Listen. Just listen."

It was painful to listen to him; I felt a tightening, a constriction in my own throat and chest, a sympathetic wave of suffocation. It seemed to get worse, George's wheezing, as I argued with him to let me get help.

"Okay, okay, George. I'll listen. Calm down and tell me what you want me to know."

"Kitty," he gasped. "Kitty. Didn't do it. Not Kitty."

I didn't interrupt him again, because then he struggled harder, and the harder he struggled, the worse it became for him. I just sat there and listened.

"All wrong. Everyone, wrong. Newspapers, police. Terrible mistake. Not Kitty. She never hurt the kids. I got it all written out. All written in letter. You tell Sam. Tell him."

I was beginning to get the message. "What letter, George? George, where are you?"

"Letter. Right here. Kitchen table. In my apartment, see. Pub. Over pub. In kitchen. Letter on table. Right here. Tells everything. Everything."

"George, let me come over. We'll talk about it. I'll bring Sam. We'll come over together and we'll talk about it, okay?"

"Too late. All too late. Letter. Tell Kitty I love her. Oh, God. I love her."

There was a terrible desperate wheezing sound as George Keeler sucked in one last deep breath before putting the muzzle of his gun into his mouth, and while I sat and listened he blew his brains out all over the walls of his small kitchen.

CHAPTER 3

T HE two patrol-car cops who responded to my urgent call had arrived in time to pull Danny Fitzmartin and Lucille Travera out of George Keeler's apartment before they had touched anything of importance, including what was left of George. There was a cop leaning against the far end of the bar, near the door leading to upstairs. He gave me one of those meant-to-be-intimidating chin jerks and narrowing-of-the-eyes cold stares as I approached.

"Hold it, buster. Where do you think you're goin'?"

I held out my hand so that he could see my shield.

"Yeah? Well, you're supposed to have it pinned on your jacket," he instructed me. "How the hell am I supposed to know who you are?"

There are so many things you can say to a hard-nosed bastard like this guy, but not one thing that's worth the bother. I pushed the swinging door to the kitchen open a few inches; Danny Fitz was slumped against a worktable; his beefy shoulders were heaving and he was sobbing and shaking his head from side to side. Skinny little redbubbleheaded Lucille, white as a sheet, turned from the sink and slammed a wet cloth over Danny's face. She looked at me and with just a slight gesture of her hand, a slight movement of her head, she let me know: Lucille was in charge; she'd handle Danny.

The young cop stationed upstairs, just outside the open door of George's apartment, saluted the shield on my jacket. There was a look of relief that he wasn't solely responsible anymore for what was inside.

"You haven't touched anything in there, have you?"

"Oh, Jeez," the kid said, "are you kidding? Holy God, there's some mess in there. Richie, that's my partner, Richie said the guy musta put the gun in his mouth. Christ, how can a guy do a thing like that?" He was babbling, looking over his shoulder toward the kitchen, then turning away; then looking back, irresistibly.

"The reason a guy puts a gun in his mouth instead of against his temple is that it's the only sure way. Straight up, right through the brain."

"Oh, Jeez, you mean that's what all that stuff is, all over the wall? Oh, Jeez, his brains?"

"What the hell did you think it was, Officer, chopped liver?"

He swallowed dryly and shut his mouth and pulled himself together a little. Even in the dim hall light, I could see that his face was a greenish yellow. He'd get over that; in time.

The scene was about what I had anticipated: George had been sitting at the small table and had toppled over backward. The kitchen was so small that he was practically wedged in between the table leg and the wall. The phone, a yellow phone, was on the counter; the receiver was hanging inches from the floor. Finally, I looked down at him: George Keeler.

The impact had knocked him back and down, and because there was no room to move, to absorb the force of the shot, he had twisted violently to one side. Had probably slammed onto the floor, then around into the wall, so that his lower body was in one direction, his upper torso in another and his head at still another angle. His face was in profile; I could see one eyeball, exposed, bulging from its socket; most of the skull on that side of the head was ripped off; hung in bits and pieces with clumps of hair and skin and brain cells on the walls and on the sides and surfaces of the stove and the sink; something was splattered on the ceiling and in sprays, like fine red mists, over the clean sheer curtains, through them onto the clean windowpanes.

His gun was probably under his body; maybe still clutched in his hand. That would be for Homicide to find and remove. There was still the smell of gunpowder, an acrid, familiar smell, intensified by the constricted space of the compact kitchen.

On the small yellow enamel table, centered and held in place by a round flowered bowl filled with sugar, was a legal-letter-sized white envelope. In small, neat, very legible writing, almost like type print, were the words "For the District Attorney"; beneath that were the words "For the newspapers."

I heard Chris Wise's voice; he had one of those voices that echo and vibrate in small enclosed places.

"Jesus, Joey," he said, "haven't these goddamn people stopped killing each other and themselves yet?"

The uniformed cop turned and stared, his mouth slightly open; he was in awe of the honest-to-god tough Homicide Squad boss, so Chris played to him a little, showing off his tough callous nature. It was hard to tell if the kid was impressed or scared to death; he was starting to turn gray underneath the yellow-green.

The homicide technicians had to take turns, one at a time: photographing, diagramming, collecting. The guy from the Medical Examiner's office showed up in about twenty minutes; he bent over George's body, fiddled around with a stethoscope; touched here and there, then stood up. He was a small, skinny guy with a bright-pink face and a head of thick bushy black hair.

He put his hand on Chris's arm and said, "Chris, I'm sorry. I did my best. But. This man is dead."

"Jesus, you butcher sawbones are all alike. Can't do a goddamn thing for a man."

The young cop took it all in; he absently leaned against the doorjamb, one hand pressing for balance.

"Jesus Christ, you dummy," Chris shouted at him, "get your fucking hands off the door! That what they teachin' these kids at the academy these days?" He shook his head and told the kid, "When the fingerprint man gets finished here, you have him take a set of your prints so we don't waste time looking for a match-up."

They finally turned George over onto his back. The gun was clenched in his right hand so tightly they had to pry his fingers open. It was still loaded and had to be handled very carefully. George's head fell over to one side; the right side of his face was still intact, undamaged, with a puzzled, sad, surprised expression.

"You caught this, Joe?" Chris asked.

I told him about George's phone call; the conversation that took place.

Chris picked the envelope off the kitchen table and handed it to me. "Then I guess this is yours; just see that we get Xeroxes."

One of the homicide men went through George's pockets and placed the various items on the kitchen table: wallet, keys, comb, handkerchief, two sticks of gum, nebulizer, small vial of large yellow capsules which I recognized as his asthma medication, a few scraps of paper with penciled notations. As he emptied the last pocket he looked up at me and said, "They're all yours, Joe. Just make sure we get a catalogue."

He gave me a large clasp envelope and I began to drop the items into it. I walked into the other room: a small bed-sitting room that had a foam-rubber sleeper couch, a chest of drawers and a small portable TV set. All neat, clean, compact. I went to the window and pushed the curtains aside for better light; went through George's wallet. Pictures of the little blond boys; I recognized the studio portrait: it was the one that had been widely publicized when they were found dead. There was a picture of Kitty, a little younger, grinning. It had apparently been cropped from a larger photograph; you could see that someone else had been in the picture and had been cut away. A picture of Kitty in cap and gown—copy of the picture on the wall in her mother's house. I checked the bill section of the wallet: three tens, two fives, seven singles. I marked the amount on the outside of the clasp envelope. I felt a slight bulge under George's driver's license, pulled out the license and a series of business cards. Checked through them, briefly: service cards from his liquor distributor, glass-supply house, a Queens real-estate agent, a wholesale butcher; a few miscellaneous business cards.

I shoved the driver's license back underneath the celluloid-covered square and gathered the business cards together. They were slightly sticky, and as I was collecting them the cards on the top and bottom of the pile stuck to my fingers and the rest of them went fluttering to the clean blue carpet. I picked them up and as I reached for the last card, a card I hadn't noticed before, I wasn't sure of what I was seeing. Because it didn't make any sense at all.

I brought the card over to the window; studied it in the daylight; it was embossed on one side:

Marvin L. Schneiderman, Commissioner of Investigation
111 John Street, New York, N.Y. 10038 267-6000

I turned the card over, and handwritten in blue ink was: "Kitty. If ever I can help—in any way—your pal, Marv (237-4401)."

I pulled out my own wallet and slid the card in among the collection I had gathered through the years. I put the rest of the cards underneath George's driver's license, shoved the wallet and the other things into the clasp envelope along with the unopened suicide letter.

Tim came up to the apartment, took a quick look at George, then found me in the bedroom. He shook his head.

"Tough, huh?"

"Yeah."

"You talked to him, Joe? You heard him pop off?"

"Yeah."

We walked down the narrow stairway, through the pub; a couple of squad guys were talking now to Danny, who looked terrible, and to Lucille, who stood over him like a tiger. Tim drove to the office in his car; I followed in my Chevy.

Tim was in his office, talking on the telephone, by the time I arrived; I'd stopped off to take care of a couple of things, including getting a container of vanilla malted milk. I dropped the envelope of George's personal belongings on Tim's desk, sat down and drank some of my vanilla malted. It was very, very sweet, which was good because I had a terrible craving for something very, very sweet. Tim finished with his phone call. He reached for the envelope, opened it and dropped the contents on the top of his desk.

"Kitty hasn't been notified," Tim said quietly. "You want to do it?" I shook my head. "No."

Tim got up, fingered through the Manhattan telephone directory, then dialed Jay T. Williams' office number; asked for the man, waited, then spoke quietly. Then he hung up. "Williams will tell her, Joe." I nodded. "Know what that corn-pone bullshit artist said when I told him what George did?" I shook my head. "He said—direct quote—'Oh, that stupid son-of-a-bitch, what the hell was he thinking of?' How about that?"

I shrugged and watched Tim arrange the items on his desk. He reached for his letter opener and slit the envelope, took out a thick wad of folded legal-pad yellow sheets, all covered with George's neat, meticulous, readable print. "Jesus, looks like he wrote a book," Tim said. He smoothed the pages flat under his hands. "Want a drink, Joe?"

I held up my container of vanilla malted.

"Look, Joe, that was a rough call you got from George. You look terrible. Would you feel better if you took off, Joe?" I shook my head. "Look, Joe, what the hell. There wasn't a goddamn thing you could have done for George at that point. There was no *way* you could have helped him. Stop worrying about it."

I leaned my head back and swallowed the last of the thick sweet, sweet malted milk, then came forward and put the container on the edge of Tim's desk and stared at him; just stared.

"Joe. C'mon, kid, pull it all together." Then he repeated what he'd said. "Stop worrying about it."

Finally I stood up, reached in my back pocket for my wallet, slid my fingers behind my driver's license and took out two small Xerox copies: one of the front of Schneiderman's card; one of the back of Schneiderman's card. I reached over, turned on Tim's lamp, and put the pieces of paper flat on his desk, with the light shining on them.

"It isn't George I'm worrying about at this point, Timmy. It's you I'm worrying about."

Tim stared at me, then looked down at his desk. I sat down again and leaned back. I was wishing I had another thick sweet, sweet vanilla malted.

CHAPTER 4

IT took Tim nearly an hour to reach his wife. She was up in Albany for some kind of special legislative meeting. His call took her away from the dinner table; I'd imagine she lost her appetite after speaking with Tim.

When she spoke to Tim in his office, all he told her was to copy down a phone number; hang up; wait five minutes; then dial the number he'd given her. We'd picked out, at random, one of the telephones in the bank of phones on the first floor. We were reasonably certain it wasn't tapped; Tim was reasonably certain that most of the squad phones were. I stood guard over the phone, although the building was pretty empty by now. It was close to nine-thirty. Tim got downstairs in time to snatch up the receiver on the first ring. He closed himself in and hunched over the phone. After about ten minutes he came out along with a cloud of cigarette smoke. Usually, Tim doesn't smoke too much.

"We're going over to Ken Sweeney's house, Joe. In Brooklyn Heights."

Ken Sweeney lives in a narrow brownstone that looks terrific from the outside and like a madhouse inside. His wife, a pretty girl named Mary, cleared a path for us, pushing and shoving at kids and scooping up toys and magazines and half-eaten candy bars all the way through a series of rooms, including one that contained not only a large dining table with eight chairs but a bed, an easy chair, a large blastingly loud color television set and about five or six kids, all arguing about what program to watch. They all looked alike, and in a quick scan I thought they all looked like their mother. They were all dressed in pajamas and flannel bathrobes.

When we reached the kitchen, Mary chased another group of kids out and told them to go to bed. She went along with them to make sure they headed where they were supposed to. Ken Sweeney stood up from the long narrow kitchen table, which was cluttered with half-finished glasses of milk and littered with crumbs and cake wrappers. He was also dressed in pajamas and an old flannel bathrobe, which was threadbare at the elbows and tied around the waist with a stringlike belt. Ken wiped a milk mustache from his upper lip.

"Either of you guys want some milk? Maybe a Twinkie if these gluttons of mine left any." He found one, held it out toward us, shrugged, unwrapped it and shoved most of it into his mouth. He collected glasses with both hands, swept the debris onto the floor and waved at us to sit down. Ken poured some more milk down his throat, finished the last bite of his Twinkie.

"Jesus, look at the mug on that guy, will ya, Joe? End of the world, Tim, right?"

Tim was breathing through his mouth, almost like he'd been running. He took the Xerox copies of the card from his pocket, handed them to me. I handed them to Ken.

He dug a pair of half-frame reading glasses from his bathrobe pocket and considered Marvin L. Schneiderman's generous offer to his friend, Kitty.

Ken pursed his lips thoughtfully, then looked up over the tops of the glasses. "Who got the original?" His bright clear blue eyes slid from Tim to me. Ken winked. "You're a cool kind of a bastard, aren't you, Joe? How come this?" He tipped the Xerox at me.

I pulled the cigarette from my mouth and shrugged. "Ya never know, right?"

Ken considered that for a minute and shook his head. "I tell ya, Tim, I don't know why this guy never took those exams. You'd be right up there, top of the heap by now, Joe."

"Not me, Ken. I'm book dumb, reality smart."

"Where it counts, kiddo, where it counts."

Tim was getting tighter by the minute. I thought he was going to blow by the time Mary stuck her head in. "Sorry," she said softly. "Ken, dear, for just a minute."

Sweeney snatched up a remnant of a marshmallow cooky, shoved it in his mouth and told us, "Back in a minute. Bedtime for the troops."

It took about five minutes, then he was back. "Okay, now, all set. We all got the last cases of the whatever-the-hell flu. All and every one of us, except, of course, Mary. We never let her get anything. Who the hell would take care of the rest of us, right, Mary-Mary?"

She beamed in the doorway, just her head in the room. Very quickly, very softly, she said, "Anything stronger than milk to drink? No. All right. And, Ken, I'll catch the phone if it should ring, don't you bother yourself. You'll have a little quiet and privacy now, boys."

"There she goes, bless her heart." He put his glasses back on again, handled the papers we'd given him, pursed his lips, drummed his fingers on the table and sort of hummed to himself.

"This is a bit of a bitch, now, isn't it? Gimme the goddamn original, Joe, I won't eat it up." He turned it over and over between his fingers. "Let's see, now. Marv was Commissioner of Investigation 1969 until 1972, up to three years ago. Yeah-yeah, until '72. Quit after his dear wife may-she-rest-in-peace passed on. Well, we got us a bit of a dilemma, haven't we, Tim?"

"Wadda ya think, Ken?" Tim's voice was thin and urgent.

"Ya mean about this?" Ken held the card up by the corner. "Ya mean why don't I just take a match and incinerate it, right here and now, and good-bye-Charlie, the hell with it, let's hold our breaths, fellas, and hope to Christ no one else in the whole entire world ever gets wind of the fact that our Marvin L. Schneiderman, our good white knight in clear and shiny armor, had at one time, under whatever circumstances, for whatever reason and toward whatever end, written in his own handwriting a little 'anytime I can be of service' to little Kitty Keeler? And in parenthesis, in his own hand, printed out for the lady his unlisted and private home telephone number?" Ken shook his head, then winked at me. "Tell him some of your 'reality common sense,' Joe?"

"I think he can figure it out himself, Ken."

Tim nodded and wiped sweat from his upper lip. "Jesus, Ken, what are we going to do now?"

"Well, number one, what we're going to do now is, tomorrow morning after a good night's sleep tonight I'm paying a visit to good old Marv, the poor dumb bastard. Jeez, never saw a guy wanted to be Mayor so bad as Marv." Ken shook his head sadly. "He's not gonna make it. No way. We're not about to live in fear and trembling waiting for someone to announce in headlines or not announce in headlines what we've all three of us just learned today. Including the lady herself, which is a bit of a puzzle. She hasn't made it known or gotten in touch with Marvin L. as far as I know."

"And then what?" Tim asked. "After you see Schneiderman."

"Ah, well, Tim, whyn't you just leave that to me?" Ken got up from the table, began collecting bits and pieces of leftover cookies and cakes from some plates near the sink. He shoved his collection into his mouth; crumbs stuck to the corner of his lips. He looked like an overgrown version of one of his own kids.

"Just leave it to you, Ken? Leave *what* to you? What the hell is there left to leave to you?"

Ken Sweeney poured himself a glass of skimmed milk. "Half the calories of whole milk, and healthier for you, to boot." He put the container back into the refrigerator. "Ah, Tim, I'd hate to be in a foxhole with you when the bullets start flying. You're ready to give it all up at the first sign of enemy fire. There's more than one way to come up on top in every and any situation. What about you, Joe? You curious, too?"

"I'd like a chance to learn from the pro, Ken."

"Ah, that's the boy. A man after my own heart." He drank some milk, licked his lips and said, "Well, our poor Marvin has a heart condition. A strange and terrible malady he didn't even know about; and he'll have a seizure, probably in about two days. And have to be rushed off to the hospital where his own brother is a cardiac specialist, thank God. He'll be able to save our Marvin, but he'll also order him to take a long, long rest. Maybe in Florida. Which means he'll have to withdraw from the primary."

Tim smashed out his cigarette and shook his head.

"Ah, c'mon, now, Tim. It won't be as bad as all that. You leave it to me to handle."

"Not as bad as all that? Jesus Christ, Ken. I was counting on that state job. With Kelleher as Mayor, you know what'll happen to me?"

"Why, sure I do, Tim, sure I do." Ken sat down and leaned back comfortably. His blue eyes glittered and a small smile twitched at his milky lips. "When Jeremiah Kelleher himself becomes the Mayor of the City of New York, Timmy-me-boyo, why, 'tis yourself as will be his Police Commissioner of the City of New York."

•

As it turned out, Marvin L. Schneiderman had met Kitty Keeler three years ago when he had taken his two little daughters and himself for a week of winter sunshine in the Bahamas after the month-long ordeal of his wife's illness and death. Along with about two hundred other guests at an adjoining hotel, he had been invited to enjoy the facilities of the New World Health Spa, a public-relations gimmick that was to be very costly for Marvin.

Prodded by Ken Sweeney, Marvin vaguely remembered a long, active day topped off by a languid tropical night when apparently the unaccustomed consumption of liquor had rendered Marvin wistful, maudlin, boastful and generous. Staring at his own handwritten message to "Kitty" from "your pal, Marvin," he recalled sitting around a circular bar with many others, listening to some beautiful girl complain about the difficulty the State Liquor Authority was giving her husband, who owned a pub in Queens. She also complained about corrupt city officials, Health Department shakedowns and the senselessness of making complaints. Marv had given her his card and his unlisted number to ensure that no one would ever trace her calls to him: he personally would institute any investigation into any of her charges.

Marvin L. Schneiderman had never seen or heard from Kitty Keeler again. Apparently, she had given his card to her husband, George, who had slipped it, forgotten, into his wallet.

"It's a damn shame," Ken said philosophically. "For what the poor bastard's paying, he sure didn't get value from Kitty Keeler. Do you know, Marvin has been so totally absorbed by his own future, he never even realized that the beautiful girl he met in the Bahamas was the same girl making headlines for the last few weeks. Poor guy, he kept staring at his card, then at the picture of Kitty in the newspaper. Ah well, that's the way it goes. It's all luck or fate or who the hell knows what. Ah, here she is now." He stood up and came around his desk when his secretary appeared, extending some letters she had just typed. He took them, scanned them, looked up and winked at the girl. "Good, good, Annie. And remember, now, you never saw these, let alone typed them, right?"

The girl's face froze. "You *really* feel you have to say that to me, Ken?" It was obvious she had handled a great deal of confidential matters for him.

"Ah, touchy, touchy," Ken said softly. "Go on, take a two-hour lunch for yourself. It's what you take anyway, but take it with my blessing today." The girl left without another word and Ken said to Tim and me, "By God, you'd think I insulted her virtue. Not that I haven't done that at times, but never with visitors in the office. Here, Tim, you fold these up and pop them into the envelopes while I get myself all prepared for my meeting with Mr. Kelleher."

Ken slipped a Miniphone tape recorder into an inside jacket pocket and adjusted the tiny microphone under his tie clip. Then he reached for the four letters, typed on the letterhead of the District Attorney of Queens County, and prepared for his signature; put the letters in a plain brown clasp envelope, which he carried in his hand. We rode down to the lobby of the building with him and out into the midafternoon spring sunshine.

"Well, a fine day for a stroll along the Battery, isn't it?" Ken said. "Well, I'll see you boys back in my office at about four, then."

Tim Neary trusted Ken Sweeney just about the way that I trusted

Tim: completely. With a few reservations. Which is why Tim had me wait a few minutes, then drive down to the Battery, where I was to secretly record, with the help of a powerful long-range movie-camera lens, the walking-along-the-Battery-in-the-sunshine meeting between Ken and Jerry Kelleher.

At 4 P.M. that day, we returned to Sweeney's office; he played his Miniphone tape for us and showed us Kelleher's signature on the four letters.

The next day, I went to Tim's apartment with the processed movie film and we more or less synchronized the conversation with their actions. There was a good deal of noncommittal banter at the beginning. Ken started reminiscing: old times, good and bad, that they had shared. It was obvious that Jeremiah Kelleher was expecting the worst. He looked tense and anxious, wondering what the hell Ken had dug up on him and how he was about to slip it to him.

Finally Ken said, "I hope you do realize that my objection to your candidacy on the party line was never related to *you* personally, Jerry. It was just a coming together of time and expectation. Those damn half-assed morons in Watergate made every known pol suspect. Even the good ones." He reached out and tapped Kelleher's shoulder lightly with his fist. "And you're one of the best, Jerry. One of the best. So. Well, I'll get right down to it, no sense in beating around the bush. For reasons of my own," he leaned closer to Kelleher, "and no questions asked or answered, I've decided to switch my support, and the support of my organization, of course, to you."

Kelleher didn't move; he had been tensed for a blow and now he just stared blankly. "*To me?*"

"Providing, of course, that we clear up a few things between us right up front."

"Clear up a few things? Up front?"

Ken dug into the brown clasp envelope and took out the typed letters. "Here, Jerry, all set and ready for your signature. To save you the trouble of trying to figure this out, I'm gonna make it very simple and clear. There has to be a certain price, of course."

Carefully, Kelleher said, "Of course."

"Well, these letters requiring your signature are merely a part of that price. Each letter, dated today and on your stationery—I think of everything to save you the trouble, Jer—spells out your intention, when you are the *Mayor of the City of New York*, to appoint certain well-qualified men to certain positions where they can best serve. For instance, what better-qualified man than Tim Neary, with two college degrees and nearly twenty years of experience, to be your Police Commissioner?"

I glanced at Tim, saw him lean forward slightly toward the movie screen. He held his breath as he watched Jeremiah Kelleher read the letter quickly, then look up, surprised but admiring, at Ken Sweeney.

He read the other letters slowly, without a word. Finally he smiled at Ken. "Well, it isn't really necessary for me to *sign* anything between us, Ken. We've been in business a long time, you and me. Isn't a handshake between the two of us good anymore?"

"Sure it is," Ken shot back. "*But a signature is better.*"

They stood and looked at each other for about thirty seconds. The tape recorder recorded nothing but the sounds of an airplane and the groans of a tug fighting the waters of New York Harbor.

"How are you going to go about dumping Marv Schneiderman?" Kelleher squinted at Sweeney; he dangled the letters between his fingers.

"Ah, not to worry, Jerry, not to worry. However, you may just learn in the next two days or so that Marv's had a sudden attack of bad health."

Gorgeous Jerry cocked his head to one side with a knowing smile. "And if you and I don't deal, Marv Schneiderman might enjoy continuing good health."

"There's no 'might' about it, Jerry." There was a hard sound coming from the recorder even though Ken's face was pleasant and smiling. He was deadly serious. "You see, the letters with your signature will be a sort of guarantee for me, Jerry. That once Marvin's health suffers and he has to withdraw, you and me are still in business." He reached out and flicked a speck off Kelleher's lapel. "And you're to deal with me *now*, Jerry. No thinking things over. No 'consultations with advisers.' None of that kind of thing. Deal with me now, *right now*." He glanced at his wristwatch. "Within the next three minutes, or it's all off. And Marvin L. Schneiderman will be your next Mayor, just like it's been expected all along." He grinned, fingered some more lint or something from Kelleher's jacket. "And incidentally, Jerry. It would be a shame at this juncture of your life, just when the road ahead could be so exciting and successful, for you to have to get involved explaining—to newspapers and grand juries and such—certain activities that you were engaged in over the last twenty-odd years. Bad time in life to start blackening a shining career. Up to you, Jerry, all up to you. I'll just walk over to that bench and leave you with your thoughts." Ken gestured out toward the Statue of Liberty. "Look at that Lady in the harbor, Jerry.

God, isn't it an inspiring sight? Aren't we fortunate to be living in the best goddamn nation in the world?"

Kelleher signed the letters and walked over to the bench, where he stood and watched as Ken Sweeney slid them into the brown clasp envelope, then stood up and thrust out his right hand.

"Well, I'll be in touch, Jerry, to work out a timetable of announcements and such."

"Just like old times, Ken, isn't it?" Kelleher said heartily. "You and me a team again, kid, just like old times!"

"Well, just like old times, *almost*." Sweeney tucked the envelope under one arm, patted Kelleher's chest quickly, pulled open his jacket and exposed Kelleher's Miniphone. "I don't remember you ever bugging a private conversation between the two of us in the past, Jerry. Or did you, and I just didn't catch wise?"

Jerry Kelleher shrugged and smiled. What the hell; he was in a good position. He disconnected the Miniphone from the holster under his arm and the microphone from his tie clip and handed it, tape and all, to Ken.

"Here, take the damn thing. You're welcome to it. The sound is so poor anyway, you wouldn't be able to make out anything we said."

Ken slipped the reel from the recorder, which he gave back to Jerry. "Thanks, kid, but I've got my own recorder." He opened his jacket and displayed his model, more up-to-date and efficient and with a better sound. "If you want a copy, I'll make one for you."

Both men started to laugh with a genuinely relieved sound of enjoyment. Kelleher, visibly relaxed, apparently had begun to believe his good luck and wasn't about to question it. *Yet*. He and Sweeney walked together to the railing, and while they both laughed and laughed Ken tossed the reel from Jerry's recorder, along with another reel of tape, into the choppy waters of New York Harbor.

Jerry Kelleher was under the impression that the second reel to hit the water was the tape from Ken Sweeney's recorder. Which is just what Ken Sweeney wanted him to think. But it wasn't. It was an extra, blank reel that Ken had shown quickly to Jerry just before he tossed it away.

Ken had played the tape of their conversation for Tim and me in his office at 4 P.M. that day.

On *my* hidden Miniphone, *I* made a tape of *Ken's* tape. Which was the one I played for Tim, in pretty close sync with the movie film, at his apartment.

As I said, Tim Neary trusted Ken Sweeney completely. With a few reservations.

CHAPTER 5

$\mathbf{T}$IM NEARY had been having mood swings since Ken Sweeney practically guaranteed him the Police Commissioner spot. One minute he was gloating and selecting his deputies, the next he was cracking his knuckles and cursing over the lost state crime commission job. Ken had told him that there was no way, at this time, that he could arrange that appointment for Tim. Support of Kelleher would put Sweeney in a difficult spot statewise, while at the same time strengthening his power in the city. He assured Tim that four years as Police Commissioner would qualify him for greater things than a state appointment. He strongly hinted at the directorship of the F.B.I.

When he was feeling optimistic, Tim generously offered me a spot in his administration: after I had officially retired at the end of November, he would hire me as his civilian deputy commissioner in charge of public relations. With my retirement pay and my commissioner's salary, I would be pulling in more money than I could ever have dreamed about. Providing, of course, that I didn't pack up and move to Florida at the end of November. And go to work in the construction business.

Tim assigned me to attend George Keeler's funeral on the unlikely possibility that the grief-stricken young widow would be so filled with remorse she would blurt out a confession which would wind up the murder case against her. No one at all gave any weight to George's meticulously written seven-page confession. I hadn't really studied it carefully yet. I don't think anyone else had either. The headlines announced: KITTY K'S HUBBY KILLS SELF: CLAIMS HE KILLED KIDS; DID KITTY "LET GEORGE DO IT"?: D.A. SAYS NO!; PALS SAY KEELER NEVER KILLED KIDS. Most of the follow-up stories more or less featured the case against Kitty and interviews with people who stressed that George loved his wife so much he'd do *anything* to save her.

I figured that if George *did* kill the kids, or if he loved Kitty so much that he was willing to confess and die for her, then he was entitled to get a serious reading of his seven-page confession. He sure as hell wasn't getting it from the D.A., who announced on the TV news that the confession was "worthless. The poor man was so aggrieved by his children's death, he obviously didn't know what he was doing." I had brought a copy of his confession home; after his funeral I planned to read it. Carefully.

Sam Catalano came into the office to type up a report; Tim had assigned him to check out some minor extortion complaint. Sam looked terrible; George's suicide really shook him badly. Not that he felt sorry for George or anything. What he felt was more like anger and frustration that George had taken this way to act on Sam's constant prodding, constant insistence that there was no way to save Kitty except to threaten her with abandonment. George Keeler had loused up Sam Catalano's best shot at promotion.

There wasn't much I could do for George Keeler, but there *was* one thing. I could take care of Sam Catalano once and for all. I took a blank file folder and in red ink I marked it CONFIDENTIAL. Inside the folder I put a copy of George's confession and several other incidental case notes. Clipped to George's confession, so that it would be the first thing seen by anyone opening the file, I put the Xerox copies of the front and back of Marvin L. Schneiderman's card. I dropped the file into the top drawer of the desk I generally work at when I'm in the office. Before I left for the funeral, I walked over to Sam and spoke to him. Very quietly.

"Sam, I'm sure nobody would go into my papers and things, but would you mind working at the typewriter on my desk? There are a couple of things I don't want anyone poking around in. I don't want to lock the desk, because there are things belonging to other guys, you know how it is. If you'll just hold the fort for me, I'd appreciate it."

Sam was more than happy to transfer over to my desk; he looked very anxious for me to leave. Driving out to the cemetery on Long Island, I thought about what Sam was probably up to. As soon as he figured it was safe, he would open the confidential file, find the Xerox of Schneiderman's card; lift it; get his own copy made; return my copy to the file. Then he would break both legs to get up to the top floor to show District Attorney Jeremiah Kelleher what a valuable man he was, delivering Jerry's enemy into his hands.

But Sam would be just about twenty-four hours too late. Had he been twenty-four hours earlier with the information, as a good spy is supposed to be, Jerry wouldn't have handed out four commissionerships to Ken Sweeney's people. Signing those letters put Kelleher irrefutably in Sweeney's hands for the next four years.

By being late with this information, Sam Catalano would lose the backing of his only supporter, the D.A. And, best of all, Sam would never know why. Which goes to prove, if you're going to be a spy, you damned well better be a good one.

As a suicide, George Keeler was not entitled to be buried in hallowed ground alongside his two young sons. As a World War II vet, he was entitled to be buried in Pinelawn Cemetery out on Long Island. There weren't many people present: just family and friends. The sensation seekers were left behind at the funeral home; not many of them could be bothered to take the long car trip for another glimpse of Kitty, in black. They would have to be satisfied with the TV news shots and stills in the newspaper. Kitty's oldest brother stood alongside her, not touching, just within reach. Her mother stood far off, with Kitty's three other brothers and her sisters-in-law between them. Every person there seemed oddly alone, isolated, solitary.

Nothing of Kitty showed; she was just an anonymous black-clad figure, behind dark veils and glasses. Not one trace of her was revealed; she stood motionless during the final, abrupt prayer, and when it was over she turned quickly and, followed by her brother, headed for the limousine. Jay T. Williams and his assistant, Jeff Weinstein, had been standing off to one side; they followed her, and Jaytee leaned forward for a few minutes, speaking to her, as she sat on the back seat of the long black car. He ducked inside the car, apparently to give her a short hug or a word of comfort. Her brother started to enter the car, but Kitty stopped him. After a few seconds of conversation, he backed off and slammed the limo door; and as though that was the signal the driver had been waiting for, the car pulled off down the cemetery lane and headed for the Long Island Expressway.

I went back to the office to write up the required brief description of George Keeler's funeral. Tim had gone for the day; Sam was gone. The tiny shred of white thread I had placed strategically on my "confidential" file folder was gone; whatever was going to happen to Sam Catalano was in the works. I collected my folder, exchanged wisecracks with a couple of squad men, then went home.

I sat with a cup of coffee and George's confession, but the memory of Kitty Keeler at the cemetery began to bother me. Or at least to distract me. She had seemed so isolated, disconnected, solitary, remote even from the Kitty I had seen before. I wondered what the heavy black veil and glasses and clothing were hiding; or were they hiding anything at all?

Even as I began to read George's tightly controlled, specific document, Kitty intruded. I thought about her annoyance with George that first morning when Sam and I responded to George's call; in retrospect, it seemed like the kind of annoyance a girl like Kitty would feel toward a man like George for pulling the same trick twice: c'mon, George, bring the kids home!

But George, on the same morning, right from the start, had evidenced a kind of anguish; a dread.

When I first questioned her that morning, she transferred her annoyance and anger from George to me; but those were the only emotions she had displayed. Certainly not panic or dread. And when the bodies had been found, Kitty's concern, her hard sudden tenderness and protection of George, were at odds with all the things we were supposed to believe about Kitty.

During later interrogation, by which time the names of her lovers had been sensationalized, along with glamour pictures of Kitty, and when her public image had been publicly accepted, Kitty had steeled herself behind a wall of anger. But I *had* penetrated it, fleetingly, a few times: at the morgue, her eyes had blazed out a kind of agony which Geraldi thought was callousness; at her apartment, when she selected the clothing for her dead sons, there was a terrible raw pain revealed before she pulled the tough skin of anger around herself; at the funeral for the boys, she had remained rigidly calm and controlled until the moment she stared from one dead face to the other, then had tried to alter reality by saying they were not her sons.

Geraldi and the others, including the news-media people and the crazy sensation seekers who dogged her wherever she went, claimed she had never shed one tear for her sons and would not grieve for her husband. But they were wrong. For whatever it was worth, for whatever reasons, Kitty Keeler was grieving deeply: a locked-in, private kind of grief which she had been able to control by tensely drawing strength and determination from the constant crowd around her who were waiting, watching, hoping to see her finally break down. They interpreted everything she did, every word she uttered, every outfit she appeared in, as evidence not only of her heartlessness but of her guilt. When she wore pink to her sons' funeral, voices had called out "Whore"; when she wore black to her husband's funeral, they called out "Hypocrite."

It's funny how your initial approach to a person can determine your feelings toward them, no matter what facts develop later on. Vito Geraldi hated Kitty Keeler. That had been his job, right from the very beginning. No matter what might turn up, if somehow it was proven that Kitty was an innocent martyr suffering for all our sins, to Vito she would always be a murderer, a bitch, a whore.

My assignment had been to offer her a shoulder to lean on, a sympathetic ear to confide in, a sort of refuge from the anger of all the others around her.

There was no way I could concentrate on George's confession. Because of Kitty. And the way my mind kept drifting toward her and the way she looked this morning out at Pinelawn Cemetery. She had seemed to be enclosed inside a vacuum, unable to touch or be touched. What I wanted to do then, what I wanted to do now, was break through the wall of that vacuum and reach out to Kitty and hold her against me. Just hold her and feel her come alive. Because, emotionally, Kitty Keeler was in the process of dying. And it seemed to me there was no one close enough to her to notice what was happening. Or, if someone did notice, no one cared.

I don't know why I cared; not exactly. Maybe because I had done what Tim Neary assigned me to do. I played good guy to Vito's bad guy, so I saw Kitty differently from all the others. She *let* me see her, in a few exhausted, unguarded moments. Now I was paying a price for having encouraged her confidence in me, for letting her turn to me: help me, Joe; get me out of here, Joe.

I felt a responsibility to her. I had to either help her carry her pain or help her get rid of it.

And, of course, it went deeper than that. There was more to it than that. There was Kitty herself, with her physical beauty, her special electric strength and energy; her tough challenging pose that didn't really hide her vulnerability but somehow enhanced it.

I wanted to protect her from the kind of mindless hostility thrown at her by the street crazies; from the cold emotionless damage of the indictments against her; from the hopeless finality of death that seemed to be overcoming her, little by little. She needed me. There was something of value I could offer to her at a desperately barren time in her life. And in my own.

About three weeks before his suicide, George and Kitty had moved to a smaller, more private apartment in a luxury high-rise not far from my own place near the Forest Hills Tennis Stadium. It was a fully furnished sublet in a building that had a large number of short-term tenants: airline personnel, Japanese businessmen, U.N. attachés, high-priced call girls. I drove over to her building, pulled into the underground garage, showed the attendant my shield. He told me her apartment number and, as I instructed, did not announce me.

Without asking who was there or checking the peephole, Kitty opened the door about two seconds after I rang the bell. When she saw it was me, she turned and walked into the kitchen, where she was boiling water for instant coffee.

"You should be more careful, Kitty. Might have been anyone at the door: thief, rapist, reporter."

"Or cop," she said flatly. She was still wearing the black funeral dress. There was an odd, vacant expression, emphasized by dark circles beneath her eyes.

"Do I have to go with you, Joe? Did you come for me?" She said it with a tired resignation; she was too exhausted to fight anymore.

I turned the flame off under the glass pot of boiling water, fixed two cups of instant coffee. "I'll tell you what, Kitty. You go inside and change your clothes. You look like hell in black. Put on something blue, that's more your color. And take your hair down." She had it twisted in a tight intricate bun at the nape of her neck.

She shrugged without asking any questions at all; took her cup of black coffee with her. When she came back from her bedroom, she looked like a college girl: she wore a blue-and-white checked blouse, with a matching kerchief on her head, her pale hair flowing down her back; a blue denim skirt; blue crepe-soled shoes; a large, soft leather shoulder bag slung on her arm.

When we exited the elevator at the garage level, the parking attendant gaped at Kitty as though she was an ax murderess on the prowl. She never even noticed him.

"I thought you might like to get out of Queens County for a little while, Kitty. Shall we head upstate for some fresh air?"

She shrugged and whispered, "Wherever. Wherever. I don't care."

I glanced at her from time to time, but neither of us spoke for well over an hour. It was getting dark, and when the radio music ended for a station break and the news I reached across her and jabbed at a button for an all-music station. She never batted an eye.

Finally I said, "I know a nice place for dinner. You interested?"

"Dinner? I don't know. Where are we?" She sounded as if she couldn't care less.

"About a mile from a nice place for dinner."

We were seated at a table toward the rear of the rustic, candle-flickering roadhouse; it was a soft, easygoing, low-pressure kind of place where everyone minded their own business and enjoyed their own quiet conversation. Kitty stared blankly at the menu, couldn't seem to make a decision. Nodded for me to make the decision for her.

"I'm not hungry anyway," she said.

But she began to nibble absently on a piece of bread, then she picked at the salad. Her appetite grew as she ate; she began to gulp wine between bites of food.

"Hey, that's good wine. Treat it with respect; it deserves to be savored."

She jerked her head up, her eyes shot reflections from the orange candle flame. She had a look of stunned surprise, like someone waking from a dream, but not sure of reality.

"It's okay, Kitty. It's okay."

When the dinner came, she stared at it, then up at me again, then she began to eat, steadily, quickly, one hand reaching for hunks of crusty bread, the other guiding her fork; she stuffed bread in her mouth, then snatched up the knife and began gouging out chunks of roast beef. It was as though she had an overwhelming hunger: an inexplicable need to stuff food, any food, inside her mouth, to force it down her throat with huge swallows of wine. She had a need to fill up a vast and awesome emptiness that was at the center of herself. She watched hungrily, greedily, as I transferred portions from my plate to hers; tapped at her glass with a fork for more wine; choked; swallowed; ate and ate, until finally the food was gone, the bread plate clean.

She sat as still as a statue, staring at her plate, then her hand went up to her mouth and she looked up at me in amazement and confusion. "How could I have done that? How could I have eaten all that food? My God, and I'm still hungry. Joe, I'm still hungry." She reached for my hand, squeezed it with a desperate pressure. "Joe, after all that's happened, I'm still hungry. I feel as though I'm starving! What's the matter with me? How can I think of food?"

She waved her hand and knocked over the nearly empty wineglass, watched in fascinated horror as the stain spread into an inch-wide line along the white starchy tablecloth. She stood up abruptly, whirled around, collided with a waiter, who nearly lost his trayful of food, then she ran a zigzag course, knocking into tables and against people seated at their dinner and out the door to the parking lot.

I apologized to the waiter, handed him enough for our bill and a good tip, explained the lady wasn't feeling well. I picked up her shoulder bag, which she had left swinging from her chair, and found her outside, her arms wrapped across her body in the cold night air. I put my jacket around her, my arm around her to lead her to my car. As my hand came to rest on her shoulder, Kitty stopped, turned toward me, her face puzzled and frightened and desperate.

"Oh God, Joe. I'm hungry, hungry, hungry." She raised her arms, her hands on my shoulders, climbing toward my neck. My jacket slid to the ground as she reached upward and I leaned forward to meet her urgent hunger.

"Kiss me, kiss me, Joe, oh God, oh God."

The intensity of her mouth on mine surprised me just a little: it was a continuation of her need to devour and consume. Her fingers were kneading and searching along my neck, sliding to my face, touching and tracing where our lips combined. Carefully, gently and firmly, I caught her hands and pulled back.

"It's all right, Kitty, it's going to be all right. Kitty, shall we go somewhere? Shall we spend the night together?"

She nodded dumbly, then walked away from me and sat quietly in the car while I picked up my jacket. I drove twenty miles farther upstate, then turned off onto a one-mile dirt road which led to the small four-room log-type cabin, set on three acres of wooded land and fronting on a nearly stagnant lake. My father had built the cabin before I was born; it belonged jointly to me, my older brother and my younger sister. When our children had been younger, we used to take three-week vacations, one group of us leaving as the other group arrived. None of us had made much use of the cabin for the last five or six years; all of our kids had grown up and away from this kind of roughing it. Occasionally my brother and I had come up for a fall weekend in hunting season: the funny thing was, neither of us had any desire to shoot at animals. It had taken a couple of trophyless weekends for us to admit it to each other.

The cabin had been empty and unused for quite a while; it had that kind of dank feel of abandonment, which was slightly dispelled by the fire I managed to rake up, starting with a handful or two of dried twigs. It took nearly twenty minutes, but finally the two small logs caught; the third one, huge and substantial, would catch and last through the night. All the time I worked, crouched down to the fire, Kitty lay on her side on the daybed, her face warm and orange, her eyes shining with glints of the flame. She seemed to have quieted down again; to retreat into that dazed unfeeling trance. I went around the cabin, turning on the water and the water heater, setting out instant coffee, which was about all that was in the food cabinet. I had given Kitty a few blankets, had wrapped them around her because she was shaking so badly, but she was still now, pensive, unmoving. I kicked off my shoes and pulled a chair closer to the fire, but before I could settle down, to wait her out, to let her make her own decisions, Kitty called to me.

She sat up, fighting the blankets from her as though they bound her. "Joe, help me." She pulled at her blouse, the buttons seemed to impede her; she couldn't manage, her fingers were trembling and shaking. I helped her; tried to calm her, but there was something so desperate about her, urgent and aggressive and insistent. Her mouth clung to mine, then moved hungrily along my face; then her tongue pushed against my teeth, then her mouth seemed to be drawing my life into herself. She whispered and sobbed and gasped over and over again, "Oh God. Oh, my God, my God."

What happened between us was something far deeper and more vital and fundamental than just a sexual act. It was assaultive and abrasive and self-seeking on Kitty's part. She had a desperate urgent strength which sought to satisfy that same ravenous, terrified empty hunger that food and wine had not satisfied. Finally she lay back, her head flung to one side, her hand, palm up, over her eyes. She breathed in deep hard gasps, and rivulets of sweat ran down her face and neck. I leaned over her and carefully blotted her face with the edge of the top sheet. She began to move her head from side to side, slowly at first, then faster and more wildly.

"No," she whispered, "oh no, no, no, no, no, no!"

I caught her face between my two hands, held it still. "It's all right, Kitty. Don't you know that it's all right?"

Her voice was eerie: a harsh whisper in the flickering light which shadowed her face and seemed to widen her eyes. "How could I be here with you like this? How could I be with anyone at all? George is alone, in that box. The boys, Georgie and Terry, they're all alone, everyone is alone. *And I'm alone!*"

The last words were a cry of terror and she pulled free of my hands and began to toss her head from side to side, as though her body was pinned by a tremendous weight and only her head was free to struggle. I stroked her face, rhythmically, began chanting to her softly, "You're with me, Kitty; you're not alone; you're with me, Kitty," and my lips on hers slowed the frantic twisting and turning and struggling, and when she lay still and wide-eyed, watchful and waiting, my mouth moved over her, my hands moved over her, tasting and kneading and arousing and whispering a sense of life back into her. She came alive again, less desperately, less urgently, and this time it was a mutual passion, this time I could join with her in a kind of lovemaking. A kind of affirmation and assurance that she was still a part of life and living and feeling.

She slept for brief periods, sliding away into an intense quietness and motionlessness. Then she would begin to move, as though drawing back from a dream. Her hands wandered restlessly to her face, her neck, then her head started to move, from side to side, negatively. Then, a soft moaning, the beginning of a cry; then she would sit up abruptly, starkly awake and confused, her eyes darting with suspicion about the room, toward the low-burning warming fire, then finally at me. I held her, eased her back down onto the pillow, my fingers tracing her dark brows, her fine fragile jawline, her slightly parted orange-flame-colored full lips, the edges of her pale hair against her forehead.

I studied her in repose. Her face, relaxed and unguarded, seemed so young and vulnerable and unmarked. Her coloring in the pale-orange shadow was delicate and exquisite, unreal. Then a frown would pull her dark eyebrows toward each other; her mouth would tighten, lips pull back revealing clenched teeth. And it would start again; and I would soothe and comfort her again.

Her body, uncovered from time to time by her struggle against sleep, was more fragile than I had imagined. She had small sharp bones, and the pale skin was pulled so tightly against her ribs it seemed transparent, the line of each bone clearly outlined. Her breasts were round and full and firm; I traced her body downward to the flat belly centered by sharp-edged hipbones; to the unbelievably white-gold triangle, wondering how this small, delicate body had borne children. She seemed at once both childlike and womanly, a disturbing combination. I studied her face intently, trying to catch a memory. She moved slightly, raised her chin an inch, then was totally motionless, and then I knew what she reminded me of. Kitty Keeler, in her absolute stillness, looked exactly like her older son had looked, in his coffin.

Toward morning, stretched and cramped in the easy chair facing the dwindling fire, I fell into a light uncomfortable sleep, then woke in confusion to a low, muffled sound. I jumped up and came beside her. Kitty was lying on her back, her eyes opened wide and staring blankly. She was crying; her whole body was convulsed by waves of nearly silent gasping. Her mouth was open, and very soft, deep, half-stifled sounds came from her. Her hands clutched at the blanket, grabbed and released with each new strangulated sound. I reached my hand out, touched her face; her eyes rolled toward me, blinked, didn't seem to recognize me or even see me. She drew her body back against the wall; sat up, knees drawn up, arms locked around them to hug herself together. She buried her face against her knees as though to hide and stifle the terrible screams that were tearing up through her body.

"Kitty, it's all right. Go ahead, Kitty. For God's sake, *cry*. Let it happen, Kitty. It's all right to cry."

She raised her face and stared at me blankly for about three or four seconds, then her face distorted as though surprised by the terrible scream that rose from her throat. All the pent-up emotion, all the held-back grief flooded her, overwhelmed her. She threw her head back against the wall and screamed until her voice was ragged. She slid her fingers up and down along her raw, aching throat, and when she couldn't scream anymore she sobbed until she could hardly breathe.

She took the tissues I handed her, but she couldn't clear her nose, and the breath came rasping from her mouth.

Finally she dropped her head; her knees slid down, her body became limp. I lifted her and placed her head on the pillow; her legs went straight out; her arms at her sides. She was wearing an old flannel shirt of mine. I buttoned it up to her chin, then covered her with a warm plaid blanket, although it wasn't the night-chilled air that sent the shudders through her body. I got a cold wet cloth and pressed it against her forehead and over her eyes until she fell into a deep, soundless, motionless sleep.

When she woke, her face was swollen and shiny. She touched her throat lightly with her fingertips and grimaced. Her voice was husky and strained.

"I smell coffee, Joe. Could I have some?"

I waited outside in the clean cold glittering morning while Kitty showered and dressed in the clothes she'd picked out from a closet filled with levis, shirts, sweaters and warm socks that had accumulated throughout the years of so many of us sharing the cabin. From the way she avoided looking directly at me, it was obvious that Kitty needed some time alone to come to terms with what had happened between us during the night. She looked wary and guarded, uncertain as to how she should act: undecided whether she was sorry or relieved that I had been witness to and participant in the emotional explosion that she had been unable to contain.

She looked very small and very young in her borrowed clothes. She had caught her hair back in a rubber-band ponytail and there were a few long damp tendrils pasted along the sides of her neck, one or two strands against her cheek. Her face, shiny and still slightly swollen around the eyes, was devoid of any makeup; her cheeks were flushed, but what made her look different were her eyelashes. They were light blond, as pale as her hair. They looked like snowflakes and gave her face a vulnerable, childlike innocence, contradicted by the deep awareness of her eyes and the tension around her mouth.

She hunched her shoulders against the surprisingly cold bright air, but didn't want a sweater or a jacket.

"Could we just walk a little, Joe?"

We set off along the overgrown path which led to the lake, Kitty striding ahead as though knowing exactly where she was going. She picked up a long narrow stick and peeled the bark off it as she walked along. It was hard to tell if we were on the old path; the vegetation was so thick and had been undisturbed for so long. Not that it mattered; we were headed downhill and that led, inevitably, to the lake.

She stopped abruptly, not to admire the view; there wasn't any, just thick foliage, tangled weeds and vines creeping around an assortment of dead or dying trees. You couldn't see the lake; could hardly see the sky for the overhanging branches. She stood perfectly still, her back to me, then her shoulders flexed and she turned, stiffening her body against the moment she had been preparing for. Her eyes narrowed and hardened with suspicion and her hands grasped the stick tightly.

"Go ahead, Joe. Ask me." When I didn't respond immediately, she clenched and twisted her hands until the stick broke with a sharp crack and she flung the pieces into the weeds as though they had suddenly turned to fire. All traces of childlike vulnerability were gone. Her expression was tense and cynical. "Go ahead, damn you. *Ask me!*"

"Ask you what, Kitty?"

She shook her head, looked around wildly, then focused her anger directly at me. "That's what all this has been leading up to, right? You've managed to do what no one else has done. You've broken me down, haven't you? Did you bring my confession along with you, Joe? Tell me how you worked it out." She smiled bitterly, a quick tight pulling back of her mouth. "Did you all sit around the office and work it out, line by line, the way you did for Vincent, or did *you* sit down all by yourself, Joe? Have you got it with you, Joe, in your jacket pocket maybe?"

I caught her wrist as she reached into my pocket. She gasped at the sudden, surprising pain, but I didn't release her. "Is that what you think, Kitty? That I brought you up here to break you down?" She raised her chin and her eyes were sharp and cold beneath the odd thick light lashes, revealing a hatred and contempt too intense for words. "Is that what you *really* think?"

Unintentionally, I had twisted her wrist, and when she winced with the pain I dropped my hold on her. She rubbed her wrist and said contemptuously, "You bet that's what I really think!"

There was nothing of the Kitty she had revealed during the night; there was only the tough, angry, smug and knowing woman, glaring at me, challenging me, provoking me to respond to her. Finally I said, "Uh-huh. You're *right*, lady, you're *absolutely right*. That's what this has been all about. *You are goddamn fucking right!*"

I walked back toward the cabin, breaking a new path, kicking and swiping at weeds and low-hanging branches as though they were deliberate obstacles put there just to annoy me. There was a sharp biting sensation just to the right of my stomach which two early-morning cups of black instant coffee hadn't helped; I figured a third cup wouldn't do too much more damage. I lit another cigarette with a vicious satisfaction: let the ulcer choke on that for a while. The minute the water began to boil, I poured it into the already stained mug on top of a spoonful of stale powdered coffee.

"Joe?" I didn't turn toward her until she spoke again. "Joe, I didn't kill my sons."

Her hand was lightly touching her throat, trying to ease the rasping soreness that made her voice so strange and intense. I poured the untasted coffee into the sink and watched as it disappeared, leaving a dark ring around the drain.

"Kitty, if you *did* kill the boys—" I held my hand up toward her and she bit back words and clenched her teeth and watched me closely. "Let me finish. If you *did* kill the boys, tell me now. Before we go any further. Tell me *now* and I'll move heaven and earth to get you the best possible deal that can be worked." My mind raced ahead, picturing Sweeney and Tim and Kelleher and all the angles and maneuvers. "I promise you, Kitty, there *are* deals that can be made. I promise you, I'll help you."

She dropped her hands to her sides and held her eyes on mine. "As God is my witness, Joe, I didn't kill my boys." Then she blinked and looked away. "But . . . but . . ."

As she wavered, I felt a sensation in my stomach like a heavy lump of ice so cold that it began to burn. There was a look of misery on her face so totally undisguised that I wanted to comfort her, to protect her, but at the same time I felt a hard, ugly anger at her evasiveness. My hands went to her shoulders, shook her insistently until she threw back her head, locked her eyes tight against seeing me.

"But *what*, Kitty? For God's sake, if there's anything to tell, tell me *now!*"

She opened her eyes, took a deep breath through her mouth, and in a shattered, ragged voice she said, "I left them alone, Joe. *I left them alone for more than two hours that night.*"

CHAPTER 6

WE spent most of the afternoon in the cabin, Kitty talking, me listening, interrupting, jotting down notes. She answered the most specific questions without hesitation and, it seemed, with a sense of relief.

It was dark by the time we reached her apartment, and Kitty looked exhausted. She was unable to speak above a whisper. When I stopped in the hall, indicating that I wasn't coming in, she said in that painful, eerie voice, "Help me, Joe. I've only got two weeks. I told you Jaytee says if I don't accept the plea-bargaining they've offered by June sixteenth, they'll put me on trial for first-degree murder with no concessions. He says if I take the offer, they'll put me in prison for maybe three or four years. Against risking the next thirty years of my life. Isn't that crazy, Joe? If I say I'm guilty, they'll put me away for three or four years. If I say I'm innocent, they'll put me away for thirty years." She shook her head, ran her fingers along her throat. "Oh God, Joe, help me. Jaytee says . . ."

I put my index finger against her lips. "Screw Jaytee. Go on inside, Kitty, and make some hot tea and lemon and a shot of whiskey and go to bed. You need sleep; you look awful." I took my finger away and kissed her lightly, lightly on the lips and on her forehead.

"You'll call me, Joe?"

"I'll call you tomorrow." And then, speaking to a flash of terror which just touched the surface of her face, "It's going to be all right, Kitty. *Trust me.*"

At eight o'clock the phone rang. Of course it was Jen. Of course I had forgotten to call her last night. And of course she was going to be cheerful about it and not mention it: martyrlike. And of course that was just my guilty conscience on the defensive.

"Hi, Joe. I was afraid you'd miss me, so I decided to call you." I could hear voices in the background, conversation, then Jen good-naturedly asking for a little quiet. "Sorry, Joe. It seems I'm holding everybody up for dinner."

"Who's everybody?"

"Oh, just Fred and Ellen," naming her brother and his wife; then a pause, then, "And Dave Waters. You remember Dave, he used to be Fred's partner out on Long Island." And then, softer, in a rush, "He lost his wife a few months ago and Fred's been after him to come down to Florida. And he finally came." Then, in a more normal voice, this part not confidential, "Guess who beat Fred and Ellen at doubles today, Joe?" I heard the laughing, the friendly groaning and teasing. I remembered Dave Waters. Big guy, blond athlete type. Yeah, I remembered Dave.

"That's terrific, Jen. I'm glad you're having fun."

"Are you, Joe? Having fun?"

"What the hell does that mean?" And then, feeling righteous to keep from feeling guilty, "Oh yeah, Jen. I'm having a helluva good time. Dinner, theater, cocktail parties . . ."

"That why you didn't get a chance to call me last night?"

She slipped it in fast, with that light, close-to-laughing sound she used when she was sore but didn't want to admit she was sore, just in case she was wrong.

"Yeah, that was why, Jen. Too much bouncing around with the beautiful people. I'm sure *you* know how it is."

"Hey, hon, I was only kidding. Listen, there are three hungry people waving fists at me. Have a good weekend, Joe. Call me Tuesday night, okay?"

We had stopped calling each other at random; we had run out of things to say to each other randomly. Our conversations on "regular call nights" had fallen into a well-regulated pattern: an exchange of basic fundamental information—health, the weather, my job, her schoolwork, did either of the kids call; and then the tense good-byes, both of us aware of too many things left unsaid, neither of us able to say them.

Tonight, she sounded young, happy, talking to me, then to the others in the room with her. She used her teasing voice; I could picture the special smile that went with that voice.

"Jen. Come home." I hadn't planned to say it; I'm not even sure if I meant it. There was an abrupt silence, but whether it was because she was listening to what the others were saying or because she was considering what I had just said I don't know.

Finally, quickly, *routinely*, Jen said, "Love ya, hon." And then she hung up before I had responded, routinely.

I took a long alternating hot-cold shower but couldn't shake the sense of wariness, remembering Jen's bright, eager happy sound: guess who beat Fred and Ellen at doubles?

I thought about Dave Waters and I wanted to call her back, to warn her: watch out, Jen; you're too innocent; you won't know how to handle it; it might become too important to you. I had a sense of being moved toward changes in my life, changes which had always seemed so far in the future that they were safe to talk about and think about. But November wasn't far off; a twenty-year segment of our lives was coming to an end. Jen had said that going back for her degree was her first concrete step toward the future, toward the rest of our lives. But I wondered if it had hit her too, this vision of our lives ending under the hot glaring Florida sun, roasting us as wrinkled and brown as baked potatoes until we just blended in with the dusty sand. I had caught something almost frantic in her voice, not just tonight, but other nights, other phone conversations when we had exchanged nothing more than information. We couldn't just keep avoiding it, just letting things happen because neither of us could admit we felt trapped by plans made years ago by the two other people we were then.

Jen couldn't let Dave Waters just "happen."

Any more than I could let Kitty Keeler just "happen."

•

It took a couple of hours just to *begin* to get an idea of how my investigation would proceed. The long narrow extension table, opened to its full length and just about stretching from one side of the living room to the other, was filled with stacks of reports, memos, case notes, statements, observations. Going through all we had previously collected, weighing one statement against another, one claim against another, one assumption against another, took total concentration. I doctored my ulcer with a cream-cheese-on-toast, two glasses of not too cold milk, a handful of Gelusils. I only took a few drags on each of the cigarettes I went through during the night.

Starting at the very beginning was Kitty's statement: brief, blunt, devoid of any details. "I put the kids to bed; I went to bed; I woke up the next morning; the kids were gone."

In her second statement, taken by Quibro, she was ready for the more specific questions which we hadn't been prepared to ask her originally: yes, she made the phone calls to Martucci; they discussed personal things; yes, she spoke to Patti MacDougal on the phone; no, she didn't believe Patti had actually come to Fresh Meadows to return the Porsche at 2:30 A.M., as claimed.

It was obvious to everyone that Kitty was lying when she said she'd called George at 10:15 instead of 11:20. It was obvious she was lying when she said she'd tended to the boys from 1 A.M. to 1:30 A.M. and that they were alive and well at that time. It was assumed she was lying because she had murdered her children and had decided to bluff it out.

We had all worked these assumptions into a rational, reasonable, believable timetable of Kitty Keeler's movements on the night of April 16–17; then we had fed these assumptions, one at a time, to Vincent Martucci and we had rehearsed him so carefully that his testimony to the grand jury seemed to cover all contingencies. I went through my notes, then typed up my own version of Vincent Martucci's statement to the grand jury:

SYNOPSIS OF VINCENT MARTUCCI'S TESTIMONY TO GRAND JURY
Kitty Keeler was supposed to have come out to Phoenix with me on Tuesday, April 15, 1975, to prepare for the Celebrity Opening Night Party the next night. She couldn't come at that time because her youngest son, George, got sick with the measles and her regular baby-sitter was sick in the hospital. Kitty couldn't find anyone else who could stay with the boys; especially since the little one was sick. Kitty said she'd try to fly out as soon as she worked something out.

On Wednesday night, April 16, 1975, at 11:30 P.M., Kitty Keeler telephoned me at my office in Phoenix. She sounded hysterical and kept saying, "Vince, I killed Georgie. I killed Georgie."

I got her to calm down and tell me what happened. She said it had been a terrible day. She and George, her husband, had been fighting on and off about Kitty coming out to Phoenix. George didn't want her to go; he was afraid Kitty would stay out there for good. And she had tried all day to get a baby-sitter, even for two or three days so she could come out, but she couldn't get anyone.

Kitty said that all day long, all night, Georgie had been crying and throwing up and she spent hours holding him, rocking him, cooling him off, getting him back to sleep. Then, she said, Terry started to complain that he had a sore throat and she knew that was how it started with the younger boy, and she knew Terry was going to come down with the measles too. She told me she gave Terry two sleeping pills, so that he would sleep through the night, because she was too exhausted to be up all night with him, too. Both boys were asleep, then at about 10:30, Kitty said, Georgie woke up. He had vomited all over his bed; Kitty changed the bed, put fresh pajamas on the kid, took care of him and all. She took him to the bathroom but the kid said he didn't have to go, so she got him into bed and like two minutes after she left the room, the kid calls her. He wet the bed; so she changed the sheets again, and changed the kid's pajamas and took him to the bathroom and kept him up awhile, maybe fifteen minutes, and the kid says, yeah, he's ready to go back to bed. And Kitty said she kept asking the kid if he was sure he didn't have to go again, or throw up or anything, and the kid says yeah he's sure and Kitty goes into the kitchen to have a cup of coffee and she no sooner takes one mouthful of the coffee when the kid calls her that he's thrown up again. Kitty rushes into the bedroom, puts on the lamp, and there's the kid sitting up in bed in a mess of vomit.

Kitty said she started to shake the kid; she said she kept yelling at him, like why didn't you tell me before this happened? why did you wait until I left the room? And she said she just kept shaking him, shaking him like he was a doll, and her hands were on his neck and then he was very quiet. And she tells me that she carried him into the bathroom and washed him off, then back into the bedroom and put him on his brother's bed while she changed the sheets again and then she puts the kid into clean pajamas and back into his own bed.

She tells me that Georgie was very quiet and didn't move and she thought maybe she was just tired, she thought it looked strange. She says she went back to the kitchen and tried to take a swallow of coffee but her hands started shaking and she couldn't hold the cup and she thought she heard the kid, Georgie, call her, so she rushed back into the bedroom and put on the overhead light, but the kid hadn't moved, so she tried to shake him, to wake him up, and then she noticed the other kid wasn't moving either and she couldn't wake him up and she thought that both kids were dead.

So she called George, her husband, but he couldn't come to the phone so she called me and she tells me "I must have choked Georgie. Vincent, I killed Georgie. I didn't mean to." And then she tells me the sleeping pills musta killed Terry and she keeps sayin' what am I gonna do, Vincent.

So I tell her to call the kids' doctor. Have him come over and she should say she doesn't remember what happened; she don't know what's wrong with the boys.

And Kitty says she can't do that. She says what kind of a mother would he think she was. Then she says, crying again, she gotta get someone to help her; she gotta get someone to take the bodies out of the house, to make it look like they been kidnapped. I tried to talk her out of it, but she got hysterical again and then she hung up.

I tried calling her back, but her line was busy. I tried calling George Keeler's number over in Sunnyside, but that was busy too. Then my maître d' comes into the office and tells me some Congressmen just arrived and I get all tied up with them.

Then, later, I don't know, they tell me it was 3:10 A.M. New York time, Kitty calls me again. She sounds very strange, very calm, like she was talking in her sleep. She says, Vincent, it's all taken care of. Someone came to help me. She says, Vincent, he did a terrible thing. He threw the boys away in the lot. He shot one of them, I don't know which one. I didn't get out of the car. She says, he shot one of them so it would look like a kidnap-murder. She asked me what she should do, so I tell her to take a couple of sleeping pills and go to bed, then in the morning to call George and act like she believes that he got the boys, just like he done that time in November, and she should just say she went to bed that night, then got up and the boys were gone. That she didn't know anything more about it and that she should stick to that story no matter what. . . .

Vincent had added that his statement was given of his own free will, in full understanding of the fact that since he had waived immunity he was vulnerable under the laws of the State of New York to prosecution as an accessory to this crime. He had insisted on adding, "I make this statement because I know that Kitty Keeler did not mean to hurt her boys. It was an accident; a terrible accident and she should not have to live with people saying she is a cold-blooded murderer and all those other things people have been saying about her."

Which was a helluva lot of help to Kitty Keeler.

Using the collection of notes I'd taken, and relying on my memory, I typed up what Kitty had told me up at the cabin. Occasionally, I jotted notations or questions on my legal pad, things that Kitty would have to clarify for me—later, when I tried to make some kind of sense out of what three different people claimed had happened the night the boys were murdered.

KITTY KEELER'S STATEMENT RE NIGHT OF MURDERS

Georgie finally fell asleep after throwing up and wetting himself I don't know how many times. Then Terry starting saying his throat was sore, which is just how it started with Georgie. So I gave Terry two sleeping pills; it was around ten o'clock. It's not the kind of thing you brag about, but I was just too exhausted to give a damn; I just wanted the kids settled down for the night.

I was feeling very low; kept thinking about what was going on in Phoenix, with me stuck here in Fresh Meadows. Finally, I decided the hell with this. I called George to tell him that like it or not, he was going to stay with the kids for the next couple of days while I went out to Phoenix. I had worked damned hard getting ready for the opening out there; I was entitled.

It probably was 11:20 when I called George, if that's what everyone says. I made a mistake the first time, when I said it was about 10:15 or 10:20 when I made the call. It was an honest mistake; not important as far as I was concerned. Then everyone kept asking me if I was sure it wasn't more like 11:15 or 11:20 when I called. I got mad; I got my Irish up and stuck with my original statement for no other reason, just that you all got me so mad. It wasn't a significant time as far as I was concerned.

Then George couldn't come to the phone and I had a go-round with that bitch, Lucille. By the time I hung up, I was really fuming. So I called Vincent, out in Phoenix, and he told me what was going on: all the movie people and sports people who were there. By the time I finished talking with Vince, I was ready to climb the walls.

So I called a guy I know. Named Billy Weaver. . . .

According to Kitty, this Billy Weaver was someone she'd met when they both worked at Mogliano's. She hadn't seen him for a couple of years, then she ran into him about a year ago at a party. He had come up in the world: from busboy to cocaine dealer. About fifteen minutes after she called Weaver, he sent a car around to pick her up.

When the doorbell rang, three short jabs, I just walked out of the apartment. Didn't check on the kids; they were quiet, so why look for trouble. There was a tall, dark young guy waiting for me at the curb, leaning against a small green car. A Datsun or Toyota or something like that. We didn't say much of any-

*thing; I just got in and he drove me to some apartment build-
ing in Jackson Heights. He took me to apartment 3-D. It was
very dark inside; there were a lot of people, mostly men. Billy
Weaver was waiting for me in the kitchen. He told me that
most of the people in the apartment were illegal aliens: from
Central America and the Caribbean islands. . . .*

Kitty said that she and Weaver snorted; that she felt good: slightly
high, very aware, relaxed, animated. She said that Weaver told her he
was having some trouble with some "people" who felt he was encroach-
ing on their territory. Some of his couriers were turning up dead. He
seemed really scared and asked Kitty to talk to Vincent Martucci; to see
if Vince could intervene for him in some way. She was there for nearly
two hours; then the driver, Benjamin the Cuban is what Billy called
him, drove her back to her apartment.

*As I opened the apartment door, the phone was ringing. I ran
into the kitchen and grabbed it before the second ring. It was
Patti. She told me about how she'd come to Fresh Meadows to
return the car and how no one answered the door. I didn't believe her, knowing Patti, but as it turns out, I guess she was telling the truth. Because she was right: I wasn't home at 2:30; I
was with Billy Weaver, getting high and listening to his troubles.*
Then I checked the boys' room. The kids were gone.

Kitty thought of George: he'd done this to her before. He must have
come over to the apartment, found the kids alone and taken them back
to his pub apartment. She started to call him, then stopped. What the
hell could she tell him: that she'd left her sick kids alone while she was
out getting high with her pusher?

*So I called Vince again. I guess the call was between 3:10 and
3:25, like the phone company records show. I told him how
I'd gone out to see Billy, that the kids were gone when I
got back, that I was ashamed to call George. Vince said not to
call George; to just go to bed; wait until daylight. Let George
cool off. So I waited. I just read magazines the rest of the night.
I was wide awake. I never did get into bed, which was why it
was made up when you police arrived. So, I called George at
7:30. And then he came over and then he called the police. And you know the rest.*

I thought about Kitty, the way she looked and sounded and moved when telling me her version of that night. It was the first time she had sounded out in the open, not trying to alibi or excuse herself for what she'd done, but also not blaming herself for what had happened to her sons. I put her statement into a file folder and got to work on George Keeler's "confession."

It was a long, tightly written statement covering page after page of neatly printed writing, and a great deal of George Keeler came through.

> GEORGE KEELER'S CONFESSION RE MURDER OF HIS SONS
> ... I went upstairs to my apartment and tried to get Kitty back on the phone, but her line was busy. I had the operator check it out. I knew Kitty'd keep it tied up all night, just to get even with me for not coming to the phone. And also for the way things worked out. I really didn't want her to go to Phoenix in the first place; I was afraid she wouldn't come back. I was glad the baby, Georgie, got sick; that way, she had to stay home. ...

But George felt sorry for Kitty and guilty for the way things had turned out for her. He was very aware of the differences between them: not just the age difference, but their outlook. He wanted to talk to her, to tell her they'd work it out. He checked out the pub: everyone was all wrapped up in the singing group; all the customers were fine. He slipped out the back way, avoiding Danny and Lucille and anyone else; he didn't want them to know he was going over to see Kitty. They would feel sorry for him.

It took him about ten minutes to get over to Fresh Meadows; he parked in front of his building and let himself in with his key.

> I could hear Kitty talking on the phone in the bedroom. I tiptoed to the doorway and figured out it was Vince Martucci she was talking to. I figured she was just tying up the line on spite, so I couldn't get through to her. She didn't know I was there, so I went into the boys' room.
> I just wanted to see them. Little Georgie woke up and saw me and he started crying. I don't know why, but I didn't want Kitty to know I was there, in the apartment. So I picked Georgie up and tried to quiet him but he started to cry more, so I put my hand over his mouth. Just to quiet him. So Kitty wouldn't come into the room.

I don't know how it happened. I never meant to hurt the baby. I just didn't want him to cry anymore. I guess I put my hand on his throat. I guess I choked him. He got very quiet. I put him back into his bed. Terry was asleep. I went back into the hallway and listened. Kitty was still talking to Vince. She was laughing about something. I think that's what made me feel sort of crazy—Kitty, laughing and talking just to keep the phone all tied up, just to get even with me. So I wanted to get even with her. To get back at her, I guess. . . .

And so, to "get even with Kitty," George Keeler stated, he picked up both of his sleeping sons and quietly carried them out of the apartment; put them on the back seat of his station wagon and drove back to the parking lot behind his pub. In his statement, he said that he knew there was something wrong with both of them, but he would think about that later. He slipped back inside; the singers were just about winding up their performance; the action among the customers started up again, and George just pitched right in with Lucille and Danny and the extra part-time help. No one seemed to have missed him; everyone assumed he had been there all along.

A couple of times, George stepped outside and checked on the boys; both of them were quiet. He kept expecting Kitty to call him, once she discovered the boys were missing, but she didn't call. Finally, when the pub closed down, at around two-fifteen or so, he dialed Kitty's number. The phone rang several times; no one answered.

Then I went out back and sat in the station wagon trying to think what to do.

I knew Georgie was dead. I knew he was dead and I didn't believe it, all at the same time. I was in a commando unit in Korea. One of my jobs, my unit's jobs, was to take care of sentries when we were on a behind-lines mission. It hardly takes any pressure at all as long as you know the exact spot on the neck and throat. It's fast and quiet. I knew that I did that to Georgie so that he wouldn't cry out. I didn't want to hurt him; I never in my life hurt my kids. I just didn't want him to cry out. . . .

George couldn't figure out what had happened to Terry. He didn't remember doing anything to him, but the boy didn't seem to be breathing, so he reasoned he must have choked Terry as well. He sat in the wagon for a while, then drove back to Fresh Meadows and kept driving around the complex. Then he pulled into his parking slot and sat there for a while, just looking at the windows of his apartment. Then he drove around some more.

> *Then I drove over to Peck Avenue and parked there and just sat. I checked the boys again. They were dead. I thought about Kitty. I thought about how I would lose her forever if she knew what I had done. I had a gun in the glove compartment. It was unregistered. I took it from a guy who tried to hold up my place in the Bronx. I never reported it to the police. I broke the guy's arm and kept his gun. I thought I could make it look like someone, some nut, took the boys and killed them. So I took them into the park and I put them on the ground. I fired at Terry. So that Kitty would think someone had taken them and killed them, there in the park.*
>
> *Then I drove over to Flushing Meadow Park and got out of the station wagon and walked around for a while. I tossed the gun into the Flushing Meadow bay, then went back to my apartment at the pub and lay down and fell asleep. I kept dreaming and dreaming, then waking up and wondering if it had really happened, or if it had all been a terrible nightmare. . . .*

Then Kitty called him and said, "George, where are the kids?" and George Keeler knew it hadn't been a nightmare; it had all been real.

> *When everyone said that Kitty did it, I couldn't speak out. I knew she was innocent and that nobody could prove anything against her, because she hadn't done it. But I couldn't tell her that I had killed the boys. And also because for that time, Kitty turned to me, the way she used to when she was a kid and I was always there to help her out. I was important to her. We were never closer. And then she was indicted. I never thought that could happen. And then the lawyer was talking about making a deal, about her copping out to a plea-bargain deal.*
>
> *So I wrote all this out, just the way it happened. I have to do it this way because of what I done to the boys and because I can't ever face Kitty again, once she knows.*
>
> *Everything I wrote here is true. God can never forgive me for what I done, but I pray that somehow Kitty can.*

And that was George Keeler's version of what happened on the night his two young sons were taken from their beds and their murdered bodies dropped in a park just off Peck Avenue in Queens. It was also the document that everyone was writing off as totally without value or validity.

I didn't get much sleep that night. My mind kept roaming over the various statements; I kept hearing the various voices, each telling a different story of how the Keeler boys were murdered. Somewhere, in all of these words, was the truth.

•

Tim Neary was in a good mood Monday morning, until he saw me.

"I've been reading over George Keeler's confession, Tim. Wadda ya say that I check it out before it goes into the case file?"

Tim's mouth got tight and he looked up from the collection of papers which covered the top of his desk. He did one of those careful, blank stares and he said softly, "I thought we had that all straightened out, Joe."

I dropped into a chair casually. "What the hell, why not let me give it a day or two?"

"You're not listening to me, Joe." He shifted to patient teacher explaining to stupid student. "You're not getting my message. The Keeler case is closed as far as this office is concerned. We got the collar; we got the indictment. Kelleher and Quibro are both happy. Everyone feels certain that Keeler will cop out and make a deal, for the name of her accomplice. Everyone's happy but you, Joe. What's your particular problem?"

I went into my act. "Jeez, I don't know, Tim. It's probably just me, not the case. What the hell, we've known each other a long time, Tim. It's, well, it's talking long distance to Jen. We seem to be getting more and more screwed up."

Tim pulled off his reading glasses and stopped tapping his ballpoint on his blotter. He leaned forward and was very sympathetic. "Hey, Joe, this has been going on too damn long. Look, why don't you take some time off? Hop a plane down to Florida, what the hell will it take you, two, three hours?"

He then reassured me, over my protests, that he could manage without me for a week or two. In fact, he insisted I take two weeks. "In that time, Joe, you'll be able to convince her to come on back up here where she belongs. I can guarantee you that job we discussed, Joe. You tell Jen that. And listen, you guys could take a nice apartment up in Westchester. I got a couple of friends up there could fix Jen up with a good teaching job." Tim's mind was racing as he listed all the things he could do for us. He leaned right back into his good mood; after all, it's a helluva good feeling to be able to do a favor for a friend.

I filled out my vacation request form and Tim endorsed it and sent me off to my second honeymoon. According to the time I requested, I'd be due back to work on June 16, 1975. Plea day—cutoff day—for Kitty Keeler.

CHAPTER 7

Danny Fitzmartin finished reading my typed extract of George's confession. He put two heavy fingers on the papers and shoved them across the polished bar toward me. He acknowledged an early-afternoon customer with a be-with-you-in-a-minute nod, then ducked down and became very busy arranging glasses and bottles.

Finally he called out, "Same thing to start the day, Tommy?," which was apparently the ritual with this particular guy. Danny's voice cracked in the middle and he tried to cover himself by coughing, like he had a dry spot in his throat. He brought the guy his drink and set the color television to a soap opera and kidded the guy because he'd missed a great hospital scene the day before.

"Tommy comes here every day to watch this crap," Danny said, not looking at me. "His wife watches it, too, but Tommy would die before he'd let her know he keeps up with it."

There wasn't anything more to say about that particular subject. And there wasn't any other trade. There was just Danny and me and he had to finally accept it. He motioned me down the far end of the bar, set up a couple of beers, glanced toward the door hoping like hell someone, anyone, would come in.

Fitzmartin has the kind of face that registers exactly what is going on behind his big honest blue eyes and he was a man who was suffering like hell and not able to handle it.

"Hey, did I tell ya that I'm thinkin' of buying the place? Me and my brother been talkin' it over and Kitty said any price we think is fair. And any terms we can manage. Did I tell you that already?"

I nodded but didn't answer. He rambled on about how he and his brother owned a place in the Bronx once and he started to describe some trouble they had with a beer distributor, but even Danny didn't know what the hell he was talking about. He looked hopefully toward the door, but no one came to his rescue. He gulped down his beer reached for my glass, but I didn't need a refill. He grabbed his own glass, started to fill it, stopped abruptly and turned his back to me. His huge shoulder muscles rippled, tightened and flexed under his light-blue shirt. He held his hand up to his face and his eyes were desperate when he finally turned back to me.

"Oh Christ," he said, "oh Jesus God." He shook his head, but the pain wouldn't go away.

"Tell me about the gun, Danny."

For a split second, he was asking himself if he should lie or not. It was obvious; it was right there on his big pink baby face, which tightened, then immediately relaxed into a kind of helpless desperation. "It was maybe ten, twelve years ago. Up in George's place in the Bronx. Webster Avenue, near Fordham Road. It wasn't like it is now, you know, with guys gettin' ripped off every other week and all. It was near closin' time on a Saturday night and just George and me and another guy was there. We were countin' the receipts and all. This guy, big nervous guy, he'd been nursing a long drink for quite a while, so you got the feelin' he was up to somethin', and anyway, finally, he pulls a gun, sticks it right in George's face." Danny shook his head. "The guy shouldn't a done that. Like if he stuck it in *my* face, then told George, gimme the money, that woulda been different. But George, well, he been through some pretty bad times over in Korea. Not that he ever talked about it, because he didn't. But I heard, ya know, ya talk around, and I heard from some guys that George . . . that George totaled a lotta enemies over there. All he ever said about it was that he'd seen enough killing to last him a lifetime, and here was this jerk sticking a gun in his face. I'd never seen George like that."

Danny was at a loss to describe George; it had been a side of him he'd never seen, only heard about. He shrugged. "All I can say is, this guy picked the wrong ginmill. George moved so goddamn fast I don't even know what he done and I was standin' right there next to him. The dummy guy don't even know what happened. Like one minute he's standin' with a gun to George's head, the next minute, faster than you can blink, swear to God, the guy is on the floor, screamin' in pain, and George is standin' over him with the gun in his hand. Then George shoves the gun in his back pocket and pulls the guy up to his feet and I make a move to the phone, ya know, to call the cops and George says, 'No, I'll take care of this,' and he shoves the guy into the back room and I don't hear a thing, then the guy lets out a terrible yell and I hear a commotion, like the guy just went through a door, and then it's quiet and George comes back into the bar and he just says, 'That bum won't be knockin' off any other ginmills for a long time.' I didn't ask no questions." Danny shook his head earnestly. "Not then, not ever. I never saw George like that, just that one time, but I'll tell ya this, Detective Peters, I believed everything I ever heard about how George handled himself over in Korea."

"And the gun?"

Danny glanced nervously toward the door, then toward his one customer, who was intently watching a doctor and a nurse, or maybe they were both doctors, I just tend to think that women in white uniforms are nurses; whatever they were, they were embracing and kissing, and Tommy, the customer, was just eating it up and wasn't looking for another drink.

Finally Danny said, "It was a thirty-eight." He looked down at his hands, twisted the clean damp bar cloth and said rapidly, "As far as I know, George kept it." And then, resigned, "Oh hell, George kept it. He pulled it one time here when a coupla bad-lookin' dudes showed up and started actin' funny. You know, makin' the kind of moves you just *know* are headin' in the wrong direction."

I nodded. Bartenders and cops can make a wrong guy pretty fast.

"Well, anyway, they was the only two left in the place, and before they can make their play George pulls the thirty-eight out and shoves it right in their faces, and they come on like George is a nut, all they're doin' here is drinking. And then the smaller guy, they were two Puerto Rican guys, the smaller guy got a smart mouth on him and he says to George, like, 'Hey, man, you think we're a coupla ripoff men, you call the cops, go on, call the cops.' And like he's daring George. And George just says, very quietly, moving the thirty-eight from one guy to the other, he says, 'You see this thirty-eight? This here is all the cops I need. I handle things myself, my own way. I take care of punks like you with this gun, I don't go botherin' the cops.' And George says, 'See, this here gun isn't registered or nothin', no way it can be traced back to me, so when they find punks like you in some alley in Bed-Stuy there's no way it comes home to me.'" Danny rubbed the back of his neck and then his damp forehead with the bar cloth. "Those guys believed him. Like they got pale under their dark skin, ya know. I frisked them and took a couple a gravity knives off them, and boy, when George told them to get lost, those guys practically disappeared in thin air they was so glad to get away from George."

Danny had gotten caught up in the reminiscence. He smiled and shook his head, then said, "Wait a minute, let me fix this soap-opera buff up."

Two workmen came in, settled heavily at the bar and Danny took care of them with the kind of rough good-natured byplay that goes on with guys who know each other for a long time.

Danny had replaced the bar cloth with a freshly laundered one and he rubbed and polished the already shiny surface of the bar.

"Where'd George keep the thirty-eight?"

Danny shrugged and polished, then raised his head. His blue eyes were swimming and he was blinking fast. "I don't know," he mumbled, then looked right at me and said, "He kept it on him."

"When's the last time you saw the thirty-eight, Danny?"

He stood there trying to decide what to tell me, and when he finally spoke I knew it was the truth because this man was hurting like hell. "The time I told you about, ya know, the two Puerto Ricans? Well, it was on April Fool's Day, ya know, April first."

"*This* April first?"

He nodded. "I remember that, because George made a joke about it, like 'Well, there goes my two April fools.' Meaning the two P.R.s."

Which placed the .38 in George Keeler's possession as late as two weeks before the murder of his sons. I think Danny knew what I was going to ask him next. He just kept staring at his hands, which were bunched together into two fists, side by side on the shiny surface of the counter.

"Danny, could George have slipped out of the pub that night the way he claimed in his letter? With all the entertainment going on and all the people moving around and singing and all, can you really swear you saw George Keeler in the pub every single minute of that night?"

Danny Fitzmartin kept his face down for a long time. When he looked up, the tears spilled from both his eyes. "I just figured," he said in a broken voice, "that he'd gone upstairs to call Kitty."

.

Ray Ortega is one of the best narcotics cops I've ever known and he owed me at least one heavy favor. A lot of guys owe me favors, which is the kind of balance I like. If you owe a guy, you never know what the hell you might get hit with; this way, it's my ball game. It was a little hard to track Ray down, because the guys in his unit play it pretty close to the vest; no one knows who's working where at any particular time of the day or night. I couldn't leave a message with anyone, since I was supposed to be in Florida and you never know who the hell just might mention your name at the wrong time and place. It is surprising how small a city of some eight million people can turn out to be. So I just kept calling around, like I was an informant with something really tight.

I finally caught up with Ray in Federal Court on Foley Square. He'd spent the whole day waiting to testify, and at 5 P.M. the judge decided to grant the defense's request for a three-week delay.

I watched Ray's reaction as the defendant sauntered up the aisle, grinning and whispering to his attorney.

"Son-of-a-bitch, they're shopping for a judge," Ray said. "He's gonna have surgery like I'm going to have surgery. I know what I'd like to cut off this bum."

The defense had interrupted the trial to submit a medical report just delivered from a very well-paid doctor which declared that, on the basis of just-completed medical tests, the defendant must be admitted to the hospital immediately for some minor but essential surgery and some follow-up tests.

We watched from the courthouse steps as a uniformed chauffeur helped the heavyset defendant into the back seat of a tremendous black Mercedes.

"A 'Cuban freedom fighter,' Joe," Ray said bitterly. "He managed to 'liberate' about two million dollars from his gambling casinos and whorehouses, as a stake to start him off in his new country. Of course by now this guy handles more than twenty million untaxed dollars a year. And you know what we bagged him for, Joe? Tax violations. And he'll probably wind up paying a fine—also in untaxed dollars. And it won't mean a goddamn thing to him. He'll make it up on his next big shipment. Then he'll make a contribution to the Red Cross or the Cancer Foundation or the Heart Fund and get a lot of good publicity for the 'Cuban exile population.' "

Ray Ortega was born in Cuba and came to the States when he was about ten years old. There are generally three ways cops deal with "one of their own." You try to give the guy a break because after all he is one of your own; you treat him exactly like anyone else in the given circumstances; or you take an absolutely hard line and come down on the guy like the wrath of God because he's giving all the rest of you a bad name. Ray Ortega was the kind of cop who was death on any Cuban, Puerto Rican or Spanish-speaking lawbreaker.

We went to a "great" health-food restaurant that Ray recommended. He had just turned forty and was on a physical-fitness kick. He gave me a rundown on calories, carbohydrates, cholesterol, protein, fiber foods. He took a two-mile jog every morning; meditated for two twenty-minute sessions every day. He also said that he had guest privileges at a midtown health club; that he was swimming ten laps twice a week and was planning on taking up tennis.

I figured he'd either outgrow the whole thing or kill himself.

The food was lousy, but I figured it was unlikely that I'd run into anyone I knew digging into a bright-orange carrot soufflé or whatever the hell it was. Aside from Ray and me at one of the two tables, there were a couple of boys or girls or maybe one of each sex at the counter exchanging gloomy information with the owner-chef, a sad-eyed kid who looked like he weighed about twelve pounds. Instead of coffee, we were served big mugs of a lukewarm herb drink. Ray gulped down a handful of vitamin pills with his drink, but shook his head when I offered him mine.

"Moderation, Joe. Moderation in everything, that's the trick." He blotted his mouth on a napkin, then asked if I would mind not lighting up my cigarette. He pointed to a large sign on the wall, behind the counter: SMOKING IS DEATH. DO YOUR DYING SOMEWHERE ELSE.

"Cute."

"Okay, Joe. Tell me, what do you need?"

"First, right up front, this is off the books. Strictly on my own."

Ray nodded; a lot of guys moonlighted on unofficial assignments.

"In fact, I'm not even here, in the city. I'm about a thousand miles away soaking up the Florida sunshine."

"I got the message."

"I'm looking to talk to two guys. They deal coke in Jackson Heights, but it's not on a drug matter. They're potential witnesses in something not really drug-related."

I could see Ray's mind working: what the hell did I hear Joe Peters was on? But he kept his face absolutely expressionless. He nodded and took a small black notebook and a slim gold ballpoint from his pocket.

"Names?"

"One guy, probably about a third- or fourth-cut dealer, is Billy Weaver. The other guy, probably a pusher or a go-fer, I get as 'Benjamin the Cuban.' "

Ray didn't even write the names down. He didn't have to; which is why I came to Ray Ortega in the first place.

"I hope you don't need to talk to Billy Weaver real bad, Joe."

"Why, what's his problem?"

"He don't have any more problems, Joe. Not since about the third week in May when he floated to the surface of the Gowanus Canal, dragging a coupla concrete weights along with him. They were tied around his neck with a coupla strands of piano wire."

Kitty had told me that Billy Weaver needed help; that she'd promised to speak to Vince Martucci on his behalf. She hadn't known what the situation was, just that "Billy was a friend and he needed help and I promised to do what I could."

"What's the story on it, Ray? Or do you know?"

Ray shrugged. "Even if I didn't know, it wouldn't be hard to figure, Joe. Cocaine has become *the* drug of choice, therefore the most lucrative traffic around. It's been a South American and Cuban monopoly for a long time, with blacks not even in the middle levels until recently. A coupla black guys figure that by now they should be able to eliminate at least one or two middle-men. Some of their *compadres* agree, others don't. Those dealing with Billy Weaver apparently didn't agree he was ready for a step up."

It hadn't occurred to me that Billy Weaver was black; Kitty hadn't said, one way or the other.

"They don't kid around, the Cubans and the South Americans, Joe. It never comes down to a question of how to handle someone who might give you trouble. You eliminate trouble before it starts by getting rid of the troublemaker, or even the potential troublemaker. It beats fair-trade rules and regulations."

"Which leaves me 'Benjamin the Cuban.' Or does it?"

"He's around, as far as I know. He's a Puerto Rican who figures he'll do better as a Cuban in the trade. Benjamin Garcia Nelson. A young handsome guy, Joe. Pretty big with the ladies. It's very possible he set up Billy Weaver." Ray shrugged. "That's how it goes, you want to get ahead in the world, right?"

The kids at the counter and the skinny proprietor were having a tasting session. The two customers took bites of a sticky-looking dark cake and tried to guess what they were eating. When I pulled out some money to settle the bill, one of the kids held a dish up to me. "I guess honey and dates and something else. It's the something else I can't zero in on."

I was starving and the cake smelled delicious. It tasted delicious, and with my change the owner included a sticky slab of his "secret recipe."

"You see, Ray," the kid said, "I told you it's better not to tell people what the hell they're eating until after they have a chance to see if they like something or not, right?"

"What are they made of?" I asked. "What is this stuff?"

The kid shrugged. I kept chewing all the way to the parking lot, trying to pick out the ingredients. Whatever it was, it was really good.

"Where can I reach you, Joe, between midnight and, say, three A.M.?"

I gave Ray my home phone number. Then I asked Ray what the cakes were made of.

"Joe, it's a basically protein-rich blend of ingredients flavored with honey and dates. This combination might one day solve the world food crisis, but I have a feeling you'd better not ask where the protein comes from."

I swallowed what was in my mouth and tossed the rest of the cake into the gutter. "I have a feeling you're right."

•

The whole room was filled with the kind of fresh-country-air fragrance they tell you about in the shampoo commercials on television. Her hair was still slightly damp, and as she sat cross-legged on the couch opposite me Kitty pulled a heavy brush through the unbelievably thick whitish mass, methodically, in a steady practiced rhythm.

All I told her was that I was on my own time for a week or two, nothing else.

"I'm going to ask you something, Kitty, and I want a straight answer." Her hair flashed beneath her brush; it was very distracting. "Look, do you think you could cut that out for now?"

She looked startled, as though unaware of the automatic ritual. "Brushing my hair? Oh, I'm sorry, Joe. I *am* paying attention."

She held the brush in her hands and watched me closely.

"Kitty, who do you think killed the boys?" She shook her head and studied the hairbrush in her lap. "Look at me, Kitty." Her face was pale and she blinked rapidly, looking past me toward the wall. "Kitty?"

"I think I've known from the very beginning."

"*Known what?*"

She focused on me now and her voice was low but controlled and steady. "That George killed the boys. There was something about him, something. When you both came back to the apartment and he said . . . he said, 'They're dead, baby, both of them.' "

"Then why the hell haven't you said anything, all this time?"

"Who would have believed me? Would you?"

"How the hell could you have faced George, every day, been with him, every day, believing he killed the boys?"

There was a curious shift between us now; I was the one who was tense and uneasy. Kitty was strangely calm, studying me, trying to learn why it was so important for me to understand her.

"It's hard to explain. It's just . . . George. Look, I've spent a lifetime with him. From the time I was a little kid I've turned to George. We've had some bad times; I've given him some bad times."

"But for Christ's sake, Kitty, we're talking about the murder of your sons!"

She studied the hairbrush, absently untwined long blond strands of hair from the bristles. "Joe, he didn't *mean* to hurt the boys. He didn't *mean* to. It was something that happened; just the way he explained it in his letter. An accident with Georgie. And Terry: he was so deep asleep from the pills, George must have thought that he . . . that he'd done something to Terry too. Joe, can you imagine what it must have been like for George to live with this? To walk around, knowing what he'd done. Joe, you didn't know George, how he loved the boys, how he loved me."

"How he loved you enough to let you be dragged through the newspapers? Enough to let you be indicted?"

"George was suffering, Joe. He was in hell. It was my fault, what happened. It really was *my* fault. I've been so rotten to him. That night. That night I deliberately tied up the phone when I knew he'd try to call me back. I knew he'd keep trying. Only . . . I didn't know that he'd come over to the apartment."

"Or that he'd kill your sons? You didn't know he'd do that, did you, Kitty?"

She jumped up angrily. "My God, it wasn't like that—that he came over to hurt the boys, or me either. You read his letter. Can't you get inside his head for even one minute and feel what it must have been like for him? The minute he . . . he . . . hurt Georgie, can you imagine what he must have felt? I can imagine it, Joe. I can understand George's suffering. Look, maybe I needed to let it all happen to me: to be accused, to be written up in the papers like that. Maybe I had to . . . I don't know, suffer for my own sins. Maybe, maybe I had to let George feel he was protecting me, that he was the only one I could turn to. Maybe . . . I don't know, maybe that was all I had left to give to him and I felt I owed him that."

"I don't know what the hell you're talking about, Kitty."

That wasn't true; I think I did know, at least partially. But one of the things I was worried about was her attitude toward George. Now that he was dead, was she still going to try and protect him? The way she persisted in protecting Vincent Martucci? There were so many things I didn't know about her; things I would have to know, if I was going to help her.

"Kitty, come on. Sit down." She had that tough cynical, wise-guy look on her face; her eyes glared, her mouth tightened, her chin came up slightly. She raked her long fingers through her hair, tossed her head abruptly so that her hair flipped back toward her shoulders.

"Did George ever tell you he did it?"

She shook her head.

"Did you ever ask him if he did it?"

She shook her head again.

"In order to prove you didn't kill the boys, Kitty, it's going to be necessary to do two things: one, prove that George did it; two, prove that you didn't."

"I thought a person doesn't have to prove innocence. I thought the great American system says you're innocent until proved guilty. Another bunch of baloney, right, Joe?"

"You better believe it's another bunch of baloney. If you were to go on trial tomorrow, with the kind of publicity you've had, not to mention the fact that you've given your attorney nothing to work with . . ." Which reminded me of another important question. "Kitty, have you told any of this to Williams? What has ole Jaytee said about it?"

"About my being with Billy Weaver?" She shrugged. "I didn't bother to tell him anything."

"You didn't *bother* to tell him? Lady, you don't need a lawyer, you need a keeper!"

"Listen, do you think for one minute he gives a good goddamn if I killed the kids or if I didn't kill the kids? You want to know about Jaytee Williams? I'll tell you, Joe. To this day," she clenched a fist, "to this very minute, he hasn't asked me, not once, he hasn't asked me if I killed the kids, if I had anything to do with it. You know what he said? You want to hear good ole Jaytee's approach to the law? 'Why, it don't matter one little good goddamn, Miz Kitty, whether a person is guilty or innocent. Don't nobody on that jury really care one way or the other. What they want is to be convinced that the person on trial either *deserves* to go free or *deserves* to go to prison.' " She spoke in a biting imitation of the good-ole-Southern-boy drawl Williams used; she had caught his inflection and pace perfectly. She dropped it abruptly and said, "I'm very *convictable* right now, Joe. People want to convict me of *something*. After all, I haven't behaved the way 'people' think I should, the way a 'mother' should have reacted, so what the hell, convict Kitty of murder if that's the only charge you can come up with." Then, remembering what I'd asked her originally, "No, I haven't told Jaytee Williams about my leaving the kids alone and meeting Billy Weaver. What for?"

"Why didn't you tell Jaytee Williams that Vince Martucci is a homosexual?"

"What for? What would be the point?"

I just stared at her, wondering when she'd start thinking about her own situation.

"Damn it, Joe. Vincent is a *friend!*"

"A *friend?*" I turned my face away, then said in a quiet neutral voice, as though giving her information she didn't already have, "Kitty, Vincent Martucci is murdering you."

"He had no choice. You know that better than I do. You were a part of it!"

If things stayed at this level, there wasn't going to be very much accomplished. "Okay, okay." Then, more out of curiosity than anything else, "Kitty, have you ever been in touch with Marvin L. Schneiderman since you met him in the Bahama spa?"

"Who?"

"George carried the card he gave you in his wallet. You haven't forgotten Marvin L. Schneiderman, have you?"

"Of *course* I've forgotten him. Joe, what the hell good could he have done me? Sure, I've seen his picture in the papers; I've seen the election posters and ads. Look, I met him once; he was a nice guy. Can you just see the headlines if someone could connect his name with mine and—" She stopped speaking abruptly; then her eyes flashed with understanding. "Oh my God. I heard on the radio last night that he'd had a heart attack. That he had to drop out of the mayor's race. Is *that* why? Because a couple of years ago he gave me his business card, with an offer to help out in any way he could?"

It sounded very cold-blooded, the way she put it. In fact, it was very cold-blooded. It added to her opinion of the American system.

"You know, Joe, it would be funny if it wasn't so awful."

She spent the next few minutes worrying about Marvin L. Schneiderman. A few minutes earlier she'd been worrying about her dead husband and how bad he'd felt about murdering their two kids. Then she'd worried about her "friend" Vincent Martucci, who had betrayed her. I wondered who she'd start worrying about next.

"A couple more questions, Kitty, then we'll take a ride to Jackson Heights."

She sat down and watched me closely with a combination of suspicion and antagonism. She was making it very difficult to get some points on her side of the balance sheet—unless loyalty counted, in which case she'd score very high. However, it wasn't proof of her loyalty we needed. It was proof of her innocence.

"Kitty, did you ever tell George that you left the boys alone that night?"

She shook her head. "No. I was ashamed." She tried to judge how I received that. "Look, I was *ashamed*, can't you understand that? What kind of mother leaves two little kids alone, and one of them with the measles?"

Compared to a father who strangles his two kids and dumps their bodies in a lot and puts a bullet into one of them, it didn't seem like the worst thing in the world a mother could do.

"All right, next question. Why the hell did you insist you last saw the boys between one and one-thirty A.M. on the night they were killed?"

"Because I figured if I *had* been home with them, I *would* have checked on them at about that time."

"But you *weren't* home with them, Kitty. Why did you stick with that time even after the Medical Examiner's report stated they were probably both dead, or Georgie dead and Terry unconscious, by that time?"

I knew exactly what she was going to say. And she said it.

"Because everyone kept asking me was I sure, was I sure, was I sure it was between one and one-thirty and . . ."

"And you got mad at everyone and said, 'Yes, I'm sure.'"

"Well, what could I do at that point, Joe? Change my story? Say, 'Wait a minute, I was wrong, it wasn't that time after all'? Then everyone would know that I was lying!"

"But everyone *did* know you were lying."

"I didn't want everyone to know I'd left them alone, Joe. Can't you understand that?"

The funny thing is, as I was getting to know more and more about Kitty, in a way I did understand.

I drove her over to Fresh Meadows and from there to Jackson Heights. She thought it was stupid not to go directly to Jackson Heights from her new apartment, but since I was driving she didn't have much choice. All I asked of her was to stop fighting me, at least for an hour or so; to let herself go back to that April night, to remember sitting next to Benjamin the Cuban in his little green car. After about fifteen or twenty minutes of riding up and down the residential streets, which were a mix of four- and six-story apartment houses and two-story attached one-family homes, Kitty picked out the building.

I knew it was the right building because earlier in the day I had checked out the phone number Kitty used to contact Billy Weaver. It was registered to a woman who I assumed—according to her name—was related to the Puerto Rican Benjamin the Cuban. Probably his mother, who resided in the six-story tan brick building which Kitty indicated.

"Don't look at me, look out the window. Where did the car stop that night?"

"I don't know, Joe. I—"

"Look out the window, Kitty."

It was a one-way street, so they had had to approach it the way we were approaching it. She just shook her head. We went around the block once more, and as we approached the tan building slowly, Kitty jerked her head up.

"Right by those garbage cans, Joe. Stop right there. I remember because I had some trouble getting out of the car."

"All right, now face the side, look out the window. You got out of the car, right? You had to get around the garbage cans, right? Did he help you, the driver, did he come around the car and give you a hand or anything? Damn it, don't turn and look at me, Kitty." I pushed her shoulder toward the car door. "I wasn't there, you were."

"Joe, I don't remember, I don't remember. I got out of the car, and the garbage cans were there. I think they were there, I don't know. It was so long ago."

"Did he come around and offer you a hand around the garbage cans? Did you rub against them? Did you get garbage on you? Did you say anything to him about it? Did you—"

"Joe! Wait a minute, wait a minute! Don't say anything. Just wait a minute."

Kitty got out of the car. I slid over to her side of the front seat, watching. She walked over to the curb, edged her way along the collection of metal cans, then around them to the sidewalk. She stood there, straining, almost willing herself to remember something.

"Joe, oh my God, Joe!" Kitty jumped into the front seat and grabbed my arm. "Joe, there were some women. Two or three, I think. Dark clothes, Joe, you know, like . . . like Italian women wear, all dark, black like in mourning. He . . . Benjamin did come around the car, and he was . . . wait a minute, he was moving toward me like he was going to help me, and then there were those women and one of them started to say something to him. I don't know what, something angry, very angry. She was talking in Italian, I think. He just brushed her off and . . . and . . . he sort of grabbed my arm and rushed me toward the building, and the woman—my God, Joe, I remember, she said something to me, something like . . . Joe, she said, 'You better stay away from him miss, that guy's a bum. You ask my daughter, miss.'" Kitty's voice was excited. "I had forgotten all about it until now. But there were those women. And they saw me, Joe, they saw me."

Which was terrific. We now had witnesses to the fact that Kitty had come to this apartment building in Jackson Heights. All I had to do was find the women, question them, get them to remember the incident. And then get them to remember the date and time it happened. And then get them to agree to sign a sworn statement to that effect and agree to testify in court to what they'd signed.

I said to Kitty, "Well, it's a start." And then I drove her back to her apartment, left her at the door and went home to wait for a call from Ray Ortega.

A little after midnight, Ray called.

"Joe, you a Mets fan?"

"I'm a fair-weather Mets fan. I root for them only when they're winning."

"That's a lousy attitude, Joe. You don't deserve the terrific box seats for tomorrow's game."

CHAPTER 8

I arrived at the designated location in the Shea Stadium parking lot about fifteen minutes earlier than the time we'd set. So did Ray Ortega. He turned to the guy with him and must have told him to wait, then Ray came over to my Chevy.

"He's pretty nifty, isn't he, Joe?" We both studied Benjamin the Cuban. "Those threads are custom-made, three hundred and sixty bucks. And his shoes, they're custom-made half boots, two-fifty. And that's through a friend." We continued to consider him for a while until he finally reacted the way he was supposed to: he fidgeted, took a couple of quick drags on a newly lit cigarette, then tossed it away; looked around, trying to be nonchalant; tried not to look at us and was obviously wondering what the hell kind of information we were exchanging about him.

Ray handed me two box-seat tickets. "I'm going to catch the game, Joe. If you don't come in, give me a call at home tonight."

He jerked his head and Benjamin strolled over to be introduced. What I could see of his face, underneath his probably very expensive dark glasses, wasn't bad if you like swarthy, square-chinned, even features, full black mustache to match thick curly black hair, and a smile full of gleaming white teeth. Frankly, I'm sure it must be a pain in the ass at times to be Hollywood handsome, but that was his problem, not mine.

After Ray left, we settled in the front seat of my car, and when Benjamin took his glasses off I could see what he'd been hiding: very large, very black eyes. Without a word, I handed him a picture of Kitty Keeler. His eyes got even wider and he gave the picture back to me with the innocent protests of a priest being asked if he'd posed for an obscene picture.

"Hey, no way, man. I don't know this chick. Never saw her in my life." A fine sweat broke out on his otherwise cool forehead; probably over his mouth too, but you couldn't tell because of the mustache.

"She knows you, Benjamin." He kept shaking his head. "She says she does." Then I slipped it to him. "She says you helped her get rid of her kids' bodies."

His eyes opened so wide at that, it didn't seem possible. "Oh, hey, wow, man. Hey, wow." He continued his eloquent protest for a while, then finally said, "Jeez, all I ever did was to drive the lady to a meet with Billy that night; and then back to her apartment. Hey, man, I don't know nothing about her kids or anything at all like that. Hey, man, you can't lay something that heavy on me. Hey, you wanna know about me, you ask Ray Ortega. Ray knows me since I was a little kid, ya know?"

He dragged on the cigarette he'd just lit, started to cough, then threw the cigarette out the window.

"You don't really enjoy smoking, do you, Benjamin?"

When he finished coughing he said, "Hey, gee, I gave up butts last Thursday. Only I got nervous today and forgot."

"You got a couple of things to be nervous about, Benjamin. Tell me about that night when you picked the lady up and drove her over to her meet with Billy Weaver."

Billy Weaver had called him up; given him the lady's name and address; told him to pick her up and bring her to an apartment in Jackson Heights. Then, a couple of hours later, Billy told him to bring the lady back to Fresh Meadows. He did and that was it.

"Like the next day, I pick up the newspaper and there's this chick's picture on the front page and the story says her little kids was kidnapped and killed. The night before. Listen, I didn't see her kids; man, I didn't even know she had kids. I mean, I couldn't care less, ya know? I never even set foot in her apartment or nothin', just ducked into the hall, hit her bell, bam-bam-bam, and waited for her. Drove her to see Billy; drove her back. That's it."

I glanced at a slip of paper, then dropped it back into my notebook. "Who's Elena Garcia Gonzalez? Your mother?"

Benjamin's curly head shook with surprise. "Hey, listen, man, that's my grandmother, ya know? Why you askin' me about my grandmother? Hell, she's a little old lady, ya know?"

"And she runs a little old cutting factory in her apartment in Jackson Heights where you delivered Kitty Keeler to meet with Billy Weaver, right?"

"A factory? A factory, what factory? My grandmother and my mother and my little sisters, they all live together in the apartment and I get my messages there and sometimes, like, it's a convenient place for a meet, ya know. But factory? Man, I don't know what you mean."

"You know goddamn well what I mean. A 'factory' where a bunch of people sit around a long table and they wear white muslin masks so they don't inhale any of the cocaine they're busy cutting with powdered sugar or whatever the hell."

"Jesus," Benjamin told me, "that's a terrible thing to say. Like my grandmother, man, she's an old lady. Like she's about fifty-five, fifty-six years old, ya know?"

"That old? And she's still *alive*? That's terrific, Benjamin. That's something for you to aim for." I decided to drop the factory line; it had been a lucky guess; from his reaction, it had been an accurate one. It was not a far-out guess as to the occupation of the women members of a family involved in the coke traffic. It was more or less considered a cottage industry; kept the women off the streets and under each other's scrutiny.

Instead, I concentrated on the first obvious lie Benjamin had handed me; this way, he would think I already knew the answers to anything else I asked him.

"Take it over again, about how Billy called you. I think you skipped the first part, about who called who."

He thought about it for a minute or so; realized I knew that Kitty obviously had his grandmother's phone number; that she had called there asking for Billy Weaver.

"Well, yeah, sure. Like, Billy moves around a lot, ya know, and so he used my grandmother's phone number, like an answering service. See, we kept in close touch, me and Billy, so okay, the chick calls him at my grandmother's. And he just happens to be there that night. So I take the call, then hang up; then Billy calls the chick back, then he tells me to go out to Fresh Meadows and pick her up. That's it. Swear to God." He raised his right hand, taking a solemn oath.

We went over his story for a second and then a third time; a few more details were added, but nothing of value: as far as he knew, no one had seen him in Fresh Meadows that night, alone in his car or with Kitty Keeler in his car.

"Jeez, I didn't even want to go to Fresh Meadows in the first place. Like I tole Billy, I don't even know the neighborhood, ya know? I get out there, and it's like a housing project, only not skyscrapers, just a whole bunch of two- and three-story brick buildings. So they got trees and grass all around, big deal. To me, it still looked like an institution, ya know?"

"You have much trouble finding the right building?"

"Hey, listen, they don't have the house number lit up or nothin'. And everything is like in a circle, ya know? I'm drivin' around and around this damn place, I'm goin' in circles. I actually passed her building twice before I asked some guy—"

He stopped speaking. We stared at each other.

"Go ahead, Benjamin, you asked some guy . . ."

He showed me his beautiful white teeth. "That's funny, ya know. I just remembered that now. There was some guy out walkin' his dog and—"

"What kind of dog?"

"What kind of dog? Man, how the hell do I know what kind of dog? I don't know from dogs. I don't like dogs. Once I got bit by a dog when I was a kid and—"

"Benjamin, don't tell me about it. I don't want to hear about it. Tell me about the man with the dog that night in Fresh Meadows."

"Hey, man, there's nothin' to tell. I ask him where the number is, ya know, the chick's apartment house, and he tells me to go back around the way I just came, that I passed right by. So I circle around and he was right; so I hit her bell, bam-bam-bam, like I tole you, and she comes out and gets in and we drive away. And the guy with the dog says, 'Hey, you found it okay.'" Benjamin snapped his fingers. "Hey, that's right, the guy with the dog seen me, that I found the building okay."

"What did he look like, the guy with the dog? Was he tall? Short? Fat, skinny, what?"

"Ah hey, man, how should I know? Just a guy with a dog. The dog looked like a sheep dog, ya know? Wait a minute. Yeah, like a sheep dog."

"A sheep dog? The kind that rounds up sheep? Like a collie? Like Lassie? That kind of dog?"

Benjamin shook his head. "Nah, nah. A sheep dog, man, a *sheep* dog. Like the dog, it looked like a sheep. Curly, like it was a sheep. They got that kinda make of dog?"

"If you saw it, I guess they do."

He couldn't remember seeing anyone else out in Fresh Meadows; we moved on to Jackson Heights and then Benjamin became evasive.

"Naw, nobody seen us; we just got out of the car and up into the building is all."

I waited for a minute or so, then asked him, "What about the Italian lady?"

"Italian lady? What Italian lady?"

His eyes were just missing mine and he was digging another cigarette out of his pack.

"What the hell did you do to the Italian lady's daughter?"

Benjamin broke the cigarette between his fingers, but he didn't seem to notice. "What I'd do to her daughter? Hey, man. I mean, just look at me, huh?" He offered himself for my inspection and very rationally asked, "I mean, do I look like the kinda dude gotta *do* somethin' to some chick don't want it?"

I had to admit that he didn't.

"Look, man, I don't wanna sound like I'm, ya know, conceited or anything, but look, it's all out there just waitin' for me. All I gotta say is yeah, okay, to some chick." He snapped his fingers; it was that easy. "I mean, look at me. I got it *made* out there. My problem is selection, if you read me. I don't gotta go forcin' myself on some girl don't wanna make it with me." He shook his head, really distressed. "I'll tell ya, I learned somethin', ya know. That it don't pay to go around with any little Italian chick. Like they're not really *ready* for the sexual revolution, ya know? They want it, and then they get scared. Like that their old lady or old man is gonna find out; and they let something slip, and right away they want to make a big deal outa something that don't mean a thing, know what I mean? She was just a cute chick didn't know how to handle the whole thing. I mean, I'm asking you right out, do I look like the kind of guy is gonna bother some unwilling chick?"

He certainly didn't. I agreed with him that he was in a very difficult situation; a dude who looked like Benjamin really had to fight the chicks off.

"Hey, how did you know about her, the old woman, the Italian chick's mother?"

I let him sit and worry for a few minutes about how much I knew about him and where I got my information, then just shrugged and said, "You know how it is," which covers a lot of territory.

"Jeez," Benjamin said slowly, "yeah, I guess the old woman come at me that night. Not that I really remember, but for a while there, everywhere I went in the neighborhood, ya know, there was this chick's mother. Like, she sees me with another chick, right away she starts yellin' about how I go around ruinin' girls and all like that. I guess she come at me that night, when I brought this Keeler girl up to see Billy Weaver."

Very reluctantly, Benjamin gave the name of the woman—the irate Italian mother.

"How do you stand, with Billy Weaver being blown out of the picture, Benjamin? You stand to gain or are you looking over your shoulder or what?"

"Me? Stand to gain? Listen, I don't know nothing about nothing about nothing, ya know? I used to do some running for Billy is all; man, I don't want to touch any part of that trade. Too rough for my blood."

I reached over and fingered the material of his suit. Butter soft. "Nice threads. You don't pay for clothes like these running errands, Benjamin."

He shrugged. "Ah, you know how it is. A little a this, a little of that. Hey, you like this suit? I mean, tell me honestly, you think this is a *nice* suit? Like, some guy says to me the other day, like, this is the kind of suit a pimp wears. You think this looks like a pimp suit?"

It was obviously very important to him; he looked very sincerely concerned. I studied him carefully and shook my head. "No way; it's a very handsome suit, Benjamin. Pimps go for flash much more; this is a very nice suit."

Benjamin looked very pleased; obviously, the worst thing anyone could accuse him of was looking like a pimp. I took out the tickets for the box seats and offered them to Benjamin.

"No way, I don't go for this game at all. Not like soccer, ya know? I go for the action. Baseball, ya got a bunch of guys all standin' around like a bunch of old ladies, all they do is wait, wait for some action, and somebody hits a ball, bam-bam-bam, one-two-three, a coupla guys toss it around a few times and then everybody settles in again. Me, I like the action. Hey, look, you ever want to see Pele play, man, you give me a call. I get you the best seats and you can even meet the Man if you wanna; I got a few connections, like."

I told him that would be fine; I gave him my phone number and told him he could feel free to call any time of the day or night when he thought of something that might be helpful.

Just before he got out of my car, he said, "Hey, man, like you were puttin' me on when you said that chick said I drove around with her kids' bodies, right? I mean, that was just, like, your *technique*, right?"

I assured him that it was just my technique and he looked very relieved and didn't even glance over his shoulder as he walked to his bright-green Datsun and drove away.

CHAPTER 9

THAT evening, when I told Kitty about the recent demise of Billy Weaver, I anticipated her reaction.

"Oh my God, it's my fault that he was killed!"

Before she offered herself to a grand jury for indictment, I tried to convince her that whether or not she had relayed his request for protection to Vincent Martucci, the odds were all against Billy Weaver surviving for very long in the cocaine traffic. It was an industry with a very high, constantly escalating mortality rate.

"When was the last time you saw Billy, Kitty?"

"That night. That night, in Jackson Heights."

"You never talked to him after that? He ever call you? You ever call him?"

She shook her head.

"Another one of your 'good friends,' right, Kitty?"

"What do you mean by that?"

"Billy Weaver never got in touch with you after the boys were found? Seems to me that unless he was deaf, dumb, blind and living alone he must have heard about it. And he must have known that he was your alibi, that you'd spent crucial time with him the night of the murder."

"Billy was on the run, Joe. There were people out looking for him. Don't judge him; you didn't even know him. When we both worked at Mogliano's, we used to talk sometimes. God, he was from the South; the things that happened to him when he was a kid, just because he was black."

"Oh, then you do realize that Billy Weaver was black?"

It didn't come out the way I meant it; or maybe it did. She just kept staring at me, so I added, "It might have helped me if I had a more accurate description of him, Kitty. That's all I meant."

"Billy Weaver wasn't one of my lovers, Joe."

She could still slip me a surprise now and then. "I didn't ask you that, did I? That's none of my business, Kitty. I don't give a damn about who is or isn't or was or wasn't one of your lovers."

In that steady, positive voice, she said, "Yes, you do, Joe. It's almost the first thing you try to find out about anybody I know."

"It's nothing to me, Kitty. It doesn't concern me."

But, of course, it *was* something to me, it *did* concern me. The problem was that there was no valid, legitimate reason why it should.

Kitty put a platter of chicken sandwiches on the coffee table, then brought in mugs of hot coffee. We began to eat in that intense kind of concentrated silence that does wonders for the digestion.

Between bites I asked her, "You remember seeing a guy with a dog that looks like a sheep?"

She pulled back, instantly suspicious. I could see her turning the question over carefully, examining it for hidden meanings.

"Look, Benjamin the Cuban told me that the night he picked you up, he couldn't find your apartment building. Some guy with a dog that looked like a sheep directed him. Then, when you got into the car, the guy with the dog walked by and said something, like 'Oh, you found the right building'—something like that. Do you remember anything about it?"

She shook her head.

"Do you know anybody over in Fresh Meadows who has a dog that looks like a sheep?"

"I never heard of a dog that looks like a sheep."

"That's not what I asked you, damn it."

We were doing beautifully. However the hell it started, it was still on. She was fighting me every inch of the way, collecting points. I don't know what the hell she thought the prize was going to be.

"This doesn't make much sense, does it, Kitty? I'm beginning to wonder what I'm doing here."

She dropped her sandwich, leaned back on the couch, folded her arms across her body and said, "There's the door. *Good-bye.*"

I nodded; went toward the door, then stopped and just stood there, my back to her. Then I turned around, went to the couch, pulled her to her feet and started to shake her. This time, she was the one who was surprised.

"Damn it, Kitty, not with me. Don't pull this act with me. I thought you knew better by now. I thought we'd cleared that up."

I held her for a long time; it took a long time before she could stop crying for Billy Weaver. Grief tore through her body as she tensed against it, until she stopped fighting and just let it happen. Finally, when she pulled back, I saw a drop of blood on her lower lip; she'd bitten down that hard, trying to hold it all inside her, the way she had always handled her emotions.

I put the sandwiches in the refrigerator and made a cup of tea for Kitty. She ran a fingertip around the rim of the cup.

"Joe," she said softly, "I did what you asked me to do today. I sat with George's confession and I read it over and over, line by line."

I felt a little crackling at the back of my neck, like when a chill passes through you and the little hairs stand up. "Yeah, and what?"

She looked up from the tea. "I think I *might* know where George threw the gun. There was a special place in Flushing Meadow Park, where he used to take the boys fishing."

•

Flushing Meadow Park had twice been the site of a World's Fair: one in 1939, the second in 1968. Between these events, it had fallen into oblivion until it was activated as the temporary site of the U.N. General Assembly. When they relocated, the old 1939 New York City Building was converted into a roller-skating rink. After the second World's Fair, the city maintained the vast park area to accommodate a growing number of New Yorkers who were willing to travel to Queens to find some touch of nature.

There wasn't much action in the park: just a couple of early joggers, a couple of bicyclists. The baby carriages and ballplayers and mothers and grandmothers would come later in the day, when the hot spring sun had dried up the morning damp grass. There weren't any rowboats being rowed across the bare, open, uninviting lake, although some of them were in the water. Others, upended, were being repaired and painted by Park Department crews.

Kitty led me away from the boating area, across a field where model-airplane enthusiasts gathered on weekends, to the edge of a stagnant portion of the bay, inaccessible to the rowboats.

"George used to bring the boys here to fish, Joe. Not that they ever caught anything. A couple of times, George brought containers of those little fish, you know, minnows? And he'd set them free into the lake. Terry thought they'd grow up into big fish that he'd catch someday." She turned back toward the field we'd just come through. "He used to bring the kids here to watch them fly those model airplanes. Then, when they got restless, George would set them up over here to fish. He sort of told them that it was their own privately stocked lake."

They had gone, the four of them, on family outings a couple of times: watched the planes awhile, fished awhile, picnic-lunched. We walked around slowly while Kitty remembered. It was the first time I had ever heard her talk about her family life. She was very controlled, very subdued. We came to a spot concealed by shrubs and bushes, an expanse of rock which jutted like a ledge into the water. When she turned to me, I saw that she had gone chalk white.

"George used to tell the boys that this was their private country spot. He used to tell them that one day he'd build a little cabin right here, and that all the little fish would be grown big by then and they'd catch them and . . ."

She turned away abruptly and walked back to the clearing.

I picked up a few stones and skipped them over the water. Then I picked up heavier stones. I hefted them for weight, then threw them, one at a time, into the water.

I don't know if Kitty realized what I was doing. She didn't ask and I didn't tell her.

I drove her back to her apartment and told her I would be in touch.

·

I found an old telephone notebook in a box of junk my son had left at the apartment on one of his overnight visits, en route between Ann Arbor and upstate friends. His left-handed, slanty handwriting had never been easy to decipher. I seemed to remember that some kid he'd gone to high school with had been a skin-diving enthusiast, but I had no idea who it was.

I grabbed the phone on the second ring. "Hello."

There was a slight hesitation, then, "Joe?"

"Jen? Is that you? What's wrong, Jen, what's wrong?"

It wasn't a "scheduled" phone call and she sounded funny; strange.

"I don't know, Joe. Maybe you better tell me."

"Maybe *you* better tell me what we're talking about."

"All right, Joe. I will. About ten minutes ago, Tim Neary called. He wanted to talk to you."

Terrific. I had had absolutely no reason to think Tim would call me. Even so, I should have covered myself.

"I kept my head, Joe. Don't worry about it. I told him you had taken a drive out to the construction site of Fred's new project. Since I didn't know when I'd be able to reach you. Or *if*."

"I'm sorry, Jen. Damn, I should have called you. Look, I've caught a private investigation from Johnny Flynn. I didn't particularly want Tim to know I was moonlighting." Flynn was a retired cop who'd opened his own agency out in Suffolk County. From time to time, I'd done a few jobs for him. "I'm really sorry I put you on the spot."

"No problem, Joe. It just took me by surprise, that's all."

She really didn't sound angry; just a little annoyed. No questions, no explanations needed.

"Hey, Jen, do you remember which one of Mike's friends used to go skin-diving? I got Mike's old phone book here, but damned if I can remember which kid it was."

"I think it was Tommy Dawson, wasn't it? The redheaded boy?"

"Hey, I think you're right. Wait a minute. Yeah, I've got his home phone number. He's the kid got the scholarship to St. John's, right?"

"Yes, I think so."

"Great, that's fine. I need someone to do a little underwater search for me. For the investigation I'm on." No comment. "You know, I might be able to come down there for a few days at least, soon as I wind this thing up, okay?"

"That'll be nice, Joe. If you can fit it in."

I really didn't need this now; particularly knowing I was in the wrong. I pretended not to have picked up on the sound in her voice.

"Okay, listen, babe, thanks again. I *am* sorry, I shouldn't have left you in the lurch like that. You really came through and I appreciate it. Listen, I'll give you a call toward the end of the week, okay?"

"Fine. Oh. Don't call Friday, Joe. I'll be tied up for a long weekend. You better wait an hour or two before you call Tim. He only called here about twenty minutes or so ago. Good-bye, Joe."

She left me with that long, tied-up weekend. As punishment. Shit. Goddamn Tim Neary.

I called the Dawson kid's number and spoke to his mother. At first she reacted very emotionally, remembering I was a policeman.

"Oh my God, has something happened to Tommy?"

I assured her that nothing had happened to him; that he hadn't done anything to interest the law; that I just wanted to get some skin-diving hints from him before I went on vacation to Florida. She was very relieved and promised that her son would call me later in the day.

I hammered out a few pages of notes and spent an hour or so trying to bring some cohesiveness and sense to the last few days' work. I gave Tim until about two-thirty for his long lunch, then called the office.

"Joe, you sound like you were right around the corner."

I thanked God for long-distance dialing. "Well, it's not costing me 'from just around the corner.' What's doing, Tim? Jen told me you wanted to talk to me about something."

Tim had had a very strange phone call that morning from Jeremiah Kelleher during the course of which Gorgeous Jerry let Tim know that he had a contract to place a very bright, well-connected, inoffensive young Italian third-grade detective in the D.A.'s Squad. Jerry, always aware of the importance of ethnic balance in a squad, let it drop, not too subtly, that he wouldn't make any noise if Tim somehow got rid of that "guinea detective, what's-his-name-Catalano."

"Can you beat that, Joe? What do you think happened to make Jerry turn on Catalano?"

"What do *I* think? You're kidding, Tim. I don't understand any of the things you political guys get into. When are you planning to unload Catalano?"

"Soon, Joe; very soon. I have about ten valid reasons all lined up. It's a matter of how I go about it."

"Very skillfully, I'm sure."

"Well, tell me, kid, how're things going?"

I told him Jen and I were in the process of working things out.

"Good, terrific, that's what I wanted to hear. You getting much time out in the sun, lover?"

"You gonna keep checking on me like this, Tim? Want me to ring every hour, or send a report in every day, or what?"

"No, no. But no kidding, Joe, you're thinking about the future, right? Have you discussed 'anything,' you know, with Jen?"

Tim was being discreet; he was positive his phone was tapped and he was probably right.

"We're discussing a lot of things, Timmy. Listen, you going to want me again? Should I hang around the apartment and wait for your calls?"

Tim promised not to bother me again while I was on vacation. He would hold all the details of his next move until I was back.

Tommy Dawson returned my call that evening. He checked his class schedule. He was free any time until twelve-thirty for the rest of the week.

At the St. John's student parking lot the next morning, Tommy Dawson transferred his skin-diving equipment from his VW to my Chevy. We drove over to Flushing Meadow Park and I parked on the service road of Grand Central Parkway. There was still an early-morning chill in the air, which was fine. We could do without an audience.

It's amazing how much difference a year makes. Last spring, when Tommy and Mike graduated from high school, they were both un-formed, gawky eighteen-year-olds. Tommy had had short, tightly curled red hair with hardly a sprinkle of beard showing through his freckles. Now, at nineteen, with one year of prelaw under his belt, Tommy had a wild mop of shaggy red hair and a really good, strong bright-orange beard which hid all the freckles. His voice had deepened and he listened closely with a sharp intelligence when I told him what he would be diving for.

"I get the feeling that this is between the two of us, Mr. Peters?"

"Right. For the time being." Then, answering the question in his narrowing reddish-brown eyes, "Absolutely nothing illegal involved, Tom. Just a little follow-up of an old case on my own time; which means this whole thing, whatever we might come up with, is just between the two of us for now."

He pulled his jeans off, then his sweatshirt, and got into his wet suit. The rock ledge, "George's private spot," gave a complete privacy which wasn't strictly necessary now, since there weren't any people around, at least not in this area. However, just to be on the safe side, since a crowd can materialize in about four seconds flat, particularly when you don't want a crowd to materialize, I gave Tom our cover story.

He was diving to try to recover a model airplane which had crashed and disappeared in this murky water last weekend. Just in case anyone asked.

It was a needle-in-the-haystack situation; I wasn't even hoping for anything, so I wouldn't be too disappointed if we came up dry. Tommy Dawson thought that was pretty funny; as soon as he laughed that cackling, high-pitched laugh, I could see last year's skinny, pale, clean-shaven adolescent.

I picked up a couple of heavy rocks and stood on the stone ledge and tossed straight out as far as I could without too much effort, then as far as I could when trying for distance. There was about a twenty-foot span between the two spots; not to mention the area covered by the possible arc: George could have thrown in any direction. We were just starting with straight out.

Tom got to the first wave of ripples, adjusted his mask and air hose, waved, then disappeared. About four or five minutes later, he broke through the surface, holding aloft a broken model airplane.

"In case we need a cover story, Mr. Peters. I'll set it down right here, then if we need it I'll know where it is."

We didn't need it. No more than ten minutes later, Tom shot up to the surface and began to nod his head up and down. He held something up over his head and got a mouthful of water when he yelled, "I got it, Joe, I think I got it!"

He handled it by the barrel and carefully inserted the gun into the heavy plastic bag I had brought along.

"That what we're looking for Mr. Peters?" He watched me closely, not too sure of my reaction.

"I'll tell you, Tom. I'm so damn used to things being hard, I'm a little uncomfortable when something comes as easy as this."

My diver went back into the water to retrieve the model airplane. It was in terrible condition, but he thought he might be able to salvage the engine, or at least parts of it. While Tommy changed his clothes, I prepared a statement for his signature.

His beard was still dripping as he carefully read what I had prepared: a simple acknowledgment that on this date, at this time and in this location, he, the undersigned, did in the presence of Det. Joseph Peters, Shield #4513, retrieve subject gun from beneath the water at said location.

"Do we have anything to mark the gun with, Mr. Peters?"

"No, I didn't think of that. Frankly, I didn't think we'd have any need to mark anything. Guess you'll have to trust me that this will at all times remain the gun in question. Like it says, thirty-eight-caliber Colt; five bullets in the chamber; one empty chamber. Go ahead, take a good long look at the gun, Tom."

I carefully slid the gun from the plastic bag, rested it on the towel the kid had brought along for his wet hair. He studied it thoughtfully and glanced up at me from time to time. Then he took the statement and read it again.

"I might have to testify in a case, about finding this gun?"

I had the damnedest feeling that this kid thought he'd been set up. There was nothing adolescent about the suspicion in his eyes or in the reluctance to commit himself to something without knowing exactly what it was. This was a very admirable attitude, but it was also a pain in the ass.

"This is a gun that may or may not be involved in a homicide, Tom. Working on information received," he didn't bat an eye at the jargon, just watched me closely, "I determined the possibility that the weapon in question might be located just about where you *did* locate it. Until I run some ballistic tests, I have no way of knowing whether or not this is the gun I'm looking for. Which is why, at this point, I want to keep the whole thing just between you and me. If it *is* the gun in question, there is a very strong possibility that you'll be called on to testify; to verify exactly what we did here today. If you're not happy with the statement I jotted down, you prepare your own statement. It would probably be better that way, anyhow."

He thought that over and nodded. "I'd rather do that, Mr. Peters. I could bring it over to you tonight, or tomorrow. Will that be all right?"

I wondered which law professor he wanted to check with; he jotted down my address and agreed to send his statement to me. When I handed him the twenty-dollar bill we had agreed on before we started, he was reluctant to take it for only a half hour's work.

"Look, if it had taken you twenty hours, the price still would have been the twenty we agreed on."

He thought that was valid. I dropped him back at the St. John's University parking lot; we shook hands solemnly and I'm not too sure what the long searching look was supposed to discover, but I do know that, if needed, Tom Dawson would be one hell of a witness.

I'm not sure of the basis of suspicion on the part of a nineteen-year-old with little or no experience of the world, but I do know what was making me uneasy. After nearly twenty years on the job, there are certain truths: the witness you have to interview never lives on the first floor of a walk-up building, it is always the top floor; if there is a stack of fifty records containing the one important piece of information, it will be found in the forty-eighth or forty-ninth, never in the first ten or twenty; if you restrain and try to subdue some nut who is beating hell out of his wife, said wife will immediately grab the first thing handy and try to beat the hell out of you for interfering.

I'm sure somewhere in the world it is taken for granted that you'll be successful at whatever you attempt the first time out. It was a new experience for me and it seemed too damn easy.

I went down to a gunshop in lower Manhattan, waited until a couple of customers left, then asked the owner of the shop if he'd set up a test fire box for me. He had a small shooting range in the basement, and while he prepared the heavy lead box with batting material I dusted the Colt for fingerprints. Nothing; a bunch of smudges, not even partially usable. I slipped one of the bullets I had removed back into a chamber and fired it off. Considering that I hadn't done anything more than dry the gun, I was a little surprised that it fired. I wrapped the retrieved spent bullet in a tissue, gave the storeowner five dollars for a three-dollar notebook and told him we were even.

I called the Police Lab and found out that my friend, Harry Sullivan, was on a day off. He'd be working an 8-A.M.-to-4-P.M. the next day.

Then I went back to my apartment; called Kitty, told her there was nothing new and that she might not hear from me for a couple of days, but I was out there, working.

Then I called Benjamin the Cuban, who reluctantly agreed to meet with me later that night; then I ate some cottage cheese, drank some milk and caught a few hours' sleep. I'd be out late and needed something to fall back on.

CHAPTER 10

I parked alongside the garbage cans in front of Benjamin the Cuban's apartment building. There were only a few cars still parked on that side of the street. If they didn't relocate by eight o'clock the next morning, they'd be hit with a stiff alternate-side-of-the-street-parking fine.

Benjamin looked almost like a stage prop: he leaned languidly against a lamppost, his long legs stretched out to show off his handsome leather boots with the high heels. An unlighted king-size cigarette dangled from his lips. During the next forty-five minutes, Benjamin worried that cigarette to shreds. When he saw the group of women approaching, he tossed it away, pulled out a fresh cigarette, lit it and inhaled practically to the soles of his feet.

"I'll give them up completely by tomorrow," he told me, sucking in the smoke for courage as the seven or eight women moved toward us.

They were accompanied by two tall skinny boys from St. Anthony's High School. It was the only way the church could continue its twice-weekly bingo games: by providing escort service at the end of each evening of play.

I had to jab Benjamin twice before he reacted. His voice sounded very thin and shaky. "Hey, Mrs. Deluca. Mrs. Deluca, could I see ya for a minute? Please?"

The whole group of women stopped, turned, gave us coordinated, expert once-overs with sharp dark eyes. Most of them were dressed in nondescript black clothing; their faces, in the dim street light, were uniformly suspicious and wary and tough, mouths were tightened into readiness as they moved in a body toward us, their shoulders and arms touching, forming a solid mass. The two kid bodyguards were shoved to the rear of the group, a fact for which they seemed grateful.

"Who is that?" a shrewd, rough voice called out. "Is that that little bum, Benjamin?"

It took me a good five minutes to convince the ladies that everything was all right. That I was a police officer; that I wanted to discuss some unimportant matter with Mrs. Deluca and that I would personally escort her to her apartment when we finished talking. The whole thing was settled when Mrs. Deluca promised to tell everyone what it was all about the next morning when they met at the market.

Mrs. Deluca and her sister, Mrs. Romero, waited impatiently and skeptically, glaring with hard eyes at Benjamin, anxious to hear what trouble he was in.

"Mrs. Deluca, you've heard about the young mother who is accused of killing her two little boys? Mrs. Kitty Keeler?"

Mrs. Deluca's right hand shot up to cover her mouth; her black pocketbook dangled against her body. Her eyes flashed to her sister.

"You see, Lucy, you see? I told you it was the same girl. I told you, didn't I?" She leaned around me, trying to see Benjamin. "This one, this little bum, was he involved?"

I assured her that Benjamin was not involved; that I just wanted to know if she remembered something that Benjamin had told me about that night.

She remembered in detail. She had seen the little bum with a pretty young woman one night as she was coming home from the games. It was later than usual because she had stopped off at a friend's house to pick up some embroidery thread. She reenacted how she had come along, seen Benjamin with this young woman. She remembered what she had said to him; and that she had called to the young woman, who had rushed into the apartment hallway.

"That bum is no good, I told her. Ask my daughter, she'll tell you about Benjamin, I told her." She stopped and nodded at her sister. "It was the woman. The woman in the newspapers. Because the next morning, I met him, this bum, and before I could ask him if he had ruined another girl, like he did my daughter, he showed me the picture in the *News* and he said it was the same girl. He said her children had been murdered and I took the newspaper right upstairs to my sister, and I showed her the picture." The sister nodded. "And I told her, 'Lucy, I seen her, this girl, the mother, last night, with this bum, Benjamin.'"

The sister said, "I didn't believe her, but we went anyway to the church and lit candles for the poor children." She crossed herself.

Mrs. Deluca was the kind of woman who would remember any unusual event in her life down to the smallest detail. There weren't many unusual events to clutter up her memory, so she hung on to the ones she had. She might not have remembered this girl at all, she said, if Benjamin hadn't shown her the picture the next day.

Did she know that Kitty Keeler had been accused of killing her children?

Yes, she knew this; but it was crazy. No mother could ever kill her own child.

Did she know that Kitty Keeler was accused of killing the children at about the time she was here, on this street in Jackson Heights, and therefore couldn't have been killing them in Fresh Meadows?

Mrs. Deluca looked at her sister, then back to me, and said, "See? I told you no mother could ever kill her own child."

Had she mentioned the fact that she had seen this woman on that night? To anyone beside her sister?

"Just to my sister. Nobody else. Nobody asked me nothing until just now, when you did. I mind my business. I don't get involved in other people's business."

I escorted the sisters to their building and up the three flights of stairs to their apartments: one lived in 3-A, the other in 3-B. I told Mrs. Deluca that I would type up what she had told me, with a confirming paragraph for her sister, then bring the statement over for them to sign. She nodded and said sure, as long as she would not be involved.

Keeler's Korner was closed up tight by the time I pulled into the parking space behind the building. Danny Fitzmartin had told me that he had taken to closing earlier and earlier, the way business had fallen off. He couldn't even afford the Irish singers more than once a week and they had kept business high. It was a vicious circle, Danny said. I sat in the car for a few minutes and jotted down the important points that Mrs. Deluca had mentioned.

At exactly two o'clock, I pulled out of the lot and drove at a moderate to fast speed over to Fresh Meadows. It took about twelve minutes from the pub lot to the Keelers' parking space. I sat and smoked for a while, allowing the time that George had indicated in his confession it had taken him to quietly enter his apartment, listen to Kitty on the phone, enter the boys' bedroom, pick up little Georgie, "quiet" him, pick up Terry, who was in a deep sleep, slip out of the apartment, back to the parking lot, put the boys into the back seat of his station wagon and head back to the pub.

In just about thirty-seven minutes, I was back at the lot behind Keeler's building.

When I got back to my apartment, I typed up Mrs. Deluca's statement, along with her sister's confirming remarks; then wrote up the result of my test run from Sunnyside to Fresh Meadows and back. I set the alarm clock for seven and fell asleep dreaming of black-clad Italian ladies with beautiful faces; they all looked like the Madonna of Forest Hills.

In my dream.

CHAPTER 11

HARRY SULLIVAN was the kind of guy who people said didn't look like a cop. Which had been one of his greatest assets when he had done undercover work. Until someone figured out that despite his skinny, concave build, pale complexion, soft manner of speaking and squinting eyes behind heavy glasses, he was a cop. At which point, what was left of Harry was found in some bad alley in Brooklyn. He survived a total of eight bullets and one broken leg. It was the broken leg that nearly put him out of the department on disability pay, until he convinced the brass he could still be of value as a lab technician, limp and all.

I stopped by the lab at twelve-thirty, which was when Harry's partner was out to lunch. When I handed over the .38 bullet and asked him to run a comparison check with the Keeler murder bullet, Harry didn't raise an eyebrow or bat an eye. He just set to work, humming a flat whining sound which never changed all the time he studied the two bullets and jotted down his findings on a note pad.

He took off his glasses and polished them with a tissue and said, "Of course, this isn't definitive, Joe. You know that'll take a while. But, as a working hypothesis, we've got a match here."

When I handed him the plastic bag with the retrieved revolver in it, before he touched it he asked if it had been dusted. Then he took the gun out and laid it on his worktable. There were a couple of tests I wanted run and Harry assured me he'd let me know in a day or two what he'd determined.

Harry agreed to keep the test bullet and the gun in safekeeping under a dummy file number which could not, at this time, be connected with the Keeler murder bullet. All he asked me was, "I'm not going to be stuck with a murder weapon for an indefinite length of time, am I, Joe?"

I assured him that would not be the case; either I would ask for it by file number in the future or someone authorized by me would ask for it.

While we were talking it over, an excited young uniformed cop came into the lab.

"Hey, Harry, ya know what just come over the ticker? That Mafioso, Vincent Martucci. He just got hit in Forest Hills. Him and his chauffeur."

•

Sometimes, not often, but sometimes, I feel a little guilty about being such a good liar. But then I soothe my conscience by reminding myself that this ability saves a lot of long-drawn-out explanations and trouble. When I arrived in Forest Hills Gardens, all I told Tim Neary was that I had flown back from Miami last night. That things were not so great between Jen and me. Which was true; that part of it anyway. Since Tim had other things to worry about at that moment, he didn't have any questions. Just a quick sympathetic hand on my shoulder.

The scene in the Martucci kitchen was pretty bad. Vincent and his chauffeur, William "Willie" Donato, had been sitting down to a lunch of scrambled eggs and peppers. The thick bright-red stuff all over the food wasn't ketchup. Vince, who apparently had been seated with his back to the outside kitchen door, must have fallen face down into his plate of food before hitting the floor. There were globs of egg stuck in his eyebrows. A long thin fried pepper was pasted on his forehead like an Indian woman's jewel.

There were golf clubs in an expensive leather golf bag leaning against a kitchen counter. It was learned that the two men had been out early in the morning and had played eighteen holes at Martucci's exclusive club in Manhasset.

It was a cinch we'd never run down who had monitored Martucci's whereabouts, but you had to admit, the job was well done. It was Mrs. Martucci's "volunteer day" at a hospital on Long Island; the Martucci children were at school; the Martucci maid was on a day off. By rough estimate, there were a minimum of four hit men. It was well coordinated and they knew exactly what they were doing. The front door was riddled—probably at the same time that the kitchen door was blasted open. The two Martucci Doberman attack dogs had been stationed in the front entry hall. That was where they were found: beautiful, sleek and dead.

Assistant District Attorney Edward M-for-Martin Quibro appeared on the scene about a half hour after I arrived. He had to be physically restrained from grabbing and touching possible evidence. He was a menace at a crime scene. He was determined to impress the importance of the catastrophe on us.

"My God," he told us, "this man was the whole Keeler case. I had it all sewn up. This couldn't have happened at a worse possible time. How the hell could you people have let this happen, Neary?"

Tim stared straight over Quibro's neatly combed head, then suddenly shoved him with a good forearm blow. Quibro went flying into a wall; before he could slide down to the floor, Tim was at his side, yanking at an arm, asking if he was all right.

"Jeez, Ed, you almost stepped in that puddle of blood. You wouldn't want to get all that mess on your nice shiny shoes, would you?"

Tim went over to one of the squad guys and said, "Get that little bastard the hell outa here."

It was a couple of hours before the two bodies could be removed. Just as the mortuary ambulance was leaving, Mrs. Martucci pulled into the driveway and parked her Mercedes behind a squad car. I intercepted her as she was about to enter through the kitchen. It was still pretty messy.

"What's happened?" she asked quietly.

I told her. Then I walked her around to the front hall. The dogs were still there, but they were covered over. She stopped for a moment, gracefully bent down, lifted the canvas covering. Then she let it drop. She turned and said to me, "I never liked these animals. Too large. Unpleasant personal habits."

Mrs. Martucci offered some brandy to Tim and me; we both declined and watched as she poured some for herself, settled gracefully on the center of a small velvet couch. With an elegant, gracious gesture, she directed us into chairs facing her.

I could see Tim's reaction to her beauty; he hadn't seen her before. She waited for us. She apparently had no questions of her own.

"Mrs. Martucci, what time will your daughters be home from school?"

She ran a fingertip around the edge of her glass and said, "Normally, they would be home at three o'clock." She checked her watch. "Just about now. But they have been invited to spend the weekend at a schoolmate's home." She paused and her cool stare seemed to dare me to question the arrangement. "This appointment," she explained, unasked, "was made several weeks ago."

"And is Friday your maid's regular day off?"

"No. Her mother has been ill for the past month. So I have permitted Pearl, that is the maid, to take off Fridays and Saturdays to tend to her mother, who lives in Brooklyn. The other days of the week are divided up amongst Pearl's sisters. Jamaicans are very devoted to their family."

"And do you do volunteer work at the hospital every Friday, Mrs. Martucci, or was it just *this* Friday?"

Her mouth turned up slightly in the corners; cool, controlled amusement. "Every Friday. I live a well-regulated life."

"And what about your husband? Did he go golfing every Friday? Did he follow a well-regulated schedule in his life?"

I could sense Tim's reaction to all this; he glanced at me, then back at the woman, trying to figure out what the hell was going on. Everything we had said, back and forth, had the light baiting tone of people who said one thing in words, another thing beneath the words.

"Vincent did whatever he chose to do; whenever he chose to do it. He never confided his plans to me."

She had nothing further to offer us. She did not know her husband's friends; she did not know her husband's enemies. She knew little of his business or his business connections. She supposed there must be many people who wanted him dead. And probably many others who wanted him alive.

"How about you, Mrs. Martucci?"

Her fingers spread around her brandy glass, and her dark eyes quickly checked out Tim, then came back to me. With a very slight movement of her shoulders, she gave her answer: one way or the other, what was the difference?

She decided she would go to her sister's home for the next few days; until "things" were decided.

She went to the leather-topped desk and on a heavy cream-colored piece of notepaper with her name engraved on it she wrote out her sister's address and phone number. When she held it out, offering it to me, I reached for it. She didn't release it immediately: it formed a connection between us.

She said softly, her eyes fastened on my lips, her tongue flicking to the corners of her mouth, "It does not really matter to me; any of this. It is all the same. He was of absolutely *no use* to me. And I am a woman of many needs." She smiled and released the slip of paper. "I shall be at that location. If you should *want* me."

She led the way to the front door; Tim gave me his impressed hey-what-goes-on-here look. I winked at him and shrugged.

The late *New York Post* headline read: KEY KEELER WITNESS KILLED. I couldn't wait to see the headline on the early edition of the *News*.

Jeremiah Kelleher generously provided one of the smaller courtrooms for a meeting of all concerned: Homicide Squad members, D.A.'s

Squad members, Paul Sutro and a couple of his fellow crime-family specialists.

Jerry opened the meeting by informing Captain Chris Wise of Homicide that he was to feel free to call upon the services of the office of the Queens District Attorney and his staff at any time, in any capacity, to assist in his handling of this homicide. Which was a very nice way of telling Wise it was all his.

Chris Wise, in a very reasonable voice, under the circumstances, asked a very reasonable question. "I would like to know why the fuck this sitting duck of a dummy was walking around without some protection?"

Edward Martin Quibro jumped right in. "It was the job of the District Attorney's office to obtain an indictment in the Keeler case. Which we did. The witness was under protective surveillance for several weeks both before and after his appearance before the grand jury, and this surveillance was called off at the insistence of the deceased. Issued through his attorney."

Chris Wise stared at Quibro blankly. Then he said, "I would like to know why the fuck this sitting duck of a dummy was walking around without some protection?"

I sat on one of the polished courtroom benches next to Tim Neary, who kept tapping his ballpoint pen on his notebook in time with whatever the hell he was whistling through his slightly parted lips. It was not his near-losing-control whistle. It was more his what's-all-this-to-do-with-me.

I leaned close to Tim. "Timmy, just between the two of us, how come you didn't continue a surreptitious surveillance on Martucci?"

Tim looked around quickly, then winked at me and pulled his mouth down with the grimace of a ten-year-old admitting he hadn't done his homework. "Jeez, Joe, with all the other stuff that's been going on," he winked, "you know, I just forgot to assign anyone."

Jerry Kelleher, who had positioned himself in front of the judge's bench, quietly made his exit in the middle of a very heated exchange between Quibro and Wise, set off by Paul Sutro's charts, which revealed that any one of approximately thirty crime-family members would benefit by the demise of Vincent Martucci.

Kelleher stopped for a moment, nodded at Tim and said, serenely, "Keep the faith, Timmy."

"You bet," Timmy answered.

The Keeler case was no longer the responsibility of either one of them. The primary was little more than a week away and Jerry Kelleher was running unopposed. He would undoubtedly become the next

Mayor of the City of New York. In which case, Tim Neary would be our next Police Commissioner.

It was Edward M. Quibro who was now on the line. He was an unknown who needed the satisfactory windup of the Keeler case to recommend him to the voters come November. Dropping charges against Kitty Keeler would hardly be considered a satisfactory windup by the voting public. Without Martucci, Quibro's case was all circumstantial, to say the least.

After about an hour more of buck passing and senseless speculation, Chris Wise picked his hat up off the counsel's table, planted it firmly on his head and announced to anyone who cared to do anything about it, "I'm not saying one more fucking word until this fucking jackass gets the hell outa this room."

At which point Tim Neary and I assisted Quibro from the courtroom with assurances that he would be kept posted on the entire situation. Tim couldn't help saying, "After all, Ed, we all realize how much you have riding on this case."

We watched Quibro hustle down the hall, buckling the straps of his briefcase as he went.

Paul Sutro was waiting for us in Tim's office. He was settled comfortably on Tim's couch, everything about him relaxed and easy. Everything except his large, dark, hooded eyes. It must have been a trick of the lighting, the way certain shadows fell on his large strong profile, or the way he held himself, but Paul Sutro could have modeled for one of those marble heads of a Roman emperor. His fringe of black hair fitted him like a wreath. He was a living encyclopedia on the structure and machinations of organized crime. He collected bits and pieces of information the way other guys collect rare, exotic stamps, and he displayed his treasures with the same kind of reverence and respect. The word was that Sutro was writing a book; the odds were that he wouldn't live long enough to see it published, but my money was on Paul. He seemed to be the exception to the "rule of silence." People talked to Paul. For their own reasons, of course. But he had a way of finding out more than people thought they were telling him.

"Well, what's the inside word, Paul? Was Vinnie's hit the start of something or the end of something? Or did somebody just do Kitty Keeler a big favor, or what?"

"Well, obviously the hit was the end of *Vinnie*," he told us, "but the word is that it's the *start* of something a helluva lot bigger than Vincent Martucci. We're going to see some blood in the streets before things settle down, Tim."

"You don't mean that someone's gonna avenge Martucci, do you?"

Sutro shook his head and rubbed his eyes. "No, Tim, no. Vincent was dead the day it was known that he testified before the grand jury. No one argues with that. And not because of Kitty Keeler. Actually, she has very little to do with it. It was the fact of his having testified at all; about anything, anyone. You don't do that and live. The word out was that he and Kitty had a falling out, a lover's quarrel, and he testified against her because of it. But no matter what the reason, the fact is the same: he broke the silence. Now, a man who does that once might as well do it again; what the hell has he got to lose at that point?"

"What about Keeler's accomplice?" Tim asked. "Couldn't this Mister X, Y or Z or whatever the hell have blasted Vincent for his own protection?"

"Anything's possible, Tim, but it's unlikely. Very unlikely. There are too many things moving behind the scenes. A few nights ago, Alfredo Veronne held a meeting with his sons. A kind of 'passing of the crown'; there are going to be power moves, shifts, a reorganization in the East Coast 'family.' A certain number of *resignations*—by execution, disappearance, 'industrial accidents'—like someone getting mixed in with the concrete foundation of a new building. That sort of thing."

"Wait a minute, Paul." I was puzzled. "Wadda ya mean, Veronne is passing the crown now? I saw Veronne what? six, seven weeks ago, and he looked to me like he'd been out of touch with things for a long time. I mean, the man was barely alive."

"He's been alive, Joe. And he's been the controlling force of this part of the organization right up until a few days ago. He's been ruling, quietly, from his bed, Joe." Paul tapped his forehead. "He's a Machiavellian, Joe; brain like a devious computer. Feed in the information, spell out the problem, and click-click-click, out come ten different solutions, each one viable. He's one of a kind, Joe. None of the other old-timers really understand any of the changes needed in the modern world. The only one to understand and appreciate the various power structures and methods of modern business has been Veronne. He was the only really farsighted one; he prepared his sons for the modern organization. Two of them have law degrees; two of them have master's in business administration. The other old-timers, it was all one big bucket of blood with money as the prize. Only Veronne was sophisticated enough, with a rare native intelligence, to understand the overlapping of the old organization into various areas of legitimate industry and government. A very remarkable man."

"Then who the hell's going to do all the killing you mentioned, Paul?"

"Oh, there are still gunsels around, Tim. There always will be. For the lower-level troops; sets a good example. Keeps everyone 'honest,' all the way up through organizational ranks. Vincent Martucci's hit was an object lesson. A reminder that at the basis of the new structure are the old rules."

"So you don't think Martucci was hit on Keeler's behalf?"

Paul shrugged. "Some people win, some people lose. I think this time Keeler just happened to luck out. That's the way it goes."

Tim leaned back and locked his fingers over his chest. "Well, how about that, Joe? The little lady's luck has changed at last." Still looking at me across the desk, he said to Paul, "Joe here has spent sleepless nights worrying about Keeler. About how we might be railroading an innocent girl."

"I never said she was innocent, Tim. I just never thought she was guilty."

"Same thing," Tim said complacently.

"You know something, Paul? It's a good thing that Tim took all the examinations that came along. He's got the perfect mentality for civil-service exams. One right answer per question. Miss X does so-and-so, therefore Miss X is (a) good; (b) bad. It's not like that in real life, Tim. There are a lot of in-betweens between (a) good; (b) bad."

"All comes down to the same thing in the end, Joe," Tim said. "On the one hand ya got good; on the other hand ya got bad."

"That's a simplistic view, Tim, of a complicated philosophical question: good–bad. Depends on where you sit, what your point of view is, what your vantage point at the moment might be." Sutro talks that way a lot; people are used to him.

"Bullshit," Tim said simply, with the same conviction he had expressed at eighteen, when I once tried to explain to him that the difference between a "good" girl and a "bad" girl might be circumstance and opportunity rather than inherent evil.

"Well, I'll tell you something interesting, Timmy," Paul said in his slow, comfortable, unflappable way. "The word I got on Kitty Keeler in all this time has been that Keeler is a 'good kid.' I haven't run into one bad word about her."

"What the hell is the definition of a 'good kid' to the people we're talking about, Paul? A girl who'll take twenty without a squawk when she's been promised twenty-five?"

I tried not to let the growing tension show; tried to lean back, listen politely, not let any of it get to me. It was very difficult; Tim's expression was so damn smug and amused.

"No, no, nothing like that, Tim." Paul leaned forward and looked from Tim to me, like a teacher including both of his students in the lesson. "There's a lot of *respect* for Kitty Keeler out there. She's a very bright girl. They respect that, brains. The world Keeler runs in is not exactly an equal-opportunity employer. These guys usually think of a woman only as a sex object, nothing else."

"Well, what the hell else would you call Keeler? Jesus, she said so herself, Paul. When was it, the first week of the investigation, some reporter from the *News* asked her, 'Hey, Kitty, how many of those guys in your little pink book are your lovers?' You remember what she said, don't you, Joe? She said something like 'Go eenie, meenie, miney, mo and you got it!'"

"I'll tell you something interesting, Tim. Keeler's the only one who's claimed any of these men were her lovers."

"Oh, hell, I'm sure according to the guys in the book, Keeler got the wrong man listed. Who the hell wants to cop out to sleeping with a girl accused on the front pages of killing her own kids?"

Paul just went on in his own quiet way, steady, not argumentative, just explaining. "Well, Tim, I have run into a couple of the Don Juan types who were anxious to tell me what a great lay Keeler was, but I never believed one of them." He held up his hand, anticipating Tim, and smiled. "Not about Kitty being a great lay or not. I just don't think any of them knew one way or the other from personal experience. The interesting thing with Keeler is that over and over again the word is that Kitty's *smart*. She's 'something special.' I guess you could almost say she's considered a sort of 'stand-up guy.'"

"Instead of a lay-down lady?" Tim couldn't resist. Then, in a hearty, buddy-buddy, you-can-tell-us-pal voice, he said to me, "Well, wadda you say, Joey? You got closest to the lady in question. She an innocent victim of her own bad-mouthing or what?"

It hadn't occurred to me before, but actually Kitty's reputation had come almost strictly from Kitty herself. She had given wise-guy, hard-nosed answers to anyone who questioned her about her sex life: police, reporters, television newsmen. She had built her own image out of her anger. But when it came down to it, I didn't know who her lovers had been.

Not Ray Mogliano; not according to his brother, John. ("Kitty was a friend, ya know?")

Not Vincent Martucci. (She fronted for Vince.)

Not Billy Weaver. (Kitty said she hadn't slept with Billy.)

"Far as I know, Tim," I said lightly, "the girl's a virgin."

Tim threw his head back and laughed, then said we should all go and get something to eat. He jabbed me on the arm and said to Paul Sutro, "Tell ya, Paul. You ever need a good guy on your side, you get my pal Joe here. When he's on your side, he's on your side all the way."

CHAPTER 12

IT was nearly midnight when Kitty called. I had been home long enough to scan the late edition of the *Post* and the early-bird edition of the morning's *News*. Both were playing up Vincent Martucci's hit as it related to the Keeler case.

It took me about twenty minutes to get to her apartment. I hadn't seen Kitty since that morning a few days ago when she'd shown me where, in Flushing Meadow Park, she and George had taken their sons for springtime picnics. I'm not sure what I expected her mood to be.

She walked from the hallway to the living room with a rigid stiffness; indicated the well-stocked bar cart. "Help yourself, Joe. Nothing for me."

She sat on the beautiful dark-brown suede couch; she looked as though the room had been designed just for her. It was all expensive, contemporary mixed with a few touches of modern and one or two really good antiques. It suited her more than anything in Fresh Meadows had ever suited her.

She stood up abruptly when I sat beside her. She stood with her back to me for a moment, then let her hands drop to her sides. She kept clenching and unclenching her fingers.

"Well, Joe," she said, finally turning to face me. She was very pale, very tense and agitated. "It's all over. The whole thing. You want to know what my 'attorney' said? My elegant-Southern-gentleman Mistah Jaytee Williams said? He had his stooge, Jeff Weinstein, sneak me out of the building through the garage this afternoon so I wouldn't run into any of those lousy bastard vultures downstairs, waiting with their cameras and microphones for my . . . reaction to Vincent's death. You know what Jaytee Williams said to me, first thing, the minute I set foot in his office?"

"What did he say, Kitty?"

"That bastard." She began to pace, reached down, snatched up a large rough-textured pillow from a chair and hugged it hard against her body. She turned and stood very still, then said, " 'Wal, little lady, you-all surely got a good Mafee-oh-so godfather lookin' after your best interests.' " She did a mean imitation of Williams. Then she dropped the pillow. "Is that your opinion, too, Joe? Is that what you think? That I had someone kill Vincent? Because if that's what you think, I want to know about it, right now. I really want to know what's going on inside your head about me, right now."

"No, Kitty. I don't think you had anything to do with it. It *does* have something to do with you, though. Vincent's death."

"You want to know something, Joe?" She began to speak again with that same intensity, the same restless energy and tension. "You want to know how I feel? I feel like every death, every single goddamn death in the whole world, somehow has something to do with me." She looked around, searching, then snatched the *New York Times* from a table; it was folded back to the obit page. She held it up for me to see. "Look, Joe. Look at this. You know what I was doing before I called you? I was sitting here, reading the names of all these people, all these dead people, wondering if any of them have anything to do with me." Her hands were shaking as she tilted the paper toward the light, blinked quickly and began to read. " 'Abramson, Judah; beloved husband of Esther, father of David and Hannah; dear grandfather of . . .' "

I took the paper from her and reached for her, but Kitty pulled back. "No, Joe. I don't need you to comfort me. You want to know why? Because I am *glad* that Vincent's dead. I am glad he's dead. *I'm glad he's dead.*"

She swiped at her eyes with the back of her hand, then held her head up, chin out. "I wasn't going to tell you that, Joe. I wasn't going to say that to you. You know why? Because I was afraid of what you'd think. That you'd think the same thing that good-ole Jaytee Williams thinks. That I just have to . . . snap my fingers or something and I make people die. You know what he said to me when George . . . when George killed himself? He said, 'Why, Miz Kitty, what the hell did you say to that pore dumb son-of-a-bitch to make him think he'd be helping you by blowing his brains out?' And, Joe, I never . . . George did what he did . . . I never wanted anything like that."

Kitty reached for my drink, took a deep swallow, then sat down on the couch, her feet under her, her arms seeming to hold her body together inside the deep-salmon-colored jersey robe. She took a deep breath, then said, "Just let me talk, Joe, all right? I feel so . . . so filled with the need to talk."

"Go ahead, Kitty. You talk."

"Look, I want you to know something. I want you to know how I feel about something. About Vincent's death. You people are as responsible as anyone else. All of you. You all set him up, and Vincent couldn't see any way out, so he went before the grand jury and he told the story you all told him to tell, because he didn't have a choice. Vincent was a dead man from the minute you found out he was bisexual and . . ."

That was funny. It was actually pretty stupid. From the minute that Vito Geraldi had announced to us that Vincent Martucci was searching for boys, we had all thought of him as a homosexual. The implications of his being bisexual just hadn't occurred to me.

Kitty had stopped speaking; she watched me intently. "What's the matter, Joe? There's a funny look on your face. What are you thinking?"

"It's just that I hadn't thought of Vincent's death in just that way. Our . . . responsibility." Which of course wasn't really true; I had thought of it; I just didn't give much of a damn, one way or the other.

"Well, it's true. Everyone knew that Vince was on borrowed time. And I'm not going to lie and say I'm sorry it was *before* the trial instead of *after*. And you know what, Joe? There isn't even going to be a trial. Williams said that Vincent was the District Attorney's whole case. That there never was one single solitary shred of real evidence against me. There was just *me. The fact of me*. And what Williams' calls my *'life style.'* And the way I shoved it to them. Williams says that no one is going to make any kind of further effort in the case. Something to do with politics, Joe. I don't understand any of that and I couldn't care less, but I do care about one thing."

"What's that, Kitty? What do you care about?"

"That we can't force them to have a trial; that I'm not going to have the chance to be tried and *acquitted*. I want that creep Quibro to bring his 'case' to a jury. He never had a case against me. He never really had to prove I was *guilty*, as long as he had Vincent. I was the one who had to prove I was *innocent*. Now it's the other way around; the way it's supposed to be. And he can't prove I'm guilty. So he'll get one adjournment after another, until after the election, Jaytee said. And then the D.A. will just quietly drop the indictment."

Her long hair surrounded her face, which was shiny and moist and very beautiful, her skin picking up a peach-colored glow from her robe. Very softly, she asked, "Joe, can you understand? Can you understand that I *want* to go on trial? I want to get it all out in the open and be acquitted."

"Yes, I can understand that, Kitty."

She dropped her chin for a moment; the long light hair covered her face completely, then she parted it with her hands, like parting curtains, and held her face up toward the light, toward me.

"Joe. I don't feel exactly the way I said. About Vincent. About Vincent's death. We . . . I knew Vincent for a long time, Joe. He was a friend. He was good to me. We trusted each other. I never judged him in any way. It was none of my business how Vincent lived. I wish . . . he wasn't dead. I'm sorry he's dead. But, at the same time, for my own sake, I'm glad, and that makes me feel awful. Like I must be an awful person . . ."

I knew that was the right time for me to sit beside her, to hold her against me. She seemed depleted; the energy had gone out of her, leaving her emptied and light and fragile and totally exhausted.

I held Kitty's hands in mine, examined the nails: bitten and ripped down to the quick, slashes of bloody ragged wounds. I put her sore fingertips against my lips.

"Joe, I don't care what a bastard like Jaytee Williams thinks. I don't care what they print about me in the newspapers. I really don't. But . . . it matters to me what *you* think, Joe. It matters to me very much that you believe I had nothing to do with Vincent's death."

"I believe you, Kitty. I believe you."

"Joe, put me to bed. I am so tired."

She seemed nearly asleep. I settled her on the bed, but when I started to leave she reached out for me.

"Stay with me, Joe. Can you stay with me? Just lie here, next to me. God, I don't want to be alone tonight."

I cradled Kitty against my body as she slept, her face turned toward the night light she wanted left on. I could see the stages of her sleep reflected on her face: the relaxation of tension as her lips parted and a kind of serenity washed over her. She had the smooth, untouched look of an expensive porcelain doll, almost too perfect to be real. As her breathing went deeper and slower, as she dropped deeper into sleep, her hands clenched into fists, her lips began to move, her dark brows pulled into a frown. I could see the movement of her eyes beneath the delicate beige lids, the flutter of those strange whitish lashes, as she went fully into her dream. Her body tensed and she began to whisper and to shake her head against whatever she was seeing. I stroked the long tendrils of hair from her damp face, and in her sleep Kitty reached and took my hand in both of hers and held on to it as she drifted closer to the edges of consciousness.

In the early morning, the room visible in that peculiar light of pre-dawn, we turned toward each other as though each of us was inside the same dream, and in a slow, almost organic connection we made love slowly, languidly, almost totally devoid of tension, as though our movements against each other were part of a perfect ritual of easy mutual satisfaction.

"Joe," Kitty said, her fingers tracing my lips, outlining my features, "could we be together this weekend? Could we go somewhere?"

"Where would you like to go?"

She shook her head. "No. *You* pick a place." She insisted that the choice be mine, as though this was very important to her.

"How about Montauk? It's about a two-, two-and-a-half-hour drive. Do you like the beach? Look, I'll take a run over to my place, get a change of clothes and be back for you in about an hour. It's six now; be ready to leave by seven, okay?"

"Okay. Joe. Just one thing. For this weekend. Let's let it just be you and me. No . . . newspapers or television. Nothing but music on the radio. Let's not talk about . . ."

I leaned over and kissed her. "Where'd you get the idea we were going to have time to talk?"

The two days we spent in Montauk were like a period of suspended time, unconnected in any way to any other time or place. Kitty was radiant, beautiful; there was a lightness about her, a kind of total freedom as she waded up to her knees in the freezing ocean, challenging me to catch her, to run with her, to slide down the dunes with her, to make love to her out in the open on a desolate, cold stretch of sunny beach.

What surprised me was my ability to keep up with Kitty. I seemed to draw energy from her, to reach her level of vitality. I felt ageless; evenly matched; exhilarated by the intensity of everything we did.

We ate seafood in a good, uncrowded restaurant, then returned to our motel room, both of us exhausted by the fresh air, too much food, too much wine; both of us feeling stuporous, both of us somehow, mysteriously, coming alive again at precisely the same moment. She filled me so completely with herself that I began to believe her when she whispered to me, "There is just *now*, Joe. Just here and now. Just us. Just you and me. No yesterday, no tomorrow. Only now. Just now."

Which is what, I suppose, is meant by the "now generation": no promises, no commitments, no questions, no past and no future. Just now. Which might, or might not, be a good way to live.

We drove back to the city Sunday night in the kind of comfortable silence that can say more than hours of conversation. As I pulled up to the front of Kitty's building, she said, "Joe, would you come upstairs with me? Just for one drink." She slid her hand along my arm. "There's something I want to talk to you about."

From the time she said that until the time she poured some Scotch in a glass, there was a growing tension coming from Kitty. I felt it as she stood next to me in the elevator, as we walked down the corridor to her apartment, as she handed me my drink and tipped her glass against mine.

I felt a reluctant wariness. For two days, I had suspended reality. For two days, she had been the most perfect woman I had ever known, and I would have liked to kiss her good night and leave without either of us speaking another word.

"Why don't you just put the drink down and say what it is you have to say?"

The line along her jaw tightened; there was nothing comfortable or easy between us now. Just an expectant silence as she seemed to prepare herself to say something to me. I didn't make it any easier; she was spoiling something I didn't want touched.

"All right, Joe. I want to ask you to do something. For me. Joe . . . since we talked about . . . since we talked up in your cabin in the country and I told you about . . . what happened that night, and we went over George's confession and all, I haven't asked you anything at all. About what you were . . . doing. About what you were finding out."

"Yeah, and?"

Finally she looked directly at me. "Joe, I want you to just drop it, now. I don't want to know anything at all about what you've found out. There's no point to it now. There isn't going to be a trial. I don't have to prove anything. About . . . George. About myself."

"Don't you want to know for sure that it was George?"

She shook her head. "There's no point to it. If my life depended on it, that's different. But this way, Joe, this way, I don't have to be sure. I don't want to have to think about George . . . hurting the boys; actually doing it. I just don't want to know for sure."

I put my drink down. "You just want me to drop my investigation? Just like that?"

"Yes."

"Look up at me, Kitty." Her head jerked up, her face confronted me, surprised, alarmed. "Is that what this has all been about? Is that what this weekend has been about? Damn it, don't you turn away from me now. Answer me."

Her chin came up, eyes narrowed and hardened: she was Kitty Keeler, shoving it to the whole goddamn world. "Sure. Absolutely. That's it, Joe. You got it. That's what this whole weekend has been about. Right."

I don't know if it hit her the same way it hit me: this was exactly the reverse of the situation between us last week up at the cabin. She had accused me of having used her emotionally; now I was accusing her. And her reaction was exactly what mine had been: anger.

I softened. "All right, Kitty, relax, let's both just relax."

"Do you really believe that, Joe? That that's what this whole weekend has been leading up to?"

"I don't know, Kitty. I don't know what to believe. But you tell me. Why has it been so hard for you to ask me to drop my investigation? Why the hell did you get so tense about it?"

"Because I knew what your reaction would be. Because you don't trust me any more than . . ."

"Any more than *you* trust *me*?"

"Joe, I am really tired. Look, you do whatever the hell you want to do. I don't care if you spend the rest of your life investigating me, investigating George. Go ahead. Do whatever the hell you want to do."

I drove back to my apartment, checked the mailbox, then sat for a long time while the weekend replayed itself: focused and refocused on certain specific moments, certain expressions, gestures, sensations, connections and touches which had all formed between us something far deeper than I was willing to admit.

Age caught up with me, my bones ached; my head ached; my ulcer burned; and Kitty Keeler was as much a puzzle to me as she had ever been.

CHAPTER 13

MONDAY morning was the start of a perfect June day. It was also the day of Vincent Martucci's funeral. He was attended by well-dressed, well-behaved men and women and neat quiet children who all maintained a sad but restrained grief throughout the funeral mass celebrated on Vincent's behalf.

There were at least ten other law-enforcement men assigned to the funeral besides me. Some of them were discreetly snapping pictures; some of them were busy copying down the license numbers of private cars. Eight limousines and a long line of expensive cars accompanied Vincent to a parklike cemetery in upper Westchester County. Everything was in good taste. There were none of the excesses of the early-day gangster funerals: no huge good-luck horseshoe of flowers, no likeness of the deceased formed by hundreds of different kinds of flowers and preceding him to the grave. Nothing "Chicago" or "prohibition" about Vincent Martucci's funeral. There was a minimum of flowers; a minimum of ceremony; a minimum of tears. Everything was low-key, doubtlessly arranged and directed and closely supervised by the queen-like widow whose eyes checked everything and everyone.

A large company then followed Mrs. Martucci and her two young daughters back to their home in Forest Hills Gardens, where a light luncheon had been prepared for relatives and friends.

Mrs. Martucci sent word, via a maid, that the police officers outside her home would be welcome to partake of some refreshments that had been especially set up for us in the kitchen. Most of us declined politely.

Before I could leave the area, Sam Catalano came from nowhere and hung on to my arm. "Hey, Joe, I've been trying to catch up to you all morning. Didn't you see me at the church? At the cemetery?"

I'd seen him all right; I'd been successfully avoiding him.

"Joe, did you hear about me? About my being assigned to Paul Sutro's squad?"

"Hey, that's terrific, Sam. Congratulations. Paul's a great guy to work for and the Organized Crime Unit is a very dedicated group."

"Joe, you gotta be kidding. It's a dead end. It's not even officially a part of the department. We're just on loan to the state committee. Nobody ever leaves that squad unless they die of old age. It's all research and paperwork and charts and stuff, Joe. The department doesn't even take that squad into account in figuring quotas for promotion, Joe. I'll never get past third grade. It's like being buried alive."

"Could be worse, Sam. Like being buried dead. The way George Keeler was. The way Vincent Martucci was this morning."

"No kidding, Joe, have you heard anything? Like, is this temporary, or what? Am I on loan-out to Sutro? You're close with Captain Neary, Joe. He say anything about me?"

"Not a word, Sam. Not a single word."

Sam Catalano glanced around, settled his shoulders, tapped at the knot in his tie. "Hey, Joe. I think I'm just gonna go inside and have a little of that 'lunch' Mrs. Martucci set out for us. You know something, Joe? That woman got a 'look' to her, know what I mean? I've been getting signals from her, right out there at the cemetery."

"Sam, you are probably just the man the widow Martucci would most like to tell her troubles to."

Sam cheered up, anticipating great triumphs. "Well, you never know, Joe. It might lead to something, one way or the other, right?"

•

I stopped by the squad office long enough to type up a one-paragraph report on Vincent Martucci's funeral. My time was pretty much my own. Tim Neary was attending a three-day law-enforcement seminar in Boston; Sergeant Gelber was in charge and not looking for trouble. I told him I'd keep in touch; he said that would be fine.

I drove over to the Jamaica branch of the New York Public Library, exactly as I had planned to do before my weekend with Kitty, and went through a couple of books about dogs.

Just as Benjamin the Cuban had claimed, there was indeed a dog who looked like a sheep: a Bedlington terrier. From the pictures, the damn dog looked like a walking lamb chop on a leash. I stared at the book for a very long time wondering what I was going to do. More importantly, wondering why I was going to do whatever it was.

Kitty was right, actually: the case was all over. Under Quibro's frantic directions, Tim had reassigned a couple of men to the Keeler case, but neither Tim nor Kelleher really gave a damn one way or the other. It was all over for them; they had gotten the necessary indictment; they had done their part of the job and there was absolutely no pressure on them, from any direction, to follow through.

It would have been very easy, at this point, to just close the book and say the hell with it. The hell with Benjamin the Cuban and the sheep-like dog; the hell with Mrs. Deluca and her unsigned statement; the hell with George's gun rusting in the Police Lab. It would have been very easy to get in my car and drive over to Kitty's apartment and say, "Yeah, you're right; *now*; no past, no future, just *now*."

But I couldn't and that was what was worrying me. I couldn't because Kitty had become something more to me than I had ever intended or could have imagined.

For forty-nine years, I have lived a pretty regular, routine kind of life with no real options: school; Army; couple of jobs, then the department. My responsibilities had always been right out front: my wife, my kids, my job. There had never been any room for any real options. There had been a few, passing nights with a few unimportant women: Jen had been right about that, but it hadn't meant anything to me. Not anything at all. There had never been anyone like Kitty Keeler in my life.

What had at first been just an assignment had turned into a real concern and then into a sense of responsibility and by now had gone past something I could just walk away from; it couldn't be something casual, random, a stop-time-out for a quick weekend at the beach. And I knew that unless I finished my investigation, unless I tied up the loose ends, there would always be a lack of total trust and honesty between us.

If ever there was to be anything more between us.

•

The manager of the Fresh Meadows development was sure there was a list somewhere of all the tenants who owned dogs. About two years ago there had been a very emotional confrontation re the rights of dogs to relieve themselves as against the rights of humans to walk without regard to such end products. The list, however, would not be very accurate, since, things being what they are, a lot of the anti-dog forces had, for their own safety, become pro-dog.

"It's funny," the manager mused, "the most outspoken person in the anti-dog forces was mugged on the subway one night. The next day, she went out and bought a Great Dane. The dog stands more than six feet high when it rears up. And it's been trained for combat. A lotta good that damn dog will do her, pacing around her apartment while she's being mugged on the subway!"

After a few more funny stories, he realized that he didn't know where the "dog material" was. His assistant had handled most of it and she was home sick, but if I didn't mind waiting he'd call her and see if she could tell him where it was.

I didn't mind. I told him I had a few things to keep myself busy with while he located the list of dog owners. I slit the envelope from Tommy Dawson; it contained a very neatly typed statement relative to his locating a certain revolver in a certain location on a certain date at a certain time in the presence of a certain detective, et cetera, et cetera. Tommy's statement was exactly the same as the statement I had jotted in my notebook and asked him to sign.

I had forgotten to tell Harry Sullivan to give me his findings in clear, concise English. The letter from him was two and a half pages of single-spaced typed data relative to certain chemical tests he had run on subject revolver. What I had told Harry was that the revolver in question had been, to the best of my knowledge, concealed in a certain location under certain conditions. From the tests he was to run, Harry was to tell me what he could about the location and conditions of its concealment.

I scanned his report quickly and picked out the pertinent information: "and it is therefore ascertainable that subject revolver had rested in a salt water solution; further ascertainable from non-visible particles embedded in handle of subject revolver that subject revolver had rested or come to rest in a substance as discussed in paragraph three (see below) rather than having been suspended in said salt water solution."

The gun had been in salt water with a combination sand and mud soil bottom.

I also caught, at the end of a detailed explanation, the statement verifying that the Keeler murder bullet and the test bullet I had given him had come from one and the same subject revolver.

"Okay, here's what we have, Mr. Peters. I got Audrey at home. God, she sounded terrible. I hope strep throat isn't contagious." The manager clutched at his own throat and extended a well-worn file folder containing ragged-edged pages of reports and lists and mimeographed flyers. There were petitions for dogs; petitions against dogs; announcements of meetings called by both sides of the issue; and, finally, an outdated list of dog-owning tenants.

"As I said, that list is more than two years old. And the issue has been academic for some time, but it's a starting place for you, isn't it?" He massaged his throat, then began to list his symptoms, in detail.

I don't know why it is, but there is a certain segment of the population that feels comfortable confiding anything and everything in a policeman: the most personal, private moments of their marital life; their most warped, dark-of-the-night impulses; their politics and religious beliefs; and their physical symptoms. This is done in the utmost confidence that such unburdening saves them the trouble and expense of a marriage counselor, a psychiatrist, a priest or a doctor.

I listened closely to the symptoms described, looked very thoughtful and concerned and advised two aspirin, bed rest and a close, continuing check on temperature; lots of fluids; gargle with warm salt water and call again in twenty-four hours. What the hell. The poor guy looked relieved.

Back at my apartment, I typed up a statement for Mrs. Deluca's signature, with a confirming paragraph for her sister, Mrs. Romero. Then I sat with the list of dog owners and a map of the Fresh Meadows development, trying to decide approximately where the man with the sheep dog might live. When Benjamin first saw him, he might have just come from his apartment and proceeded to walk his dog toward the Keeler apartment building. Or, he might have come from the area of the Keeler apartment, walked his dog over to where Benjamin saw him the first time, and been returning home when Benjamin saw him the second time.

Or, of course, he might have come from a mile away and just been walking his dog in circles.

I planned my next day's work around what I regarded as the four prime dog-walking times: between six and eight in the morning; between three and four in the afternoon, when school kids walk the dog; 5:30 to 6:30 P.M., when business people without kids walk the dog; between 10:30 P.M. and 1 A.M., when most people give Rover a last time out for the night.

•

By the time I called Sergeant Gelber on Tuesday morning, I had already been working for more than three hours, but I didn't tell him that. I didn't tell him anything; just that I would be in touch, which was fine with him. One way or the other.

I started ringing doorbells in the area where Benjamin said he had first seen the man with the sheep dog, hoping that had been his starting point. It seemed that every dog owner on the list who I checked with had the names of two or three other tenants who had gotten dogs in the period of time since the dog protests. The reasons were always the same: fear. Of muggers, housebreakers, rapists, lunatics, kidnappers, murderers. Instead of shortening my list, for each name I crossed off I had to add several more.

At about one o'clock, I headed over to Jackson Heights with Mrs. Deluca's and Mrs. Romero's statements to be signed. It was impossible to find a parking space. The alternate-side-of-the-street-parking regulations didn't end until 2 P.M., but long before then, neighborhood cars had been jockeyed from temporary locations to choice spots in front of apartment buildings. I drove around for nearly twenty minutes before I found some guy pulling out.

The neighborhood looked different in daylight. It was a very active "people" kind of scene. Young mothers stood around, talking, rocking baby carriages with one hand and hanging on to a squirming kid with the other. Older women walked among the younger people; stood gossiping, giving advice, showing what bargains they had found at the local stores.

Mrs. Deluca and her sister had just returned from shopping. They had unpacked their bags on Mrs. Deluca's kitchen table and were sorting and dividing the various items when I arrived. It was easier to accept the coffee and pastry that was offered than to refuse. It was also smarter. It set a more congenial, hospitable mood of cooperation. Mrs. Deluca read over the statement, then her sister read it. They conferred with each other, then with me. Yes, that was exactly the way it happened, just as it said on the paper. But why should they have to sign anything? Wouldn't that mean they would be "involved"?

I accepted some more heavy pastry and assured both women that it was merely routine; just to complete my records. Mrs. Deluca signed her statement; Mrs. Romero signed her added paragraph.

Mrs. Deluca asked me if I didn't think that Benjamin the Cuban was going to end up badly. I agreed; very badly; her sister agreed.

I walked along the warm sunny street toward my car absorbing the scene that was so different in the dark—almost as though it was two entirely different locations. It took a minute or two for me to realize that one of the differences was that along the edge of the sidewalks, where the collection of apartment house garbage cans had been set, there was a collection of women, sitting on folding chairs, enjoying the spring afternoon. Ignoring the bits and pieces of debris that the not overly zealous Department of Sanitation men had left behind. One young guy, maybe eighteen, nineteen years old, leaned against the alternate-side-of-the-street-parking sign and seemed to be arguing with one of the young mothers, who kept shaking a baby carriage. Finally a heavy old woman, clicking and shaking her head, dug into her large black pocketbook and came up with a folded bill, which she extended to the boy. He grabbed the bill with one hand, turned and, in a kid's exuberant excitement at having gotten what he wanted, swiveled around, leaped up and hit the parking-regulations sign, right smack in the middle of the words "Tuesday and Friday." Then, he kissed the older woman on the forehead and said to the younger woman, "You'll see, Angie. I'm gonna hit me a winner."

From the look on the younger woman's face and from the triumphant gleam in the older woman's eye, I figured the boy's mother had just shelled out five bucks over the protests of the boy's little wife.

Nice little sidewalk family scene.

Back to Fresh Meadows, where I talked to a couple of kids with dogs: big dogs, little dogs, common and uncommon dogs. No Bedlington terriers. I hung around; watched some teenagers playing basketball for a while; drove around; rang doorbells; watched the five-thirty-to-six-thirty crowd of dog owners. It was interesting: the nonchild dog owners had the more expensive breeds and were more anxious to talk about their pets. I got a pretty good education on the care, feeding and emotional problems of a variety of dogs. Not one of them looked like a sheep.

I decided to skip the late-night dog walkers for a while, hoping to get lucky in daylight hours. After all, why risk scaring a dog-walking citizen to death in the dark? Or getting myself bitten or reported to the precinct as a strange or menacing character in an already jumpy neighborhood.

I went to bed early after a long hot shower. It wasn't so much the long hours that were exhausting; it was the long empty periods of waiting, of empty time in between active time. I set my alarm for five-thirty to make sure I'd get up and out in time for the first dog of the morning.

I thought of Kitty. I hadn't spoken to her since Sunday night and we had both been angry when I left her. I thought of finding Benjamin's sheep-dog man; who would confirm what Benjamin had told me; who might also remember having seen Kitty in the car with Benjamin; who might also, if I was very lucky, just happen to have seen George Keeler in the area on the night the boys were murdered. Then I would type up his statement and put it into my own private files. Then I would go to see Kitty and tell her she was right; it was all over; all in the past; the hell with it; let it all die a natural death.

I thought of Kitty. Of how beautiful she was; of how unbelievably beautiful she had been out at Montauk. I felt myself slipping into a light, pleasant semi-sleep and thought of Kitty. And saw her, getting out of my car, describing and recalling exactly how it was the night she'd gotten out of Benjamin's car and walked around the garbage cans, and Benjamin came around and offered her his hand and then the Italian women came along.

Kitty, getting out of my car recalling exactly how it was that night, the night her children were murdered.

Which was a Wednesday night. *Wednesday night.*

I sat up; switched the lamp on. Lit a cigarette.

What the hell were the garbage cans doing set out along the edge of the sidewalk that night? Pickup for that neighborhood, according to the alternate-side-of-the-street-parking signs, was scheduled for Tuesday and Friday mornings. Which would mean, normally, that the janitors of the various buildings would set out the cans on Monday and Thursday nights.

I checked through the day-by-day notes of my investigation: it was a Monday night that Kitty and I had driven around and around the Jackson Heights streets until she spotted the building where she'd met with Billy Weaver. Monday: therefore, the garbage cans were set out for pickup the next morning.

Checked some more: I had met with Benjamin on a Thursday night. We waited together for Mrs. Deluca on a Thursday night. And the garbage cans were set out for pickup on Friday morning.

Which did not explain why—or if—there were in fact garbage cans set out along the edges of the sidewalk on the night the Keeler boys were murdered.

•

Between six-fifteen and eight-forty-five the next morning, I encountered four German shepherds, one Doberman pinscher, two very old cocker spaniels, one fat beagle, one blond Labrador retriever, three mixed-breed mutts, one mouse-sized, surly, snappy Chihuahua. Not one of them could pass for a sheep; not one of the dog owners knew of any such in the neighborhood.

Since I didn't feel like ringing doorbells just yet, and, more importantly, since the matter of the garbage cans was bothering me, I took a ride over to the Queens County Department of Sanitation administration office and requested a check of their records relative to pickups in the Jackson Heights area for a three-week period: April 7 through April 26, 1975.

Ever ready with a good cover story, I told the worried-looking supervisor that I was investigating a claim against the city by some irate motorist who claimed that a Department of Sanitation truck had clipped one of his fenders right off his car at the Jackson Heights location. I made it a *good* story: this same irate motorist was known to have instituted various minor lawsuits against other city agencies and private companies in the past few years. The D.A.'s office was building a frauds and larceny case against him, and this time we were pretty sure we had him.

According to the records, there had been no change or variance of pickup days during the period checked. There hadn't been any public or religious holidays in that period that could account for an alteration of pickup days.

"Can you think of any other reason why a janitor might put out the cans, say, on a Wednesday night, for pickup on Friday morning?"

He didn't come up with anything better than I had: possibly the superintendent or janitor of the particular building was going to be away for a few days and set them out in advance. Possibly there was an unusual amount of garbage piling up and he wanted to get the cans away from the yard area of the building. Possibly there had been a change-over of staff in the building and through some misunderstanding—maybe the guy was used to Monday/Thursday pickups on his old job—he had put the cans out the wrong night.

Maybe. Maybe not.

That would have to be checked out with the janitor of the Jackson Heights building. Later.

I went back to Fresh Meadows and decided to try to change my luck by changing the location of my inquiries. I started now close to the Keeler apartment building, going with the possible assumption that the man with the sheep dog had been heading back toward his home when he met Benjamin, rather than away from it.

Two dog owners, both on the original list, were home: one had a growling German shepherd; one had a mixed-breed cross between a beagle and a cocker spaniel.

There was one more name on the list of dog owners residing in the three-story garden-apartment building immediately adjoining the Keeler apartment: Arnold Nadler; Apartment 3-B. Top floor.

When I pushed the upstairs buzzer, there was a soft chiming sound and a woman's voice called out, "Be with you in a minute." She was as good as her word; about a minute later, a pleasant voice asked, from behind the locked door, "Who is it?"

"Mrs. Nadler? I'm Detective Joe Peters, D.A.'s Squad. Could I see you for a minute?"

She examined my i.d. through the opening of the chained door, then undid the chain and told me, "I'm not Mrs. Nadler. I'm Mrs. Arons. The Nadlers moved out almost two months ago."

She was a very pregnant, very beautiful, glowing young woman of about twenty-three. She did not have a dog. The Nadlers, who had moved to New Jersey, *did* have a dog, but she didn't know what kind of dog it was. She'd never seen it.

"Are you checking on dogs because of anything to do with those two poor little boys? Does it have anything to do with that?" She folded her arms uncomfortably over herself and said, "It's an awful thing to say, and I probably shouldn't say it or even think it, but because of that terrible tragedy, we got lucky. We got this apartment nearly two weeks earlier than we were supposed to."

When I expressed a cautious interest in that circumstance, Mrs. Arons invited me into her sunny, cheerful kitchen and offered me coffee, tea or skimmed milk. She checked her watch and told me, "I'm about to have my second glass of the day." She wrinkled her nose. "I never, ever drink milk for myself; but, well, this isn't for me. It's for the baby."

I accepted a glass of milk with thanks; not for me; for my ulcer. "What do you mean you got this apartment two weeks early because of the Keeler murders?"

"Well, not actually *got* the apartment. Got *access* to the apartment. We were to have taken over as of May first. The Nadlers' house in New Jersey wasn't quite finished. But then, I guess houses are never really all ready, even on the date they're promised. Well, anyway, we really did want at least a few days to paint the apartment before moving in. You know, we had to be out of our old apartment by May first; if we had to wait until then to take over this apartment, it would have meant moving into an unpainted apartment; having to be unsettled and all while the painters were here. You know, a whole mess."

I agreed. "Sure, it's much better to be able to have the painters in when the place is empty."

However, the Nadlers were not planning to vacate until April 30. But then on April 18 the development manager called the Aronses to report that the Nadlers were moving to New Jersey over that weekend; the apartment would be vacant as of Monday, April 21, so that the Aronses could arrange to get the place painted prior to moving in on May 1.

"We were delighted, of course. They sure moved out in a hurry, the Nadlers. They left an awful lot of things behind: some books, a few clothes, pillows, a teapot, you know, small things. Anyway one day during the week, while we were having the place painted, Mrs. Nadler came by to collect her things. That poor woman. She was really frazzled. It hadn't been *her* idea to move out like that, in such a hurry. And she told me she was going crazy with all the workmen all still busy all over her new house. She said that some of the plumbing had been hooked up wrong and she had had a flood in the playroom, and . . . all kinds of minor catastrophes. She looked like she was ready to climb the walls. I felt so sorry for her."

"It hadn't been her idea to move out in a hurry?"

"No, it was Arnold. Her husband. Poor Mrs. Nadler. She said, 'Arnold just wanted us to pack up and get out of here, after that awful thing that happened.'"

"Meaning the murder of the Keeler children?"

Mrs. Arons sipped some milk and nodded. "I only met Mr. Nadler once, the first time we saw the apartment, and he seemed like a very nervous kind of man. His wife said he was a very nervous-type man; so nervous, he had an ulcer." Mrs. Arons clamped her hand over her mouth.

"That's okay, I'm not offended. After all, I *do* have an ulcer, so I know the type. Was there anything in particular, anything specific, about the Keeler case that seemed to bother Mr. Nadler, that you know of?"

Mrs. Arons' large dark eyes widened. "Something *specific?* Good grief, Mr. Peters, the whole terrible thing *generally* was bad enough. Who'd need specifics? He just said, according to his wife, that he wanted to get away from here, from all the crime and all. Right away."

Mrs. Arons found the Nadlers' address in New Jersey; then she found a number for Mr. Nadler in Manhattan.

"He's a C.P.A., and this number, I think, is an answering service, because he moves around a lot. But if you call they'll give you a number where you can reach him. Or they'll have him call you back."

I took a few minutes to assure young Mrs. Arons that despite what had happened to the Keeler children and despite the wave of fear that seemed to permeate the area, Fresh Meadows was still one of the safest neighborhoods in the city.

Which isn't exactly saying much.

I went to a phone booth and dialed Arnold Nadler's answering service. After nine rings, the phone was answered by a bored, slurred voice which repeated the last four digits I had just dialed.

"Do you have a number for Mr. Arnold Nadler?"

"Ya got a pencil?"

"Yes, I've got a pencil."

"Okay, ya can reach him at this number."

She mumbled a number which I had to ask her to repeat. Then I dialed said number.

A switchboard operator identified the new number as belonging to

"Heilweilder, Simkowitz, Kelly, Smith and Ito, Importers, good morning. Could you hold please."

I had to feed another dime to the telephone company before the cheerful voice got back to me; asked me to wait while she checked on Mr. Nadler's whereabouts; then informed me he had left their office about two minutes ago; I'd just missed him. Call his answering service for his latest whereabouts.

I went through the routine all over again; dialed; nine rings. Do-you-have-a-number-for-Arnold-Nadler? Do-you-have-a-pencil?

He wasn't at this number either, but a gravelly smoker's voice told me that Mr. Nadler was en route; that this was his office on Lexington Avenue and Fifty-fourth Street and that he would be there for the rest of the afternoon, would I leave a message?

No message.

I decided the best way to contact Mr. Arnold Nadler was to drive into Manhattan and show up at his office, which is what I did.

It was a very crummy-looking old building with long dark halls lined with crinkled-glass-topped doors bearing multi-inscriptions: Thomas and Thomas, Atty's-at-Law, Hillard Mfg. Co., Inc.; Nu-Skin Facial Products, Benson Belt and Buckles; Arnold Nadler, C.P.A., Bernard Jackson, C.P.A.

I tapped on the glass portion of the door with my knuckles, then walked into a small square room filled with desks put back to back and file cabinets side to side. There wasn't much floor space showing. A plump, badly preserved woman with a cigarette stuck to her lip turned from a coat rack and raised her eyebrows at me.

"Yeah? You're looking for someone?"

It was the gravelly telephone voice. Before I could answer her, the phone rang. She grabbed it, listened, put her hand over the mouthpiece and yelled toward an inner office, "Arnie, pick up. It's Mr. Kaye." She listened for a moment, then hung up and continued putting on her coat.

"Some time for lunch, huh? Eleven-thirty, who's hungry at eleven-thirty? You know how long this is gonna make my day?"

The phone rang again. She rolled her eyes toward the ceiling, then at me for sympathy, which I gave her by a slight shake of my head.

"I'm not gonna talk to you, Sheldon, I'm going out to lunch now, so you're talking on *my* time. Listen, you call me tonight at home and I'll talk to you then." She hung up and said to me, "He can't talk to me from his own home, his wife objects!"

I reached over and held the coat for her.

"His own mother, he gotta call me on the sly, nice, huh?" She opened the inner door and called out, "You want me to go to lunch early, Arnold, so I'm going to lunch early!"

She shook her head at me; undoubtedly a martyr in an uncaring world.

About three minutes later, Arnold Nadler came from the inner office. Before either of us could speak, the phone rang. Nadler spoke in quick staccato bursts of words. "I told you already, Ralph, you got nothing to worry about. Will you listen to me? When they call you, you say, 'Here's the name of my C.P.A.' Okay? All right? That's what they expect you to say. And, Ralph, stop worrying; you paid to the penny. Believe me, you're in good shape. I'm the one who faces them, not you. It's no big deal. It's everyday I.R.S. practice. Stop worrying already. Yeah, yeah, good-bye."

Arnold Nadler was a well-built, compact man in his early forties. He had a thick fringe of dark-red hair around the base of his head, and a long strand had been allowed to grow and was then pasted across the top of his skull to simulate a normal head of hair. He looked frazzled; harassed. He looked like a C.P.A. The sleeves of his shirt were rolled up halfway; collar opened; necktie pulled down; eyeglasses slipping down his small nose. He shoved his pencil behind his ear, then offered me his hand for a quick, moist, hard grip.

"Come into my office, we'll talk there."

The inner office was more cluttered than the outer office. There were stacks of file folders everywhere: on chairs, on the floor, on the surface of the two back-to-back desks, under the desks. He lifted a stack of folders and ledgers from one of the chairs, put them on the floor, indicated the chair for me.

"So, okay. You brought the books, didn't you?" He looked at me carefully for the first time, leaned forward as I extended my gold shield. "You're not Stanley Beck?"

"Detective Joe Peters. Queens District Attorney's Squad."

Nadler took a long deep breath which seemed to catch in his throat as he tried to exhale. He turned his head away and coughed; dug a handkerchief from a back pocket; dabbed at his mouth, then at the beads of sweat over his upper lip. He balled the handkerchief in his hands and made absolutely no effort to disguise his sudden nervousness and agitation.

Very quietly and calmly, hoping to give him a chance to get a better grip on himself, I said, "It's all right, Mr. Nadler. You've been sort of expecting me for a while now, haven't you?"

He nodded, then dabbed the damp handkerchief along his forehead. I offered him a cigarette; he didn't smoke. Since he seemed to be having a little difficulty breathing in the close stale air, I didn't light up, either.

I leaned forward and said, "You were walking your dog that night, weren't you?"

Nadler stopped blotting his face and stared at me. "Walking my dog? That night? What walking my dog? Is this . . . is this something about my dog?"

Either we were thinking of the same event or we were thinking about two different events, in which case I was as confused as this guy was.

"Mr. Nadler, what do *you* think this is about?"

He was also smart enough to not volunteer anything unless and until asked. "I don't know what this is about, Mr. . . . . Detective Peters. Tell me."

"You moved into your house in Somers almost two weeks before you had planned to, Mr. Nadler. You packed up and moved the weekend after the Keeler children were murdered."

He nodded vigorously. "Yes. Yes, we did. Yes."

"It was a very sudden decision, wasn't it?"

"Yes. Very sudden."

"Why, Mr. Nadler?"

"Why? Why? I just wanted to get my family away from there, out to Somers. I just . . . wanted to move away from Fresh Meadows, right away."

"Because you didn't think it was safe there anymore?"

He nodded.

"Not safe for you? In particular?"

Arnold Nadler stood up and looked around, but there wasn't any floor space for him to pace, if that's what he wanted to do, so he just sat down again in his swivel chair and turned first one way, then the other, all the time shaking his head and blotting his damp face. Then he stopped moving around, pulled off his glasses, dug at his exhausted, reddened eyes, smeared at his glasses with his dirty handkerchief.

I just waited him out.

Finally he calmed down, slowed himself down, took a deep breath and said, "Sooner or later, I knew you'd come. If not one of you, my God, maybe one of *them*. I guess I should be glad it's you instead of them."

"Well, since *I'm* the one who's here, how about talking to me? About that night?"

He nodded; bounced his pencil on the surface of his desk. It flew from his fingers and landed somewhere on the floor. He put his hands, palms down, on the desk blotter. It started to get damp.

I helped him. "Let's start with that night, Mr. Nadler. You took your dog out and . . ."

"My dog? My dog? What does Pom-Pom have to do with anything?"

"Tell you what, Mr. Nadler. Let's do it this way. It's your story. You tell me what happened the night the Keeler boys were murdered."

He folded his hands one over the other but couldn't control the trembling. There was a small tic at the corner of his right eye, and from time to time he reached up, adjusted his glasses and lightly touched the jumping nerve.

"I was coming home. I had parked my car in the parking lot. It was late. In April I work late hours, long hours. People think, after the fifteenth, things slack off, but I have clients who need extensions and I only *begin* to get to work on their taxes after my regulars. And it piles up. So through most of April and May, sometimes even in June, I work late."

He reached for his calendar appointment book, opened it to the week of April 14–April 20, 1975. The small boxes were filled with an illegible collection of notes. He pointed to Wednesday, April 16.

"All day, I worked. First in the city. Then I had to go over to Brooklyn. Then, in the evening, here, look, see . . ." He turned the book towards me and showed me his schedule. "See, 'P.M.: Christie's Lounge, N.J.'—I already had a few accounts in Jersey, near Somers. But we were still in Fresh Meadows, so I had to travel. Fifteen, eighteen hours a day in April, May. That's standard for a C.P.A. at tax time. So that night I had to go to Jersey. And the books were in worse shape than I expected. I just took them on as a new client. What a mess; so it was very late when I came home. Maybe two-fifteen, two-twenty in the morning, so—"

"Wait a minute. Are you sure of the time? Was it that late? Couldn't have been closer to midnight? Maybe twelve-thirty?"

Nadler shook his head emphatically. "No way. Maybe two-twenty, somewhere around there."

Which didn't make much sense; Benjamin picked Kitty up at about twelve-thirty. But then, maybe Nadler had seen Kitty returning home; which had been closer to 3 A.M.

"Could it have been later, Mr. Nadler? Say . . . three A.M.?"

Nadler looked blank.

"Mr. Nadler, I'm sorry. Look, you just go on and tell me what you saw. We'll worry about the timing later, okay?"

"Well, so I parked my car in the parking lot and I walked toward my building."

Which is the building adjoining the Keelers'.

"Before I got to the first court, as I came around the side from the parking lot, I noticed a car. Parked at the curb. The headlights were on and the motor was running. And what made it seem strange to me was that the doors were open. Back door and front door."

"All of the doors? All four doors?"

He nodded. "Yeah, yeah. No. Not all four doors. Two doors, at the sidewalk side. And . . . I would have just kept going, right past, only there were voices. And they sounded, you know, they sounded angry. Very angry."

"Angry?"

"Like they were fighting. Arguing. They came from the building, a man and a woman, and it was like they'd been arguing inside and just kept on as they walked outside toward the car."

"What building did they come from?"

"From the building where the Keelers lived."

Neither Kitty nor Benjamin had said anything about arguing. "All right. Then what? What did you do?"

"Well, I realized they couldn't see me, I was in the shadow. I guess I took a step or two back, so they wouldn't see me. You know, I was embarrassed. Maybe I thought they'd be embarrassed, arguing when they thought they were alone, and then, if they saw me, it would be . . . embarrassing."

"Go on."

"So, anyway, I stepped back and waited. For them to get into the car and drive away."

"And? Did they get into the car and drive away?"

Nadler didn't look at me; he looked at his hands.

"Mr. Nadler, what kind of car was it?"

He shrugged. "I don't know. I don't know cars. Dark. It was a dark car."

"Big car? Small car? Compact? What?"

"Oh, it was a big car. Big."

"Big?" A Datsun? Big? "You sure of that? It wasn't a small car?"

Nadler shook his head. In a dull flat voice he said, "It was a big black car. Cadillac maybe; or a Lincoln. Something like that."

"A Cadillac or a Lincoln? Not . . . not a green Datsun?"

"A Datsun? No. No, that's a small car. This was a big car."

He was waiting for me; he would answer whatever I asked him, but he wasn't going to volunteer on his own.

"Did you speak to either of the people you saw walking toward this car? To the man? To the woman?"

He shook his head. "Oh, no way. No way. I just stood there in the shadows and waited. Until . . . until they got into . . . until they . . ."

"Mr. Nadler." Those small hairs stood up at the base of my neck; my throat felt dry and tight as Nadler squared his shoulders, licked his lips, and let his hands fall into his lap. There was a kind of final resolve in his posture: a decision finally made. He turned his face toward me and watched me closely.

"Arnold. Tell me *exactly* what you saw and heard that night." He nodded and kept focused on me. "Get it all out and over with, you've been living with it long enough."

His voice came out steadier than it had been; there was a sound almost of relief at finally telling what he'd kept bottled up.

"I stood and watched them come toward the car. I was not more than ten feet away from them. They each, the man and the woman, they were each carrying something." He looked down at his hands, sucked in a deep breath. His voice broke, but he kept on. "Detective Peters, they were each carrying a child. They looked like they were sleeping. The children. The man, he . . . he was a big man. Very large. Look, I'll be honest. I was scared to death. Something about him; about both of them. He sort of pushed the woman toward the car, then he, my God, he sort of threw the child he was carrying into the back seat." Nadler twisted his fingers together and licked at his lips. "There was, like, a thud when he threw the child into the back of the car. The woman said, I don't know, something like 'My God, you hit his head.'"

The welt on Terry Keeler's forehead; the unexplained abrasion that was never publicized.

"And what did the man say, or do?"

There were tears streaming down Arnold Nadler's cheeks. He seemed unaware of them; his voice was ragged and thin. "The man just sort of pushed her into the car, into the back seat, and he said something like 'What difference does that make now?' and when the woman got into the back seat, with the child in her arms, he, the man, slammed the back door. Then he slammed the front door and walked around and got into the car, on the driver's side, and drove off. I waited until the car turned the corner. And then . . . I went . . . I went home. To my apartment."

Arnold Nadler was soaked by the time he finished talking. I had seen a box of tissues on the gravel-voiced woman's desk; I stepped into that office and came back with the box, which I handed to him. He took a wad of tissues and blotted his face, blew his nose, then wiped the inside of his shirt collar. His hands trembled so badly that he dropped the tissues onto the floor, started to reach for them, then stopped and held out his hands.

We both watched the terrible trembling.

"This is how I've been ever since that night. The next day, of course, we all heard about . . . about the Keeler boys and all. And then all the newspapers printed stories about . . . about Mrs. Keeler and all her . . . gangster friends. I was afraid, Detective Peters," Nadler said. "I was scared to death. I still am."

I did not want to ask Arnold Nadler one more question. Particularly, I did not want to ask him *the* single most important question.

But I asked him.

"Mr. Nadler, did you recognize the woman you saw carrying a child into the back seat of that car?"

"Oh, yes. It was her."

"*Her?*"

He nodded and blinked rapidly. "The mother. Kitty Keeler. I recognized her. You know, from the neighborhood. I recognized her right away. I don't think I'd ever seen the man before. It wasn't her husband, that much I do know. He was a big, dark, heavyset man. He looked . . . like . . . a gangster."

Yes, a police officer did come to his apartment the next day, but he had already left for an early-morning appointment with a client. Nadler showed me his appointment book in confirmation. His wife had nothing to tell the police officer; Nadler didn't tell her anything until a few days later, when he insisted they move out to New Jersey without delay.

Just out of curiosity, to tie up a dangling loose end, I asked him what kind of dog he had.

"Pom-Pom? Oh, she's a Pekingese. She's very old; nineteen years, something like that. My wife had her since before we were married."

So Arnold Nadler wasn't even the man with the sheep dog.

And there was still something else he hadn't told me and wanted to tell. He was just waiting for me to ask.

"Mr. Nadler, what else do you know that might be helpful?"

He knew the license number of the large black automobile that was used to transport the bodies of the Keeler boys to the dumping ground on Peck Avenue.

He might not be on top of all the various makes and models of automobiles, but when it came to numbers, Arnold Nadler had a brain like a computer.

CHAPTER 14

THE car, a 1975 black Lincoln Continental, was registered to Lorenzo Pellegrino.

Lorenzo Pellegrino was the companion, bodyguard, chauffeur and henchman of Alfredo Veronne.

•

I sat in my apartment for hours reading and rereading every report, interview, speculation, confession and statement regarding every aspect of the murder of the Keeler kids.

For the first time, I read Harry Sullivan's report in its entirety and caught what I had missed by skimming. I underlined the key finding with red pen: "*. . . therefore it is the conclusion of the undersigned based on above described tests, that subject revolver has been submerged in salt water solution as described in paragraph 3-subdivision b, for a period of no less than one week and no more than two weeks.*"

No more than two weeks.

According to George Keeler's confession, he had tossed his unregistered .38 revolver into Flushing Meadow Bay on the night of the double murder of his sons: sometime around 3 A.M. on Thursday, April 17, 1975. Nearly two months ago.

There was a pattern of events dating from May 27, 1975, the date of George's suicide and detailed confession.

The pages and pages of typed and handwritten reports began to blur; word ran into word; line ran into line. I began to feel disconnected: by fatigue; by an unwillingness to admit and analyze the growing discomfiture and suspicion I had been feeling for several days.

One of the basic rules when concocting a false story is to keep it loose; keep it easy; keep it fluid; avoid too many precise details; incorporate your surroundings; use what you see at the moment to reinforce your claims.

Like garbage cans on the edge of the sidewalk late at night.

Kitty. Kitty.

When I switched on the television, I was surprised to catch the eleven-o'clock news. It felt more like three o'clock of a very bad morning.

None of the international horrors made any impression; too far away, remote, impersonal.

On the national scene, some poor dope tried to hold up a bank in Cleveland, using a little gun he'd carved out of *soap*. A bright-eyed grandmother-type bank teller laughed into the camera when praised for her courage in standing up to the would-be bandit: "Why, for heaven's sake, the paint was coming off all over his hand. It wasn't anything but a cake of Ivory soap and that's pretty much what it looked like." Laugh-laugh. "I'm not about to hand over my day's receipts to someone who waves a bar of Ivory soap in my face!"

I must have nodded off for a minute or two when the newscaster's voice cut through my dulled exhaustion with the words ". . . Alfredo Veronne has been in seclusion for most of the last three or four years, living quietly at his estate in Kensington, the most exclusive enclave in exclusive Great Neck."

The overvoice described what was being shown: old news clips dating back to the days of the Kefauver hearings. A younger, steel-faced Alfredo Veronne respectfully declining to answer. A straight-backed, Homberg-wearing Veronne deferring to his attorney as he bolted from court steps to waiting limousine. A quick rundown of some of his more sensational arrests, illustrated by shots of Veronne being escorted in handcuffs from squad car to precinct for booking; follow-up shots of Veronne hurrying, head down and face concealed in time-honored gangster fashion, from Criminal Courts Building to a taxi while his attorney expressed indignation over "excessive bail."

Then a live shot to outside the Veronne mansion; quick interviews with guarded, reluctant neighbors: "I really never met the family. We all tend to stay pretty much to ourselves in this community." A woman caught off guard: "A gangster? You're kidding. I always thought he was a retired European film director. Now, where could I have gotten that?"

The live shot picked up on several nuns being hurried from a station wagon to the front door and then inside the mansion. Attempts were made to identify them: from what order? for what purpose?

Finally a young priest stepped outside the door and responded to the persistent questioning: "Look, gentlemen. Mr. Veronne has personally contributed millions of dollars, literally millions of dollars, to so many charities, I doubt if he could remember them all himself. Because of his charity, thousands of children with deforming diseases have been restored to a useful life. Elderly indigents have been guaranteed dignity and protection in several homes financed solely by Mr. Veronne. There are many, many people, in religious orders and outside of religious orders, who want to offer prayers on his behalf this night."

The priest smiled, nodded, ignored questions and disappeared back inside the Veronne home.

"And so, Jim," the newsman on the spot said, "we have the strange and conflicting picture of this man Alfredo Veronne. On the one hand, the vicious and feared crime lord, known for his brilliance and ruthlessness; on the other hand, philanthropist and benefactor to untold numbers of helpless. His family and friends and beneficiaries from religious orders all over the country arrive at his fortresslike home in Kensington, Great Neck, Long Island, to keep the watch through the night, as Alfredo Veronne prepares to face that final, ultimate judge, who will not accept the plea of the Fifth Amendment. . . ."

I switched to another channel and caught another wrap-up of the career of Alfredo Veronne: an interview with Paul Sutro, who stated that in his estimation Veronne had one of the most brilliant, Machiavellian minds he'd ever encountered. That, given the opportunity and the education, in a different setting Veronne would have been able to move mountains or arbitrate the most complex international disagreements to the satisfaction of all concerned.

As Paul Sutro's voice droned on, repeating almost verbatim what he had already told Tim Neary and me about Alfredo Veronne's brilliant, problem-solving mind, I began to dig through pages and pages of reports, then remembered that I hadn't typed up what I was looking for: it was still just a series of cryptic notes in one of my notebooks.

I read it over carefully.

> *Jamaica Hosp. 12/23/70; Dr. J.Lattimore-neuro-surg. R.Mogliano—contusions/abrasions; C.Mogliano—possible concussion; X-ray work-up; curious re condition—why girl cripple? why no past corr.surg. & therapy? Lattimore opin: girl should have had surg. 8–10 yrs. ago; too late now; patient transf. via priv. ambul.*

What Dr. Lattimore had told me was that the young husband had been puzzled by his questions; had assumed the girl had been hopelessly crippled as a very young child. When Ray had approached Alfredo Veronne with questions about the lack of corrective treatment of the girl's condition, Veronne had made it very clear that the matter was not open for discussion in any way. Lattimore's educated guess, without any other information, was that Veronne had deliberately neglected therapy for the girl, possibly as a means to keep her close to him, dependent on him.

Before I left my apartment, I gave myself the once-over in the bathroom mirror: freshly shaved, clean-shirted, dark-suited and -necktied, I looked as respectable and respectful as any other "family man" coming to pay my last visit to Alfredo Veronne.

I parked a couple of streets away from Veronne's mansion. I didn't want my Chevy to stand out among all the Continentals and Cadillacs and Mercedes.

Small quiet groups of people were being admitted as other small quiet groups were leaving the mansion. I just walked along, right past the uniformed private guards, the television and newspaper cameramen; just kept my head down sadly, stepped back politely so that the lady next to me could enter first. We were all ushered into the dimly lit marble reception hall. A tall slightly graying, beautifully tailored and well-tanned guy thanked us all for coming and shook each hand. Apparently he was one of Veronne's sons; I heard someone call him by name, so that when he took my hand I just said, "Anthony, Anthony. Terrible, terrible." He agreed with me and we both looked sad.

"After you've seen Papa," Anthony told us, "please, join my sister and the others in the library for a moment or two."

Through the open door of the library, I could see the back of the girl's head and shoulders as she sat in her wheelchair. People were standing around her, bending to whisper, to kiss her cheek. At this point, I wasn't sure what the hell was going on: was the old man still alive or was this the beginning of a wake?

Before I could ask anyone, our little group was escorted to Alfredo Veronne's bedroom. The scene would have done justice to the last hours of a medieval lord of the realm. The massive, ornate bed was covered by a beautiful pearly-white satin cover, underneath which, in the smallest possible mound, propped up by four-foot-wide satin pillows, was Alfredo Veronne, very much alive. His scrawny arms, inside red satin pajama sleeves, were neatly placed outside the cover, and his swollen fingers moved restlessly, clutching and releasing the cover. All around the room, at respectful distances, were the heirs and inheritors of the still-breathing and alert *padrone*. I scanned the room quickly, but didn't spot Lorenzo.

A young priest stood at the bedside and acted as a sort of go-between for the host and his guests, and one after the other the visitors bowed reverentially to kiss the slightly extended left hand offered them by

Veronne. Finally there was no one behind me; my group had left; the next group hadn't arrived. The priest nodded at me; he had a very glassy-eyed look and I wondered how long he'd been standing at Veronne's bedside.

"He is conscious, isn't he, Father?"

"Oh, yes. Indeed, yes. Won't you approach Mr. Veronne now. There are so many others waiting to pay their respects."

Veronne looked dead, but he was just resting his eyes. I grabbed his hand and squeezed and leaned close and spoke directly into his left ear.

"It's Joe Peters, Veronne. You're going to tell me, right now, about the killing of the Keeler kids."

The small watery eyes snapped open; the loose mouth pulled back with a gasp. He tried to pull his hand from my grip, but I leaned in close again and said, very quietly, very directly, "Because if you don't, the minute you're dead, old man, I'm going to tell your daughter how you kept her a cripple all her life, just so you could keep her close to you. And I'll get five doctors to back me up."

Again, a gasp; again, an attempt to pull his hand from mine. The young priest smiled questioningly.

"Mr. Veronne just said he wants to talk privately to me," I said. The priest kept smiling, but he was looking around for someone to intervene. He wasn't used to making decisions like this on his own.

Veronne's voice cracked through the carefully hushed, soft voices as another group of visitors approached the foot of his bed.

"Get out," Veronne said sharply. With great effort, he waved an arm at his son, Anthony. "Get them out of here," Veronne ordered. "Goddamn it, do what I tell you and take him with you. I got something to discuss. Get out, get out!"

In less than forty seconds, we were alone. "My daughter," Veronne began in a croaking voice, "only the best for her, always, always. For her protection, to prevent her from suffering, to . . ."

"I don't give a goddamn why you kept your daughter a cripple, Veronne. Tell your reasons to your priest. All I'm telling you is this: we trade. Now. My silence for your talking. You tell me about that night or I'll see to it your daughter spits on your grave."

His hands leaped up, one on either side of his narrow body. It was an involuntary movement, spasmodic. He tried to shrug; he coughed, then passed his tongue dryly over his dry white lips. His head slipped to one side; his profile was that of a broken-down, decaying mummy.

"Kitty called you that night. Because she knew you'd help her."

"Yes, yes." He spoke into the pillow, but I could hear every whispered word. "It was an accident. Truly, an accident. She did not mean to hurt the child. The child was so fragile."

"I know that. Go on. Talk."

"And she gave the second child the sleeping pills to quiet him because he was so frightened, so hysterical. It was all a sad and terrible accident."

"So you sent Lorenzo?"

He nodded; sighed. "I sent Lorenzo. It took me a long time to find him. He had been visiting in his brother's home out on Long Island. That was my mistake, sending Lorenzo. He never . . . trusted women. He trusted no one but me. All his life, he has been with me. Devoted all his life to me." Veronne jabbed a bony hand at his temple. "He is a simple man, Lorenzo. He has always done exactly, *exactly* what I tell him to do. When Kitty called, she said they were both dead, both of her boys. So I told Lorenzo to go, take the bodies, drop them somewhere nearby, maybe in a park. And to put a bullet into one of the kids' heads, so it would look like a kidnap-murder." Veronne coughed, a dry hacking scraping sound. He shook his head. "Kitty called me as soon as Lorenzo left. She was hysterical. She said that the second boy hadn't been dead after all, from the sleeping pills. That when they were in the car, the child cried out. She tried to save him, to tell Lorenzo, 'No, don't shoot this child,' but . . . but Lorenzo, he pulled the child away from her. Because he would do what he had been told to do. Exactly, *exactly* what I had told him to do. There was nothing Kitty could do. Nothing. It was all so terrible, so sad, the whole thing, all a terrible, terrible accident."

"So you told her to go to bed. To say nothing. Until you thought up a good story for her?"

"I told her to trust me. She could always trust me. Don't you see how I felt? That it was my fault, my responsibility, the death of this second child. Because of Lorenzo, who all his life did only what I told him to do and nothing else. My poor Kitty, my beautiful, beautiful Kitty. What a tragedy."

I stared at Veronne, and a strange idea began to form. This old, dried-up, dying and powerless man had not always been old and dried-up and powerless. Not too many years ago, he had been strong and healthy and dynamic: an ugly man whose known charm and courtly manners and attentions had made him attractive and sought after by women from many levels of society. My first thought in coming here was that Kitty had used what I was using: knowledge of his daughter's condition. She could have gotten that from Ray Mogliano. But Veronne was smiling, whispering to himself: "My beautiful Kitty."

Slowly, carefully, Veronne confirmed for me what I had all but figured out: he had told Kitty how to make use of George's confession. It had been almost a game for him: so easy, so easy, he said. You make up a good story, you get witnesses to confirm what you say. Witnesses were easily come by.

"Billy Weaver was dead; in his whole life, he never done nothing good for nobody. Why not let him do a good deed for Kitty in his death?"

Benjamin the Cuban: "For money, for a good suit of clothes, a good pair of boots, Benjamin would swear to anything."

And Mrs. Deluca?

There was a strange gagging sound working its way up Veronne's throat; for a second, I thought he was dying, but he wasn't. He was laughing.

"Ah, ah, Mary. She was always the tough one in her family, that Mary. Her husband, Salvatore, he handled the numbers. Penny-ante stuff, but he was loyal and a goodhearted slob, from the old days, you know? He could be trusted. But when he died," Veronne tapped his chest, "bum ticker, ya know, but then, when he died, his wife took over. A clever woman; clever, clever. Could trust her with anything, anything."

Danny Fitzmartin: Veronne's thin lips turned down into a sneer. Every man had his price. In a year, two years, the pub would be his; free and clear.

"But a hypocrite, ya know," Veronne said softly. He winked and tapped his nose with an index finger. "He tells Kitty he'll go along only because of George. Because George was willing to give his life for Kitty and it wasn't up to him to spoil George's story. Hypocrite." Veronne made a dry, hacking spitting sound. "Hypocrite."

"But just to be on the safe side, after all the scheming and plotting, after all the game-playing, you had Martucci hit anyway?"

The bright eyes froze; the thin lips pulled back into a wolflike grin. "Vincent was a dead man all along. It was only a matter of time. He knew that."

"Then why all this? Why drag me into all this?"

Veronne shrugged. "Why not?"

Quietly, two of his sons had entered the room with a third man, the doctor. Veronne looked past me and gestured vaguely for the doctor to approach.

"Mr. Veronne, you're exhausting yourself, sir. Have you finished speaking? All of this, all of these people coming to visit, it is all too much for you."

"I'll tell you what is too much for me," Veronne said in a hard, strong voice. "You. You're too much for me, coming in here and telling me what I am able to do and not able to do. Get out of here, you'll get me soon enough. But for now, get out. Tell my friends I want them to come and see me. Send them in, send them in, it's too damn quiet in here.

"And you . . ." Veronne grabbed my sleeve and pulled me toward him. "Look, Peters. What I done for my daughter—all her life, the best, the best of everything in the world."

"Except the surgery she really needed."

The small clawlike hand tightened its grip. "That's not for you to say, bastard," he hissed at me. "What do you know of it? It's not for you to judge."

I leaned in close again, so that the people who had come into the room could not hear anything that I said to him. Only Alfredo Veronne could hear, which is exactly the way I wanted it.

"I'm not going to judge you, Veronne. I'm going to tell your daughter the truth the minute you're dead. Then, let *her* judge for herself."

His hand fumbled up my sleeve as I pulled back and plucked his fingers from me. He made a terrible, strangling sound, and two of his sons and his doctor rushed toward the bed. He looked right past them, trying to find me. I just stood back, mingled with the rest of the observers.

Somehow, he found the strength to shove the doctor aside, to pull himself upright in his bed and to turn his head from side to side, trying to find me. He looked around wildly, his eyes bulging slightly as they found mine and he realized that he had no way of controlling the situation.

Veronne sat absolutely rigid; then he raised one arm and pointed in my direction. "Jesus Christ," he gasped, "Jesus Christ, you . . ."

Then he fell over back onto his four-foot-wide pillows, and the doctor leaned over to confirm what we all knew. There was a general sighing, a muffled, soft sort of grief, a whispering: get the daughter, get the grandchildren.

Then, over all the polite, controlled sounds, a woman, some heavyset, black-clad old aunt, screamed out, "He saw God. Did you hear? He called out the Savior's name with his last breath!"

The woman fainted and was carried away. In the general commotion, I backed out of the room, stood back carefully as the daughter was wheeled into her father's death scene. I mixed with the rest of the company; kept my face down after I spotted Lorenzo Pellegrino approaching Veronne's room, his long dark face streaked with tears.

It took me about five careful minutes to slip out of the house via a side door. After that, it took me about one minute flat to get to my car and head for home before someone decided to ask questions about old man Veronne's last private conference.

CHAPTER 15

THE various documents and statements and notes and street maps and reports were still scattered all over the surface of the extension table, just where I had left them. I collected everything, tapped edges of papers into some semblance of order, then ended up just shoving and stuffing all of it into the red manila accordion file folder. I wrapped the frayed red string around the folder, then dumped it into a top drawer of the bedroom bureau.

Then I went to bed and fell into one of those unbelievably deep sleeps that don't leave you feeling rested, just confused and disoriented: the kind of sleep usually accomplished with sleeping pills or booze, neither of which assisted me. I imagine the lack of proper food, irregular habits and exhaustion had plunged me right past the supposedly therapeutic r.e.m. and into the void.

It was nine-thirty the next morning when I woke up; I called the office, asked Gelber if anyone was looking for me. He said no; I said fine, I'd keep in touch; he said okay, fine.

I showered, shaved, got dressed. Then I packed a few things into an overnight suitcase; just a few things.

Then I called Kitty and told her I was coming over to see her. She sounded very soft, very vague.

She looked fragile and beautiful and delicate and pastel in a long pink cotton robe. She had just a touch of moist pink lipstick on; no other makeup. Her long beautiful thick light hair was pulled back from her face. Her cheekbones gleamed like fine polished porcelain.

She went through a ritual with coffee cups and a plate of biscuits. The coffee was fresh perked and we both drank it black; neither of us touched the biscuits. For the first time since I'd met her, she was wearing no jewelry: none of the clittering silver bracelets, none of the intricately twisted silver rings.

"Are you all right, Kitty?"

She nodded without looking at me. Her hands rested motionless on her lap. Her face was turned toward the sunlight which cut from the window in a wide band along the carpet and across her feet. Her profile showed a clear-cut perfect beauty. She turned without expression and I studied the fragile face marked with the anguish and pain of too many deaths, too much grieving, too many losses. There was something puzzled, a bewildered innocence and remoteness which made it nearly impossible to form the connection between this Kitty and all the things that had happened because, on one long, sticky, unpleasant, exhausting and disappointed night in April, a sick and irritable little boy had thrown up one time too many. And that had led to the death of two little boys; to the death of their father; to the death of Vincent Martucci; to the "retirement" of Marvin L. Schneiderman; to the guaranteed election of Jeremiah Kelleher; to the appointment of Tim Neary as Police Commissioner. And my own future? Whatever I wanted, I guess.

Finally she blinked and regarded me with a patient faint smile. "What is it, Joe?"

"When's the last time you spoke to Jay T. Williams?"

She frowned and tapped a finger along an eyebrow, a trick she used sometimes when she was trying to remember something; or trying to decide *why* she was being asked to remember something.

"Jaytee. I guess it was last Monday night. When he and Jeff Weinstein and I got together."

"Monday. That was the day of Vincent's funeral."

Her dark-blue eyes took on a strange intensity: a kind of *listening,* a sharpness of concentration. "Yes, Joe, that's right."

"And that was when he told you that you'd plead not guilty when you go to court next Monday. And that then you'd just ride out all the delays and postponements until such time as the D.A. feels it would be politically feasible to let the charges against you drop."

"Yes, Joe. And I told you that I wanted him to force the D.A. to bring me to trial. That I want to be tried and acquitted, once and for all."

"Do you remember, Kitty, a couple of weeks ago, when we were up in my cabin, you told me that Jaytee had passed along a deal to you? That the D.A. offered to reduce the double murder-one charge to manslaughter, one count. And promised you wouldn't serve more than three to five years. In return for the name of your accomplice?"

She leaned forward slightly, alert and wary. "Yes, Joe, I remember telling you about that offer."

"Do you know where Jaytee Williams is right now, Kitty?"

"Why?"

"Do you know where Jaytee Williams is right now, Kitty?"

"Yes, Joe. He's in his New York office." She came over to the couch, reached down for my hand, turned her head to one side to look at my wristwatch. "He's probably at his desk right now."

I caught her hand, which still rested lightly on my wrist; studied the long white fingers, the wounded nails; held her hand to my mouth, pressed the knuckles against my lips, against my teeth, tasted lightly with my tongue the sweet flower taste of her soap, held her hand in both of mine and, not looking at her, said, "Call him, Kitty. Call him and tell him you'll take the District Attorney's deal."

She slid her hand from my light hold and stepped back to get a better look at me. There was a steady, quiet demand in her voice. "Why, Joe? Why should I do that?"

The jagged-edged knife point stabbed and twisted at the raw, untreated ulcer with a pain that shot both down and through my body before it subsided into a familiar dull throb that I could hold with my hand.

"Because, Kitty, if *you* give him Lorenzo, then you still got a pretty good deal going. If *I* give him Lorenzo, then the double murder-one charge will stick and you'll risk the next twenty to thirty years of your life as against a guaranteed three to five with a probable early parole."

I don't know exactly what I expected: hysteria, maybe; indignation, protest, denial. At least questions, a demand to know how, what, why. Not this quiet acknowledgment of what she'd been denying for all these weeks.

"What would be the point, Joe? What difference would that make, to anything? To anyone?"

I tried to see beneath this calm unsurprised surface. She repeated softly, almost encouragingly, "What difference would it make, Joe? To anyone?"

I shook my head, because I really didn't know. She reached out and pressed my arm in some strange, irrational gesture of sympathy. As though *I* was the one who needed support; needed someone to lean on.

"It won't change anything, will it, Joe?"

"I guess not."

"I *know* not." She spoke with a quiet certainty; a calm, steady assurance. "The boys will still be dead. George will still be dead. Vincent will still be dead. I loved my sons, Joe. I really loved them."

"I know that, Kitty."

"It was something that just happened so fast, so quick. It wasn't something deliberate or cruel. I loved them, both of them. I never deserved any medals as the best mother of the year, but when it gets down to it, who the hell does? *I did love them.*"

She spoke with a quiet passion, as though it was her love of her sons that she had to convince me of, nothing else.

"It happened, Joe. It was an accident. And from then on, things got out of my control. It was all out of my hands. I went to pieces completely. Nothing like that had ever happened to me, Joe. I couldn't get George. Vincent talked and talked and tried to calm me down, but then I went back into their bedroom . . . I started to fall apart all over again. I . . . called Alfredo." She shrugged. "And then it was all out of my hands. One thing happened after another . . . Joe? What would be the point, at this stage?" For the first time, her voice broke. She brought her hand up quickly, pressed it against her mouth, to steady herself. "I have a lot of living left to do, Joe. I have a lot of life left to be lived."

She moved against me; her cold hands sought warmth. Her body shuddered with a terrible, suppressed fear. Her heavy clean hair gave off the fragrance of flowers and fresh air and innocence. Her voice was warm and husky, her words inaudible as her tongue flicked my ear, lips brushed my cheek, slid to my mouth. Her lips tasted of some pink sweetness. I locked my teeth and stiffened.

Kitty pulled back abruptly, her hands on my arms, her face puzzled, her voice shaking. "Joe? Joe, please."

For the first time since I'd met her, there was the sound and look of terror about her. "Joe, I haven't told you this before, but I have some money. I have a great deal of money. I own property in the Bahamas, Joe, free and clear, and a percentage of a development company down there. We could wait, Joe, until all of this blows over. We could go down there together, Joe, you could take over my share of the company. . . . We could—"

I shook my head. "Not this time, Kitty."

"What do you mean, Joe? What do you mean, 'not this time'?"

"I'm not George-to-the-rescue, Kitty. And I'm not Papa Veronne."

The words had a strong physical effect on her. She pulled back from me and studied me closely, her eyes narrowed and dry and hardening. Everything about her changed: the growing panic was gone, submerged beneath a cold, controlled anger. "You goddamn hypocrite," she said slowly. "It isn't what happened to the kids that night, is it, Joe?" She whirled around, found the *New York Times* which had been left at her door this morning. It was folded back to the obituary page, a continuation of the front-page story of Veronne's death. Kitty jabbed at the article.

"You see all this, Joe? All this crap they've had waiting to print about him for such a long time? None of it, none of it even begins to tell about him." She jabbed at the paper. "Here they tell all the 'bad' things: connections with this crime family, with that crime family. Now, here, Joe, here they tell about all the charities he supported, all the people he helped. Words, words, that's all. Nothing here about the *man*, Joe. Nothing here about *the man*."

"My beautiful Kitty," Veronne had said; "my beautiful Kitty."

It was almost as though she could read my mind. She said, "Ask me about him, Joe. God, go ahead and ask me. You want to know, don't you? It's killing you, isn't it, Joe?"

"You don't have to tell me anything, Kitty."

"And if I don't tell you, you won't have to think about it, later on, when you're alone with your thoughts, right, Joe? It won't get inside your head for you to live with and think about. Well, I'm going to tell you—"

"Kitty, it isn't going to change anything. Nothing's going to change anything."

She stiffened. "Don't you think I know that, Joe? That's *why* I'm going to tell you, because it doesn't make any difference. So you're going to hear about it, damn you." She dropped onto the couch, leaned back, crossed her arms, her hands massaging gently. "There was *only* Papa. Only Papa. No one else. No one. After him, there could be no one." She stopped speaking, closed her eyes, then abruptly shook her head and reached for a cigarette. She leaned forward, her hand on mine as I held my lighter to her.

"Thank you, Joe. Nothing you want to ask me, Joe? Good, then I'll just tell you everything I want you to know. You know why no one ever linked his name with mine, Joe? Ever, not ever? Because he wanted it that way; no one ever knew. I was of value to him, Joe. Not just my body. God, he was the only one who loved me for my brain. Yes, *loved* me. And trusted me, Joe. You know what it's like for a man like Alfredo to *trust*, completely, totally?"

"He knew you'd sleep with whoever he told you to, right?"

"Be very careful, Joe," Kitty said softly. "Be very careful or I might go further than you really want to hear."

"I know all I want to hear, Kitty. How Veronne worked out a story for you, based on George's suicide; how he got you witnesses; and how he finally had Martucci hit, just as insurance."

"You're skipping important parts, Joe."

"Kitty, let's cut this short. Call Williams and—"

"You're really not going to change your mind are you?" She was reconciled; there was nothing pleading about her. "All right, then, Joe. There's no point in my *not* telling you. Just between the two of us, Joe. Just to satisfy your curiosity about me. And Papa Veronne."

"I don't want to—"

"I know you don't, but I'm going to tell you. You only saw him now, when he was dying, Joe. You never saw him when he was *really* alive. Five years ago, after Terry was born, I went to work out in Mogliano's place and I met Alfredo. He treated me . . . the way no man ever treated me."

"Not even George?"

Kitty smiled and shook her head. "You don't know anything about George. Or me. George . . . treated me like I was made out of . . . spun sugar. Like I would melt, disappear. Like I was a dream, not a woman. Alfredo Veronne was the only man I ever knew who treated me like a woman: a real woman. A whole woman. I could have had any-thing I wanted, but he knew I didn't want to be set up in an East Side apartment somewhere, waiting for when he had some free time. I wanted . . . I wanted to be independent, Joe. To be involved. I wanted to run my own business. He let me learn, he taught me so that one day I could open my own place: a health spa, maybe, a restaurant, a club, whatever I wanted."

"And part of the on-the-job training was sleeping with his son-in-law, Ray Mogliano."

Kitty leaned back, drew a last lungful on her cigarette, then crushed it out in the large blue ashtray she held. Slowly, she shook her head. "No, Joe. I never slept with Ray Mogliano. Alfredo asked me to try to keep him straight. For his daughter's sake."

I remembered that John Mogliano had said Kitty was special; a friend; the only woman he'd ever known who could be considered a friend.

"He was very concerned about his daughter, wasn't he, Kitty? A re-ally good father; made sure he kept her home. In her wheelchair."

Kitty's eyes flashed with cold anger. "You don't know anything about that. He adored that girl. He protected her."

"Kept her crippled for her own good?"

"I know about that. I know what Ray tried to say, that Cindy could have had an operation years ago, when she was a kid. But there was more to it than that, Joe. Cindy . . . is retarded, Joe. She never got past about eight or nine years old. She trusted everyone. Alfredo was afraid for her. He made it up to her, Joe. In so many ways. Except for Ray, Cindy never had an unhappy day in her life."

"A devoted and loving father. Very touching."

"It doesn't matter what you think, Joe. It doesn't matter. But it matters to me, that a man like Alfredo loved me; respected me; trusted me . . ."

"Set you up with Vince Martucci, right? Trusted you enough to set you up with Vince."

"Vincent Martucci was Alfredo's cousin's son. You didn't know that, did you? Alfredo . . . had heard things about Vince. That he was bisexual. He asked me to . . . watch out for Vince. Keep him straight—or discreet."

"Didn't even ask you to sleep with Vincent? To keep him 'straight'?"

"God damn you, Joe. Alfredo asked me to sleep with two men, in all these years." She held up two fingers and leaned forward. "One was George. And the other was . . ."

She shrugged and put her hand down.

"George? Alfredo asked you to sleep with your husband? George?"

"Alredo said that George deserved to have a son of his own; God knows, he was good to Terry, but Terry wasn't really his."

"You *gave* George a son? Like a present? For being a good man?"

"George never complained about our life together. He had his pub. Alfredo put up the money for the pub."

"And poor old George killed himself to save you?" I shook my head.

Very coldly, Kitty said, "George did exactly what he wanted to do. *Exactly.*"

"And in the end it was unnecessary. Because Alfredo had Vincent hit after all."

"Joe. Things are where they are. Nothing can be changed. Nothing can be undone." She went soft again, her voice became warm and tempting. "Joe. Why can't you just let things be at this point?"

I didn't answer. She studied me carefully, then smiled and said, "Okay, Joe. The second man Alfredo told me to sleep with was you, baby. We both sized you up pretty good, Joe. You played good guy pretty good. You were *easy*, Joe. You were a pushover. You went for everything, Joe. Everything I told you; every little trick, every little story. Exactly, exactly the way Papa said you would."

Which by now I realized all by myself.

"But why, Kitty? Why all the stories, all the bits and pieces, when it was all so simple: just hit Martucci?"

"Because Papa felt responsible for me; for the situation I was in. He wanted it proved that I was innocent."

"And I was the likely one for the job?"

She shrugged. "You were good, Joe. We both agreed that you were good." She shook her head. "Better than I needed you to be."

"What about the sheep dog, Kitty? What the hell was that all about?"

She clenched her teeth and shook her head. "That stupid son-of-a-bitch, Benjamin. He ad-libbed. He just stuck that in, for authenticity, I guess."

"How come Veronne didn't set up someone with a Bedlington terrier? How come he slipped up there?"

Kitty shrugged. "He said let it go; if Benjamin's extra witness turned up, it might be too perfect. You might become suspicious. And that's why you kept going, Joe, wasn't it? To find that one last witness."

"There was more to it than that, Kitty. There were . . . other reasons why I wanted to finish the investigation."

"Oh, Joe. It wasn't the way I thought it would be. With you. Going away with you; spending time with you. That was something I hadn't anticipated. How I would feel with you."

I believed her; only because I wanted to believe her.

"Joe, you've a right to feel angry with me. To feel used. Sure, I used you. People use each other every day of their lives. But there was still more to it than that. You know it and I know it. Oh, Joe, can't we let it be the way we said, out at Montauk? Get it all over with, and then just forget the past and live day to day. One day at a time, Joe, no plans, no long-range anything." She stopped abruptly, studied me and shook her head. "My God, Joe, what the hell in your life makes it so hard for you right now, at this minute? What the hell have you got here that you can't just walk away from, turn your back on?"

I wasn't able to answer her or to answer myself.

"Kitty, call Williams."

She stood very still, not breathing, searched my face, puzzled, unable to understand.

"Kitty," I said once more, softly, before I left, *"call him and take the deal."*

CHAPTER 16

BACK at my apartment, I called Jen. I told her I was coming down later in the day. She sounded surprised, disinterested: if-you-feel-you-want-to-Joe. That kind of thing. But then, just before I hung up, she said, "Joe, I think it's a good idea. We have to talk."

Then I called the airline and made a reservation; tourist class; round trip; return flight open. I threw a few more things into my suitcase and turned and stared at the telephone as it rang and rang. I counted the number of rings: fifteen. Then the phone stopped ringing and I called the office.

I told Gelber that I had just gotten an emergency call from Florida; tell Tim Neary when he returned from Boston that I had to take a few days off and fly south. He knew where to reach me.

Tim would want to reach me on Monday morning, when Jay T. Williams entered a plea of guilty to manslaughter on behalf of his client, Kitty Keeler. And then I'd tell Tim to call Harry Sullivan. I would give him the code number to ask for; then Tim would have the Keeler murder gun.

The really ironic part I don't think I'll ever tell him: that we were right all along. Right from the very first day, when we all sat around in the office and discussed the way it must have happened. That the story we fed to Vincent Martucci, line by line, was correct. That our educated guesses were pretty damn accurate educated guesses.

The phone began to ring again. As I closed the suitcase and checked my wallet, I began to count the rings, automatically.

All the way out to the airport in the taxi, I could hear that phone ringing inside my head: I could see Kitty's stricken, beautiful face.

When Tim calls on Monday, I'll tell him what I guess both of us have known all along. There's no way that I can retire to Florida. What I'll do is what I've always done: hang in there and follow where Tim leads me. I don't know about Jen. That's going to be strictly up to

Jen. I do know that I want her to be happy and that I'm going to try and help her be happy with whatever decision she makes for herself.

Even on the plane, settled back, waiting for takeoff, I could hear that phone ringing: I could see Kitty. In an hour or two, she'll come to the conclusion that she'd be better off with a guaranteed deal than to take her chances on calling my bluff.

The funny thing is, right now, at this exact moment, I really don't know what I'd do if she decided to tough it out.

About the Author

Dorothy Uhnak, a native New Yorker, spent fourteen years as a police officer—years during which she was promoted three times and twice awarded medals for "services above and beyond."

Ms. Uhnak, an Edgar winner in 1968, had her first book, *Policewoman,* published while she was still a detective. She is currently working on a new novel titled *The Crime.*